PERFECTLY ADEQUATE

Jewel E. Ann

This book is a work of fiction. Any resemblances to actual persons, living or dead, events, or locales are purely coincidental.

Copyright © 2019 by Jewel E. Ann
ISBN: 978-1-7337786-5-7
Print Edition

Cover Designer: Sign.Yra
Formatting: BB eBooks

Dedication

To Marley

Playlist

"Our Love" – Judah & the Lion
"If You Ever Wanna Be In Love" – James Bay
"Arms" – The Paper Kiss
"Magnetised – Acoustic" – Tom Odell
"Hold Me While You Wait" – Lewis Capaldi
"7 Minutes" – Dean Lewis
"The Shores Of Scotland" – Max Richter
"On the Nature of Daylight" – Max Richter
"Rosalee Theme" – Max Richter
"I'm Gonna Be (500 Miles) – Blake Stratton
"Don't Give Up On Me" – Andy Grammer
"Only To Be With You (Unplugged)" – Judah & the Lion

"The spectrum is *human.* It's not autism."
–Dorothy Mayhem

CHAPTER ONE

She's Gone

Elijah

A WOMAN BROKE me, so I chose a woman to put me back together.

Probably not my most brilliant idea.

"It's been a year." I stare at my folded hands, ignoring cloudy downtown Portland just outside the window to my right.

August.

My wife left me at the end of summer, two days after our son's second birthday. Impeccable timing. I'd say out of the blue, but that would be a monumental understatement. She seduced me the previous night, after we shared a bottle of wine—and dare I say the best sex of our entire married life.

We met in high school and attended the same college. Medical school. Residency. Hobbies. Shared life goals.

Check.

Check.

Check.

"Yes. Time to move on. Julie's not coming back to you. Have you thought about dating? You're surrounded by women all day. Surely someone has a friend that might be a good match for you."

"You're the worst psychiatrist ever." I close my eyes, shaking my head.

"My colleagues would disagree." Dr. Lori Hawkins brushes her chin-length, silver hair away from her face etched with a few soft wrinkles. Her hazel eyes peer at me from over the black frames of her glasses. She excels in all the mom looks.

Sit down.
Shut up.
You're lying.
Don't be a baby.

The family discount comes with an extra-large side of sarcasm and hardcore truth. My mom's attention lingers a whole two seconds before returning to her salad.

"I haven't dated since high school. Do you know how many years that's been?"

"Twenty since you graduated. Twenty-four since you started high school. I'm good with math." She dips her fork into basil-lime dressing before stabbing a grape tomato.

"It's all online dating now. No one gets fixed up. I don't think. I'm not really sure." I rub the tension from the back of my neck.

"You're a millennial. You'll figure it out." She blots her red lips with a napkin.

"I'm a millennial by fourteen days." Leaning forward, I rest my elbows on her desk, framing my face with my hands. A deep sigh escapes me. I have lots of deep sigh moments. The previous year has felt like one big, deep sigh.

She fights her grin. "You look like the little dirty-blond-haired boy that your grandma used to bring into this very office thirty-plus years ago to have lunch with me. That baby face and cute nose." The tip of her fork bops my nose as I wrinkle it. "Of course, now you're all grown up. A tall, handsome doctor who needs to shave more often and could use a haircut. I wish your grandma was here to see you now. She'd be so proud."

After a few seconds, I frown, scratching my scruffy face. "I hate her. I thought after this much time I'd stop hating her, but I think I hate her more now than I did then."

"Grandma? That's not very nice ... she was a bit stubborn, and she liked to swat your ornery little ass sometimes, but—"

"Julie." I roll my eyes.

Mom smirks. It quickly settles into a sad smile. "Why? What purpose does it serve to hold on to that hatred?"

My shoulders lift toward my ears, an excruciatingly hard feat given the way I've carried the weight of the world for so long. "I'm not sure it will ever make sense to me. We waited until our mid-thirties to start a family. Roman wasn't an accident. We planned for him. We planned every part of our lives to fit around him. Julie scaled back her surgeries because she wanted to be home more with him. I turned down a promotion because the added hours would have taken away from time with my family. Then one day she's just ... done? I go from seeing my son every day to being a part-time parent? What is that? Who does that? Who just walks away because they're..." I shake my head "...what were her words? *Not that woman anymore?*"

Mom bites her lips together, returning the lid to her salad. "I saw Julie with Roman the other day at Shemanski Park, buying flowers for her mom's birthday. Julie has a tattoo on her ankle, a lotus. When I complimented her on it, she showed me Roman's name tattooed at the nape of her neck with a heart next to it. Did you know about the tattoos? Or that she's a redhead now instead of a blonde?"

"Yes. I know. My sophisticated wife—ex-wife—who obsessively ironed our clothes and wore her hair in the same long, straight style since we were in high school, has wavy, red hair, tattoos, and the wardrobe of a teenager."

And boobs. I don't say it aloud and neither does my mom, but Julie got breast implants six months ago, and she likes to show them to the world. Turtlenecks ... she wore turtlenecks with me.

"Rhonda's daughter recently turned twenty-four. She's an architect who just got out of a lesbian relationship because she's questioning her sexuality again. She's had some health issues that have played havoc on her hormones. Poor thing. But she's doing better, and Rhonda thinks she's ready to try dating men again. Loves adventure. The nicest girl you could ever meet." Mom takes out a compact, checks her teeth for lettuce, pops a mint into her mouth, and applies a soft pink shade of lipstick.

"Your secretary's maybe-possibly-not-sure-if-she's-a-lesbian daughter? I feel like you're disregarding my emotions." I stand, angling my arm to see my watch. "But we'll save that for next time. I have to get back to work."

She pushes back in her chair, making her way around the desk to give me a hug. "I love you, Eli. And not just because you bring me lunch every Friday."

I drop a quick kiss onto her cheek. "But that makes me the favorite, right?"

Mom chuckles. "You're my favorite boy."

I grin, being the youngest of three ... and the only boy.

Releasing me, her glossed lips turn downward. "You met Julie when you were sixteen. That's pretty young to expect forever."

I nod. She's been my other half, my better half, my morning cup of coffee, and my favorite goodnight kiss for so long I stopped counting. We were supposed to be forever—that unreachable number. Yet, here I am starting again at zero.

One ... I have Roman. He is my one, and one is enough; it's officially everything.

"She wasn't everything, Eli."

How did she read my mind?

"Julie is the mother of your child. That makes her something ... but not everything."

✧ ✧ ✧

I GRAB A coffee and make my way toward my lab. Rounds went well this morning. Some good research results this afternoon is all I need to make Friday officially the best day of this week.

A shiny pair of red sneakers with red soles and red laces snag my attention when the doors open on the second floor. The sneakers move toward me, and my gaze slides up the blue scrubs to the young woman with shoulder-length, sable hair and a friendly smile. She makes eye contact for two seconds before turning toward the doors and pressing the button to the fifth floor.

"Nice shoes," I say.

"Thanks, Dr. Hawkins." Her blue eyes make a return to me with her surprisingly enthusiastic reply to my compliment.

My lips curl into an unavoidable smile. "Have we met?"

She tucks her dark hair behind her ears. "Yes. No. Well, I hear a lot about you. And I've delivered mail to your office and test results to your lab. We've passed in the hall, but clearly you don't recognize me, maybe because I'm usually pushing a patient or a piece of medical equipment. So … we have not *officially* met."

"I see…" I glance at her badge "…Dorothy?"

She doesn't look like a Dorothy. Maybe a Lauren or an Elizabeth. Maybe even a trendy name like Poppy.

Her hand goes straight to her badge. "Yes. I'm a patient transporter and a nursing student." Blue eyes roll toward the ceiling as she bites her lips together. Dorothy's cute. Young. Petite. My mom and sisters would say something like "simply adorable, cute as a button," or something crazy like that.

My grin swells by twenty percent. She has a forced confidence. I think it's forced. Maybe just nerves. I can't tell for sure. "What do you hear about me?" My head cants to the side just as the elevator stops on the fourth floor—my floor.

She points her finger upward. "I'm the next stop."

"You're not off the hook. I'll catch you later."

"You will?" she blurts as I step off the elevator.

"Yep." I don't turn back.

Dr. Warren, my intern, glances up from his tablet, peering over my shoulder as the elevator doors close behind me. "Dorothy Mayhem. Now there's an odd duck."

Mayhem? I keep my amusement to myself. Dorothy seems like an oxymoron to Mayhem.

"Odd how?" I brush past him toward my lab, and he follows right on my heels.

"She has like a million pairs of tennis shoes and they always match her undershirt. I saw her in the cafeteria last Sunday, eating lunch. She had a red metal lunch box, all prim and proper looking on one side, but the other side was covered in stickers. Decals ... like Nike and Taylor Swift. I tried to say something to her, but she had earbuds in and was reading some textbook. Willow said she's on the spectrum. I can totally see that. I once dated an Aspie. It lasted all of two weeks. Damn eager to please in bed, so it wasn't completely awful."

"You're a dick. Did you know that?" I swipe my badge to open the lab door.

"I'm just saying … it's a tough personality. Grating and annoying."

"It's ASD, not Aspie, and you're annoying me. Does that mean you're on the spectrum?"

He chuckles. "Point made. I was just making conversation. Don't get me wrong. She's cute. Kinda has that innocent sex appeal. Plain but forbidden in some ways."

I pull up the previous day's test results on my laptop. "Placebo is performing better. Go figure. Tell me why the placebo is performing better, and I'll forgive you for being a dick."

Warren deflates as I smirk at him.

No one wants to cure cancer more than me … except Warren. His younger sister died of a malignant brain tumor a year earlier. My motivation isn't as personal. I just want to stop offering painful and oftentimes false hope to young people who should have their whole lives ahead of them instead of fighting for a chance to have one more Christmas, a high school prom, or the opportunity to fall in love and have their hearts broken.

CHAPTER TWO

Catch and Release

Dorothy

I PUSH BODIES and equipment around the hospital the rest of the afternoon. That's all I do every weekend—push, deliver, wait, return. It doesn't require in-depth conversation, which is good since conversation is not my best honed skill. Sometimes, I deliver mail and lab specimens, but most of that is done digitally. I feel certain the future will have robotic wheelchairs and gurneys to transfer patients without the assistance of an actual human—like autonomous cars.

With one year left of nursing school, I want to work in plastics. But after talking with Dr. Hawkins, I'm reconsidering my goals. Dr. Elijah Hawkins, pediatric oncologist, complimented my shoes. And what was that promise of later? Later when?

Today?

Tomorrow?

The dilemma plays out as different scenarios in my

mind. I consider finding him to see if he wants to set a specific time to discuss my being on a hook. After one brief encounter, I'm indebted to him for some unknown reason.

I push Gavin Hamlin's wheelchair back to his room after his MRI. He's twelve and doesn't say much. He has a tumor in the upper right quadrant of his brain—probably not cancer. They're unsure if surgery is an option. I transported him three times last week.

If they find out it *is* cancer, then he might have Dr. Hawkins as his oncologist. And for a full second I think this would be great because then I might get to see Dr. Hawkins more often if Gavin needs more tests. But right after that second passes, I think, "What the fuck just went through my mind?"

The upside to this young kid having cancer!

Not a finer moment for me.

See, my parents think I need to put myself out there and be more available, but after one interaction with the hottest doctor in the hospital, I've let my thoughts seep into the darkness, wishing death sentences upon young kids. What's next? Running through the halls, telling all of the kids the Easter Bunny isn't real and that most of them with rare cancers will not live another five years?

"Do you think I'm going to die? I mean ... it's a tumor. In my brain. It's going to kill me, right?"

"I'm not your doctor." It's not my job to discuss medical information with patients. It's not really my job to discuss anything with them. But kids don't know one set of scrubs from another, so sometimes I field these life and death questions.

"Yeah, but you work here. I'm sure you see this a lot."

"Sick kids? Yeah. I see a lot of sick kids. But not all of them die. Most live. That's all you need to think about."

I make conscious efforts to censor every word I say to kids at the hospital. My mind abandons all emotion when asked questions that have factual answers.

Neat and tidy.

Black and white.

Only, kids don't do well with the truth. Scratch that. Parents don't do well with the truth.

Lie to my child. I don't want to scare them.

Code for: I'm not ready to face reality.

I can't imagine having children. Keeping track of my own shit, my own issues, and my own anxiety gobbles up all twenty-four hours.

"Why do you think I have this tumor?"

"Because you have cells in your body that are dividing at an excessively rapid rate."

"Duh … but why?"

Before I can entertain him with my theories—based on solid research by some of the world's leading doctors and medical researchers—his parents greet him just outside of his room. I give them a smile and make sure he gets safely back into his bed.

Several hours later, I take a quick break to get a coffee from the cafeteria. And talk about timing … Dr. Hawkins is in front of me in line. He doesn't see me because of that unfortunate evolutionary flaw in humans—no eyes in the back of our heads.

My mouth falls open to say something, but then I clamp my jaw shut and replay the dialogue in my head one more time to make sure it's not stupid.

"Hey, Dr. Hawkins. I have ten minutes if you want to catch me now."

Catch me now … hmm. I'm not sure that's what I mean or he meant. But since I don't really know what he meant—

Whoa! Dear lord he smells good.

Like herbaceous good. Not woodsy, vomit-worthy cologne stench. More like he rolled around in a patch of my dad's herbs, that kind of herbaceous good. Maybe … rosemary?

I lean in and take a generous whiff. "Fuck!" I yell as his elbow lands in my nose when he turns to reach for a wood stirring stick.

"Shit!" He jumps forward, arching his back after I spill my hot coffee down his backside—but only because he elbowed me in the nose.

My eyes see stars and burn with those unavoidable tears that always spring out the instant someone rams you in the nose. I look at my hand.

No blood.

I touch my nose again.

No blood.

Damn! That hurt like a motherfucker. How is there no blood? I actually wish blood would gush from my nose so my reaction that's silenced the area around us might feel a bit more justified.

Dr. Hawkins grimaces, pulling the wet material away

from his skin while he inspects my non-bleeding nose. I grab several napkins as does the lady behind the coffee counter, and we hand them to him to blot the coffee. Then I grab some more napkins and blow my nose really hard.

No blood!

I've never wanted to bleed so badly in my life.

"Are you okay? I'm sorry. I had no idea you were so close to me."

That's because I was sniffing you.

I laugh at my own thoughts. How appropriate that I got elbowed in the nose for sniffing him.

"Is it bleeding?" He keeps his focus on me.

The older woman behind the counter hands him more napkins. "Are you okay, Doctor? That had to burn your skin."

He gives her a polite nod, taking the extra napkins.

"I'm …" I shake off his question while removing the wad of napkins from my nose and showing him the clear mucous on it. "There's no blood. See?"

The barista grimaces. I take her cue and dispose of the napkins. Maybe showing my snot is not the right approach.

"But yeah … no … I mean good. I'm good. Your ass is probably scorched from that coffee. Hope you have on thick briefs." I do my best to show my concern for his wellbeing instead of focusing on my complete embarrassment and lack of blood coming out of my nose.

"It's just skin." He wipes his leg as the barista cleans the mess on the floor so the line can keep moving.

I place a five on the counter for my coffee.

"Let me get you another cup of coffee."

"What?" I shake my head so hard it hurts my brain. "Let me pay for your scrubs. Your medical bills for treating your burns. New briefs. Shoes. Everything! Let me pay for everything."

He laughs in spite of the slight grimace on his face as he moves forward several steps. "I'm good. Really, Dorothy. I'd better get cleaned up and have someone take a peek at my backside."

"Want me to take a look?"

He lifts an eyebrow. "You're a patient transporter."

"Yes. And a nursing student. But I have my CNA license, and I was an EMT for a while. Also, I listened to a podcast a few months back on cutting-edge burn treatments that can prevent permanent nerve damage, reduce scarring by sixty-three percent, and cut recovery time in half."

Dr. Hawkins blinks for several seconds, eyes narrowed a bit. "Dr. Hathaway is head of the burn unit. I think I'll have her take a quick look."

"Your ex-wife?" I'm certain the whole cafeteria hears me, but his suggestion strikes me as odd. I mean … all the rumors about his marriage. His wife leaving him.

Wrinkles form along his forehead.

Yes, I know everything about him because the sexiest doctor in the hospital getting a divorce was the hottest topic for months. The divorce saga settled down, but *he* remains a hot topic.

"She is. Why?" he says slowly.

"I realize she's a doctor, but it has to be weird letting your ex-wife see your naked ass … butt … buttocks … gluteus." I smile, my go-to when things get really awkward—which happens way too often.

His thick eyebrows dip. "She's seen it a few times before." An odd grin plays along his lips.

I'm not sure if *I* amuse him or if it excites him to think about his ex being forced to look at his ass again, a reminder of what she gave up. Sucking my top lip between my teeth, I nod several times. "Okay. But make sure she listened to that podcast. I can send her the link if she hasn't heard it yet. But I'm sure she knows all about it. She's brilliant and my favorite boss bitch in the whole hospital."

"Dorothy …" He scratches his chin, lips corkscrewed to the side.

"I mean bitch in a really good way. Take charge. No nonsense. Get shit done."

Dr. Julie Hathaway is my idol in so many ways, but I stop short of making that confession. Real progress on my part. "Yes?" I whisper.

He hands me his cup of coffee. Pressing his finger to the bottom of my chin, he lifts it, guiding my head to one side and then the other side, gaze focused on my nose. Then he gently pinches my nose while pressing the surrounding area with his other hand. It's a bit sore, but not broken … or bleeding. Or scorched from hot coffee.

Ugh …

It's not that I'm not concerned about my nose. I am. This isn't my first nose injury. By now I could have irreversible damage to structures and tissues in my nose. I can't even think about the long-term problems I might experience, like stuffiness and breathing issues or sinus, bone, and other nose infections. This could be really bad for me.

"Sorry about your nose." He releases my chin and smiles before heading toward the elevators.

"Your coffee!" I hold it up.

"Keep it." He presses the up button.

✧ ✧ ✧

Elijah

JULIE KNEW SHE wanted to be a plastic surgeon from the moment her older brother had surgery on his cleft lip. She knew she wanted a successful career as a doctor. She knew she wanted to change lives by giving kids confidence again. I, on the other hand, floundered around, unsure of a specialty, unsure of where I wanted to live and work, unsure about if and when we should start a family.

Julie was my compass.

"I need a favor." I tuck an extra pair of scrubs under my arm.

She glances up from her phone, just outside of her office on the second floor. "I'm not switching weeks with you. Roman has been looking forward to—"

"A large cup of really hot coffee was just spilled down my backside."

Her eyebrows shoot up. "Oh. You want me to take a look?"

"No. I just wanted you to know in case I die from sepsis."

She rolls her greenish-brown eyes and smirks. "Follow me."

We find an empty room down the hall, and she closes the door with her back to me. "Let me know when you're ready."

"Wow! Fifteen years of marriage and you want me to undress while your back is to me? Put on a gown, only so you can pull it back and inspect my bare ass. We've had sex so many times in this hospital, I stopped counting. Yet ... here we are. Cordial and professional."

"Eli ..." she whispers on a sigh.

"I'm ready, Dr. Hathaway."

Dr. Hathaway ... there was no question that she wasn't going to take my name when we got married. I didn't need her name to be the same as mine. I just needed her.

On my stomach, I glance at her over my shoulder. She focuses on my burns. Always professional. I focus on her new red hair color and her crisp, purple button-down under her lab coat revealing her larger cleavage. I'm sure some eager plastics guy jumped at that opportunity for professional reciprocity with the world renowned Dr. Hathaway.

"Hope you can learn to sleep on your right side or your stomach." She cleans the burns as I clench my teeth.

"I'm a back sleeper. You know this."

Julie frowns, dressing my wounds. "That's why I said it. But we've been apart for over a year." She shrugs. "I thought maybe having the bed to yourself might have changed that. Or do you have company in bed?"

"Yes. Roman finds his way into my room, heating my bed by about ten degrees."

For the first time since she started tending to my bared backside, she shoots me a quick glance with a nervous smile.

Yeah, I'm an idiot.

I turn my head, staring at the wall with my arms folded under my chin. "That was your way of asking if I've had another woman in my bed? Smooth, Jules ... so smooth I didn't catch it."

"You're a wonderful man, Eli. Any woman would be lucky to be in your bed."

"Except my wife."

"I'm not your wife anymore."

I grunt. Maybe I should have let Dorothy deal with my burns. "God ... you're so clinical, Jules."

"I'm professional."

"Cold."

"Thorough. Focused. What is your deal? Did you think I was going to treat your burns with a hand job?"

"If I thought you were going to address my burns with the same fumbling ineffectiveness as your hand jobs, I would have let the patient transporter treat me."

Her gloves snap as she peels them from her hands and tosses them into the trash can. "Have your mommy change your dressings."

The door opens. The door closes.

I remain on my stomach, eyes shut as I blow out a

slow breath. Had I not loved her right down to my soul, I wouldn't hate her so much. After easing on a pair of clean scrubs, I slip out of the room and find Julie in her office.

She glances up from her computer as the door clicks behind me. Guilt wars in her eyes, weathering her face and weighting her posture. It's always the same look. Even when I provoke her like I did a few minutes ago, she bleeds more pain than anger.

"Will the day ever come that I fully understand?" I stroll around her tiny office, inspecting the diplomas, professional licenses, and achievement awards that I've seen a million times before, the photos on her desk of Roman, and the Zen garden my mom gave her.

"Probably not."

Keeping my back to her, I stare blankly at the bookcase filled with medical journals. "Are you happy, Jules? Is this new life everything you hoped it would be?"

"I don't know how to answer that. It's hard to feel happy being the villain."

I turn slowly as she closes her laptop and leans back in her desk chair, hugging her arms to her body like a shield.

"I never said you were the villain."

Julie grunts. "I'm not sure our families would agree."

"Families? You mean my family."

"Your family. My family. Our mutual friends. People here at the hospital. Don't act like you don't see it. Perfect Elijah abandoned by his awful wife. The looks. The whispers. They don't go unnoticed by me. And that's fine. I made a very conscious decision to walk away *knowing* this would happen. But it's been a year. Haven't

I served my time?"

I can't answer that question. I just ... can't. One night we were making love with so much intensity I felt like a damn virgin, falling in love with this woman all over again. It felt pivotal. Something so out of our ordinary that I knew things would be different between us. But my different was not even on the same planet as her different. Before I could suggest we ask her parents to watch Roman so we could get away, maybe renew our wedding vows, and work on giving Roman a brother or sister ... BOOM!

"*I need out, Eli.*"

Need.

Not want. NEED.

Julie needed out of our marriage. And when she broke down crying, I actually felt sorry for *her*. She sounded like a victim pinned beneath an overturned car. Begging me to help her.

"*What do you want me to do, Jules?*"

Anything.

I wanted to do whatever she needed. All I could focus on was helping her out of her pain. Lifting that proverbial car from her so she could breathe ... so she'd stop crying. It was always instinctual to take away her pain.

"*I need you to let me go.*"

She wanted me to let go of fifteen years of marriage, just like that. Live with joint custody for the next sixteen years. Untangle my life from hers. Julie wanted me to stop breathing. She'd been so adamant about my lack of understanding her motives, her feelings. But I just couldn't understand why you'd work so hard to have everything you ever wanted and then just … let it go. Because that's what I believe. The life we had was everything. How do you let go of everything?

Taking two slow steps, I pick up the framed photo from her desk. Same frame. Different picture. It used to be a photo of our family at Disney World. It's been replaced with a photo of Roman at the zoo with Julie. "You know the patients who survive the unimaginable? The ones who, by all rights, should be dead? And yet … they hang on. As doctors we have no explanation for the heart that's still beating in a body that's broken beyond repair. We remove our hero cape and toss it aside because we're not worthy of taking credit for something that's clearly greater than our most honed skill. It's the fight. The patient fights for something they refuse to lose, even when to everyone else it's over."

I return the photo to her desk and continue. "I never saw you fight. You just … let go. And the only explanation you've ever given me is 'I just can't explain it. You won't understand, and it won't change anything.'"

"Eli …" She bows her head, closing her eyes.

"If you could give me *something* … the tiniest of clues … it would profoundly change my life." Emotion hits me in the form of desperation. I refuse to blink and let her see me cry again, but fuck … it still hurts.

Julie opens her eyes but keeps her chin tipped to her chest. She won't even look at me. "I fell out of love."

"With me …" I whisper.

She slowly shakes her head while lifting her own teary

gaze to meet mine. "With myself. I fell out of love with the woman I was with you. And to this day, I still can't explain it because the words sound so selfish and utterly ridiculous in my own head. I just wanted to be someone different. And I couldn't do it when I felt anchored to you. And as much as I wanted to just forge ahead, I felt this ticking clock counting down the hours of my life. And every day felt like a missed opportunity to honor myself by living the life I wanted to live."

"The hair. The tattoos. The new clothes. The..." I glance at her chest "...the implants ..." I shake my head. "Did you think I wouldn't be okay with them?"

"Don't do this ..." she whispers.

"Do what? I don't understand why you can't tell me—"

"Because it's embarrassing!" She presses the heels of her hands to her head before running her fingers through her red hair. "I wanted a new start. A rebirth. I felt like a butterfly dying to emerge from my cocoon, and you were the cocoon. I didn't want to *become* something in your eyes. I wanted to simply *be* someone in the eyes of a man who didn't watch me stumble through my awkward teen years. Who didn't have a firsthand account of how much I hated sex for months after I lost my virginity because I didn't have the confidence to be sexy and adventurous. I want a man who didn't see me break down a million times during medical school. It's like you were the contractor who built me. But I don't want to be with someone who knows every single part of me. I want to be exciting and new. I want to have a man look at me with curiosity and wonder. I want to keep a part of me for myself. An unsolvable mystery, not a forgone conclusion."

Her words hang heavily in the air as my mind struggles to process them. They would make sense to me if we were fifteen again. But we are grown-ass adults with jobs and a child. Still, I just want my life back. My wife ... my family. "Fine. Let's meet at a bar. Let's date like we're meeting for the first time. I'll act like you've looked this way forever. You can tell me as little or as much as you want to about yourself, and I won't bring up our past."

After several unblinking seconds, a tiny smile works its way up her face. "I love you, Eli. I will always love you. But you just said it yourself, it would be an *act*. We both deserve something better than that. We could go through the motions, but they would mean nothing because we both would know they were an act."

She looks at me like a dog she plans to leave at a shelter. It's the way she looked at me when she said she needed out. A terrible look. I'm good with that being the last time she gives it to me.

"I'll have Roman's bag packed Sunday night." I turn and exit her office without looking back. I'm done looking back at the wreckage of my marriage.

❖ ❖ ❖

Dorothy

THE FOLLOWING MORNING, after a twelve-hour shift, I wait inside the parking garage entrance. I have it on good authority that Dr. Hawkins will be here at 7:00 a.m. It's not his weekend to work, but (also on good authority) he has a patient in a special chemotherapy trial, and he needs to check in on her.

"Dr. Hawkins!"

His head snaps up as he walks through the automatic glass doors, holding his son's hand. The little boy looks about four from his height. Tall. Probably his dad's genes. Dr. Hawkins has to be at least six-four—a full foot taller than my five-four stature. But I know, in spite of his height, little Roman is only three. Lots of rumors about the hottest doctor at the hospital float around. I'm fairly certain the age of his son is correct.

"Dorothy …" he says my name slowly, like the smile that grows on his face.

"For you." I hold out a large reusable shopping bag, but it hasn't been used before. I bought it for his stuff. He can reuse it. He can think of me when he reuses it. Unless it brings back memories of me spilling coffee on his ass and down the back of his legs. Then maybe I prefer he not think of me when reusing the bag.

He releases the little boy's hand and takes the bag. "What's this?"

"What's in the bag?" Roman says in choppy increments. He's a spitting image of his dad. They both have the same dirty blond hair. A little longer on the top and shorter on the sides. They have the same rich brown eyes too. His shirt reads TROUBLE.

"Dorothy …" Dr. Hawkins shakes his head, lifting his gaze from the contents of the bag to me. "Why did you do this?"

"I ruined your scrubs. So I bought you new ones. Underwear ... just took a guess on the size. Hope you're good with boxer briefs in black. And the shoes are in two sizes. I guessed either a ten and a half or an eleven. Am I right?"

Dr. Hawkins nods slowly, wearing a distorted mask of confusion. "Eleven. But ..."

"Donate the other pair." I shrug.

"You ..." He shakes his head again, brows knitted together. "You should return them and get your money back. You should return all of this and get your money back. And what is—" He pulls out the superhero cape.

"Oh!" I laugh. "That's not for you. I heard you usually arrive with this little guy because he goes to the hospital daycare. Apparently, a lot of the nurses' ovaries explode when this happens." I roll my eyes. "Seems a bit farfetched. Anyway, I had an uncle who used to include me whenever someone in the family had a special occasion like a birthday. He'd get them a gift, and he'd get me some sort of dress-up gift. My mom said he was spoiling me, but he said fostering a child's imagination is an investment into the future, not the spoiling of a generation."

Dr. Hawkins opens his mouth, but nothing comes out for several seconds.

I glance at my watch. "I have to get upstairs. Hope everything fits. Especially the cape." I grin at Roman. He's adorable, hugging his dad's leg and watching me with big brown eyes.

"Thank you, Dorothy. Really ... I don't know what

to say."

"Daddy ... go." Roman tugs on his leg.

"Yeah, buddy. We'll go." He shares a big smile, not the confused and guilty expression from just seconds earlier. Dr. Hawkins has a great smile.

I can tell he's a flosser. Tall and he flosses. Journal-worthy.

"I'll give him the cape later. If I show it to him now, he'll want to take it to daycare, and there will be a meltdown when I don't let him."

"That's cool. So ... later." I turn and push open the door to the stairs.

"You're taking the stairs?"

I glance over my shoulder. "Yep. I like to close my movement and exercise rings before noon." Lifting my wrist, I show him my watch.

He holds up his watch. "I already closed my exercise ring this morning." He winks.

Tall. Flosser. Fit. Yeah, totally journal-worthy.

CHAPTER THREE

Accidental Babysitter

Elijah

"CUTE CAPE." MOM smiles at Super Roman as he flies around my parents' backyard, chasing Elmo their golden retriever.

I nod, sipping my Sunday brunch mimosa, finding it impossible to hide my grin while looking at that cape and thinking about the woman who gave it to him. "The burn incident…" I glance at Mom, leaning to my right since the burns on my left butt cheek and the back of my left leg prevent me from sitting with my weight evenly distributed "…the culprit is a patient transporter at the hospital. She replaced my items of clothing … including new underwear."

Mom's eyebrows inch up her forehead.

"Yeah." I chuckle. "She also bought Roman that cape, having never met him."

"I already love her. When are you bringing her to Sunday brunch?"

I laugh some more. "In another life where I'm not emotionally stunted from my wife leaving me and only spending half the year with my son. Or when I'm not buried in my lab or attending funerals of deceased patients."

"Well…" she taps my leg with her toe as she bounces one leg crossed over the other "…in that pathetic spiel you call an excuse, you failed to mention that you're not interested or *attracted* to this woman. That's progress, Eli."

I scratch my jaw, focusing my gaze on Roman. "She's young."

"How young?"

I shrug. "Maybe late twenties. I'm not sure."

"Married?"

"I don't know." I grin. "Our interactions have been limited."

"Wedding band?"

"No. But she might just not wear it to work."

"Ha!" Mom throws her arms in the air like someone scored a touchdown. "You looked! Eli, you actually looked to see if she was wearing a wedding ring. That means something, my dear boy."

Great. Yes, I looked to see if she had a ring on her finger after she went on about the podcast on burn research. For the tiniest, fleeting moment, I wondered if she went home to some guy who got to listen to her sexy, nerdy-girl chattering about medical research.

Jesus…

Did I really just think "sexy?"

"You should ask her out on a date."

"I work with her. Not a good idea."

Mom pulls her glasses down to the tip of her nose to look at me over the frames. "She's a patient transporter. I'd hardly call that *working with her.*"

"I'm not ready to date."

Mom drains her drink and sets it on the mosaic tile table between us. "Roman sure does like that cape."

On a sigh, I bite back my grin. "Yeah, yeah … it was the perfect gift. I'll write her a thank you."

"You do that." Mom nods slowly. "Make sure you leave your cell number on that thank you."

"Aaannd … I'm out of here. Where's Dad?"

She juts her chin toward the detached garage. "Playing with grease, as always. You know, you'll never get over Julie if you don't crack open the door to other possibilities."

"Yup, I think I'll go help Dad." I make my escape to the garage to help my dad. He doesn't ask questions beyond *what's up*—a man of few words, always under a car, covered in grease. My parents are opposites in every way possible—the mechanic and the psychiatrist. But somehow it just works. Maybe Julie and I were too much alike. I never thought that really could be the case, but the list of things I never thought seems to grow every day.

✧ ✧ ✧

"I ASKED DOROTHY out on a date," Dr. Warren informs me two seconds after I walk into the lab Monday morning.

My forward motion comes to a halt, crashing into a strange reality. It's not that he asked her out on a date. It's the way my hands ball into fists because I want to strike him square in the nose. And I'm not a violent person. Relaxing my fists, I stare at them for a few seconds before shaking them out, shaking out the completely irrational sense of anger he spurred in my unstable mind.

"Why would you do that? You were making fun of her just last week."

"I wasn't making fun of her. Just making observations. But I sensed it pissed you off, so I thought what better way to make you see that I'm not a dick than to ask her out. Buy her dinner. Show her a good time."

How did he make it through medical school? Why did our educational institutions not require an ounce of common sense to receive a diploma? "Your level of ignorance knows no boundaries."

"I graduated top in my class."

"Good for you. I hope you find the cure for all cancers because your chances at finding success as a decent human are pretty slim."

He chuckles like I'm joking.

I'm not joking. Clearing my throat, I thumb through some papers next to my computer. "Did she say yes?"

"I'm not sure. I think she needs to check her calendar, but she didn't say calendar. She actually said 'list.' Do you suppose Dorothy Mayhem has a waiting list for dating?" Warren laughs, shaking his head.

"Maybe it's a sex offender list."

"Real funny." He tips his chin, looking through the microscope.

"Did you…" I play it casual like it's not bugging the hell out of me "…just ask her out this morning?"

"Yesterday. She only works Friday through Sunday. She's a nursing student. Willow said she lives on a farm with emus. I'm not buying that rumor, but I'm sure as hell intrigued. It's been a while since a woman really intrigued me. But she wouldn't hand over her phone number, so now I have to wait until Friday to see where I fit on her *list*."

"Who is Willow?"

Warren's head snaps up. "Dude, she's your nurse."

"Willa. Not Willow."

He shakes his head, enjoying some sort of laugh at my expense. "No one calls her Willa."

My head jerks backward. "I call her Willa because that's her name."

"I stand corrected. No one *except you* calls her Willa."

"Why not?"

"If you were a woman in your twenties named after your great grandmother Willa, would you actually go by that name?"

My lips twist, eyes squint. "Huh … how did I miss that? I'll try to remember to call her Willow from now on."

"No. Don't. I'm pretty sure the only thing keeping her from jumping you is the fact that you call her Willa. If you call her Willow, she'll probably start dry humping your leg." Warren glances at his phone. "I have to check on Opal."

"I want her lab results ASAP."

"You got it." He tucks his phone into the pocket of his coat and slips out of the lab.

My brain hurts more than my burnt ass. Warren and Dorothy. Dorothy and emus. Willa is Willow. Willow wants to hump my leg.

✦ ✦ ✦

THURSDAY NIGHT, JULIE picks up Roman. Her mom watches him while she works—because only his awful father sends him to daycare ... which he happens to love.

Friday morning I arrive early to the hospital and park by the entrance where Dorothy gave me the bag of clothes. I may have pried a little to see what time her shift starts, and I may have been told that she usually arrives thirty minutes early for her twelve-hour shift that begins at 8:00 a.m. So I arrive by 7:15 to play it safe and not miss her.

At exactly 7:30 a.m., a white Audi Q5 zooms past my blue Tesla and makes a ninety-degree turn into a parking spot. How did it not crash into the car next to it? A miracle.

"Damn ... didn't see that coming," I whisper to myself when Dorothy emerges from the vehicle—blue scrubs, pink undershirt, matching pink tennis shoes. She curls her dark hair behind her ears, hikes her bag onto her shoulder, and shuts the door.

Dorothy Mayhem drives a luxury car like a bat out of

Hell. On all accounts, I'm in shock. It takes me a few seconds to close my gaping mouth and climb out of my vehicle.

"Good morning."

She turns just before the entrance. "Oh, hey! Good morning."

"That was quite the parking job."

Her gaze flits to her car. "Thanks. I've had a few issues with parking. So once I got my Q5, I decided to slow it down a bit."

I try not to react, but I feel my eyebrows inching up my forehead all on their own. *That* was her slowed-down version of parking? "Here. You really should not have done what you did last week. So the least I can do is give you this." I hand her the thank-you card. "By the way, Roman loves the cape. Wears it all the time. You hit a home run with that gift."

"What's this?" She takes the card from me.

I feel stupid. Is the card a bad idea? Do people no longer give thank-you cards? Is everything communicated via text and email? "It's uh…" I slip my hands into the pockets of my gray pants "…a thank-you card."

"Oh." She inspects it. "Should I open it now? Or do you want me to wait?"

I have no clue. Now, so she'll see my number? (Thanks, Mom.) Or later, so she doesn't have to acknowledge my phone number? Since common sense has a tradition of arriving late to the party, I want to pluck that thank-you card from her hand and buy a new one that doesn't have my phone number scrawled on the inside of it.

"Oh. It doesn't matter. Whenever."

She shrugs and rips it open, making my stomach twist with regret. The phone number was a terrible idea. (Really ... thanks, Mom.)

I can't stand here like an idiot waiting for her to react. "Thanks again. I'd better get to my office. I have rounds soon." Slipping past her, I breeze through the automatic doors.

"Is this your phone number?"

I stop. Closing my eyes, I curse my mom and her terrible idea ... that I didn't have to take, but she's smart and usually right, so ... "Uh, yeah." I cringe, unable to turn around like a grown man and face her.

"I'm in school during the week, and I work twelve-hour shifts over the weekend, but—"

"No." I turn, feigning confidence mixed with indifference. "It was stupid and impulsive of me. I'm not really sure why I felt compelled to do it. Just—"

"No. I mean ... as long as it's after lecture and clinical during the week. Or I guess if you're thinking late on the weekends. I can totally babysit Roman for you."

Oh, for the love of ...

I'm just that oblivious to reality. I have been since the day my wife left me. How can I be just that stupid? Dorothy is younger than me. Of course she thinks I'm looking for a babysitter, not a date. Dr. Warren is closer to her age. And what a dick move of me to even leave my number after Dr. Even Bigger Dick asked her out.

"You uh ... have a lot on your plate. I wouldn't

dream of asking you to babysit my son."

"Well ..." She waves the thank-you card. "Clearly, you thought of it at some point."

Nope. Just thought we'd grab a drink this week while Julie has Roman.

"My intern said he asked you out." If in doubt, throw your intern under the bus. When you fail at properly asking a woman out on a date, you move to plan B—discuss other men who are waiting for her to answer their date invitation.

I'm clueless. Maybe I should stick to looking for a cure for cancer. I honestly think it might be easier than asking Dorothy out on a date.

"Dr. Warren." Her face scrunches. "Yeah, I'm not sure about him. I've thought about it, and I don't know what we might discuss. And there are rumors that he's the hospital's man-whore, which makes his invitation to take me out on a date that doesn't involve the on-call room feel a little suspicious."

Her lips twist. "On the other hand, I've heard he's good at what he does."

"Mmm ... yes. Dr. Warren is an excellent doctor."

"Oh." She grins. "I meant what he does in the on-call room."

Rubbing the back of my neck, my gaze drops to my feet. "Well, I can't vouch for *that*. You'll have to get other references for that."

"Did the underwear fit?"

I need to get out of here. The conversation has taken way too many sharp turns. My brain hurts from the whiplash. Why didn't I stick with a simple, verbal "thank you?"

Babysitting.

Dr. Warren's inappropriate behavior in the on-call rooms.

The gifted underwear from a stranger I've known for all of two seconds.

Really—no words.

Yet, I gave her my phone number. And at the time, my only explanation was impulse ... and my mom. I'm not ready to date. But I *need* to date. The commiserative looks from everyone around me chips away at my sense of self-worth. Yes, my wife left me. But those looks stopped months after it happened and have evolved into "poor thing can't get over her" looks.

No thank you.

"Yes. They fit just fine."

"Good." She nods, a pleasant smile stealing her face for several seconds before it simmers into cork screwed lips. "You need my phone number. I mean. If you want me to babysit, you need my phone number. It's not like I'm going to call you and tell you when you need a babysitter. Right?"

Why? Why the phone number? Do I really expect her to call me and ask me out? I would have paid top dollar for a shot of clarity and common sense while writing that damn thank-you.

She slips her phone out of her pocket and moves her thumbs along the screen. A second later, my phone vibrates. I glance at the text.

Hi, Dr. Hawkins. It's me, Dorothy Mayhem. Now you have my number.

My grin grows exponentially. It feels good. Better than good … it feels pretty damn amazing as I glance up at her. "Thanks. I'll add you to my contacts."

"Cool. I'll see you around."

"Oh … Dorothy?"

She turns. "Yeah?"

"Is Dorothy your grandmother's name?"

She wets her lips and rubs them together a few times while her brows pull toward her nose. Then her face relaxes, welcoming back that contagious smile. "No, silly. It's *my* name." And just like that, she heads up the stairs as I replay the train wreck in my head.

Cool. Julie never says cool. And she never calls me silly. She speaks to me on a need-to basis, scowling at me like a tumor protruding from her neck, giving her a perpetual frown.

CHAPTER FOUR

On-call Room

Dorothy

"Just the person I was looking for."

I cringe at Dr. Warren's deep, confident voice. "Hi." I continue pushing Lizzie Williamson toward radiology.

"Do you have an answer for me?" he asks.

"No, but I have a few questions."

"Such as?" He creeps up beside me so his arm brushes mine.

"Why dinner and not just the on-call room?"

He chokes on a laugh. "Um …"

"I asked Jana, Evie, and Kari where you took them for dinner. They said you don't do dinner. Yet you specifically said dinner to me. And you don't fit my list, other than good genes."

"I'll take good genes as a compliment."

"Why? You didn't have anything to do with it."

He chortles. "This list … tell me more about it."

I shrug, pressing the button at the elevator and smiling at Lizzie. "Traits. Qualifications. Minimum requirements. I don't like getting into awkward situations." The doors open, and I push Lizzie's wheelchair onto it.

Dr. Warren gives her a curt smile as he follows me. He says nothing more until I drop Lizzie off for a CT scan. "What do mean by awkward situations?" He corners me ... literally in a corner outside of radiology.

He smells kinda good, kinda bad. Coffee good. Strong-hair-product bad.

"In the on-call room, you don't have to say much ... I imagine." Heat rushes up my neck as I stare at his green scrub-clad chest. "But dinner requires conversation, which is not my specialty. So if you don't have a lot of material planned in terms of conversation, then dinner could be awkward."

I don't have to look up to know he's grinning. Dr. Warren bleeds confidence, and it drips all over me like sticky honey that I need to wash off. Wavy black hair. Dimples. It's almost too much. "Would dinner be less awkward if our first date were in the on-call room?"

"That makes no sense." I look to my right at the nurse headed our way. "That would give us one topic to discuss—sex. And if you don't live up to the expectations, I'm not going to be able to pretend that you did. And I don't want to hurt your feelings, but I'm not great at lying."

Warren barks a laugh. "Dorothy, I can guarantee that won't be an issue on my part. As for you, I have no idea, but I'm willing to give it a go."

My head jerks up to meet his mischievous, hazel eyes. "I'm very well-read on the subject. Probably more so than you."

"Well-read?" Dr. Warren laughs more. He laughs at *me*.

It seems highly unlikely that I will join him for dinner or meet him in the on-call room. Although, the latter stands a better chance because I'm pretty competitive. And at this point, I want to show him I'm nothing to laugh at in bed.

He leans closer, sharing his coffee breath on a whisper, "Dorothy ... are you a virgin? A well-read virgin?"

I stumble backward, hitting the wall. "No. I'm not a virgin!"

Warren's eyes widen as he looks around the hallway at the few bystanders silenced from my answer that may have been a bit louder than necessary. Does he really believe I'm a virgin at thirty?

An unsettling amusement ghosts across his face as one side of his mouth curls into a smile, showing off one dimple. "When you take lunch, page me. We'll see who does it better." He pivots, strutting toward the elevator.

"I only have thirty minutes for lunch."

"Then find me quickly." He keeps strutting.

"But I have to eat my soup and carrots."

"Bring them with you." His shoulders shake, and I know he's laughing at me ... again.

✧ ✧ ✧

OVER THE NEXT five hours, I pass by different on-call rooms, and my skin begins to itch. I have to be allergic to Warren. Or he gave me something. He did breathe on me, and he's around sick kids all day long. It's disgusting how many doctors don't follow proper protocol to prevent cross-contamination. I bet those on-call rooms are breeding grounds for every infection known to man.

Just what I need, some fatal infection that causes bleeding from all of my orifices. I inspect my skin for bruising—indicative of internal bleeding.

Since it's a sunny day, I take my lunch outside instead of paging Dr. Warren. I prefer clean bedrooms ... and half-deflated blowup mattresses, but that's a story for another day. Planting my butt beneath a maple tree, I slip in my earbuds and re-listen to a podcast on flesh-eating infections. Just in case ...

"Canned, no-chicken soup?"

Plucking my earbuds from my ears, I glance up at Dr. Hawkins and his god-like aura as he squats in front of me, sipping something from a YETI mug. He's hot. My mind reaches for something better, a better word than hot because I like words—words like synecdoche and scaturient. But I have to call it like I see it. And the more I see it/him, it's hard to not fixate on his hotness.

Tall, athletic build.

Bright eyes that shine with more green than brown in the sunlight.

A flosser's smile.

And large hands—the strong, capable kind that can break something, not just the kind with freakishly long fingers dangling like jellyfish tentacles from bony appendages. Dr. Hawkins has hands that don't just hold shit. They command everything they touch.

Or so I imagine.

"Yes." I spoon another bite of my chicken-less soup.

"You're eating that cold out of the can?"

I shake my head. "Room temperature."

He chuckles. "There are microwaves in the break rooms."

"Yes. But have you seen them? Disgusting."

Rubbing his lips together, he nods slowly. I try to focus on the bridge of his nose, the safest place to look at people to give them the impression you're looking them in the eye even when you're not. However, Dr. Hawkins has no safe zones on his body. I can't look at him anywhere without physically reacting with a flushed face and racing heart because, if my intuition is right (50/50 chance), I think he enjoys looking at me too. So I keep my focus on my soup, tonguing my teeth to make sure I don't have parsley stuck between them.

My luck involves miscommunication catastrophes. I think he likes looking at me, but really I just have shit between my teeth—these kinds of miscues.

"Did you eat lunch already?" I ask between sips of soup.

"Yes. I have lunch with my mom on Fridays." He nods across the street. "She works in that building. I get her favorite salad and take it to her."

I squint at the building—another medical building. "What does she do?"

"She's a psychiatrist."

I nod and swallow. "Talk doctor."

He grins before bringing his red mug to his lips, still balancing in his squatted position. "Yes, she's a talk doctor." Dr. Hawkins clears his throat. "Listen. I just wanted to set something straight. The phone number in the card wasn't for a babysitter." He shakes his head, glancing down at the grass between us. "It was because I thought it might be a good idea if I bought you dinner. And I should have just came out and asked if I could buy you dinner, but instead, I put the number in the card and found myself fumbling for the right words ... like I am now." He rubs a hand down his face and whispers to himself, "Jeez, Eli ..."

"No!" I set the rest of my soup in my lunchbox because there's no way I'll finish it before I need to get back to work. It's laughable that Dr. Warren thought we could have sex *and* have time for me to eat my lunch in thirty minutes. "I know you think I shouldn't have bought you those things ... that I shouldn't have spent the money on you, but I'm financially okay. Really. So please don't think you need to buy me food. I just went to the store last night. Fridge is fully stocked. Definitely no need to buy me dinner. But thanks anyway."

Dr. Hawkins drops his head, giving it a slight shake while running his hands through his messy, dirty blond hair. It's not a new gesture. I seem to bring out that reaction in a lot of people.

Missed cues.

Misunderstandings.

What did I miss?

"I'm terrible at this." He sighs.

"I don't know what *this* is, but I think it's probably me. If you need to buy me dinner, that's fine. Just don't get all … stressed." My nose wrinkles. "And if you need a babysitter … I can do that too."

He stands, turning his back to me, scratching his head while surveying the area.

I so desperately want to read his body language, the unspoken words between the lines that I can't see. Is he mad at me? He looks frustrated.

"Dorothy … Roman likes the cape. I like your shoes and your smile. Both feel like something I need …"

"I got the shoes online. Amazon."

Dr. Hawkins turns. "Amazon," he whispers before chuckling an odd chuckle like a crazy man on the verge of losing his mind.

I stand, brushing off the grass from my butt and the back of my legs. "Yes. And my smile is from Dr. Crowe. He's an excellent orthodontist. I still wear my retainers three nights a week. But you have nice teeth, so I don't think you need Dr. Crowe."

He digs his nice teeth into his lower lip, eyes narrowed a bit. "I think you should spend some supervised time with Roman before you babysit him for me. He's with his mom this week. Would you like to have dinner with us when I have him again?"

"Sure." Okay. Thank god. It's not me. It's him and his concern about a stranger watching his son. That's cool. Too many parents blindly leave their kids with complete strangers from babysitting services. I respect his approach. If I planned on having kids, it would be my approach as well.

"Sure." He grins. "I like sure. So I'll call you after I check my schedule."

"Or text me. We don't have to talk. No one calls me except my dad. He doesn't like to text."

"What if I *want* to talk to you?"

I can't imagine why that would be. Maybe he doesn't know how to text, like my dad.

"Then you better call after I get home from school during the week … so after three, except on days I have clinical. Then it's after four. Or you could call me after I get home from work on the weekends … so after eight-thirty." I shake my head. "That's not true. I walk for an hour and a half, so tack on ninety minutes to both of those times."

He smiles like my parents smile at me and maybe a few friends I used to have, like Nicole. It feels comfortable like … acceptance. "Noted. I have to get back to work. I'll *call* you."

"Okay." I start walking toward the hospital entrance. He walks beside me. "Did Dr. Hathaway listen to those burn podcasts? I bet she did. She's so brilliant."

"I didn't ask, though I'm sure she did. Because, yes, she's brilliant. She's always on top of cutting-edge treatments in her field." He exhales like his ex-wife, Boss Bitch, amazing doctor isn't a great thing.

But she is. Julie Hathaway is the pinnacle of achievement for any woman in the medical field. I'd give my right nipple and even my clitoris on most days to feel *that* successful, confident, and generous.

"Was it weird? Asking her to look at your burns? I heard she left the exam room a bit aggravated."

He pushes the elevator button and turns to face me, arms folded over his chest. "Just how much gossip about me do you hear on a daily basis?"

The doors open and I step onto the elevator first. "I'm not here that often. But if you divide the gossip into a daily amount and multiply it by seven, then I'd say it's a lot."

He follows me onto the elevator and leans against the opposite wall. I stare at his shoes. They're older blue Nikes. Not great, but far from awful. And not on my No Way In Hell list. His sinewy arms and his genetically sculpted face make up for the worn Nikes.

"People feel sorry for me?"

"I don't know. Maybe. They just talk about you and your ..." I stop before saying *hotness*.

"My?" His eyebrows lift.

They're good brows. Not a unibrow and not like some of the older doctors who get one long-ass brow that's like an inch long and standing straight out, ready to stab someone. Whenever I see that, I just want to pluck the damn thing from their face. Do they not have a mirror or close friends to tell them about it?

"I don't know ... really." And I don't know for sure. I know a lot of the nurses whisper inappropriate comments about him. Inappropriate because of sexual misconduct rules at the hospital and inappropriate because they're married with kids and attending church on Sundays.

My opinion of his hotness stays in my head. No one can fire me for my thoughts ... except when I let them slip out to patients like, "Yeah, you might die." A rare occurrence that happened only once, just after I started and at the end of a very long day when my brain felt ready to explode. In my defense, the boy was fifteen and knew he was dying. He just wanted one person to give it to him straight. And that just so happens to be my specialty.

But I never join in the break room chatter about Dr. Hotness Hawkins (not my label) and the speculation of his penis size in relation to his hand size and finger length ratio. There is nothing scientific to back that up. *That* I did mention in the break room once, but it wasn't well received by my coworkers. I think they used the word "killjoy" to describe me.

"Finish what you started to say."

"Oh shoot." I grin as the doors open to my floor. "No time. Bye, Dr. Hawkins."

CHAPTER FIVE

Meatballs

Elijah

FIVE DAYS AFTER our chat outside of the hospital and in the elevator, more alluding to my gossip popularity, I decide to call Dorothy. No solid reasoning backs my decision. I just know that my incessant need for things in my life to make sense has gotten me nowhere.

No clarity.

No family unit.

No wife.

No hope that it's all just a bad dream.

So I change directions and let instinct guide me. My instinct says Julie would shed several tears if I died, but short of that, she wants nothing to do with me. My love rubs her like a splintery piece of wood someone impaled into her chest. Every move I make only intensifies her pain and angers her.

"Hi, Dr. Hawkins." Dorothy answers on the first ring, probably because I've followed her guidelines for the best time to reach her. I have a feeling she has a lot of guidelines. Fine by me. I'll take all the cues and guidance I can get. If she doesn't brutally murder me with the truth first, I find it quite possible that her honesty could unshackle me from my self-doubt.

That self-doubt sucks. It's a creepy little bastard that lingers in a dark corner waiting to chase me into the street, where I have a high probability of getting struck by a bus. When someone says "It's me, not you," it's a blinking neon sign that there's something so fundamentally wrong with you, that they'd rather take the blame than let you find out how they really feel about you.

"Dr. Hawkins?"

I clear my throat. "Yes. Hi. How are you?"

"Tired."

"Oh, is this a bad time? I can call you when you're less tired."

"Okay."

I stare out my bedroom window at the sunset over downtown Portland, a ridiculous grin pinned to my face. Maybe Dorothy is on the autism spectrum, lacking the social filter of neurotypical people, or maybe she prefers complete honesty over frivolous lies.

On my days off, I like to sleep in as long as Roman will allow. But my mom has a gift for waking me up with an early phone call. She asks if I'm sleeping. I always lie and say no because I don't want her to feel bad for waking me. Maybe I should say yes and follow it up with an honest "but that's okay."

"Or I can make this really quick so you can get to

bed."

"Okay." Her personality continues to feed my amusement—my joy.

Even if she is honest to a fault, she at least has an aptitude for agreeability.

"Great. Would you like to have dinner next week?"

"I like to have dinner every week," she deadpans.

I chuckle. Is she joking? Serious? I don't know. I *like* that I don't know. It makes the possibility of getting to know her that much more appealing.

"Me too. Roman is a fan of dinner too. He likes spaghetti. We'd love for you to have spaghetti with us next week on a night that works with your schedule."

"Well, Mondays are chaos. Tuesday might work if I put some extra study time in on Monday. Wednesdays don't work because it's pet night at the car wash. When you purchase the Better or Best wash, you get a free pet wash. And Thursdays I glean at the farmer's market. The other three nights I don't get off work until eight, and I'm sure you don't want to eat spaghetti that late. Although … I'm not opposed to carb loading after a long shift. I pretty much eat around the clock when given the opportunity. My mom wondered if my insatiable hunger was a parasite issue, so I did some extensive research on it and had myself tested. Turns out I have no parasite issues. I'm just hungry a lot."

Pet washes. Gleaning. Parasites.

While so many questions race in my head, I promised one quick question before letting her get to bed. The other questions will have to wait until spaghetti night.

"Tuesday sounds like the perfect night."

"Um ... yeah. Maybe." Indecision seeps into her words. "I'll see if my dad will feed Wilbur, Orville, and Gemma."

Okay. Even with the time restraint ... I have to ask. "Wilbur, Orville, and Gemma?"

"Yes. My emus and my dog."

So much for rumors.

I have no idea where Dr. Warren and Dorothy stand. It never feels like the right time to ask him, especially since I've been planning my own date—dinner—invitation. And he doesn't bring it up, so I assume (secretly hope) she rejects his invitation. But he is right about one thing, Dorothy Mayhem evokes an unavoidable curiosity.

I close my blinds and head downstairs to the kitchen. All the food talk makes me hungry. "Tuesday at six work for you?"

"I'll check with my dad."

"Fine." I open the fridge and grab a bowl of grapes. "Tuesday at six, *unless* your dad can't feed your pets. Then you feed them, and we'll have dinner at seven instead."

"But what time does Roman go to bed?"

"Eight."

"So I'm coming over for an hour? Two if my dad feeds Wilbur, Orville, and Gemma?"

"You can stay later than his bedtime."

"Why?"

I chuckle. "I don't know. To talk to me."

"About what?"

"Maybe you can tell me about your emus."

"I can tell you about them while we're eating dinner."

"True." I have no great response. She makes nothing easy for me. "I guess if we have nothing to talk about after Roman goes to bed, then you'll go home."

"Okay."

Okay. So difficult and agreeable at the same time.

"Okay. I'll text you my address. Maybe I'll see you around the hospital this weekend."

"Okay."

I grin again.

Not true. I just haven't stopped grinning.

"Goodnight."

✧ ✧ ✧

Dorothy

"HEY." I PLOP down into my dad's recliner since he's chosen to sit on the sofa with my mom. Apparently they will have sex tonight. My mom let it slip that Dad only sits next to her on the sofa when he wants sex.

Things I *never, ever,* in the history of mankind, needed to know. So basically, walking in on them sitting on the sofa together always feels like the opening credits of a porn film not appropriate for anyone of any age.

They pause their Netflix show and glare at me with wide, expectant eyes.

"What?" I shoot them a wrinkled-nose look.

"What are you doing?" Mom asks, setting her bowl of popcorn on the coffee table.

"I'm sitting in this chair."

"Why?" She prods.

Funny story … my uncle died (not the funny part) and left me a lot of money.

Me.

Not my mom or my grandma. Not my other cousins.

So I bought some land with a small house on it and added a parents' quarters off to one end. I figure since they housed me for twenty-six years, the least I can do is return the favor. Besides, I like having them there. It's not that we spend hours bonding, watching TV together, and sharing meals. I just like having the company. So we share the kitchen and laundry room, but they have their own bedroom, bathroom, and family room.

"I just got off the phone with a doctor from the hospital." Did I mention the only time I visit them in their family room is when I have something to share?

They return slow nods in unison—good listeners—another bonus to having them in close proximity.

"He wants me to do some babysitting for him. He has this three-year-old son named Roman. You'd love him. He's really adorable. But now he's invited me to dinner next Tuesday to get to know Roman better. I guess so he's comfortable around me before I watch him. I respect that. Do you know how many parents don't think twice about leaving their kids with strangers?"

More nodding from them.

I wait for more than a nod. "So?"

"Oh …" Mom jumps. "It's our turn to speak?"

I roll my eyes.

"That's great, Dorothy. I hope you hit it off with the little guy. He's in your preferred buddy age range."

"No …" I shake my head while retracting it a bit. "What's that supposed to mean? And that's not what I was asking."

"You do well with people a lot older or a lot younger. That's all."

"That's not true." It is one hundred percent true. I understand mentor-mentee relationships. They feel clearer to me. One teaches. One learns. Black and white. Interacting with people closer to my age gets a little murky. Am I to impart my knowledge upon them? Do they think they have something to teach me? Who is the mentor? Who is the mentee? It just seems like an awkward power struggle and competition for knowledge.

"Okay. Whatever …" Dad clears his throat. He hates conflict even more than I do. Mom will bicker with me longer, until I get frustrated and stomp out of the room.

My dad is a get-to-the-point kind of guy. "What was the question? I think we missed it."

I sigh. It's like they don't even know me. The question is perfectly clear. "Dinner at his house. No restaurant. No menu to study online before Tuesday. He said it's spaghetti. But does that mean with meat? Meatballs I can handle. Those can be slid to the side … unless they're greasy and they leave a pooling of oil on the pasta. But if it's ground meat … like what if it's a meat sauce? Or what if the sauce is too spicy or too chunky. Ugh …" I gag on my tongue. "Chunky tomato sauce. Gross."

It sucks being a thirty-year-old woman on the autism

spectrum. I obsessed over my diagnosis for years, my obsession being another confirming factor.

Autism.

OCD.

ADHD.

Depression.

I'm a cluster-fuck of issues. My parents sighed with relief when I received an official diagnosis of Asperger syndrome. For them, it's a label to explain *everything* that isn't quite right with me. A catchall.

She's too messy.

Too organized.

Too energetic.

Too lazy.

Too picky.

Too indifferent.

Basically every time I'm "too" anything to them, it gets filed into the "she's an Aspie" catchall category. Of course, as with all labels, *Aspie's* political correctness became extinct years after my diagnosis. Everything got dumped into ASD—Autism Spectrum Disorder. But to my parents and even myself, I will always be an Aspie. And let's be honest, aside from the word "ass" phonetically present in the word Aspie, it at least has the possibility of being something extraordinary, like savant or genius.

ASD … not cool at all. Even if the average person can look past the autism spectrum part, the second anyone hears the word "disorder," game over. Something is clearly wrong with an ASD person. A fault. A defect. Not normal. Just … wrong.

So while I've spent many hours studying autism, to the point of feeling like an expert, I still can't always hide the fact that I am, in fact, on that fucking spectrum. I mean ... you don't have to tell someone you're a diabetic. You can keep that a secret until you pass out from low blood sugar. Then it's like, "Oh, yeah ... sorry I passed out on you. Did I forget to mention I'm diabetic?"

My "disorder" doesn't cause me to pass out. It just contributes to really poor social etiquette choices and occasional meltdowns over things like spaghetti dinner invitations. But unlike the diabetic, I never say, "Oh, did I forget to mention that I'm autistic?"

"Just tell him you're a vegetarian." Mom smiles her see-I-just-solved-your-problem smile.

"So, I'm supposed to call him *just* to tell him I'm a vegetarian? What about the spice level and the chunkiness? He's not going to ask me to watch Roman. He's going to think I'm crazy. Especially since his mom is a talk doctor. You guys are no help."

I march out. Why? Why did I think they could help? I give them too much credit for understanding things they clearly don't understand.

CHAPTER SIX

Dr. Hawkins doesn't work every weekend. And the one weekend I need him to work ... he isn't scheduled. That means I have one day, one chance to talk to him about the spaghetti dinner. Friday is my day—my only day.

I type out texts, but delete every single one. It isn't something that can easily be discussed with a text no matter how many emojis I use to convey my feelings. And my feelings are strong. I want him to invite me to dinner.

> *Thanks for the dinner invitation. (high-five emoji)*
>
> *I don't eat meat. Cheese is my drug of choice. (living cow emoji, cheese emoji, smiley face emoji)*
>
> *If you and Roman like meat, maybe consider balls instead of a meat sauce. (eggplant emoji) LOL. (wink emoji)*

My humor isn't everyone's taste, but I feel a connection to Dr. Hawkins, like maybe he might appreciate it.

> *I'm not great at picking out wine, but I could bring the sauce. (spaghetti emoji, tomato emoji,*

high-five emoji)

Something not too spicy—for Roman. (high-five emoji)

JK about the wine. Ice water is great. (water emoji, high-five emoji)

It's a lot of high-five emojis, which is great if he likes that emoji. But what if he doesn't? Then I'm the girl obsessed with high-five emojis. And while I know it isn't a date, I like him enough to care what he thinks of me.

Which is why I need to handle the spaghetti situation in the most neurotypical way possible.

Face-to-face.

Forcing eye contact.

Reciting my words just as I've practiced them.

I want to help him out with Roman. I just don't want to seem ungrateful for his efforts if the meal involves a meaty, chunky, spicy sauce.

"Dr. Hawkins!" I chase him out the door just before 7:00 p.m. He gets off an hour before me. Lucky.

He turns, a grin immediately finding his lips. It plunges into a flat line as he looks over my shoulder. "Is she your patient?"

I know who has his attention—Layne Gibson and her possible concussion from a gymnastics accident. We were on our way back to her room when I saw Dr. Hawkins leaving for the day.

"No. I don't have patients. She's Dr. Freeman's patient."

"Waiting in the atrium for you. Did you abandon

her? I think that's a big rule. Don't ever leave a patient unattended in a wheelchair."

"Gary's watching her. If she looks like she's about to puke, he'll give me a heads-up."

"Who's Gary?" Dr. Hawkins cocks his head to the side.

"Security guard."

"Why don't you get Dr. Freeman's patient where she's supposed to be and call me when you get off work?"

"I can't. That's why I ran after you. If what I have to say could be said over the phone, then of course I would have just called you. Not really. I would have texted you."

His focus stays glued to Layne. "Make it quick."

"I'm a vegetarian." By some miracle, I manage to hold back the full vomit—my love of cheese, meatballs verses meat sauce, and tomato chunks.

His attention shifts to me, and the smile returns. "*That's* what you couldn't say over the phone or in a text?"

I nod. "See … I'm smiling." I point to my face. "I still want to come to dinner. I'll bring my own sauce if it makes things easier. Or even plain spaghetti is great. If you have parmesan cheese, I'll put that on it. I love cheese. God … I love it so much. All dairy really. I just didn't want you to mistake me for a vegan."

He blinks so many times, I start counting them. By ten, he slides his key fob from his pocket. "Get back to work, Dorothy. I won't feed you the hog."

"Not just pork!" I call as he turns, heading toward his car. "Beef. Poultry. Fish …"

It didn't go as planned. I hate when things play out one way in my head and another way in reality. One of my many special gifts involves either giving zero shits about something or completely obsessing with a laser fixation on whatever catches my attention. I'm easily distracted one minute, and the next the world could be ending, but if I have something to say to someone, the world will just have to end.

Yes, by thirty I have a solid grip on my personality traits even if I don't get why some of them seem so odd to everyone else. It's the difference between empathy and sympathy—imagining and experiencing. Under certain non-threatening situations, I can look at myself with a small percent of objectivity, but it's not a superpower that changes my thoughts or actions.

I should have texted him. Instead, he's driving off while I have ten more emoji faces to express and a half dozen high fives.

✧ ✧ ✧

DURING THE LAST hour of work, everything intensifies to a degree I haven't experienced in years. All of my coping mechanisms for dealing with sensory overload fail me. Flickering lights in the hallways, excessive chattering, Dr. Overton's bag of spring rolls sending bile up my throat, the contour of my new shoes rubbing just below my ankle, a fraction off from where all of my other shoes hit my legs, just ... everything.

"How was work?" Mom asks from the kitchen, the

PERFECTLY ADEQUATE

second I walk in the door.

I make no effort to respond. Instead, I march into my bedroom and lock the door. Floor to ceiling bookshelves cover the wall opposite my bed. I'm a voracious reader, but I also have rows and stacks of journals.

My sanity lives in those journals. I sort my life out in words on pages. Sometimes just one word on each page for big problems. After my uncle died, I used four journals to describe the funeral, each page with one word. Four hundred and thirty-one words later, I had my feelings neatly sorted into those four journals. My script size matches the size of my problems. So my journals aren't just a compilation of words with meaning. The way they are arranged on a page says as much as the actual words themselves.

I grab a brand-new journal (I purchase them in bulk and in various colors to match my mood) and deal with everything swimming in my mind, rescuing each thought one at a time until the waters calm into a manageable ebb and flow.

> **Spring rolls should be banned from the hospital.**
> **LED lights on dimmers should be used in every work place.**
> **Shoe designers don't need to redesign a shoe if the original design works.**
> **Humans talk too much.**
> **Layne Gibson didn't have a concussion, therefore, Dr. Hawkins didn't need to worry about me leaving her with Gary the security**

guard.

Spaghetti should be the most simplistic dish in the culinary world—one box of pasta, one jar of non-chunky, mild marinara sauce. Why did Dr. Hawkins insist on making it so difficult?

Ask Dr. Hawkins if he grew up on a farm. Who says, "I won't feed you the hog?"

I will eat before I go to dinner at his house. After all, I don't need to eat to get to know Roman.

Problem solved.

"Bad day?" Mom asks as I emerge from my room, trekking a straight line to the front door to go take my walk.

"Yes. No. Just … ugh!" I slam the door behind me.

No more late-afternoon honking horns and bumper-to-bumper traffic. No chattering coworkers. No antiseptic smells. No flashing monitors. Just … quiet.

"Woof!"

Except for Gemma. I open my eyes. "Hey, Gem." I bend down and give my chocolate Labradoodle some love before making my way to the three acres of fenced-in field with a pond at the far end. Orville and Wilbur race out of their shed when they see me open the gate. I press music on my watch and click on my Max Richter playlist.

Space.

Solitude.

Air.

Setting sun.

Sky.

As I walk the parameter of the fence with my dog and two emus in tow, the lingering stress of the day evaporates from my mind, unburdening my senses. My lungs welcome a full breath of air since I've spent most of my day holding my breath to keep it together. With each step, my day unscrambles into manageable moments that I can piece together in my own way, free from the urgency to quickly process the onslaught of ... *everything*.

Ninety minutes later, I feed Wilbur and Orville and push through a gate behind their shed that opens to rows of raised-bed gardens. Dad tosses a handful of weeds into a bucket and scratches his chin as he glances up at me. It leaves a smattering of dirt clinging to his short, gray whiskers, only slightly shorter than his buzzed salt and pepper receding hairline.

He was army, police force, and private security before retiring to spend part of his day gardening and the other part driving my mom crazy.

"How was your walk?" He sits on the edge of one of the garden beds and wipes his hands on his dark gray cargo shorts.

I shrug. "Good. How was the reheated lasagna?" I smelled the burnt grease the second I got home. My mom can't even use a microwave properly.

"Well, considering it was frozen when your mom bought it and she's served it and reserved it for the past three days ... it was disgusting. Nuked mush."

"How do you flirt with a girl?"

He blinks several times before his lips curl into his

usual smile. My dad has one smile. Nothing that beams, nothing tiny like a smirk, just a cheesy, one-size-fits-all smile. "Are we going to have the lesbian talk? I feel like this conversation is better suited for your mom."

"What is the lesbian talk?"

He scratches his head, leaving more dirt in places it doesn't belong. "Rewind, since I'm not *really* sure what that is. How do *I* flirt with girls? Well, very carefully if I want to keep my nuts intact. Your mom acts like a confident woman, but she has a lethal jealous bone."

"How did you flirt with Mom?" I sit on the edge of the opposing garden bed.

"Are you asking me how to flirt? Again, this might be a subject that you should discuss with your mom."

"No. I don't need to flirt. I'm sure I can flirt if the situation arises. I'm just wondering if this doctor at the hospital has been flirting with me. I'm sure he *hasn't* been flirting with me because he's older and really successful and his ex-wife is my idol, but while I was walking, the thought came to mind. But …" I shake my head. "Just forget I asked."

"What did he do?"

"Nothing … I don't know. He just smiles at me … a lot. Maybe excessively. I'm not sure."

Dad chuckles. "Remind me again why you're having this conversation with me?"

"Because you're a guy. Who better to know how guys flirt?"

"Okay, sweetheart. If I'm going to be honest with you, then I have to confess that I'm no longer an expert on flirting. Your mother beat that out of me years ago. I walk straight lines, with a straight face, looking straight ahead at her—the only woman for me."

"Bullshit. What about your favorite waitress at The City Grill? I've watched Mom elbow you in the ribs at least a hundred times. I just always miss what you do to make her react like that."

The latch to the back-screen door clicks. Mom has two bottles of beer and a fruity wine cooler. "He looks at her boobs when she's taking our order and watches her ass when she leaves the table." She hands a beer to Dad and the wine cooler to me before frowning at the brown basket of harvested goods—four small tomatoes, a tiny head of cabbage, and a gum-ball sized onion.

"Lies. All lies." Dad shakes his head just before wrapping his mouth around the amber bottle's neck.

"How did you get on this topic?" Mom asks, squinting against the setting sun while swatting at a fly.

"A doctor has eyes for our Dorothy." Dad winks. "If he hurts my baby, he'll get his ass handed to him."

I spit out my drink, earning me two unappreciative scowls from my parents wiping at the splattered wine cooler and saliva on them. "Oh my god! You have to rock three times to get enough momentum to get out of the recliner. I don't see you handing Dr. Hawkins his ass. He's at least six-four and much younger. And I heard someone say he's done the Iron Man competition."

"Whoa ... wait." Mom peels her index finger from her bottle and points it toward me. "This wouldn't happen to be the same doctor who invited you to dinner, would it? A young, athletic, and *tall* doctor. Tell me more, Dorothy." My mom taps her mouth with the beer bottle to hide her smirk.

"There's nothing to tell."

"Is he cute? Did you tell him you're a vegetarian?" She nudges my dad's elbow. Why? I don't know. Is she asking *him* to answer her question?

"His wife ... ex-wife is Dr. Julie Hathaway."

My parents look at each other with wide eyes before sharing knowing expressions with me.

"Boss Bitch?" Mom asks.

I nod with a grin. Dr. Julie Hathaway isn't a new name in our house. She's a familiar fixation of mine. I try to emulate her confidence every single day ... with little success. Dr. Hathaway knows her stuff, owns her job like a bad-ass, speaks with intelligence and authority, yet focuses her goals around surgeries that give children a sense of confidence and belonging. She heals them in ways that go way beyond surgery.

"Yes." I sigh.

"So Roman is her son?"

For a high-functioning person, it shouldn't take me so long to really think about that. Dr. Hawkins asking me to babysit his son is—on a mind-numbing scale—the equivalent of asking me to look after a piece of my idol. Quite possibly the most important piece of her life.

I'm nauseous, so nauseous I have to sprint to my room, take out another new journal, and list all of my fears. My predictions never come to fruition, so I list every possible fear to prevent anything bad from happening.

Roman gets kidnapped ... on my watch.

Roman chokes and dies on a grape ... on my watch.

Roman gets attacked by a mountain lion ... on my watch ...

CHAPTER SEVEN

Mixed Signals and Matching Bibs

Elijah

"B LUE OR GREEN?" I hold up two shirts as Roman jumps on my bed.

"Boo!"

"Blue it is." I slip on the short-sleeved shirt and button it while my mini-me giggles with each jump.

The spaghetti is done, resting in a strainer while the sauce simmers on the stove.

Salad in the fridge.

Roman's favorite homemade cherry popsicles in the freezer for dessert.

Why am I so nervous I can barely button my shirt? Oh, that's right. I haven't been on a date with anyone but Julie. Does six kids in the eighth grade going to a movie together count as a date as long as I held Candice's hand? God, I hope so. Otherwise, my dating track record is pathetic.

"It's not a date," I mumble to myself in the full-length mirror. "It's dinner with Roman and a woman that might babysit for me." I laugh at myself while ruffling my damp hair into something resembling a stylish look. When did I start talking to myself? And why are my hands sweaty?

"Listen, Daddy! Listen!" Roman jumps off the bed and runs toward the stairs.

The doorbell rings again.

"Slow down, chief." I follow him down the stairs. Dorothy is thirty minutes early. "Rules, Roman. You don't answer the door. Remember?"

He fights with the deadbolt, yanking on the lever handle. "She's here. Babysitter's here! Open the door!"

I had to explain the reason for our dinner guest, so I told Roman we were thanking Dorothy for the superhero cape, and that if things went well, she might babysit him sometime. I don't need a babysitter. I have joint custody of Roman, parents to help out, and two older sisters in Portland who jump at any chance to watch Roman.

"Oh, hey, guys." I smile at the two young kids at the door, selling something. Someone is always selling something. I have a credenza by the door with cash in a drawer for all the kids in the neighborhood who come around raising money for activities like Little League and band trips.

We make our usual exchange of money and a handshake promise that they'll eventually return with ten tubs of popcorn or whatever I just purchased for thirty dollars. Just as I start to close the door, a familiar white Audi Q5 parked across the street catches my attention.

"I think that's Dorothy's car. Think we should go see?"

"Yes! Come on, Daddy. Let's go!" He runs into the yard, no shoes. I quickly catch up to him, scooping him into my arms. "Let me down. Down, Daddy!" He giggles as I vibrate my lips onto the tiny areas of exposed belly. "Stop!"

I shift him upright onto my hip and knock on Dorothy's window.

She jumps, closing the visor mirror and meeting my gaze with her wide eyes. Dorothy's freshly glossed lips pull into a tiny smile as she rolls down her window. "Hi. I'm early. I just wanted to make sure I knew where I was going."

"Hi." I have more to say, but I just want to stand here and let her obvious excitement to see me soak into my skin, all the way to my bones. I've nearly forgotten what that look of adoration—from someone who isn't my mom—feels like. It's pretty damn good.

"Hi, Dorfee," Roman greets her while pressing in on my cheeks, making my lips into fish lips.

"Hi, little Romeo." The corners of her mouth continue to climb up her face.

He giggles. "My name is Roman!" My cheeks take the brunt of his excitement as he relaxes the pressure on my lips, but only to play a tough game of patty-cake with my face.

"Let's ask Dorothy if she wants to come inside."

"Dorfee, you come inside. Pa-sicle, Daddy!"

I step back and open her door, unearthing a bit of

ingrained manners. "Pasta before popsicles, little man."

"Thank you." Dorothy climbs out, wearing a pink skirt that flows just below her knees, a pink and yellow floral, sleeveless blouse, and white flats.

"You uh …" I clear my throat. "Have something on your cheek." I point to my own cheek in the same spot as the brown smudge on her face.

Her hand flies to her cheek, rubbing it furiously. "It's chocolate. I was just checking my face when you knocked on my window. I stopped for ice cream on my way here."

I chuckle. "You're making this tough on me. I won't let Roman have a Popsicle before dinner, but you stopped for ice cream?"

"Yes. In case dinner doesn't go well."

I head toward the house with Roman on my shoulders and Dorothy right beside me. "*Not well* as in my culinary skills, or *not well* as in bad company?"

"I don't know yet."

I glance over, but she gives nothing away. That's okay with me. I want to discover the layers of Dorothy Mayhem by following her pace. Julie crippled me in a way that feels equally devastating and pathetic. There's no switch to turn off my love for her, all those years of marriage, college, careers, a child … I wonder if I'll ever find a switch, or if I'll simply have to find a brighter light.

At the moment, Dorothy shines, and it thrills me because I can't pinpoint what it is about her that brightens my day.

"Mmm … it doesn't smell bad in here." Dorothy closes her eyes, taking a slow inhale after I shut the front door behind us and set Roman down to go play with his toys.

I wait for her to open her eyes. One, because I like looking at them. Two, because I like how they look at me.

When she grins, I can't help but wonder if she tastes like chocolate, if she closes her eyes when she kisses, or if her mind goes to the same questionably inappropriate places mine does.

"I'm trying really hard to think the best of your comments. Can I take the *not bad* as meaning good? Or is that too presumptuous? Does your not bad mean not awesome but it could be worse?"

Slipping off her flats, she wiggles her toes painted in white toenail polish and stares at them while she delivers her answer. "Definitely good. Not meaty or spicy. I'm already regretting the tacos." Her nose wrinkles.

"Tacos?"

She nods. "I got home early, *and* my dad fed Orville and Wilbur, so I had way more time than originally anticipated. My parents were going out for an early dinner because they're old. I've discovered that's what old people do. So I followed them to their favorite Mexican restaurant. But I only had three tacos and a basket of chips and guacamole. So I can probably take down some pasta."

God ... my cheek muscles ache. I can't stop grinning. "I have two older sisters, I was married for years, and I see plenty of young female patients. But I'm not sure I've ever been around a grown woman, as petite as you, making references to *taking down* pasta."

"I've mastered the art of burning calories."

"Oh? Then you should sell that secret. People make a lot of money off weight loss breakthroughs." I jerk my head toward the kitchen for her to follow me.

"Not mine." She laughs. "I just walk, hike, and bike the trails. Bounce on my trampoline, and chase Gemma, Orville, and Wilbur. People don't like those weight loss tips. I broke my leg several years ago and gained fifteen pounds because I stopped moving but didn't stop eating."

"How'd you break your leg? Trampoline?" I lift a glass. "Can I get you something to drink? Wine? Beer? Lemonade? Water?"

"Water, please. And I broke my leg on a Segway. One of the city tours."

"You took a Segway city tour?"

"No. A tourist on one hit a pothole in a crosswalk and crashed into me." She curls her hair behind her ears, gaze surveying my kitchen. "You like to cook?"

"Yes. Ice water?"

"Yes, please."

I hand her the glass of water. "Are you serious about the Segway?" Another unexpected chuckle rumbles my chest.

"Uh … yeah." She lifts her skirt and traces the scar on her leg. "I had to have surgery."

"Nice scar."

Legs. I say scar, but I mean legs. Dorothy Mayhem has incredible legs. Not legs for miles like a runway model. Nope. I'm done with those legs, especially since they walked away from me. The legs on display before me are petite, muscular, sun-kissed, and riddled with more than one scar and several scrapes and bruises. They look like the legs of a hardworking woman. A woman who doesn't give up. A woman who sticks it out during the hard times. And the fact that she dresses them in flowing, girly skirts only makes them that much sexier.

Yes, my fascination (slight obsession) with Dorothy Mayhem has happened quickly—a toxic mix of hating my wife and going so long without getting laid. At least, that's what I tell myself. I tell myself a lot of things to get through the day. Eventually, I can't distinguish truth from intention. If I look and act like a functional male, I'll actually be one. It sure sounds good to me at the moment.

"Did you get a fair settlement from the lawsuit?"

"What lawsuit?" She sips her water.

"The one against the Segway tour company."

"It wasn't their fault. Something was worked out between the woman who crashed into me and the Segway company. Honesty, I'm not sure who paid for what. I just know that my medical expenses and time off work were covered." She gives me a shoulder shrug. "That's all that mattered to me. It's not like I was permanently disabled. And I'm sitting just fine financially." Another shoulder shrug.

"How un-American of you."

"What do you mean?"

"Everyone sues for everything."

"Oh. Ha! Yeah, I suppose that's true. I'm not a fan of conflict."

"Are you a fan of cooking?"

She uses the glass to hide her smirk as she pauses it at her mouth and shakes her head. "I can make like … three things."

"Do tell." I run warm water over the pasta in the strainer, dump it into the serving bowl, and pour the marinara over the top of it.

"Grilled cheese. Mac and cheese. Bean and cheese microwave burritos. That doesn't count pouring cereal into a bowl in the morning. Oh! Peanut butter sandwiches and microwave nachos too. That's five." Dorothy grins, chin tipped up with so much pride.

"Not pasta?"

"I suppose I could, but I usually make more single-serving meals unless my mom cooks for all of us, which is risky because she's not any better than I am at cooking. But she's too stubborn to admit it. I rarely eat with them unless we go out or get takeout."

"So you live with your parents?" I hold up a finger to pause her response while I call Roman to dinner. "Spaghetti, Roman!"

Dorothy takes a seat at the table as Roman careens around the corner, nearly crashing into me.

"Slow it down." I pick him up, set him in his Stokke chair at the table, and fasten his bib.

"Do you like spaghetti?" Dorothy asks Roman as I set out the salads and bottles of dressing.

"Um … yes. I like … I like sketti." He tugs at his bib. "Take it off!" Tugging harder, he growls at me.

"You'll have sauce all over your clothes if I take it off.

Just leave it on."

"No. I won't!"

"Roman …" I frown at him.

He closes his eyes and throws his head back. "Daddy, listen, listen, listen!"

Dorothy bites her lips to keep from smiling. I blame Julie for his constant, "listen, listen, listen." She always shushes him and tells him to listen. And in the process, she's created a defiant little monster that tries to get his way by always interrupting me and telling me to listen, even when he has no follow-up to his chanting "listen."

"I'm listening."

Roman opens his eyes, and just as I anticipated … nothing.

"Do you have another bib?" Dorothy asks.

I nod. "It won't matter which bib, he just doesn't want *any* bib."

"I want a bib. I want a bib like little Romeo's bib." She removes his bib and fastens it around her neck. It never would fit around my neck, but Dorothy is petite. And cute … and sexy.

Gah!

Yes, she's sexy. And it's the last thing I should think about with my son sitting just inches from me.

Roman studies her for a few seconds. "Daddy, I want a bib!"

Dorothy … Dorothy … Dorothy …

The girl with an old lady name, an uncensored tongue, and the most contagious grin has managed to flip my world on its side. Only, she thinks she's here for a possible babysitting position, not a date. Things are complicated.

After retrieving a bib and serving up the pasta and salads, I take a seat on the other side of Roman. "So you live with your parents?"

"Yes. But it's not like you probably think," she mumbles over her food.

Dorothy eating with a Cookie Monster bib around her neck ... I can't stop grinning. It shouldn't surprise me. After all, she abandoned a patient, risking her job, just to tell me she's a vegetarian. My mind stopped speculating anything about her long before she arrived at my house.

"I have no thoughts on the matter." I twirl spaghetti around my fork while eyeing her.

"My uncle died. Left me a lot of money. Since I lived at home well into my adult life, I decided when I got a place of my own the right thing to do would be to let my parents live with me. I bought some land with an existing house on it and added onto it so they could live with me without actually living with me. We share a kitchen and laundry room. That's it."

"More, Daddy! More sketti!" Roman reaches for my plate.

I dish part of my spaghetti into his bowl. "You like it?" I smile at him before shifting my focus to Dorothy. "I hope our guest likes it."

She pats her mouth with her napkin, cheeks puffed out with a mouthful of pasta, and she nods. After she swallows, she takes a drink of her water. "It's good. Not chunky or too spicy. And the water is good too. It doesn't have a funky taste to it ... just how I like it."

I tap my bottom lip with my fork, eyeing her for a few seconds, holding back the full shit-eating grin I can't seem to control.

"What?" she asks.

"Nothing." I shake my head, forcing myself to return my focus to my food. It's hard to do because I love staring at her, waiting for her next look, her next smile, her next words.

We finish dinner and popsicles with Roman interrupting all attempts at conversation. Dorothy entertains his every murmur with enthusiasm. I expect nothing less from the woman who wears a bib for dinner.

"Little man, you can watch one show while I clean up the kitchen and talk with Dorothy."

"Kratts! Dorfee, wanna watch Kratts?" Roman squirms as I wipe his face.

"Sure." She grins while removing her bib.

"You don't have to watch—"

"I love the Kratt Brothers. Show me the way, little Romeo." She follows Roman as he runs to the living room.

"The remote is complicated. I'll be in to turn it on in a—" Before I finish, the Kratts are already playing.

"I know my way around a remote, Dr. Hawkins."

I nod, stealing a few more seconds to just ... look at her. "Dorothy Mayhem ..." I whisper on a content sigh as I collect the dirty dishes from the table.

Thirty minutes and one Kratt Brothers episode later,

the kitchen is clean and Roman is ready for bed.

"Goodnight, Dorfee." Roman yawns as I scoop him up and carry him up the stairs.

"Night, Romeo."

"Dorfee has super pow-wows." Roman's smile beams, much like mine.

"Super powers? Really?" I tuck him under his covers.

"Yes! She can see my bones!"

"X-ray vision?"

Roman nods.

"That's pretty cool." I kiss all over his face until he giggles. "Night, buddy. I love you to the moon."

"Night, Daddy." He yawns again.

"Bye, Dr. Hawkins! Thanks for dinner," Dorothy calls before I even get out of Roman's bedroom.

Bye?

I run down the stairs, catching her just as she slips on her white shoes. "Whoa, wait! Leaving already?"

"Yeah. Did you need something else?"

Yes. I need more than five minutes alone with her that doesn't involve cooking or Roman interrupting.

"We never discussed your emus." I slip my hands into the front pockets of my jeans and lean against the cherry banister.

"Oh. Yeah." She rests her hand on the front door handle, ready for a quick getaway as soon as the emus are explained.

What is it with women desperately trying to run away from me?

"The previous homeowner had the emus. I was actually there looking at the property the day they hatched. I mentioned how much I like emus ... you know, since they're basically little dinosaurs. So he let me name them. And the next thing I knew, papers were signed, and he moved out. My parents and I arrived with a moving truck, and the two emus were still there. A gift from the previous owner. When I tried to contact him to say I couldn't accept the gift—for obvious reasons—he never returned my calls."

"Wow. And I thought I scored when Julie and I rented an apartment just after we graduated from med school and the previous owner left an expensive leather sofa."

"I bet the sofa cost less money to maintain than Orville and Wilbur."

"Probably." I laugh.

"Welp, now you know." She opens the front door.

"Dorothy?"

"Yeah?"

I push off the banister and erase half the distance between us. Not enough to invade her space, but enough to grab her if she tries to leave. Yes, I realize how creepy that sounds. But it's exactly what I think. She makes me feel like a child really wanting something, torn up with anxiety at the thought of not getting it ... of leaving the store without it.

"I really enjoyed you being here for dinner."

"Oh ..." She nods a half dozen times. "Yeah, Roman is great. I think we got along perfectly. I'd be happy to babysit him anytime it works into my schedule."

"Yes. Or maybe you could just come over again and

have dinner with us? Or we could grab ice cream some evening. Take a hike. Go to a park." Ask my mom to watch Roman. Make out on my sofa.

Sex deprived pervert!

"Um …" She scrapes her teeth along her lower lip and nods slowly. "Sure. You can never be too safe. I get it. You'd like me to spend a bit more time with him while you supervise."

Breaking news … Elijah Hawkins scores an F in asking a woman out on a proper date. Why am I using Roman as a crutch? He should be my wingman. I should have him say something to Dorothy that is super sweet and impossible to resist. Like … "Dorfee, my dad is awesome. You should go to dinner with him."

Too pathetic?

"Welp, goodnight!"

I don't even get "goodnight" out before she makes it halfway to her car.

"Smooth … real smooth." I close the door and thump my forehead against it several times.

✧ ✧ ✧

OVER THE NEXT few weeks, I manage to demonstrate how *not* to date Dorothy Mayhem.

Step one: Lie to her and say you need a babysitter when you don't need one.

Step two: When she continues to turn your date invitations into playdates with your son, don't correct her.

Step three: There is no step three.

Yeah, not dating Dorothy Mayhem is pretty much an easy two-step process. And I'm good at it, maybe the best at it.

I ask her to have coffee one morning, and she suggests a cafe that has great chocolate milk and donuts for Roman.

I ask her to have lunch with me in the cafeteria at the hospital, and she brings lunch for Roman in a brand-new lunch box that matches hers. Only it's blue and has superhero stickers on it. So ... I smile and go get him out of daycare to have lunch with us.

It's been three weeks, and I have no idea how to end this playdate streak—honesty seems too obvious.

My final attempt is another dinner date (playdate) at my house. It goes well. I put Roman to bed. And as usual, Dorothy tries to escape. But I manage to catch her at the door, determined to make it clear that I don't need a babysitter.

"Dorothy?" I lower my voice and take a step closer, breaching the safe zone, the one I'd normally keep with a potential babysitter for my son. But she's not my son's babysitter. She's the young woman I've obsessed over for weeks. She's the smile I catch on occasion in the hallway. She's the "Hey, Dr. Hawkins!" that makes my dick stir when she says it while applying lip balm in the elevator.

Dorothy stares at my chest. Looking at me would require her to tilt her head up. Her eyes double their blinking rate and her cheeks turn red. Dorothy looks stunning with pink cheeks. She releases the door handle and retrieves a tube of lip balm from the pocket of her skirt. Still focusing on my chest, she applies it then rubs her lips together while returning it to her pocket. Coconut scent invades my nose... everything Dorothy Mayhem is coconut.

"Dr. Hawkins?" Her curious eyes glance up at me, wide and expectant.

I want to kiss those glossed lips. Of course it's impulsive, a product of emotional displacement and abandonment. The stupidity of it all flashes blinding neon in my head. Still ... I really want to know if Dorothy Mayhem tastes like coconuts. I want to silence all my scattered emotions, desires, pain, and need with one kiss. My need to feel something new, something promising, nearly kills me.

"You can call me Eli."

She swallows hard. "I don't actually think I can."

"Why not?" I force my gaze away from her mouth.

The second our eyes meet, she averts her attention to her feet. "Because you're half of the Hathaway-Hawkins duo."

This is a new one to me. "I'm divorced."

"I know. I ..." She makes an attempt to look at me, but her attention shifts to my temple then maybe my ear. "I mean you're a brilliant doctor, and Dr. Hathaway is too—so brilliant. God, she's just phenomenal. Like there are no words. But still ... you change the lives of young children. You save them. You're what every young person entering the medical field can only dream of becoming. You've earned the title. I can't call you by your name. It's too personal. I don't know ... almost intimate."

She has Julie on a really high pedestal. Me? Down a few pegs. Sounds about right for my life at the moment. It's not that Julie doesn't deserve to be on the pedestal. No matter how much I hate her, I still love her. And her skills as a pediatric plastic surgeon are unmatched. She deserves Dorothy's admiration.

But I don't want to talk about medicine, accolades, and saving lives. I know … I know … how terrible of me. Sorry, but I need something for myself. Something personal and maybe a little selfish.

Definitely intimate.

"I don't need a babysitter for Roman."

She jerks her head back, giving me her full attention, eyes squinted, gaze locked to mine. "What?"

I trap my top lip between my teeth, drowning in coconuts as my heart races, sending ample blood to all regions of my body. God … I just want—need—to kiss her.

"Oh jeez …" She shakes her head, closing her eyes for a breath. "You invited me to dinner to … flirt." Her eyes open to their widest point.

A tiny laugh escapes me. I can't help it. Everything about this woman feels like a rebirth. "I invited you to dinner because Roman really likes you. And I just can't thank you enough for all that you've done for him. You're so generous."

Gah! I suck at this!

What is my problem? Yes. The answer is yes! *Yes, Dorothy, I invited you over to flirt, maybe even kiss. And other things …*

"Oh." She takes a step backward, stumbling a bit as the front door catches her, and more embarrassment tints her cheeks. "Well, now I feel stupid. Yes, of course you invited me here because Roman likes me. Duh. Now I just look like an idiot for assuming you wanted to flirt with me. And really, no need to thank me. My generosity is selfish. It makes me feel good to do nice things. That's all. And really, you've bought me coffee and made me dinner again. It's like I should be thanking you again. But that's probably weird. So … I'll just go now."

Really, *really* weird shit goes through my mind as she fidgets. Dr. Hawkins is nowhere to be found. Neither is Roman's dad. Raging-puberty-hormones Eli Hawkins invades my head—both of them really. And I just want to kiss Dorothy. That's the PG version of my thoughts. Most of them are R-rated. Worse than the R-rating. *All* I can think about are the ways Dorothy and I can be generous with each other, leading to never-ending thank-you's that don't involve stationary, replacement scrubs, superhero capes, pasta dinners, lunch boxes … or clothing.

"Should we call it even? No more thank-you's," I suggest.

"Okay." She lifts her gaze, eyes going a little cross-eyed like her focus is centered on the bridge of my nose.

"Okay." I release a slow breath, but it does very little to relax *all* of my body. "Can I ask your age?" I'm not sure why I've been so chicken about asking her age. I think it worries me that she's too young, and I'll feel like a dirty old man having really inappropriate thoughts about her.

"I'm thirty. Why?"

"You just look young."

"I wear massive amounts of sunscreen."

I nod slowly.

Just kiss her, you big chicken!

What if she doesn't want to be kissed by me? Or flirt with me? I internally laugh at the memory of her comment and at myself for being just as awkward. Why does something so simple have to be so complicated?

"I have an hour-and-fifteen-minute drive home."

And school the next day. Where is my head?

Oh, that's right …

"Of course. I'm sorry. I lost track of time."

"Okay." She smiles.

I love her okay's. They feel like more than the average okay.

"I'll walk you out."

"Have you not closed all of your rings?" She holds up her wrist, signaling to her watch.

I chuckle. "All rings were closed hours ago."

"We could track each other. Share our rings. Did you know that?"

Rings. Kisses. Trips to the on-call room for sex.

For the love of God … get your shit together, Elijah!

"Never mind. That's weird." She shakes her head, rolling her eyes at herself just before opening the door and scurrying ten steps ahead of me. Her pace gains momentum with the hill of my driveway.

My long strides catch up to her at the bottom of it. She looks both ways and bolts across the street to her car, clicks the locks, and opens her door.

"Goodnight!"

"Dorothy Mayhem … you're killing me."

She turns just before ducking into the driver's seat.

"What do you mean?"

Resting my hands on my hips, I drop my chin in defeat and stare at my untied gray canvas shoes. "What if I did ask you to dinner tonight to … flirt?" I glance up, digging my teeth into my bottom lip on a slight cringe.

Her body remains stoic as her eyes shift from side to side, like she's been caught on a hidden camera. "Well … the wrong outfit." She refuses to look me in the eye.

"I think you look amazing."

"Yes. But this is a playdate outfit. Maybe even one I'd wear to apply for a babysitter position. It's fun, but wholesome. Practical and safe."

I just want to spend one day in her head. Everything about her fascinates the hell out of me. The curiosity gives me such a high.

"Tell me about your flirting outfit."

"Well …" She clears her throat, keeping her focus on the big hill leading out of my development. And of course … her cheeks are perfectly flushed as she talks to the wind. "Since Romeo was involved, I would have chosen my red dress with white stripes. It hits just below my knees, but it's strapless. And I would have worn my blue cardigan with it and matching blue wedge sandals with straps that tie around my ankles. Flirty … but appropriate for young eyes."

"And if Roman wouldn't have been here tonight?" I

stare at the side of her head, wondering if she'll look at me again before driving home.

She narrows her eyes. "I would have taken off the cardigan after you invited me into your house."

The picture she paints in my head does all kinds of wicked things to me. Why imagining her in a striped strapless dress has such a physical effect on me is a mystery. It's not like she suggested showing up wearing nothing but high heels and a trench coat. Dorothy Mayhem possesses her own brand of seduction, and I'm completely entangled in every part of it.

"And in this scenario, would you have kissed me after I walked you to your car?"

She turns *completely* red. I feel certain even her toes hidden in those blue shoes have to be red. "You're making fun of me."

Her comment knocks me back a good ten steps, even if my body remains right next to her. Why would she say that?

"If you want me to watch Roman, just let me know. I need to go home now."

"Why would you think I'm making fun of you?"

She slides into the driver's seat. "Because it's ridiculous."

"What's ridiculous?"

"You. Me. This! The doctor and the transporter. Dr. Elijah Hawkins and ... me! My idol's ex-husband. Dr. Hottie Hawkins. This is just ... a joke. And I don't think it's funny."

As my thoughts snag on *Hottie Hawkins*, she tries to

shut her door, but I block it with my body.

"Whoa, whoa, whoa ... no. Just ... no." I duck my head into her vehicle.

Her eyes nearly pop out of their sockets as her head presses firmly to the headrest, unable to avoid my face ... my total invasion of her personal space. My lips ... inches from hers. "If I don't do this, I won't be able to sleep, or think, or function at work tomorrow, or focus on anything but why I was too chicken to kiss you."

"You're going to—"

Yes. I kiss her. I kiss her because it's all I can think about. She turns me into a child, much like Roman with his one track mind when he wants something.

Dorothy doesn't kiss me back. She doesn't move at all. So I pull away and swallow my pride, standing tall so she can't see my anguish as I run a frustrated hand through my hair and sigh, ready to bang my head on the top of her car. I'm out of practice with ... everything. And it sucks. It makes me hate Julie that much more.

Julie took her time, sorting her feelings, slowly detaching from me without me knowing, planning her escape and new life. I feel like someone kicked me out of a moving vehicle—tattered, bruised, and lucky to be alive. But clearly I have no clue how to navigate after what felt like a near-death experience.

"I'm sorry, Dorothy. Please forget that happened." I talk to the roof of her car like she talked to the wind. And there is little doubt that my face matches the red dress she described to me.

You're an idiot, Elijah.

"Goodnight." I make a one-eighty turn and cross the street, not looking in either direction as if I don't care if a car hits me—because at the moment it would be a quick way to put myself out of my misery.

CHAPTER EIGHT

Kiss and Tell

"IT MUST BE Friday!" Mom greets me from her desk as I open the door to her office, holding her favorite salad.

"Favorite day of the week."

She makes her way to meet me in front of her desk, taking the salad from my hands and planting a kiss on my cheek. "Emily's funeral was yesterday. Did you go to the funeral?"

"You know the answer." I take a seat as she shuffles back to her desk chair. With very few exceptions, I attend my patients' funerals—if I can't save them.

"No. I *assume* you did, but sometimes your schedule doesn't allow it. So I didn't know for sure. How's Mary Ann doing?"

Mary Ann, Emily's mom, lost her husband and daughter within six months of each other. I referred her to my mom when she asked if I had a recommendation for a psychiatrist. She also wanted me to keep my mom updated on Emily's progress.

"I'm surprised you weren't there." I sip my coffee, focusing on the photo on her desk of Roman and me.

"I'd planned on it, but I had an emergency."

I nod slowly, feeling melancholy from the past few weeks. It's not just Emily dying or even the botched dates (or whatever they were) with Dorothy. Everything has simmered into a feeling of failure and loneliness.

"Do you want to talk about it?"

"Emily?"

Mom nods, peeling the lid from her salad.

"No."

"Okay. Is Roman excited for his trip?"

"Yes."

She shoots me a half grin and a single lifted eyebrow. "That's it. Just yes? What's wrong?"

"Why does something have to be wrong?" I stare out her window.

"Because this is where you fall apart. This is where you tell me how unfair it is that Julie is taking Roman to Texas for the first time, and it upsets you that she's experiencing a 'first' with him because you didn't sign up to be a single parent and miss out on half of his childhood."

I shrug. "See. You already know my feelings on it, so no need to repeat it."

"So this mood is about Emily. I know you had high hopes for that new chemo, but—"

"It's not about Emily," I reply with a little more aggravation than she deserves. "And I didn't have high hopes. I simply had concrete reasoning to believe that it would work. It worked on five other patients. So my hopes aren't dashed. I'm simply pissed off and ready to get to work on figuring why it didn't work for Emily."

"Well, okay. It's not about Emily. I'm here if and when you're ready to discuss what really has you worked up today." She takes a bite of her salad.

I blow out a long, slow breath, keeping my gaze away from her knowing inspection of me. "I've been kinda seeing Dorothy recently."

"Transporter Dorothy? Superhero cape Dorothy?"

I nod.

"Wonderful! Is that going well?"

"Yes and no. She gets along really well with Roman. She calls him little Romeo, and for whatever reason, that makes me like her that much more. But I've failed at asking her out on a real date. I mean … I've tried, but she always assumes it's a playdate with Roman—like I'm vetting her for a babysitter. And I've had serious issues getting the nerve to say otherwise because this part of me wonders if she thinks I'm too old for her, or maybe I'm just not her type. And yes, I'm afraid of rejection."

Mom chuckles. She doesn't extend me the same level of professionalism as she does to her patients. Another downside to the family discount.

"So did you hire her to babysit Roman?"

"No!" My frustration even surprises myself. I rub my temples. "I kissed her. And by kissed her, I mean I think I scared her to death or completely offended her. Hell, she'll probably file a sexual harassment complaint against me." I shake my head. "I'm out of practice, for reasons you know. So I won't rehash all of it, but this single life doesn't fit me. Or maybe it does. Maybe the point is I'm supposed to stay single. Clearly something about me drives women away."

"Okay. Time out. I draw the line when you start picking on my baby. My handsome, talented, caring beyond words, baby boy. There is nothing wrong with you. There is nothing wrong with Julie or Dorothy. We've been over this. Relationships are fluid and ever-changing. *People* are fluid and ever-changing. Honor who you are, not who you aren't. Let people come and go from your life without feeling the need to catch them and keep them. Stop looking at the wrong reflections. Your happiness is a reflection of you and only you. I'm sure you've broken many hearts without even knowing it. I *know* nurses at the hospital think you're a god. If you don't give them a second glance, does that mean something is wrong with them?"

I rub my chin, letting her words sink in, but it's hard because all I can think about is Dorothy Mayhem. "I can't stop thinking about her. And I have no idea why."

"Julie?"

"Dorothy." I give Mom a sheepish glance.

A record breaking grin steals her whole face. "Tell me more."

I feel my own grin do its thing, and I don't even try to hold back because my Dorothy grin has a mind of its own—an uncontrollable force. "It's ridiculous. Just so ridiculous. We've had a handful of interactions, but if I'm completely honest, my addiction ..." I roll my eyes at myself. "Yes ... an *addiction* that started the second she walked onto the elevator weeks ago wearing these outrageous red shoes and a look on her face that did something so profound to me in that moment ... I can't find the words to explain it. I just knew something in my life shifted and would never be the same. And *yes,* I know how completely ridiculous that sounds. How girly, chick-flick movie that sounds. But again, if I'm honest, that's what happened. And now I can't stop thinking about her. When I'm physically near her, I feel like I did before I met Julie."

"You were a teenager when you met Julie."

"Exactly! Dorothy makes me feel like a stupid, word-fumbling teenager. But she also makes me feel like I have a new chance at life. One where I see things through her eyes."

Mom chews her salad, head cocked a bit. Then she points her fork at me. "And how do things look through her eyes?"

It's hard to articulate. My gaze returns to the window as I look for even a few inadequate words to describe the indescribable. "Life is more vibrant through her eyes. Simple things like matching undershirts and tennis shoes bring about unfathomable joy. In her world, everyone is equal. And words are poor expressions of feelings. I could just stand in a room with her, not saying a single word, and feel deliriously happy. Her eyes ... she has the bluest eyes, and the way she rolls them when she talks animatedly just makes me search for absolutely any excuse to make her talk. And the tiny smirk that seems to be her resting face is like being on the receiving end of the best secret ever."

Mom's eyebrows slide up her forehead.

"I know!" I shake my head, laughing at myself. "It's insane. Just commit me now. I've known her all of two seconds, and most of our time together has been with Roman. I'm delusional, just say it. This is a side effect from my breakup with Julie. Maybe my own midlife crisis. Before long, I'm going to be one of those people claiming to see the Virgin Mary in my cereal bowl, or aliens taking me to their planet at night and implanting chips into my brain. Tomorrow, I'll probably turn into a werewolf on my morning jog through the forest."

"Or ..." She wipes her mouth and leans back in her chair, working her tongue over her teeth a few times. "You have an undeniable chemistry with this young woman. It can be that simple, Eli. I didn't need three years to fall for your dad. It happened in a single moment. He came out of his shop, covered in grease and sweat, to tell me my brakes were shot. I didn't care that I was a poor college student who didn't have the money to replace them. All that mattered was the world tipping on its side, doing all kinds of weird things to me when he smiled at me. A smile, Eli. I knew my life would never be the same *from a smile*."

I love that story. So do my sisters. Probably because fifty years later, our dad still smiles at our mom the same way. And she still blushes every time he does it. I thought that would be Julie and me.

"He could cheat on me tomorrow."

I blink several times before squinting my eyes. "What?"

"Your dad. He could cheat on me tomorrow. You know how people say they could die tomorrow? They do it to give today better perspective, to lessen their worry over an unpredictable future. Break apart lifetime into two words—Life. Time. You spent a time in your life with Julie. Let it be a lifetime. Then move on and give someone else a chance to be part of your time in this life. I've spent a lifetime with your father, but that doesn't mean I won't spend a lifetime with someone else. If something is meaningful … impactful … then it can be a lifetime. Think about phobias. For someone with a fear of something, facing that fear, even if it's for mere minutes or even seconds, can feel like a lifetime. It's an impression that stays with you forever. Someday when you find yourself in a really good place again, you will look back at the years you spent with Julie, and it will feel like a lifetime ago."

I love my psychiatrist because she never talks to me like she talks to her patients. She gives me seventy-five percent heart and twenty-five percent mind. As much as she wants to give me her professional side, it's a conflict of interest. Her mom side always wins over.

"She didn't kiss me back."

Mom grins.

"Dr. Warren told me she's autistic."

She shrugs. "Does that matter?"

I frown. "You know it doesn't."

"But you're wondering if that's why she didn't kiss you back?"

I nod.

"Has she had other relationships?"

"I don't know. I'm too busy being infatuated with her to really *know* her. I need to slow down."

"Don't slow down. Then you'll think … *overthink*. And trust me, if she has ASD, then she's overthinking enough for both of you."

CHAPTER NINE

Never Enough Journals

Dorothy

THE KISS DISASTER took up two entire journals—blue and hot pink. Starting with bold, all caps, one word per page of:

**I
WASN'T
READY!!!**

He wasn't making fun of me. He wanted to kiss me.
Legit.
No sick jokes.
Dr. Hottie Hawkins hot for Dorothy.
One hundred percent wanted to kiss me.
And …

**I
WASN'T
READY!!!**

I just sat there frozen, completely unmoving. I couldn't have been less responsive had I been dead. And that wasn't a bad idea.

Seriously … kill me right NOW!

What's next? I have no idea. A different zip code, on the opposite coast, seems like the best idea. He either thought I didn't want to be kissed or that I didn't know how to kiss. Both are untrue. Both scenarios are embarrassing. And both possibilities leave me with no options.

The finicky vegetarian who didn't like chunks, spices, or kisses.

Nooo!!!

I spend the next forty-eight hours coasting through classes while contemplating my options.

One: New zip code.

Two: The afterlife.

Three: New profession.

Four: Ask for a redo.

Five: I have no five. I just like options I can count on one hand. I like the number five.

Friday morning I arrive fifteen minutes earlier than usual to avoid any possible encounters with Dr. Hawkins. And because I have the luck of a one-legged mouse in a room full of cats, my first transport after lunch is Dr. Hawkins's patient. His nurse calls me to his floor.

I wait outside the room while he finishes talking to the patient's parents. My head remains bowed, hair covering most of my face. Maybe I can literally be a wallflower when he comes out.

"Good afternoon, Dorothy."

No such luck.

"Hi," I murmur as he walks past me, talking to Dr. Warren.

"Page me when you take a break, Dorothy," Warren says, glancing over his shoulder, wearing a cocky grin that Dr. Hawkins seems to ignore.

I stick my tongue out at Warren before pushing the wheelchair into the room to get Jasmine for an MRI. If only my tongue would have worked properly when Dr. Hawkins tried to kiss me.

Tried ... that eats at me. The poor guy had to *try* to kiss me.

I failed.

So he failed.

It was textbook definition of a complete disaster.

How did that happen? I'm not a bad kisser. Just the opposite. I've studied kissing through girly magazines, romance novels, movies, and even several documentaries on the chemistry behind kissing. I've practiced on inanimate objects before testing my technique out on actual humans. And when I did find a living recipient to test out my special kissing method, it was well received. So well, it led to early ejaculation.

On his part, of course. Not mine.

The rest of my day involves dodging Dr. Hawkins and his sidekick Warren. By eight I'm ready to jet home, take an extra-long walk, and journal while eating an abnormally large quantity of food.

"Dorothy?"

I cringe at the sound of Dr. Hawkins's voice as I unlock my car. "Hmm?" I open my door.

"I don't want things to be awkward between us. I misread the situation. I overstepped a boundary. And you—"

"I wasn't ready!" I turn toward him, balling my fists with so much pent up energy and anxiety. After a twelve-hour day, that's pretty much my norm. But the anxiety doubled as soon as he said my name.

He has on blue pants and a white button-down with gray canvas shoes and a look of total confusion as he stands at the back of my car. "What do you mean?"

"I wasn't ready for the pasta to taste good. Or to discover you live off Skyline Drive, where I've wanted to live my whole life—but my dad's knees are not great, so I chose a flatter location. And I wasn't ready to flirt. And I definitely wasn't ready for you to kiss me. I just ..." My fingernails dig into my palms. "I wasn't ready."

I remain quiet, just long enough to make my rambling as awkward as my corpse kiss.

"Wasn't ready or didn't want it?"

I force myself to make eye contact with him. "Wasn't ready."

"Do you plan everything?"

"No. I just like to be prepared."

"Is there a difference?"

"Uh ..." I jerk my head back. "Yes. I don't plan on there being leftovers in the fridge when I get home, but I'm always prepared to eat them. I don't plan on getting a flat tire, but I'm prepared with my roadside assistance membership in case it does happen."

He rubs his lips together, nodding slowly. "You're just not prepared for men to kiss you."

"If I'm on a date, then I would be prepared. Lip balm, mint gum, sizing up the height difference, calculating the probability of it going past a kiss. I wouldn't plan on it, but I would definitely be prepared for it."

He tries to hide his grin, but I see it. And it makes me nervous because it feels mischievous. I don't do well with mischief. It's immune to all planning and preparation.

"Well, maybe you should prepare to be kissed."

"When? Where? By whom?"

He turns, pulling his key fob from his pocket as he struts toward his sleek, blue Tesla. "Soon. Could be anywhere. And I sure as hell hope it's me. Goodnight, Dorothy."

Oh the anxiety …

✧ ✧ ✧

"Mac and cheese in the fridge." Mom smiles when I come in the door after my ninety-minute walk with Gemma, Orville, and Wilbur.

"Happy hour special?" I slip off my shoes.

"Yep." She scoops up ice cream for her and Dad. "How was work?"

"Dr. Hawkins kissed … or tried to kiss me the other night. Like … out of nowhere. Not creepy rapist out of nowhere. He just planned a date and failed to mention it was a *date* date and not a playdate, and then BOOM! I get in my car, he ducks his head in, and kisses me! Can you believe that?"

Mom halts mid scoop, unblinking.

"But I wasn't ready. And I was so mad that he did it when I wasn't ready. It made me look like the world's worst kisser because I just froze, completely unmoving. The one doctor who is not only very hot but wears normal shoes tried to kiss me. So I told him. Tonight after work, I told him I wasn't ready. And you know what he said?"

Mom blinks once. No nod. Just a single blink.

"He told me to prepare to be kissed. How am I supposed to do that if he doesn't tell me when and where? Am I just supposed to walk around the hospital all day doing my job *and* have myself ready to be kissed by him? Why? Why would he do that to me?"

"Are you done?" Mom gives me a tiny smirk.

"Yes …" I sigh.

"I know you don't like to hear this, but you're overreacting. You didn't screw up. Clearly, if he told you to prepare to be kissed, then he wants to give it another shot. And a lot of people, women in particular, like spontaneity. I do, but your dad doesn't know what that means. He asks me at three-thirty in the afternoon if I want to have sex that night. Maybe that's great for you. Maybe you need that, but most women don't. So a guy just kissing you is a really great thing … as long as it's not the creepy rapist thing you mentioned."

I don't need a 3:30 p.m. warning that a kiss will happen later that night, nor do I need to know more about my parents' sex life.

Gag!

"You're no help." I return my signature scowl and brush past her to the fridge. Her smirk and taunting eyes follow me. I can just *feel* them on me as I put the leftovers on a plate and grab a glass of water before taking it to *my* TV room on the opposite side of the house. They are basically banned from going into my space.

My big screen.

My recliner.

My gaming systems and virtual reality equipment.

After I finish the leftovers and play Xbox for an hour, I grab a shower and hop into bed with a book in my hand and Dr. Hawkins dominating my thoughts.

Just as I double-check the alarm set on my phone, it rings. It's *him*.

I contemplate letting it go to my voicemail, but since he's all I can think about, it seems silly to ignore him. Maybe he wants to give me a better heads-up on the kiss.

"Hello?"

"Hi, Dorothy. Are you in bed yet?"

"Why? Are you calling for phone sex?"

He coughs on his "no."

"Good. I'll need a heads-up on that too. Well …" I giggle. "I suppose you'd be calling for a *heads-up*, so …"

"Wow, maybe I should call back when you're a little more groggy. I didn't anticipate this level of … feistiness."

"Sorry. Why are you calling me?"

"I was feeling pretty good about myself. I had a great day at work, especially in the lab. I got in a long jog this morning and an evening hike. The rings on my watch have circled so many times it would make you dizzy. Anyway ... I felt the need to be knocked down a few pegs, so I thought, who better than Dorothy Mayhem to do the job. And sure enough, within five seconds of answering your phone, I'm feeling completely cut off at the knees. Thank you."

I like his brand of sarcasm, which says a lot since, in general, I don't like sarcasm. It's like the smallest letters on the eye chart. I have to focus pretty hard to read them, and even then, there is a little guessing involved. They use those really tiny letters just to make sure no human feels perfect.

Dr. Hawkins takes his sarcasm way over the top, delivering it in an unmistakable package. No guessing involved.

"I'm glad I could help. Is there anything else you need from me?" I fold over my pillow and prop my head up on it with my phone glued to my ear and a smile pinned on my face. Part of me finds it odd that he called. I mean ... no one talks except on a need-to basis and usually only in person. But I like his voice, and for that I'm willing to forgo my favorite form of communication—emojis.

"Julie has Roman this week. And I'd really like to see your striped flirting dress and those wedge shoes that tie around your ankles. What are the chances you could make that happen for your favorite doctor?"

"Ha! I'm not sure Dr. Hathaway wants to see me in my dress and wedges, but if you'd like to see me, then I could check my schedule. No promises."

"And there I go ... slipping down another peg. Thank

you."

I laugh, beaming with pride because I'm joking with him, and it's actually easy. "You're welcome."

"Bring the dress to work tomorrow. And the shoes. We're going out when your shift is over."

"It's not over until eight."

"I know."

I pinch my lower lip and tug on it, wrinkling my nose. After work I walk. Then I eat and journal. Then I game while eating more food. Shower. Bed. I'm not sure how going out will fit into my schedule.

"Maybe."

"Great! I'll be waiting by your car."

"I said maybe. And let's meet at the restaurant ... *if* we meet."

"*When* we meet. And just text me your favorite restaurant. Goodnight, Dorothy." He ends the call before I can get in another protest. Another maybe. Another reason to cancel on him.

"Great ..." I mumble, setting my phone on my nightstand. Just what I need, something to obsess over at work tomorrow.

CHAPTER TEN

Going Down

I CLOSE MY exercise and activity rings before seven Saturday morning. Nervous energy alone would do it, but I take a long bike ride just to be on the safe side.

Sleep?

It evaded me at all turns. I'm a night owl and a terrible sleeper anyway, but Dr. Hawkins calling me sent me over the edge. Sleep didn't have a chance against my brain working through all the possible scenarios to our Saturday night date.

Are we going to eat? I need to know this so I can study the menu.

A bar? If he expects me to drink, I will have to get a ride home. Total light weight. But then I won't have my car for tomorrow, so drinking isn't a viable option.

Conversation? Gah! Without Romeo there as a buffer, what will we discuss? We already covered the topics of my inheritance, my animals, and nursing school. I hope he likes discussing recent medical journal articles because that's what I have teed up for our main conversation topics. I also have a small list of things to ask him so I don't dominate the conversation with my interests.

Are you originally from Portland?
What is your favorite color and why?
If you weren't a doctor, what would you be?

All solid choices from a conversation starter article I found online.

I manage to not see him all day, but I heard he was working in his lab earlier this morning. At eight, I change into my red and white striped dress and wedge, close-toed shoes. By ten after eight, my stomach starts to feel uneasy. Is he at the restaurant? Does he think I'm late? Hailey, a nurse in the ICU, went home midday because she had a bad stomach ache.

Fever.

Vomiting.

Diarrhea.

I probably have what she had. I *know* that's it.

Dr. Hawkins doesn't want to get what Hailey and I have.

I shoot off a text to him.

Me: *I'm sick. You don't want what I have. Maybe we try this another time.*

My phone rings. It's *him*. Why does he insist on calling me? A simple "okay, feel better" text is the appropriate response. Not calling me. For all he knows, I could be in the middle of vomiting or on the toilet with the squirts.

"Yes?" I answer with a bit of annoyance.

"What are your symptoms?"

I sigh. "Fever. Vomiting. Diarrhea."

"What's your temperature?"

"I don't know. I haven't taken it yet."

"Then how do you know you have a fever?"

"Because I feel warm."

"When did you last vomit?"

"I haven't vomited yet. But my stomach feels uneasy, so I know everything will come up soon."

"And the last time you had diarrhea?"

"Again, it's on its way. My stomach is *very* uneasy."

He chuckles. "You're just nervous."

"You don't know shit."

"True. I only have a medical degree. What do I know?"

"Just go home. If you get sick, then Romeo will get sick. And I refuse to be responsible for the spread of infection."

"Roman is with Julie this week."

"And you? What happens when you get sick and can't see patients? Lives are at stake, Dr. Hawkins."

"Eli."

"What?" I wrinkle my nose.

"When we're not working, you should call me Eli."

"Well, I'm still at work. So, Dr. Hawkins, I suggest you go home."

"Call me Eli. And I'm already at the restaurant you suggested."

"Jesus ... Fine! Eli, go home!"

"That was better than I imagined." He chuckles.

"You're crazy." I slide my bag over my shoulder and grab a mask from the empty room by the exit. "I'm on my way home."

"Come to the restaurant," he says like a command, like he's in charge. I like knowing who's in charge; I'm just not sure if I want it to be him at the moment.

"This is stupid. I'll stop by the restaurant—*just* so you can get a quick glimpse of my deteriorating health. I'm not actually going to get out of my vehicle. Then I'm heading straight home before the vomiting and diarrhea start." I press *End* and slip on the mask.

As expected, he's standing outside of his car in the parking lot of the pizza place, wearing a stupid grin.

"Go. Home. Dr. Hawkins. This could be something big. If the CDC gets notified tomorrow, and I'm quarantined, you're going to regret this cocky stubbornness," I yell out my window that's cracked half an inch.

"Unlock the door, Dorothy." He tries to open it.

"It's bad. I could start bleeding from my eyes," I shake my head.

"I'll jump onto the hood of your car and wait for you to open the door, so why don't you save your paint from a few scratches and just open the door?"

"You're stupid and reckless." I shut off my car and get out, adjusting my mask to tighten it a bit.

"Damn, Dorothy … just … damn …"

"Damn what?" I mumble beneath my mask.

"That dress looks incredible on you."

"I know. It's my go-to dress."

Dr. Hawkins laughs. "Go-to for what?"

"Everything. I have it in two other colors, but the red gets the most compliments."

He slides his hand along the back of my neck, cupping it and pressing his lips to my forehead.

"What are you doing?"

"Checking your temperature," he murmurs with his lips firmly pressed to my head.

"Did they teach you this in medical school?"

He chuckles as his other hand removes my mask. "No fever."

"You don't know that," I whisper, feeling oddly breathy and incredibly anxious. His touch is definitely intrusive and out of line for a doctor's examination, but it isn't completely awful. He smells good. Those herbs I like. A miracle because there are very few scents that don't make me legitimately want to vomit.

"I'll take my chances." His lips move to my cheek. "Dorothy …" he whispers.

"Huh?" I close my eyes so we don't have to look at each other so closely. It weirds me out a bit.

"I'm going to kiss you now." And he does. He attaches his mouth to mine. We are a good fit. I keep my jaw set to a position that won't allow his tongue access into my mouth. Of course, I assume he tastes as good as he smells, but after the corpse kiss catastrophe, I don't want to risk another bad kiss if the way he tastes makes me gag.

His hand ghosts down my arm, and his thumb grazes over my breast—I think by accident. It overstimulates my nipple, just that simple graze, because my strapless dress doesn't accommodate a bra. And while I don't want him to touch my breast again, accidental or not, I feel an urgency to orgasm.

No more foreplay.

No more teasing.

Just the orgasm, please!

He releases my lips. "You seem to be feeling better. I think we can still have our date."

I can't stop thinking about his thumb grazing my nipple area. Was it an accident? My body reacts oddly to different touches. That tiny thumb graze sends my hypersensitivity into overdrive. It's all I can think about. I need to get my body back in balance, but it's like he pushed a button, and he can't reverse what needs to happen to balance my body at this exact moment.

Dr. Hawkins takes a step back, rubbing his lips together before turning up his signature grin. "So, what do you want to do first? I was thinking—"

"I want you to go down on me."

He freezes for several seconds. Not a single blink. Then his jaw unhinges so slowly I expect to hear it creak.

"I-I was going to say drinks at the bar and then dinner."

"Then why did you kiss me and run your thumb over my nipple?"

He covers his mouth with his fist and coughs a laugh. "I uh …" He shakes his head. "I'm sorry. I …"

I sigh. Clearly, I misread a cue. Sexual cues are the hardest for me to read. Either I completely miss blatant attempts men make to get me into bed, or I misread something as simple as a misplaced thumb during a first kiss. "Dinner is fine. I'm not drinking alcohol tonight."

Dr. Hawkins continues to inspect me with what I think is confusion, based on his wrinkled brow, but I'm not sure what's confused him so much. I'm not the one who made a confusing sexual advance.

"What?" I tear my gaze away from him because my inability to read his expression feeds my already out of control anxiety.

"Did you really just ask me to go down on you?"

"Asked? No. Suggested? Yes. But if you don't do that sort of thing, it's okay. Let's just get pizza? They have an amazing Caesar salad too."

"I ... we ..." He closes his eyes for a few seconds and shakes his head.

"What? I can't keep up with your stuttering and head shaking. I'm not good with that kind of communication. In fact, it drives me crazy. So use your words. What are you thinking? Have I done something wrong? Offended you? What?"

"You're unexpected."

"I'm weird."

"Refreshingly honest." He smiles. It's the good one again, not the grimace he had on his face just seconds ago. "I'm trying to be a gentleman."

"Okay."

He breathes the essence of a small laugh from his nose. "Okay."

"So pizza?" I ask.

"Uh, yeah ... option two is fine."

"Option two?" My head cocks to the side.

He smirks.

"Oh …" I laugh. "The moment for option one passed. I'd rather have pizza now."

"Should I be offended?"

I narrow my eyes. "Well, I don't think so. Why would you be offended?"

Someone walks out and climbs into the car next to mine. Dr. Hawkins gives them a nod and a polite smile. I mimic his reaction to them.

"Why would you be offended?"

"Dorothy, I was joking. I'm not offended."

"Huh …" I grunt. "I missed the funny part of that joke."

"It was poorly delivered. Just forget it. Let's get pizza."

I follow him into the restaurant, and we wait for someone to take our name before waiting in the bar. He doesn't try to fill the wait time with small talk. And I keep my conversation starters to myself, knowing I'll need them during dinner. No sense in wasting them on a ten-minute wait while they get our table ready.

"Can I get you something to drink?" he asks.

"Water. And a Dr. Pepper."

He relays my order to the bartender.

"They don't have Dr. Pepper," he says, glancing back at me.

"Figures." I frown. "Just water then."

We take our two special order bar waters with us to our table.

"What do you want to eat?" He opens his menu.

I don't have to open my menu. In fact, menus drive me crazy. Too many choices and too much pressure. That's why I like frequenting the same places or scoping out online menus in advance for new restaurants.

"Pineapple with extra cheese."

"Great. And a Caesar salad?"

"Yes," I reply slowly. I can't explain how this makes me feel. I mean ... he doesn't even blink when I suggest a pineapple pizza. He doesn't suggest we each get our own pizza or do half and half.

The waitress stops at our table.

"A large pineapple pizza with extra cheese and two Caesar salads," he says, handing her our menus.

He ordered a large! Nothing chaps me more than people who want to split small and medium pizzas.

Leftovers are life. Not that I can't easily take down half a large pizza.

My affection for Dr. Hawkins triples in that moment. He makes a huge leap toward catching up with Boss Bitch.

"So are you originally from Portland?" he asks, crossing his arms on the edge of the table.

That's my question. He stole my question, leaving me with two original questions.

"Yes." I try to grin past my slight irritation.

"Me too."

Gah!

He doesn't give me a chance to ask it.

"My dad owns his own auto repair shop. He's had it for over fifty years. We keep thinking he should retire, but he loves it. He'll go to his grave covered in grease. All of my family live in the area. I have two older sisters, three nephews, and two nieces. My oldest niece is getting married in a few months. Roman is the ring bearer. He has an electric blue suit he's wearing. About the same color as my car—my favorite color."

"If you weren't a doctor, what would you be?" I cut him off before he finishes the word color.

He pulls his head back as his eyebrows lift into peaks. I may have blurted out the question in a rush, but I knew his next words would be *"Before I decided to be a doctor, I wanted to be ... "*

"Sorry." I laugh. "But you're stealing my questions. I planned three questions to ask you tonight, and you've already taken two. I don't want to sound uninterested in you, but you already ruined two of my questions. I wanted a chance to ask at least one."

"Is that code for I'm talking too much?" He chuckles.

"No. It's not code for anything. Talk all you want, just don't tell me everything I was going to ask you before I get a chance to ask it."

"Dorothy ..." He scratches his chin. "You are ... unexpected. Like balloons, flowers, and winning lottery tickets."

I have no response to that. It seems like a weird compliment, and I majored in weird, but it's a different kind of weird.

"If I weren't a doctor, I would have been a kayaking or white-water rafting tour guide. I love both equally. I grew up coasting down rivers, hiking trails, skiing the slopes." He holds up his watch. "That's why I get my rings closed every day."

"Let's share our activity progress." I go into my activity app and invite Dr. Hawkins to share his activity with me.

Several seconds later he glances at his watch and grins. Tapping it once, he accepts my invite.

I have an activity buddy!

"It's on, Mayhem. Watch out. I'm a fierce competitor."

"You mosey from one patient room to another all day, sit at your desk, or stand hunched over a microscope. I move *all day long*. You don't stand a chance of outdoing me."

We fall into an easy conversation, something I only do with my parents because they know me better than anyone else. And even then, some days they wear a zombie look when I go off on things they don't understand.

Just as our pizza arrives, Dr. Hawkins holds up his phone.

"Did you just take a picture of me?" I ask after the waitress delivers our salads and pizza.

"I did. For my contacts. I wanted you in that dress."

I lift my phone and take a picture too.

He laughs. "Did you just take a photo of the pizza? Are you one of those foodies who photographs your meals?"

"Me? No. I just eat the food. The pizza photo is going to be your contact photo. When I think of you, I always want to remember that you ordered my kind of pizza—a large at that—without saying anything that made me feel guilty and weird."

Dr. Hawkins nods in small increments, eyes slightly narrowed, lips turned into a tiny smile. He dishes up a slice for me and one for him. Then he folds it ... JUST LIKE ME! And he eats it. I follow suit, easily shoving half of it into my mouth. We grin at each other over our full mouths.

Pizza.

Salads.

Fun.

Yes! I'm having fun with Dr. Hawkins. Not awkward-date-fake fun. Not crowded party, overstimulation fun.

Legit. Easy. Fun.

"I'd suggest ice cream if you didn't have to work in the morning," he says as we exit the restaurant.

The crisp evening air captures my breath, or maybe it's his hand on my back. Dr. Hawkins possesses a touch that I can't put into a particular category. It sparks anxiety, confusion, and maybe something else. The grazing my nipple kind of something else.

"Yeah. If I'm going to kick your activity ass in the morning, I need to get some sleep."

"Well, in that case, let's grab some ice cream since you won't need a good night's sleep because you have no chance of kicking my activity ass in the morning."

He beats me to my car, opening my door. "Dinner was amazing."

For someone who has issues sorting emotions, I feel

that ... the giddiness over good food with really good company.

He continues, "I can't believe I've lived here my whole life and never eaten here. I mean ... I've driven by it hundreds of times. It makes me wonder what other hidden treasures around Portland that I'm probably missing. I really need to stop being such a creature of habit. Get out more and try new things."

"If you can do that, then you probably should." I shrug. "Not me. I need my habits, familiarity, predictability."

"And friendly exercise competition." He shoots me a sexy grin.

"Yeah." I nod, wearing my own grin as I start to slide past him to get into my car.

He rests his hand on the top of my car to stop me. "So ... the pizza and salad were the best I've had. But..." he leans in, reducing the distance between us to approximately twelve inches "...so was the company. Roman excluded." He winks.

"Okay."

"Okay," he repeats on a whisper. "Is okay good?"

I force myself to hold his gaze since he's so close to my face. "It's perfectly adequate."

His firm, pink gums and nice teeth steal the show as he grins.

Yep, total flosser.

"I'm going to kiss you goodnight."

"I figured. I wore the dress for it. And that's why I ate that mint after dinner and offered one to you." I rub my lips together. They're still lubed from my post-dinner lip balm application.

He sure does smile a lot at me. It beats the usual snickering and eye rolls. When our mouths connect, he tastes like mint. I like mint. Peppermint, not spearmint. Cinnamon is okay in a pinch, but too much cinnamon irritates my tongue. Hot Tamales at the movies leaves my taste buds fried for days. But totally worth it.

Dr. Hawkins presses his hand to my neck and slides it up to cup my jaw, taking the kiss to the next level with a little tongue. French kissing isn't usually my thing. Too much saliva. But he's not salivating like a dog, or suffering from a painful case of dry mouth, so the kiss is acceptable. Such a Goldilocks moment. Dr. Elijah Hawkins is my just right.

When the kiss ends, he lets me slide into the driver's seat. Then he ducks inside and kisses me again. A hungrier kiss. Instead of wondering how long the kiss will last or planning what I will say when the kiss ends, I cup his face and fully participate.

I let myself revel in the fact that the sexiest doctor at the hospital is kissing me. He smells good. Tastes even better. And makes me want sex, not something I want on a regular basis. Yet, it's *all* I can think about right now.

Breaking the kiss and breathing heavily, I keep ahold of his face. "I vacuumed the crumbs from Gemma's dog treats out of the backseat."

His eyebrows pull together.

"And she doesn't shed, so we wouldn't get dog hair all over us."

"Are ..." His gaze shifts over my shoulder for a few seconds. "Are you suggesting we get in your backseat?"

"I got the Q5 because it's roomier than the Q3. Not for having sex, for Gemma. But since the room *is* there ... well." I shrug.

Please say yes. I'm dying a little here, buddy.

"Sex? In the backseat of your car? Now? In this parking lot?"

"The windows are tinted."

"Dorothy ..." He chuckles, shaking his head. "I'm a doctor at the children's hospital. My son goes to the daycare there. We are within miles of it. Patients ... their parents, other doctors or administrators could happen to stop here to eat. We could get arrested for lewd acts ... public indecency."

"Okay." I release his face, but he doesn't move. So we're just two people not planning on having backseat car sex, hovering really close to each other. "Welp ..." I pull my mouth into a tight-lipped grin. "Thanks for dinner. Say hi to Roman for me."

He gives me a look ... a real emoji, but I can't decipher its meaning. Confusion?

CHAPTER ELEVEN

Mild Insanity

Elijah

"GOODNIGHT, DOROTHY." WHAT can I say? My Dorothy Mayhem high hits a level so high I'm not sure my feet feel the ground beneath them.

The lesson for the night?

Expect the unexpected—whiplash with a deadpan delivery.

Did passing up the opportunity to *go down* on her, followed by hardcore adult reasoning for not having sex with her in the back of her car, make me the most responsible man in Portland or just a run-of-the-mill dumbass?

I ease my upper body out of her car and give her one last smile and easy nod. "Drive safely."

"Sure thing, Dr. Hawkins."

"Eli. Dorothy ..." I shake my head. "You can't suggest what you just suggested and then call me Dr. Hawkins."

"Well, as you just reminded me, we could see people from the hospital, and I should keep things professional."

"Touché. Goodnight." I shut her door. As she fastens her seat belt and plugs her phone into the charging outlet, I just stand here, like a stalker.

I love my job, in spite of watching so many young people suffer and sometimes lose their battles with cancer. The fight to find a solution keeps me motivated. I love being a dad to Roman, even if I have to give him up every other week. I love lunch on Fridays with my mom. Family dinners. Morning runs and evening hikes along the dense forest trails.

But ... something's missing. For a year I thought it was Julie.

It wasn't.

It's Dorothy Mayhem and the backseat of her Audi Q5.

Sliding my fingers along the side of her clean car, I stop at her back door, take a deep breath—the kind you take before doing something mildly insane yet totally exhilarating—and open it. As I ease into the backseat and shut the door, Dorothy and her big blue eyes watch me with uncertainty.

"I don't have a condom, but I can fulfill your predinner request."

Her lips part, and her eyes widen a fraction more for several blinks. "Okay."

Brilliant.

Had she said anything but "okay," I would be disappointed. But Dorothy Mayhem doesn't disappoint ...

ever.

And because opening and closing two doors would be too easy, she unfastens her seatbelt and crawls over the middle console, landing like someone dumped a bag of arms and legs onto my lap.

She straightens herself onto the other seat and reaches under her arm for the zipper to her strapless dress. "I have a condom. I always pack a condom when I wear this dress. So, we can do both. And I don't have a bra on, so this will not be a strip tease. I'll quickly go from clothed to naked. You good with that?"

Um … yeah. This is Heaven. *She* is Heaven. At thirty-eight, it's hard to imagine something old ever truly feeling new again.

Wrong.

Dorothy makes breathing feel new again. And something tells me she's about to make sex feel new again. And I don't give a single fuck that we're only on our fourth date (first official one).

We're consenting adults.

Julie got fake boobs and tattoos.

I haven't had sex in a long time.

And if the world ends without me getting into the back of Dorothy Mayhem's car, I will regret it in the afterlife.

"I'm good with that." I try to keep my voice steady, but anticipation and complete disbelief shake my words.

Zip.

She lets her dress fall to her waist. I stop breathing. Part of me surrenders to the distraction of the logistics.

Sure, her car model isn't the smallest, but it's far from roomy in the backseat.

On a smirk, she leans back and lifts her butt off the seat, shimmying her dress past her hips, and stepping out of it before slinging it over the seat in front of her.

Wow ...

Here she sits in nothing but a delicate pair of white panties. And she doesn't appear the least bit self-conscious. Looking me in the eye seems to pose a bigger challenge to her than taking off her clothes.

"Good thing I'm short, huh?"

Yes, she's short, and my dick is long and so very very hard.

"Panties on or off? You can slide them to the side to access everything." Her lips twist. "But I don't want them getting really wet, so let's just take them off."

It *has* to be a dream. There's no way this conversation is taking place. She makes oral sex sound clinical. I anticipate her giving me a quick tour, pointing out specific things like her clitoris. Yet ... I can't blink. And for whatever unexplainable reason, it's the most erotic moment of my life.

Dorothy unties her shoes and removes her panties. She folds them and sets them on the center console. I'm in the back of Dorothy Mayhem's car, and *she is naked!*

"Are you going to lose your clothes so we can go right from one to the other? Or do you want to leave yours on while you do me?" She scoots to the far corner of the backseat, which isn't that far at all, and draws one leg toward her chest, resting her foot on the seat like someone might do while getting cozy on a sofa. Only ... we're not on a sofa. And her new position completely opens her up to me.

Everything about her paralyzes me. Only my eyes can move, and they can't decide where to land. She is fucking beautiful.

"Dr. Hawkins ..." Her nose wrinkles. "I don't want you to feel rushed to the point that you can't perform. But I do have to work in the morning. So ..."

"Let's go back to kissing." I lean in and kiss her.

She cups my face again and kisses me back in a way that sends my hands into a frenzy of need.

Needing to explore her naked body, but the time crunch nags at my conscience, I cup her left breast while my other hand cups her between the legs.

She moans into my mouth, and I nearly come in my damn pants. I slide my middle finger inside her and massage her clit with my thumb. But Dorothy knows exactly what she wants ... she knew it before dinner. Her hands on my face guide my head down her body, only my long torso doesn't allow me access. And she's pressed to the door. Maybe she needed to go with a bigger backseat to accommodate car sex with someone over six feet tall.

"I'll scoot onto the floor. You lie down, and I'll straddle your head."

I laugh a bit, in spite of my efforts to remain serious. After all, I have a naked woman offering me sex, all different kinds of sex. But there's just not enough room. And her words are sexy, but still very matter-of-fact. A how-to manual instead of raw and needy.

My carpe diem begins to fade. Really, what if one of my colleagues gets a craving for pizza and walks by the car and happens to glance back through the windshield into the backseat?

"Dorothy …" I let my head flop against the head rest, closing my eyes and rubbing my face. It's not that I'm not ready. The possibility of my cock breaking from the strain against my pants remains a serious threat. "I thought I could, but if someone walks by your car …"

She sighs, scooting back onto the seat while hugging her legs to her chest with her chin resting on her knee. "You're probably right. The last thing you need after the chaos of Boss Bitch leaving you is a viral rumor about you snacking on Dorothy Mayhem—patient transporter—in the back of a car parked outside of a restaurant."

Kill me now. Snacking on Dorothy Mayhem?

My fisted hand flies to my mouth as tears fill my eyes. I don't want to laugh at her. Really, truly, sincerely do not want to laugh at her. But I do. And it isn't a slight chuckle; it's the kind of laugh that makes me cry, makes it hard to breathe, makes the muscles in my stomach hurt.

To make things worse, I peek open an eye after wiping my tears, and she's just … waiting there. No big deal. Still naked like sitting in her car naked happens all the time. Her nose scrunches, but she doesn't seem offended. Maybe a little amused by my reaction and equally confused.

"Do you always laugh so hard you cry?"

"No …" I shake my head and hold my stomach with one hand while my other hand wipes my face. "I'm not …" I breathe hard to keep from laughing more. "I'm not sure I've ever laughed so hard in my life. Thank you."

"For what?" She leans forward and grabs her folded panties, slipping them on slowly with a bit of lethargy or resignation in her movements.

I regain my composure, wiping my eyes one last time as she puts her dress on and slides her feet into her shoes. "For you." I grab her waist and pull her onto my lap, her legs straddling my legs—not my head. "You are the very best of humanity." Then I kiss her, keeping my hands on her waist instead of snaking them up her dress like I want to do.

The night got away from us in the most bizarre way imaginable. But it's turned into something so unforgettable, I feel reborn. Someday, I will look back and remember this night—the night Dorothy Mayhem crawled into my existence in a way that would change me forever.

She could bring me back to life.

She could show me a world I never imagined possible.

Or … she could destroy me.

If I only knew …

CHAPTER TWELVE

Playing Hooky

Dorothy

THE CAR INCIDENT requires more than one journal, but I only have one red journal left! And it has to be red, since I wore my red dress.

WE
WILL
NEVER
HAVE
SEX!
!!!!!!!

That takes up the first six pages.

Sex is not a priority for me.
BUT ....
I don't like to fail.
I don't like to disappoint.
How did this happen?

?????????????????
I just don't get it!
The books.
The movies.
The blogs.
I've read
EVERYTHING!

Eighteen pages. And I just keep writing. So many emotions. Thoughts. Things to work out and sort through. I replay the entire evening on paper, including dialogue, so I can reread my entry. Study it. Figure out a way to repeat the good stuff and avoid the disasters.

Knock. Knock.

"Yes?" I slam my journal shut with two blank pages left. I'll add *THE END* later.

Mom cracks open the door and pokes her head inside. "You sneaked in without saying anything."

"Nothing to say. And it's late. Didn't figure you'd still be awake."

"You had a date tonight. There has to be something to say."

"What do you want to know?" I crawl into bed, knowing there is a good chance I might fall asleep during her interrogation.

She sits on the end of my bed. "Did you have a good time?" Her questions sound generic, but my answers rarely are.

"Yes. He was so easy to talk to. It was like talking to you and Dad. And he ate my kind of pizza *and* ordered a large."

"That's great. So there might be another real date?"

I sigh. "I don't know. I mean … well, it's just hard to say. He doesn't function like most guys I've dated. I've been able to do the same thing and get the same results. Not with Dr. Hawkins. It's like he plays with rules from a different rule book. Ya know? But I really like him, so I'd like to see his rule book. Would it be really weird if I asked Dr. Hathaway?"

Mom grimaces. "I'm inclined to say yes, but you said it's been a long time since she left him. So I suppose it depends on what you want to ask her."

"I want to ask her about his … preferences."

"What kind of preferences? Foods? Activities? Sports? I'm not following."

"Gah! You just don't get it. Sex, Mom! I want to know what does it for him." I throw my arm over my face, half from frustration, half from embarrassment because the moment I said it, her mouth fell agape. Why does she have to react like I'm a little girl?

"I'm just …" She stutters.

"Just go." I turn onto my stomach and bury my face into my pillow.

"Dorothy, I'm not mad. I just wasn't expecting you to say *that*."

"Oh … wow." I lift my head to speak but keep my gaze on my headboard. "Thanks for not being mad that your *thirty-year-old* daughter is sexually active."

Is? Was? Can I say I'm sexually active if no sex is involved?

Truth. I'm actively seeking sex with Dr. Hawkins. That counts. Right?

I almost lost my virginity at twenty-three to a guy who was also a virgin. He thought he was inside of me. I thought he was in the vicinity. His cock slid between my folds, quite vigorously, and I kept waiting for it to take a sharp turn into the first hole. It never did.

When it was over, he asked if it was good for me. I said yes. And it wasn't a lie. That kind of almost-but-not-really sex involved constant clitoral stimulation. I orgasmed. Twice actually. However, the partial lie ate at my conscience for a week, so I texted him:

Me: *Hi. U didn't find the hole. Just FYI for future reference. I still enjoyed it. Good luck on your finals! BTW Charlie's food truck has peanut butter fudge today. (tongue-licking emoji)*

"Dorothy, I'm not mad. Just surprised. You told me last month that sex was overrated, messy, and mentally exhausting. Now you're thinking of asking a man's ex-wife about his sexual preferences. So, take a breath, baby girl. I'm just surprised, but also happy for you. The fact that you want intimacy with him is good. Right?"

I flip around again to look at her. "Sex. Not intimacy. I just like hanging out with him. He gets me ... I think. We like the same food. We work together. We both love exercising. I mean ... we follow each other's rings now. I love that. It's the greatest motivation. And he's competitive too. But the sex is just getting in the way. I know he wants it. I just don't know *how* he wants it. And yes, most of the time I don't think I want sex because it usually is overrated, messy, and exhausting. But when Dr. Hawkins kisses me, I feel like the messy exhaustion could be worth it."

Mom grimaces again. "I'm not sure what to say. Maybe you can ask him. That's what all the experts say. Right? I mean, your dad and I don't—"

"LALALALA …" I pinch my eyes shut and plug my ears. "I don't want to hear this!"

I open my eyes when she kisses my forehead. "Understood. Truth be known, I don't like to talk about sex with your dad either. You'll figure things out with Dr. Hawkins. Stressing over the sex at this point might not be the best thing for a relationship in the early stages." She winks and leaves my bedroom.

After trying and failing for hours to get to sleep, I text Dr. Hawkins.

Me: **I should have purchased the Q7, huh?**

It's not that I expect him to answer, after all, it's after one in the morning. I just need to find a way to figure out the sex thing. And not because I want it all the time. I simply want to be good at it in his eyes.

Dr. Hawkins: **Hi**

I jump when he responds so quickly.

Me: **Whoops. Figured you were sleeping.**
Dr. Hawkins: **I don't think you need a Q7. I think you need to call in sick tomorrow and come to**

brunch at my parents' house.

"What?" I mumble, reading his text.

Me: ***I'm just having issues sleeping. I'm not sick.***

Dr. Hawkins: ***Good. I'd hate for you to get my parents sick at brunch tomorrow.***

I'm not tired enough to sleep, but I'm too tired to write in my journal. And here he is, texting me an invitation to eat food with his parents.

Food.

Unknown food.

Food made by other people.

Food not at one of my regular restaurants.

Me: ***You want me to lie?***

Dr. Hawkins: ***I want you to meet my parents tomorrow.***

Me: ***I have never called in sick.***

Dr. Hawkins: ***Do it for me.***

Me: ***I'm not good at lying.***

Dr. Hawkins: ***Pretend you're sick and it won't feel like a lie. That's what you did earlier when you tried to cancel our date. I'll write you a doctor's note.***

Me: ***Really. I'm a terrible liar.***

Dr. Hawkins: ***Text your boss, then you don't have to say the lie aloud. It will be easier.***

Me: ***Do you lie about being sick?***

Dr. Hawkins: ***No. I'm a doctor. I have to work from my deathbed.***

Me: ***I'm a patient transporter. If I don't show up to work, who will transport YOUR patients?***

Dr. Hawkins: ***Please (folded hands emoji)***

Me: ***(eye rolling emoji)***

Dr. Hawkins: ***I'll make sure everything is vegetarian. I'll even order you a pizza or a dozen tacos from your favorite restaurant so you don't have to eat my mom's cooking. Which would be a shame because she's an excellent cook. (three folded hands emojis)***

Dr. Hawkins is an emoji man. That makes him exponentially more attractive to me. Still ... I'm not a good liar. But since it will be Sunday, maybe having four days at school before seeing my coworkers again will make it easier to deal with the guilt and not spew my confessions the second someone at work asks me if I'm feeling better.

Me: ***Send me the address and time. Will Romeo be there?***

Dr. Hawkins: ***Sending ... and yes, Julie will drop him off.***

The next text is his parents' address and the time: 11:00 a.m.

Drop him off. That means Dr. Hathaway will be there. Right? At least long enough to let him out of the car. Or will she walk him to the door? Come inside? Meet me?

Hi. I'm Dorothy. Does your ex-husband require any-

thing out of the ordinary to have sex? I tried a sexy dress, stripping for him, offering both oral and vaginal sex. Not sure where I went wrong. Would you mind giving me a few tips? Oh ... and I think you're brilliant. I want to be you when I grow up. Me? Yeah, I'm thirty, but in the Aspie world that's like twenty ... so barely a grown-up."

I imagine her feeling flattered by my compliments, suggesting we be friends who share knowledge of their favorite scientific studies and tips on pleasing men. My friend list is pretty short. Accommodating Dr. Hathaway seems doable.

Dr. Hawkins: **Did you fall asleep?**

His text brings me out of my roleplaying.

Me: **No. Going to try again now. See you tomorrow.**

Dr. Hawkins: **Night, Dorothy. Can't wait to see you again.**

"I don't mind being me.
No one else can do it better."
–Dorothy Mayhem

CHAPTER THIRTEEN

Frittata Fingers

SLEEP ISN'T ON my side, so I make the most of my Sunday morning by texting my boss—lying to her. Then I load up my bike and drive to the trailhead. Two hours later, I return to my car and check the activity app on my watch, fully intending to message Dr. Hawkins to brag about my early start to meeting my activity and exercise goals.

"What the hell?" When I look at my watch, there are notifications that Eli has already completed an eight-mile run and a weight lifting workout—exceeding all of his daily goals.

Before I can figure out a response, my watch chimes with a message from him.

Dr. Hawkins: *Good job! Keep up the hard work.*

That's his response to the notification he got about the workout I just completed.

"Oh, I'm keeping it up." I breathe a determined sigh,

securing my bike to its carrier. On the way home, I stop by the gym to make sure I exceed his weight lifting workout. Then I hustle home to get a shower since the drive to his parents' house is forty-five minutes, and I don't want to be late.

"Hey, what are you—"

I hold up my hand to my mom as she pours coffee for herself and my dad. "No time to talk. I have to get showered."

"Why aren't you at work?"

"I'll explain later." I jump into the shower, trying my best to multitask—suds and shave while planning out the appropriate outfit. Settling on a dark eggplant skirt and a pale pink button-down blouse with matching flats, I blow out my hair, and then apply my lip balm while pulling out of the driveway.

The traffic isn't too bad late Sunday morning. Things I wouldn't know because I've always been at work by now. The guilt of not being at work continues to eat at me, but the idea of getting to spend time with Dr. Hawkins and Romeo numbs the agitation grinding against my nerves. I pull into their circle drive at 10:30. The blue Tesla is nowhere to be seen, so I wait.

A red Lexus SUV pulls up behind me ten minutes later. I know that car and the woman getting out—Dr. Hathaway. She unfastens Roman from his car seat and walks up beside my car, giving me a polite smile. I smile back and slowly open my door. If I stay inside, she might tell his parents. Then I'll be the weird woman sitting in their driveway. There is no disputing my slightly weird personality, but I try to avoid consciously putting it on display to the whole world.

So, instead of being the weird stranger sitting in my car, I turn into the weird stranger staying five steps behind Dr. Hathaway and Roman as they walk up to the front door.

"Dorfee!" He smiles, looking back at me.

Dr. Hathaway glances back as well.

"Dorfee, why are you here?"

"I'm here to have brunch with you, Romeo."

"Hi." Dr. Hathaway smiles. "I'm Julie. When did you meet Roman?"

"Dorfee is a superhero!" He tugs on Julie's hand, jumping up and down with excitement.

"Shh …" I hold a finger to my lips and wink at him. "That's a secret. Remember?"

Julie's smile morphs into something a little uneasy. Clearly, I don't look familiar to her. And I shared secrets with her son. Nothing creepy about that.

"Dorothy Mayhem. I'm actually a patient transporter at your hospital … and a nursing student." I stop. Someone needs to send me a high-five emoji for having such self-control. I want—*really* want—to talk about her work and studies. The million things she's done to help kids.

"Oh, then I've probably seen you there." The line along her forehead eases a bit.

"You have."

She nods slowly, inspecting me—the woman who calls her son Romeo and is having brunch with her ex in-laws. "Sorry I didn't recognize you. I see so many faces."

"You don't need to apologize."

"So … how is it that you know Roman? Wait …" She narrows her eyes. "Dorothy the superhero. X-ray vision. Roman did mention you. He said you ate spaghetti with him and wore a bib. I thought you were an imaginary friend."

"Oh. Ha! No. I'm real."

"So you're a friend of Eli's?"

"Grandma!" Roman runs into the house when the door opens.

His grandma hugs him while her gaze ping-pongs between me and Julie. "Hi. Julie. And you must be Dorothy."

"Hi. Yes. Nice to meet you." I brush past Julie and hold out my hand, not that handshakes are my thing, but I want to blend in at brunch. I want his parents to like me.

"I'm Lori. It's a pleasure to meet you too, Dorothy."

"Bye, Roman. I love you," Julie calls, but he's already rushed into the house. "Okay. So, nice seeing you, Lori. And nice officially meeting you, Dorothy."

I feel bad for Julie. She seems nervous. Not at all like my boss bitch idol.

"You too. See you around at the hospital."

She nods, sliding on her sunglasses as she walks back to her vehicle, dressed in fitted jeans, a gray sweater, and black ankle boots. Her red hair hangs long and wavy around her shoulders instead of in a ponytail or messy bun like it does at work. At least she looks like I imagined

Boss Bitch would look like outside of the hospital—casual but still very classy.

"Come in, Dorothy. Did you get Eli's message? He had an emergency. He'll get here as soon as he can. We didn't know if you'd show up or not. He said he'd give you the option of coming another Sunday. But I'm so glad you decided to come today."

I glance at my watch. Yep. There's a message from him. How did I miss that?

> Dr. Hawkins: *Hi. I've been called for an emergency. I'm hoping to still make it for brunch. You're welcome to go there and hang out with Roman and my parents, but I assume you'll choose a different day when I'm not running late. Call you later! Or I might see you at the hospital if you decide to go in now.*

Just ... great. I smile. "Missed his message. I'll reschedule for another Sunday." I turn, taking steps toward my car.

Oh my god! I didn't have to be here! Why am I here?

"Wait? No! You should stay, Dorothy. I would absolutely love for you to stay. My daughters couldn't make it today, so it's just Roman, Kent, and me ... and of course Eli when he shows up."

I don't want to stay.

Nope.

No way.

Five years earlier, I would have kept shaking my head, slid into my car, and skidded out of their driveway. But I no longer act on total impulse all the time. I've practiced deciphering neurotypicals, imagining what they would do in my situation, and reacting/mimicking accordingly.

"Thank you for the kind offer." I turn, plastering on a smile. "But I'm a vegetarian. I'd hate for you to have to deal with my dietary restrictions. Have a lovely day."

Have a lovely day seems to make everything okay, like the time I told Kelsey, one of the X-ray techs, that her deodorant had worn off and she was emitting an offensive odor. At first she gasped, which led me to believe I'd worded the FYI incorrectly, but then I followed it up with "have a lovely day," and she nodded slowly while hugging her arms to her chest. Aspies may not be best friends, but we are the most honest ones.

"Eli told me. Everything I made for brunch today is vegetarian with lots of cheese. He said you have a thing for cheese."

He did, did he?

She has a better hand of cards today, so I take a deep breath and retreat toward the house. There is nothing I love more than spending time with strangers, eating food they make that I probably won't like, and making small talk—the hardest thing in the world for me to do.

Lori leads me to her kitchen. It's big and clean. Tons of food fills a buffet table behind a large dining room table adorned with a sprawling bouquet of fresh flowers, real plates and flatware, and cloth napkins. It looks like a nice restaurant. Even the trays of food are garnished with herb springs and fresh fruits.

"Whoa, this is quite the brunch. I honestly imagined

coffee, bagels, bacon, and maybe a few donuts."

"Sounds like continental breakfast at a hotel." She laughs. "I'm all about presentation."

Me too.

Only, I have to work really hard at it, and rarely do I one hundred percent nail it.

"Kent?" she calls out the back door. "Let's eat. Bring Roman."

"What can I get you to drink, Dorothy? Do you like mimosas?"

"Yes. But I'm driving so I'll pass?"

"You can just do orange juice. It's fresh squeezed."

Fresh squeezed, as in she fondled the oranges and squeezed them ... maybe with her hands. "I have my water bottle in my bag." I pull it out of my handbag.

"You sure?"

I nod.

"Please, grab a plate and help yourself."

First through the line. I can do this. Yes ... she probably touched everything on these platters, but I choose to believe she wore gloves. And first through the line means no one else has had a chance to touch the food first or sneeze on it. I grab a plate and silverware. Real silverware, not the plastic kind that tastes like plastic. *Yuck!*

"Dorfee!" Roman rushes in with a tall, older version of Dr. Hawkins behind him—a few more wrinkles, gray mixed with dark blond hair, and a more pronounced receding hairline. He's dressed in jeans and a Trailblazer sweatshirt.

"Dorothy, this is my husband Kent. Kent, this is Eli's

friend, Dorothy."

"Papa, Dorfee is a superhero." Roman reaches for a plate behind me. Kent quickly grabs it from him.

"Nice to meet you, Dorothy." Dr. Hawkins has his father's smile.

I return a genuine grin. It isn't awful here—yet. Just the four of us. I can do it. With a few deep breaths ... I can handle brunch with strangers.

"Show me what you want, Roman," Kent adds food to Roman's plate after Roman pokes the things he wants with his finger.

I keep reminding myself I'm first in line, and clearly there will be no second trip for me, even if I do like the food. It's not that I don't adore Romeo, but I know darn well the chances that he spent most of the ride to their house with that same finger stuck up his nose are pretty good.

"Stop touching everything, silly." Lori rolls her eyes at Roman. "We have company, and I don't think your friend, Dorothy, wants your little fingers touching all the food."

A small amount of bile works its way up my throat. I just want to ignore his fingers and stay one step ahead of them without imagining eating toddler contaminated food.

"It's a little chilly out, but we have the porch heaters on, so you can head out that door." Kent nods to the door that he and Roman came through earlier.

"Okay." I head out the door and take a seat on one of the comfy outdoor chairs. After I steady my plate on my lap, I text Dr. Hawkins.

> Me: ***I didn't get your message in time. I'm at your parents' house. Hope you're going to make it soon. Don't kill a patient to get here, but please hurry. (grinning face with sweat emoji)***

"I sit by Dorfee!" Roman crawls into the chair next to me.

"Maybe you should sit at your table. It might be easier for you to eat, buddy." Kent puts Roman's plate on the little table in the corner of the porch.

"No! Listen, Papa, listen! I sit by Dorfee!"

"I'll sit by you, Romeo." I grab my stuff and move to the toddler table, twisting my lips at the little red chair for a few seconds. Surely it will hold me. Easing into it, I smile. "Coming?" I ask him.

Romeo jumps out of the big chair and runs over to the table, taking a seat next to me in the blue chair.

"You really don't have to." Kent grins while chuckling.

"I prefer the kids' table." I shrug. It's one hundred percent true.

Lori makes her way out to the porch, letting out a little laugh when she spots me sitting next to Roman. "Your dad's going to be jealous of you, Roman. You're stealing his friend."

Roman plays with his food, ignoring his grandma.

"What's dis?" Roman jabs his finger into one of the tiny piles of food on my plate.

I freeze, trying to play it really cool. "Um ... I'm not

sure."

"Roman Alexander ... keep your fingers out of Dorothy's food!" Lori scolds him. "It's frittata. Do you want some?"

He removes his finger from my little square of frittata, sticks it into his mouth, and nods.

Lori starts to stand.

"Here. He can just try some of mine." I lift my plate and hold it next to his while scooping *all* of it onto his plate.

"You don't need to give him all of it." Kent frowns at his grandson.

I expect Lori to rush to get me more, which I don't want. No. She just smiles at me like I did something right, and she isn't going to play fixer with the food. Does she know I need to give him *all* of it after he stuck his finger into it? Maybe. She is a talk doctor. She probably knows my type. But I don't announce my Aspie status or show them my medical ID bracelet that I *don't* have for my neurodivergent condition.

Have I already fucked up my pursuit of acting neurotypical today? Hmm ... what tipped her off? Probably the water bottle. I should have just drank the mimosa and asked my parents to come drive me home. That's what most people would do, right?

"How much more schooling do you have, Dorothy?" Lori asks.

"For nursing?"

She nods. "Yes. Are you getting a degree in something else as well?"

"Not yet." I shrug. "I have a bachelor's degree in science. And I'm a CNA and EMT. I hope this nursing thing works out. I'd like to work in the plastics field with Dr. Hathaway. She's so brilliant."

Lori continues eating, giving me no visual feedback—that I catch anyway. Maybe she doesn't realize how brilliant her ex-daughter-in-law is.

"Eli is a brilliant doctor too," Kent says, first glancing at Lori before smiling at me.

"Yes. He is. But oncology is pretty draining. It's not like okay versus better—disfiguring scar verses no disfiguring scar. It's always life versus death. It's watching parents grasp for false hope. I mean ... when the treatment works, it's phenomenal, but when it doesn't, it becomes the worst job in the world. 'How long does my child have?' Really? Could there be a worse question to have to answer?"

"It's terribly hard on Eli, but he's the best at it. He's always been our most compassionate child, which is interesting since he's our only boy. And I love that you have such respect for Julie. She *is* incredibly talented. You couldn't have a better professional role model." Lori sips her mimosa.

Professional. Lori stressed that word. At least that's how it sounded to me. It's possible they don't think highly of Julie after she left their son. When I heard the news of their split, I journaled it because everyone wouldn't stop talking about it. So I worked it out in my mind and put it on paper. That's when I realized they were too alike. No alpha or beta. No teacher and student.

That would be hard for me.

Dr. Hawkins's physical stature alone gives him an air of dominance, let alone his professional accomplishments. But Boss Bitch could never be a student ... a beta ... or submissive. No way.

Since she acknowledged the awesomeness of Dr. Hathaway, and has a medical degree of her own, I feel it might be appropriate to list a few of the things I admire most about Boss Bitch. It seems like the perfect conversation and much better than small talk.

"I actually heard Dr. Hathaway speak years ago at ..."

CHAPTER FOURTEEN

Doggy Style

Elijah

TWO HOURS LATE, I arrive at my parents' house. Dorothy's car is still parked in the driveway. That makes me happy. I want to see her. I want to see her around my family.

"Hey." I smile at my mom as I turn the corner into the kitchen. She looks up from her phone.

"Hi. Leftovers are in the fridge. Everything go okay?"

"Yeah, fine now. Everyone else out back?"

"Uh huh …" She slides her phone onto the counter. "Sorry. I'm on call this weekend. And of course it's been nonstop. Yes … your dad is out back with Roman and Dorothy."

"Everything go okay?"

She laughs. "It went well. Really well. We like her. She adores Roman, even though he stuck his fingers in her food. And she sat at his little table with him."

Of course she did. Dorothy is awesome like that.

"And ... Dorothy thinks Julie walks on water."

I chuckle. "Well, I don't know if I'd say she thinks Julie walks on water."

"No." Mom shakes her head. "I'd definitely say she thinks she walks on water. Dorothy knows more about Julie—professionally—than you and I combined. But ..." She holds up a finger. "At first it caught me off guard, and I wasn't sure how this would all play out. But now I think it's a good thing. If you and Dorothy get serious, I think her respect for Julie will be a positive for everyone involved. Dorothy could be the glue that holds everyone together with respect."

I can't figure out how to properly have sex with Dorothy. A serious relationship seems a ways down the road. And she works three long shifts a week and goes to school. The last thing Dorothy needs is to be anyone's glue.

"Let's not get ahead of ourselves. I just wanted you to meet her, since she's met Roman. And I, at the moment, enjoy her company." I retrieve the food from the fridge, specifically the plate my mom made up and saved for me.

"Okay. I have to call in a prescription. I'll be right out."

I nod, grabbing a glass of orange juice before shouldering my way out the screen door to the porch, where my dad's sitting with a satisfied grin as he watches Dorothy and Roman play ball with Elmo.

"I like her, Eli."

My shit-eating grin doubles. How could anyone not like Dorothy Mayhem? "Yeah, I do too. How've you been?" I sit next to him instead of interrupting the yard play.

"Not bad. Your mom's bugging me to take time off for a vacation. She wants to go to Costa Rica after Christmas."

"Well, then take Mom to Costa Rica."

"I hate to travel."

I chuckle. "You hate anything that takes you away from your shop. I'm amazed you're sitting here right now."

"You know she threatened to do something very brutal to my balls if I didn't stay … what were her words? Oh yeah, *fully engaged*, during brunch with your friend."

"Dorothy will give you a pass if you want to change your clothes and get a wrench in your hands. I'm certain she wasn't thrilled about meeting you and Mom all alone."

"You wouldn't have known. She's quite chatty when you get her started about something she loves … like your ex-wife."

A grunt makes it past the spoonful of frittata in my mouth. I wipe it with a napkin. "Was Dorothy here when Julie dropped off Roman?"

He shrugs. "Beats me."

"Yes," Mom answers as she pushes open the screen door. "They all arrived at the same time. I gathered there was a conversation happening on the porch before I opened the door. All friendly and amicable. Julie looked a bit thrown by Dorothy being here, but not necessarily angry. Just like it was unexpected."

I wonder if I'll get a call or message from Julie. They must have discussed my inviting Dorothy to brunch. "Well, too bad it's not any of her business."

"Now, Eli, Roman is her son too. She should be concerned enough to want to know that the people you bring into his life are good for him, and you should have the same concerns about the people Julie dates."

"I don't think she dates. I've heard she just has random hookups when I have Roman. Go, Julie! It's never too late to be a slut."

"Elijah Alexander Hawkins!" Mom whisper yells.

"Too far?" I smirk before taking a sip of my juice.

"Yes. Too far. That's your child's mother." Mom frowns. On Fridays, in her office during lunch, she adheres to a slightly more professional tone with me. But at her house, she isn't Dr. Lori Hawkins, she's just Mom. Brutally honest and just as opinionated as any other mom is of their child's behavior.

"Oh ... woman down!" Dad cringes.

I shift my attention to the yard.

"Dorfee! You okay?"

I set my plate on the ottoman and jog out to the landscaped area of shrubs and river rock where Dorothy's on her ass, hissing as she pulls her scraped knees to her chest.

"Daddy! Dorfee's bleeding! Call 9-1-1!" Roman squats next to her.

"Roman ..." I grab his hand just as his chubby little finger reaches for the blood on her knee. "Don't touch her booboo. It will hurt her. Okay?"

"It's fine." She starts to stand.

I grab her arm, helping her to her feet. "We'll get it cleaned up. What happened?"

"Elmo cut me off. Not his fault. I was looking behind me at Romeo chasing me."

"Well, I know a good doctor." I help her toward the house.

"Dr. Hathaway already left."

"Not funny, Mayhem." I roll my eyes.

She laughs. "I didn't know if you'd get the joke. Well … not totally a joke."

"You okay, Dorothy?" Mom asks as soon as we step onto the porch.

"Yep. Fine. I'm clumsy by nature."

"First aid kit is upstairs under the sink, Eli."

"Thanks, Mom."

"I'm fine. Really. We can just blot it with a paper towel."

"Or we can wash it properly and put some antibiotic ointment and a Band-Aid on it."

Dorothy rolls her eyes. "Sure. Or that. Nice of you to make it, Dr. Hawkins."

"Eli. And I'm sorry. Really."

"It's okay. I like Roman … and even Elmo in spite of recent events."

"Not my parents?" I give her side-eye as we reach the top of the stairs.

"They're okay too, but clearly it was only Roman and Elmo who wanted to play chase in the backyard. It's not an activity on my watch, so I logged it in under outdoor jog. Did you notice I'm kicking your ass now?"

"The day's not over." I give her ass a playful slap as I usher her into the guest bedroom. "Take a seat on the bench. I'll grab the supplies."

Dorothy gives me a wide-eyed look over her shoulder. "Getting a little sexual for a family brunch, Dr. Hawkins." She rubs her ass where I lightly tapped it.

"That wasn't sexual. It was playful." I grab the first aid kit and a hand towel.

"Would you spank your mom like that?" She sits on the bench, crossing her arms over her chest.

"Really? You casually undressed for me last night in the backseat of your car, but a playful pat on your ass has what ... offended you?" I kneel in front of her.

"I was dressed for sex last night. My mind was focused on sex."

And ... there goes my dick, doing its own thing.

"But today, I'm dressed for brunch with your family. So I wasn't expecting the sexual advance. That's all."

Grinning, I shake my head and clean her knees. "I love your rules. Even if I haven't mastered them yet. I still love that you have them."

"You love to break them." She rubs her lips together when I glance up at her. They have luster, like she recently applied her lip balm. They look kissable. I apply two Band-Aids and part her legs just enough to wedge my body between them, placing my hands in the safe zone just above her ass.

"This feels inappropriate." Her words would carry more weight if she weren't staring at my lips. "Your parents and Roman could sneak up here and wonder what's going on."

"Is something going on?" I kiss her neck.

She sucks in a sharp breath. "You have to stop teasing me. I can't figure out what's a playdate and what's a sex date, not that we've had sex, because I can't figure out how to make you have it with me. And that's very frustrating. But anyway ... you should behave. It feels like the right thing to do. Maybe I'm not the best judge of that all of the time, but this one is pretty obvious."

"Wait." I pull back, cocking my head to the side. "You can't figure out how to *make me have sex with you*?"

"Duh ..." She shrugs. "If getting completely naked for you and bringing my own condoms doesn't work, I'm not sure anything will work. So I just need to know, are we ever having sex? Or are you just looking for companionship—a hand to hold, a few stolen kisses ... an ass to pat? I'm fine with whatever. It's just I don't like not knowing. I *need* to know. So if it's never happening, that's cool. Totally cool. I can stop obsessing over *when* it's going to happen. I can focus on my activity rings. I don't have to deal with sexy panties that itch. I can wear my soft and perfectly worn cotton ones." She blows out a long breath.

Amazing ... since she used so much oxygen to get all of that information out in such a short amount of time. I didn't think a woman could think about sex more than a man.

Wrong.

"You name the place and time."

She squints. "For sex?"

I nod, sliding my hands an inch lower to scoot her closer to the edge of the bench so she can feel how much I want to have sex with her.

"Now. Right here. Do you have a condom? My handbag is downstairs."

"Now?" I laugh. Maybe she doesn't understand flirting and foreplay. "Two seconds ago you gave me a speech about this being inappropriate and someone sneaking up on us. But *now* you want to have sex? Here? While my parents and Roman wait for me to bandage your wounds?"

She twists her lips to the side for a few seconds. "It's not ideal. But it's doable if you don't take too long and if you cover my mouth if I start to make noise—but I won't if it's nothing spectacular. And really, I just think we need to do it, so you know."

Every single one ... every single conversation with Dorothy turns into the most bizarre exchange of random thoughts. Fifty percent inappropriate. Fifty percent gut-splitting funny.

"So I know what?"

"That I'm good at it."

I try to control my eyebrows shooting up my head, but they do it before I can control my reaction.

This woman ...

"I mean ..." She rolls her eyes. "Clearly, I lack in the seduction part. I didn't think that was the case until I met you. But if you ever give me a fair chance, you won't regret it."

Seriously ... For. The. Love. Of. God! The woman

speaks of sex with the demeanor of conducting a job interview.

Yet … yes … I am so fucking turned on at the moment. I press my hands to the bench on both sides of her lap and push myself to standing.

Pivot.

Take three steps.

Shut and lock the bedroom door.

"It's going to be quick because it has to be. You do *not* under any circumstances tell anyone that we had *quick* sex. I don't need that rumor going around." I unfasten my jeans and fetch a condom from my wallet.

Yes, I learned my lesson the previous night.

"These are not my sex panties. Just so you know." She stands, lifts her skirt and shimmies out of her panties.

"No fucks given as to what your panties look like, Dorothy. Just take them off and pick your position."

Her eyes light up just like her smile. "I get to pick the position?"

When I had sex with Julie for the first time, it started with a kiss that progressed into heavy foreplay that led to my hand sliding down the front of her panties, finding a little nub, and wondering if it was her clit. She stroked me on the outside of my gym shorts so much that it pulled them down a few inches in front. We were a hot mess of teenaged hormones. The sex was awkward, and the groping was sloppy. I couldn't steady my hands to put on a condom, and Julie worried that we'd be part of the tiny percent of condom failures.

She came on my hand before I put my cock in her,

and I came two seconds after said cock entered her.

Decades later ... here I am, pushing down my jeans just enough to pull out my cock and roll on a condom with steady hands while Dorothy crawls onto the bed, skirt around her waist, ass in the air.

Doggy style. I didn't see that being her choice. Interesting ...

I stand at the side of the bed and grab her hips, coaxing her to move closer to the edge. So this is thirty-eight, post-divorce, millennial sex. Nothing fancy, just sex a la carte.

My ... how times have changed.

"Wait!" She sits back on her heels, back to me, wrist close to her face. "Did you press start yet?"

"What?"

She whips her head back, eyeing me over her shoulder, wearing a spectacular grin. "On your watch?"

"For sex?" I cough a laugh.

"Um ... yes. Under your health app on your phone, you can manually add sexual activity. See?" She holds up her arm and presses *Go*. Then she shrugs. "Don't worry, yours will just record it as movement."

I let the "snacking on Dorothy" statement end our quest for sex the previous night. I could easily let the sexual activity tracking on her watch make me pause just long enough to let my thoughts catch up with me.

My parents.

Their house.

Roman.

But ... I don't. Because the second she leans forward

again and readjusts her skirt, exposing her bare ass, I can't stop my hand from sliding between her sexy legs to feel if she's ready for me.

Her breath hitches when I find her clit, circling my finger over it several times before sliding that finger into her.

"Dr. Hawkins ..." She moans my name and jerks against my hand.

"Eli ... you *have* to call me Eli." Dr. Hawkins makes me feel like a dirty old man doing something really inappropriate to a patient. I work a second finger into her and kiss the curve of her ass.

"Eli ... don't lick my butthole. Okay?" she asks in a breathy voice.

I grin against the soft skin of her perfect ass. "Okay." My fingers work her faster, and she rocks on her hands and knees to set the pace. I want her naked again. I want to feel every inch of her skin. I want to slide my head between her legs and give her exactly what she wanted the previous night.

But ... we have to be quick. So I replace my fingers with my cock, grab her hips, and push into her with just enough force to make her whole body shift forward.

"Eli—" I cover her mouth to muffle her cry.

"I guess this means I'm pretty spectacular, huh?" I whisper, leaning close to her ear.

With my hand still over her mouth, she nods.

I won't reveal just how quick we finish. But it's too quick. So quickly that I have a hard-on again by the time she slides her panties back on.

"Forty calories is all?" She frowns at her watch before slipping her feet into her flats again.

After I dispose of the condom and fasten my pants, I grab the back of her head and kiss her. I kiss her like I want to have sex with her—slow and deep. Exploring every inch of her mouth the way I want to do to her body.

Her hands claim my shirt, keeping me close. And she hums into the kiss, softer than earlier, but just as sexy. Seconds ... maybe minutes later, I pull away a few inches, admiring the pink blooming in her cheeks and her slightly swollen lips licked clean of all her coconut lip balm.

"Dorothy Mayhem, you are full of surprises." I curl her hair behind her ear on one side. Apparently foreplay and seduction are not her game. Or maybe it's a thing of the past. Jesus ... am I really that old and clueless about dating and sexual trends?

"Told you I was good at sex." She smirks.

"Easy, champ. I wouldn't call forty calories good. I give points for stamina. We're going to need a redo under better circumstances with more time to really burn some calories."

"Daddy?" Two little feet slap the stairs in a slow rhythm.

I straighten my shirt and my erection as Dorothy tries to absorb some of the heat from her cheeks with her palms pressed to them. Then I quickly unlock the bedroom door. The last thing I need is Roman telling my mom that the bedroom door is locked.

"Daddy! Where are you?" Roman runs straight into my legs, making me wobble a bit to keep my balance.

"I'm right here, buddy. Are you ready to go home?"

"Dorfee! Your knees are beeding."

I turn just as she leans down to reattach the Band-Aids. Then my gaze darts to the bed and the two blood smudges on the off-white quilt. My face twists into a grimace as Dorothy's gaze follows mine.

"Oops ..." She looks back at me, mirroring my grimace.

"I was just getting Dorothy new Band-Aids. They came off because they were too small." Giving Roman a quick shrug and oh-well face, I pull two new Band-Aids out of the first aid kit.

"Sit." I wink at Dorothy.

"Ruff!" She barks and grins at Roman while taking a seat on the bench again.

"Uh ... interesting position choice, given your recent knee injuries," I mutter under my breath as I replace the Band-Aids, more upset with myself for completely forgetting about her knees once sex became the topic.

"Does my doctor son not know how to put on a Band-Aid?" Mom's voice creeps closer as Roman climbs onto the bed and starts jumping.

"Down, Roman. Now ... please."

Please, child! Get off the bed before ...

"No little monkeys jumping on my bed." Mom heads toward the bed.

"I've got him!" Before I manage to replace the second Band-Aid, I stand, plucking Roman from the bed and turning to face my mom, hoping to block her view of the blood smudges.

Dorothy finishes the second Band-Aid.

"We couldn't imagine what was taking you two so long."

Roman squirms out of my arms and runs toward the stairs.

"Sorry. We were talking … that's all." I smile my very best oh-shit-I'm-in-trouble smile.

Dorothy stands and Mom inspects her. "Dear, you have blood smeared all over your knees. Didn't Eli clean your knees first?" She clucks her tongue and shakes her head.

Dorothy remains statuesque, eyes wide.

"Sit, Dorothy. I'll get a wet washcloth." Mom points to the bench at the end of the bed.

"Don't speak. Okay?" I whisper after Mom leaves the bedroom.

Dorothy nods stiffly.

I move the gray throw blanket up the bed to cover the blood smudges and quickly turn back toward the door when Mom comes in with a wet washcloth. She squats down in front of Dorothy and cleans the dried blood around the Band-Aids.

"There. Much better." Mom stands straight, smiling at Dorothy. Her smile fades when she sees the throw blanket situated in the middle of the bed.

"Thanks, Mom. I need to use the restroom. Can you take Dorothy downstairs? Maybe package up some of those leftovers for her. She *loves* leftovers."

"Sure …" She steps toward the bed.

"What are you doing?" I block her attempt to move

toward the bed.

Mom narrows her eyes at me. Yes, I'm acting incredibly weird—extremely paranoid. "I'm just fixing the blanket on the bed."

"I thought you were going to get Dorothy leftovers." I plant my fists on my hips to widen my body like a gate she can't pass.

"Yes, Eli. I just want to straighten the—"

"Mom! Dorothy doesn't have all day."

The room falls silent.

Mom's head jerks backward as Dorothy grimaces, trapping her lower lips between her teeth, wringing out her hands in front of her.

"Elijah Alexander, what is wrong with you, child?"

"Nothing," I say as calmly as possible. "You just … go. I'll fix the blanket and use the restroom. You get Dorothy some leftovers."

"What is under that blanket?" She crosses her arms over her chest?"

"What?" I narrow my eyes.

"I wasn't born yesterday. You're acting like you used to act when you broke something and didn't want me to find out. You might be a grown man now, but you still lie to your mom like a ten-year-old boy. What is under that blanket? Did Roman get it dirty with his bare feet?"

"Yes. Just let me have it cleaned. I don't want you to worry about—"

"No!" Dorothy yells before cupping her hand over her mouth.

My mom turns toward her while I shake my head so

hard it makes my neck hurt. Dorothy's eyes ping-pong between us. I silently plead with her.

"No ... what, dear?"

"It wasn't Roman," she mumbles from behind her hand.

"Dorothy, it's okay. He's not going to get into any trouble." A nervous laugh infiltrates my words.

"It was me," she says, dropping her hand from her mouth. "I got blood on your quilt. I'm really sorry. I will replace it if it doesn't come out in the wash."

"Dorothy, I'm not worried about a few drops of blood. I'll get them out." Mom shoulders past me and removes the throw blanket. "Oh ... I guess it's more than a few drops. Did you faint face-first or something?" She cocks her head, inspecting the smudges too much ... way too much.

"Yes, a little lightheaded." I grab Mom's shoulders to steer her out of the bedroom.

She brushes me away, shooting me a scowl before returning her attention to Dorothy. "Well, looks like you have plenty of color in your cheeks now."

Dorothy presses her palms to her cheeks, patting them gently.

"Better get used to a little blood, dear. You could potentially see a lot of it as a nurse."

"I'm fine with blood." Dorothy acts a little offended.

It's not the right time to get offended.

"Just not your own. That's pretty common." Mom heads toward the stairs.

Thank god!

"No. I'm fine with my own." Dorothy chases after my mom like she has a point to prove.

No points need to be proven. We just need to get the hell out of here.

"I didn't get lighthea—"

Dorothy claws at my hand covering her mouth.

"Let it go!" I whisper in her ear.

"Elijah Alexander!"

Here we go …

I remove my hand.

"What in god's name are you doing to her?" Mom stands halfway down the stairs with a look of horror etched into her face.

Dorothy curls her hair behind her ears and lets her hands flop to her sides as she releases the world's biggest sigh. "We had sex. I chose doggy position, totally forgetting about my knees. I'm so sorry. I should have said missionary."

Closing my eyes, I rub my temples and drop my chin to my chest. How is this my life?

"Oh …" My mother stretches that "oh" out for many seconds. "I see. Dorothy, we'll meet you downstairs. I need a few minutes with my son."

"Okay."

Okay …

Damn! Dorothy holds no remorse in her voice. No embarrassment. No concern for the fact that I'm about to be grounded for life. Yes, I feel certain my mother would ground me—at thirty-eight.

The *pat pat pat* of Dorothy's steps fade, but the slight

creak of the steps gets louder as my mom inches toward me. I can't look at her. There is a good possibility I will never be able to look her in the eye again.

"Eli?"

"Mom, I—"

"I'm so incredibly proud of you."

"What?" My head snaps up.

Yep, it's pride that shines along her face, feeding her smile, glistening in her eyes.

"Way to go! I've wanted this for you for months. The right woman who would drag you out of your cave of desperation and depression. A woman so completely different than Julie, but who would adore both you and Roman. A woman with a zest for life. A woman willing to take risks like a quickie at your parents' house."

Blink.

Blink.

Blink.

"Um ..."

Blink.

Blink.

Blink.

"I don't know if Dorothy is necessarily a risk taker. I think that *if* she's on the spectrum, then she just became a little fixated on ... proving something," I say.

My mom won't stop grinning at me. Normally parental pride is a good thing. Not now. Not when fucking Dorothy Mayhem doggy style is the reason for Mom's glowing pride.

No.

Just … no.

"What was she trying to prove?"

"We're done talking about this." I brush past her to the stairs.

"You'll tell me Friday."

"I'll never tell you. Sorry, *Mom*."

Mom packs leftovers, but I can tell by the horrified expression on Dorothy's face that she will not eat them.

"Thanks for brunch. It was better than I imagined." Dorothy gives my mom a sincere smile.

Mom chuckles. "You are most welcome here anytime, Dorothy—with or without Eli."

I roll my eyes and corral Roman by tossing him onto my shoulder. "Thank you, Mom, for another great Sunday brunch and your hospitality." I kiss her cheek. "Tell Grandma bye, Roman."

He giggles, upside down over my shoulder as Mom kisses him goodbye.

"Tell Dad bye."

"Oh, I will. The stinker already snuck out to his shop."

We follow Dorothy to the driveway.

"Bye, Dorfee!" Roman yells next to my ear just as I set him down by the back door to my car.

"Bye, Romeo. See ya around."

"Hop into your car seat, buddy."

While Roman climbs into his seat, I meet Dorothy at the driver's door to her car and lean back against it so she won't run off quite yet. "Thank you. I know playing hooky, lying to your boss, eating with strangers, and letting Roman contaminate your food is probably way out of your comfort zone, but I really..." I lower my voice "...*really* enjoyed this brunch date."

"Okay." She grins.

"Okay ..." I challenge her with my very own guilty-as-hell, shit-eating grin. "So, what's on your agenda for the rest of the day?"

She glances at her watch. "Aside from keeping a close eye on Dr. Hawkins and his daily activity, not much. I'm supposed to be at work, so I might get some extra reading time in and gaming."

"No studying?"

"Nah, I don't have to study much. I mean sometimes I have to study, but nothing today."

"Smart girl, huh?"

Dorothy shrugs. "I suppose. It's just easy stuff is all." She curls her hair behind her ears and stares at her feet.

"You know ... Roman has never seen an emu up close."

"Really?" She glances up at me, squinting against the sun.

"Really."

"He'd love them."

I nod slowly while she goes back to staring at her feet because I'm blocking her from getting into her car.

"If only I knew where he could see one ... or two."

"Mmm ... hmm." She nods a few seconds before snapping her head up to meet my gaze again. "Oh ..." She laughs. "You mean Orville and Wilbur. You want me to show him my emus."

I lift my shoulders, stuffing my hands into the pockets of my jeans. "Only when it works in your schedule. Like on a day you're unexpectedly home instead of at work."

"Ha ha. Okay, I get it. You mean today." She wrinkles her nose while nibbling on her lip. "I didn't plan on visitors today."

"You didn't plan on not working today. But ... so far so good, right?"

Dorothy studies me for a few seconds. "I suppose."

"What happened in the bedroom deserves a higher ranking than *I suppose*."

"Okay."

"Okay we can follow you home?"

She nods.

"You're sure? I don't want to make you uncomfortable."

"Ha! This whole morning has been really uncomfortable."

I frown. "I'm sorry. We can go home. We don't have to impose on your day anymore." Stepping away from her vehicle, I open her door.

"Dr. Hawkins—"

"Eli," I say with more bite than I intend.

"Eli…" she repeats on an exhale "…I'm not the best at articulating things correctly. It's hard to explain. I just express things differently. But I do want you to come to my house. And I do want to introduce Romeo to Orville and Wilbur, even if it's been a stressful day. All my days are stressful in a way you can't understand. Okay?"

"Okay." I rub my lips together, studying her for a few

seconds, trying to figure out if now is the right time to say something. "Warren said you have ASD," I lie. He didn't say it correctly.

"Dr. Warren?" She twists her mouth. "Huh … he wanted to screw an Aspie. Interesting."

No. The interesting part is that's her reaction. So Aspie is an okay term with her. Who knew?

"What do you think, *Eli*?" Her head cants to the side.

Is this a test? What does she expect me to say? And is it a reference to her ASD or Dr. Warren wanting to screw an Aspie? I don't know, and it shouldn't matter. There is no way I will stumble over her question. Brushing my fingertips over the palm of her hand, I lean down close to her ear and whisper, "I think you're an extraordinarily spectacular *human*. Drive safely. We'll follow you." I let my lips graze her cheek, wondering if young eyes are watching and if Roman will say anything if he does see me so close to Dorothy.

Dorothy watches me, unblinking.

"Okay?" I ask.

After a few more seconds, she blinks and nods.

"I have a surprise for you, Roman," I say, grabbing him from the floor of my car where he tries to hide from me.

CHAPTER FIFTEEN

Me-yous

Dorothy

INTERESTING TRAIT OF most Aspies—we don't multi-task well. Not physically or mentally. I shouldn't be driving home. My brain distraction has to be more dangerous than impairment from alcohol. But I have three things vying for my attention, my thoughts … my natural tendency to obsess.

I had sex with Eli, and he wants a do-over.

Dr. Warren knows I'm an Aspie, and he wants to have sex with me.

Eli doesn't care about my Asperger's.

By some miracle, I make it home without crossing the center line or driving off a bridge. Did I stop at red lights? Presumably so, since I can't remember anyone honking at me.

I glance in my rearview mirror before pulling into the garage.

No blue Tesla.

The screen of my car shows a string of messages and two missed calls from Eli.

Slow down, please.

You just ran a red light.

Jesus, Dorothy! Slow down!

You lost us. Pulling over to wait for you to answer your phone or reply to this message.

Maybe you can give me your address?

"Oh, fuck …" I murmur while texting him my address with a grimacing emoji.

I take my accidentally earned extra time to run into the house and make sure my parents aren't sitting together on their sofa or making a mess in the kitchen. Or dressed in weird clothes.

"Dr. Hawk—" I shake my head. "Eli and Roman will be here soon."

Mom looks up from her book. "That's exciting."

"No. It's …" I grimace shaking my head. "It just … never mind. Where's Dad?"

"In his garden, of course. Do you want to tell me now why you're not at work today?"

"No." I rush out of her living room to check on my bedroom. There's no way I will let them into my bedroom, but sex at his parents' house wasn't on my radar either. I have to submit to the fact that Eli has his own agenda that doesn't always match mine. Was sex at his parents' his idea or mine?

Either way, I like his agenda—our agenda—

sometimes ... like earlier. I liked the hell out of it. I wanted to like it again, right after I liked it the first time, but that seemed greedy and maybe disrespectful to his parents and Roman.

"They're here!" Mom calls.

I straighten my journals and run a hand over my bed to smooth out the comforter.

"Dad's chatting with them."

"No!" I run toward the door.

Is Eli upset about me telling his mom about doggy style sex? Will he get revenge by telling my dad? My dad is not the kind of guy you joke with about his daughter and definitely not about pounding her from the backside.

"Hey!" I practically burst out the front door, a little out of breath and a lot anxious about the situation.

Eli and Roman on my property.

Eli and Roman meeting my parents for the first time.

Eli with that I-just-fucked-your-daughter look on his face.

Okay, I might be incorrectly reading into that look, but it still *feels* like a real possibility.

"Hey. Glad you made it home safely." Eli smiles at me.

"Sorry, I totally got distracted and didn't pay attention to the fact that you were no longer behind me."

"Your phone didn't ring in your car?"

"She drives like a bat out of Hell." Dad shakes his head. "And if she's distracted, a fire alarm could fall on deaf ears."

"You should introduce us, Dorothy." Mom's voice

chimes right behind me.

"Randy already introduced himself. I'm Eli and this is Roman." Eli holds out his hand to my mom.

"Kellie. Nice to meet both of you. Dorothy talks nonstop about you."

"Mom …" I mumble between gritted teeth.

Eli winks at me as Roman tugs on his arm.

"Daddy, look!" He points to my Orville and Wilbur strutting toward the fence. "Listen, Daddy! Listen!"

I laugh. "Let's go see them, Romeo." I hold out my hand, and he takes it. "You can come too, Eli."

"I'm good. I'll just stay here and chat with your parents."

"No. You need to come meet my emus."

He chuckles along with my parents, but after a few seconds, I hear the rocks behind me crunching beneath his footsteps.

"Big bird! Daddy, look at the big birds!"

"Yes. What did I tell you they're called?"

"Me-yous."

Oh my god … this kid is so damn adorable. "Emus." I lift him up as we approach the fence.

"This is Wilbur. He's a lover." I stroke Wilbur's neck. "And this is Orville. He's a little ornery. You'll see what I mean. He's a little more spastic."

Ruff!

Gemma runs toward them. "And this is my girl, Gemma. She has access to the fenced-in area and the house. Orville has managed to get himself caught in Gemma's access door more than once."

"Soft …" Roman says with reverence as he pets Wilbur. "Look, Daddy! A doggie."

As soon as the emus catch sight of Gemma running toward them, they take off like two robbers fleeing a bank.

"And so the chase begins." I laugh.

"Who wears out first?" Eli asks.

"Gemma. Those birds can run for hours and then cool off in the pond or kiddie pool."

"Daddy, look at the me-yous run!"

"They're fast, huh?"

"Yes!" Roman punches the air with his little fist. "Daddy, look!" He points to my trampoline.

"Oh … that looks … dangerous." Eli shoots me a tight-lipped smile.

"Daddy, let's bounce."

"Tiny fracture to my arm, but other than that, it's been pretty safe. Let's check it out while those three wear themselves out."

I set Roman down, and he runs straight to the trampoline. We jog to catch up to him. I help him in through the mesh doorway and crawl in behind him.

"This view might be worth a tiny fracture."

I glance back at Eli's smirk as he stares at my ass. He's seen his share of it today.

"Perv." I roll my eyes.

"It's not my fault you keep putting it in my face."

We take turns jumping with Roman, having a fun day I didn't expect. Then we play with Gemma, Orville, and Wilbur once their energy settles into something more manageable for Roman. And by manageable, I mean they are perched on their clean blankets in their shed, letting Roman love on them. I take at least fifty photos.

"What are you going to do with all of those pictures?" Eli asks as I flip through them.

"Put them on their Instagram page."

"Whose Instagram page?"

"Orville's and Wilbur's."

"What? Your emus have their own Instagram page?"

I hold up my phone.

Eli's eyes try to pop out of his head as he leans closer to my phone. "Your emus have over five hundred thousand followers? Is that for real?"

"Real." I shrug. "What can I say? People like animals better than humans. I know I do."

He chuckles. "Clearly, you might not be alone." He nods toward Roman asleep between Wilbur and Orville.

I have to snap ten more pics.

"Do you have a personal account? A Dorothy Mayhem account?"

"Yeah."

"And how many followers does it have?"

I pull up my account and show him.

He lifts his right eyebrow at the screen. "Thirteen people?"

"It's a private account. I don't let that many people follow me."

"So your mom and dad ... who are the other eleven?"

"Couple people from work and school. My chiropractor, who my mom has a huge crush on. And several patients who share my taste in awesome tennis shoes."

He pulls out his phone and moves his thumbs over the screen. A few seconds later, my phone vibrates with an Instagram follow request from Eli Hawkins. I close out of my screen and set my phone down to give Gemma some love since she's managed to worm half of her body onto my lap.

"Um … did you just see my request to follow you?"

I nod, staring at my emus being all sweet to a sleeping Romeo.

"But you didn't accept it."

"I know. I usually think on requests for a while."

"Are you serious?"

"Yes."

He lowers his voice. "I was physically inside of you just hours ago, but you have to think about letting me follow you on Instagram?"

"Whoa … do you honestly think had I let Warren have sex with me that I would also let him follow me on Instagram?"

"I think it's messed up that your standards for sexual partners are lower than your standards for people who follow you on a social media site."

"It's *way* easier to stalk someone and harass them on social media than it is to do it face-to-face. I could get a restraining order against you easier than I could shake you from my Instagram life. Do you realize how many creeps have multiple accounts? I mean … some psycho could steal a bunch of photos of say … emus and set up an adorable little account to attract unsuspecting victims."

"Well ..." He flaps his wordless jaw a few times before finishing his thought. "Okay. You think about letting me follow you. Clearly, you weren't ready for me to follow you to your house, so I waited. And I will wait for you to let me follow you on Instagram."

"Not funny. I wasn't trying to lose you. I just had too much going on in my head."

"Well, I'd love to crawl into your head sometime."

"No. You wouldn't. It's a dark hole with blundering ideas. It's where good intentions go to be suffocated. It's a freight train with no brakes. It's a million scenes from movies, books, and real-life observations, all trying to find where they fit into my own life—all waiting to be acted out at the right time. It's an incessant replaying of missed cues and misspoken words."

He narrows his eyes.

I look away and shrug. "I don't mind being me. No one else can do it better."

CHAPTER SIXTEEN

The G-spot

Elijah

I COULD FALL in love with Dorothy Mayhem. Even though my analytical brain won't go there, not even a tiny bit. I'm a father. The woman I thought was the love of my life left me because she wants to be someone else without me. My mom is right—I reside in a cave of desperation and depression.

Dorothy doesn't attract me with her attempts to mimic neurotypical people. She captures little pieces of my heart with her whispered honesty. I feel it, just in a different way.

Good.

I've been good.

"How are you doing, Eli?" concerned friends ask.

"I'm good."

"How's it going being a single dad?"

"It's good."

"How's your relationship with Julie?"

"It's good."

"How's Roman adjusting?"

"Good. Good. Good. He's good. I'm good. Julie's good." *It's all so fucking good.*

Except ... it's not.

"I'm going to run to the restroom," Dorothy says.

I snap out of my reflections of goodness. "Oh. Okay. I'll wait here. I don't want him sleeping much longer, but another thirty minutes will make the rest of my day easier because he'll be in a much better mood on the ride home."

"Stay as long as you want." She smiles. "Come on, Gemma."

Thirty minutes later, Roman is still asleep between the two emus, and Dorothy hasn't returned. She must have some gastrointestinal issues. I hope it has nothing to do with brunch. She'll never go back to my parents' house for brunch. And I definitely want her to go back.

"Roman ..." I rub his back as Orville inspects my hand with his beak. "Time to wake up, buddy."

He stretches out on the blanket, startling Wilbur, who quickly stands up as does Orville. I snatch my son out from between them and carry him to the house. After ringing the doorbell twice, Kellie answers.

"Oh, hey." She lifts onto her toes to look over my shoulder. "Where's Dorothy?"

"She ran to the restroom—a half hour ago. Might want to check on her."

"Oh jeez ... she probably thinks she's dying. That girl is such a hypochondriac." Kellie steps aside for us to come into the entry.

Everything is tidy. Not overly decorated, pretty basic white kitchen, a few framed photos on white walls. Hardwood floors etched with scratches, probably from Gemma.

"Dorothy?" Kellie knocks on the bathroom door several times then turns the knob. It opens to a dark, empty bathroom. "Dorothy?" She nudges open another door.

All I can see is the bottom of a bed.

"Maybe she went out the back door and you just missed her." She walks down a short hallway and opens one more door. "Oh my god … what are you doing?"

I slip off my shoes and Roman's shoes and creep down the hallway behind Kellie.

"What?" Dorothy pulls wireless headphones from her head and pauses her Xbox game.

"You have guests, and you left them to play Xbox?"

She shrugs, glancing past her mom to me, wearing a curious look on her face. "How was nap time?"

"I'm …" Kellie turns toward me, shaking her head and rubbing her temples. "I'm so sorry. I really thought we taught her better than this."

"Better than what?" Dorothy stands, making her way to us.

"Nothing, Dorothy. Nothing." Kellie shuffles past us and just keeps walking.

"Romeo, do you like Xbox?"

"I like EssBoss." He squirms out of Eli's grasp.

"I bought you a Toy Story game while you were napping." Dorothy brings up the game while Roman grabs the control.

Julie would crap her pants if she knew Roman was playing electronic games. At least that's what thought comes to mind. I have no idea what Julie would or wouldn't do anymore. All I know is Dorothy bought my son a game so he can play it on her Xbox.

"Want me to show you how to play?" she asks, starting to take the remote from him.

"No! I do it."

"Okay, that's cool. Have at it." She backs away, watching him with a grin on her face.

I move behind her and slide my arms around her waist, resting my chin on her shoulder, both of us out of Roman's view. Not that anything is going to tear his attention away from the huge TV screen and his fascination with the remote, which I don't think he knows how to use. Still, random things happen on the screen when he presses the buttons, and that seems to entertain him.

"You left me in the barn."

"It's a shed. And I had to use the bathroom."

"And play Xbox?"

"You weren't saying much. So I assumed we were done talking. Roman was sleeping. What's the problem?" She turns in my arms, pressing her hands flat to my chest.

"I don't mind being me. No one else can do it better."

Her words belong painted on the walls of every children's hospital, every church, every school. If *every* human could possess Dorothy's humble confidence, the world would be a much better place.

"No problem."

"You're mad that I didn't go back out to the shed."

"Nope."

"You are. My mom's mad too. Go figure. Dorothy failed Social Etiquette Rule #473."

I take several steps back and pull her with me, to take us a little farther away from young ears. "I failed to keep my marriage of thirteen years together with a two-year-old child at the time. I attend countless funerals of children who I failed to keep alive. I probably know a lot of social etiquette rules, but they don't save marriages and they don't save lives. So fuck the rules. If you want to play Xbox while I'm in your shed, play Xbox. If you want to cancel a date because you're not prepared for something that might happen, then cancel the date. If you need to take weeks—or months—to decide if I'm worthy of following you on Instagram, then take the time."

"Now you're making fun of me."

"No. Just really hoping I get to see your secret social media posts."

She looks at her watch, narrowing her eyes before scraping her teeth along her bottom lip.

"We should go." I release her from my hold.

"I want to get my walk in. That's all. You can stay."

"We can walk with you." The second the words come out, I know better. I feel her body stiffen even without touching her. And her face contorts into a nervous grimace. "On second thought, we're going to head home."

Dorothy makes no attempt to argue, no attempt to make it seem like walking with her would be okay. That is my lesson today. Dorothy needs time alone. It isn't personal toward anyone else. It's her personality. More of a good thing is just that ... more. Not necessarily better. So even if I crave more time with her, I need to wait. I want the desire to be mutual. The last thing I can handle at this point is having feelings for another woman who wants to get as far away from me as possible.

"Go walk. If it's okay with you, I'm going to give him a five-minute countdown. He does better if he knows his time is almost up instead of me grabbing him and hauling him out the door."

"Yeah. Sure. Absolutely. Stay as long as you need to."

"Thanks." I slide my hand around her neck to the back of her head and pull her to me for a slow kiss.

She steadies herself by holding my arms. I peek past her to see if Roman is still entranced by the Xbox. When I determine that he is, I slide my other hand to her face to deepen the kiss. Dorothy used to stiffen at this point, like it bothered her to swap saliva or let our tongues touch. But things have changed, and right now she seems perfectly willing and even a bit eager to let our kiss build into something that might require a bucket of cold water to extinguish.

I pull away first because I want to keep her wanting me. And that sucks. Julie stifled my confidence in a way that feels permanent. Will I always wait for the other shoe to drop? Will I bring paranoia with me to every relationship? Will I become the needy person in the relationship who requires constant affirmation that everything is fine? That everything is *good*?

Dear god ... I hope not.

"Thank you for buying Roman that game."

"Oh. Yeah. I'll buy him all the games he wants."

"Well, let's start with just one."

"Yeah, don't want it to turn into an addiction like it has for me."

"You're addicted to Xbox?"

"Xbox. Netflix. Certain music. I have a lot of obsessions. If you're lucky, you might become one of them."

I swallow hard and clear my throat. "Roman, five minutes, and then we're heading home, buddy."

"Six minutes. Listen ... listen, Daddy. Six minutes."

I shake my head. "I'm not sure when and how he learned to negotiate, but the kid is hardcore."

"Hmm ... six minutes. Just enough time to show you my room." She pulls me toward her bedroom.

"Stay there, Roman. I'll be just around the corner."

"K, Daddy."

Dorothy softly closes the door to her bedroom and leans back against the door. I glance around at the massive amounts of books and journals.

"Do you have HPV?"

"What?" I turn back toward her just as she's shimmying out of her panties.

"Dorothy ..."

"Yes or no."

"Um ... no. Why do you—"

"I don't either." She folds her panties and sets them on the edge of one of the book shelves before leaning back against the door, one hand on the handle. "Kiss me."

Roman is definitely down to five minutes, maybe four, not that *he* is keeping time. But the fact remains that my three-year-old child is ten feet away from the door at Dorothy's back. She wets her lips, and I can't say no, so I kiss her. She kisses me back for two seconds before turning her head to the side to break the kiss.

"Lower," she says in a thick voice that I barely recognize.

I kiss her neck, inhaling the lingering scent of coconut on her skin.

"Lower ..."

I kiss along the open area of her button-down shirt, just above her cleavage.

"Lower ..."

I start to unbutton her shirt.

"Low..." she fists my hair and pushes my head down "...er."

My knees hit the ground. Dorothy releases my hair and grabs her skirt, gathering it up an inch at a time. She doesn't look at me. Her eyes close as her lower lip remains trapped between her teeth as if the need is almost painful.

The moment my tongue breaches the apex of her legs, she grips the door handle and seethes, biting her lip harder as her hips buck away from the door. I know how this will go down—literally and figuratively. I will give her the best oral sex she's ever had. The six-minute timer will go off in my head, or if we are incredibly unlucky, a little fist will bang against the door and try to push the lever handle down. She will slide her skirt down like nothing happened. The door will open and my painfully hard erection will bust right out of my jeans and jab my kid in the eye.

It's possible I have issues with feeling like luck is *not* on my side.

"Fuck … fuck … fuck … fuck," she whisper chants as she releases her skirt and grabs my hair again, jerking it in the direction she wants me to go like my head is an Xbox controller. "Do you know where my G-spot is at?" Her eyes open as she gives me a pointed look.

I nod, keeping my tongue moving.

"Then find it."

Mayhem synonyms: chaos, havoc, madness, trouble, disorder, pandemonium.

Yep. All of those fit Dorothy.

I slide two fingers inside her—nothing like being put on the spot, or having to find it. A real-life *oral* pop quiz. For ten extra credit points, find the G-spot.

"Mmm!" She bites her lips together and nods repeatedly as her eyes pinch shut. "Mmm hmm …" Her right hand tears at my hair until I coax an orgasm from her. Then she loses all control of her legs.

I pull my fingers out so I can grab her hips to keep her from collapsing while my mouth stays between her legs. Our gazes meet. Her eyelids are heavy, and her fingers stroke my hair, a silent thank-you.

I slowly climb to my feet.

"No!" Dorothy jerks her head to the side when I lean in to kiss her. "I don't want to taste myself. Yuck … nope. No way." She peeks open one eye.

"But you wanted me to do that to you."

"Yes. But I don't want to do it to myself."

I step back, adjusting my cock before it pokes a small child in the eye. "Okay then."

"Are you mad?"

"No. Painfully turned on? Yes. But that's why God made cold showers and three-year-olds."

"Okay. Well …" She shrugs. "Thanks."

I shake my head on a small laugh while using the back of my hand to wipe Dorothy's "yuck" from around my mouth. "Anytime."

"We can hug."

I laugh again. A hug—the ugly stepsister to the French kiss and the blowjob.

"Okay." I try to wrap my arms round her, but it's like we're two people trying to get past each other instead of hugging. She can't decide which way to take her head. If she were my height, we would bonk heads.

It's an odd hug. I can't explain it. Before, when I'd held her to me and kissed her passionately, she grabbed my arms or my shirt, sometimes even the back of my neck, and pulled me to her with such need and desire. We had doggy style sex earlier today. And I just went down on her for about four and a half minutes including a successful conquer of her G-spot.

But after all that, the one thing Dorothy Mayhem truly sucks at is hugging. So I hug her to me like I do to Roman when he doesn't want to be hugged. And she gives my back a very awkward series of pats.

Pat pat. Pat-pat-pat-pat.

It doesn't even feel like a hug, more like two strangers

forced to move together in a tight space to let someone else by.

"We'd better go."

"Yep." She quickly releases me, not that she was really holding on to me. "I'll get him off the Xbox while you wash your hands."

For the record, I planned on slipping into the bathroom to wash my hands before getting Roman. I swear. But the fact that Dorothy insists on it before I have the chance to do it, only magnifies the huge difference in the women I've chosen to be in my life.

During the end of our marriage, when Julie was evidently experimenting with her new personality, the one she tested a few times with me (unbeknownst to me), she sat naked in bed, back against the headboard, legs spread wide, and she masturbated in front of me. Then she stuck her wet fingers into my mouth and told me to taste her. But never did she suggest either one of us go wash our hands.

"Great. Thanks." I grin as Dorothy opens the door.

"Sure. No problem."

I love this. It fills me to the brim with happiness—the way that Dorothy shifts from a vixen telling me to find her G-spot to a polite "no problem," like I just spilled a few drips of coffee on my shirt and she's going to watch Roman while I slip into the bathroom to pretreat the stains.

As much as I want to believe I know Dorothy Mayhem, I've only caught tiny glimpses of her. Each one so luminous, I know she's too bright for anyone to ever truly see all of her.

After I wash my hands, I make Roman go to the bathroom before the car ride. Dorothy waits outside for us, already changed into yoga pants and Nikes that match her burnt orange T-shirt.

"Bye, Dorfee. We ... we will be back. I will play Ess-Boss."

"Bye, Romeo." She hunches down in front of him and gives him a wrinkled-nosed smile.

Roman tackles her with a hug. She falls backward, lying stiffly on the ground with Roman's arms encircling her neck.

"Whoa, buddy. That's enough hugging." I peel him from her body and hold out my hand to help her up.

She brushes off her backside and laughs. "He's quite the little hugger. I'll be ready next time."

I bite my tongue as the words "you could learn a few things" sit idle between my pursed lips. But she said she'd be ready next time, and that means she welcomes more hugs from my son.

"Have a great walk."

"Okay. Thanks." She holds up her hand in an awkward wave as I carry Roman to the car. "All these leftovers sat in my car."

"Oh ... shoot. Can't eat them if they haven't been refrigerated." She shrugs.

"Sorry. I know you were really wanting them." I smirk.

She returns a tight smile, her weak version of lying.

CHAPTER SEVENTEEN

Gleaning 101

I MAKE IT three days before pressing SEND on my phone to call Dorothy. Aside from her random sexual demands, which happen with a moment's notice, she qualifies as the world's least needy girlfriend.

Girlfriend.

That's a weird word for me to have in my thirty-eight-year-old head. Is she my girlfriend? I'm nearly two decades behind on the dating scene, so maybe girlfriend is an outdated term.

She doesn't answer my call, even though it's past her scheduled time at the car and dog wash. Maybe she's still walking. Before I can speculate anymore, my phone vibrates with a text from her.

Dorothy: *What do you need?*

Me: *I need to talk to you.*

Dorothy: *Texting not work for you?*

I chuckle.

Me: *I like the sound of your voice.*

Dorothy: *"What do you want?"*

She sends a voice text. I mean … *of course* she does.

That makes me laugh more. It makes that infinite happiness bubble to the surface again.

I return a voice text. *"I need a babysitter for Roman tomorrow night."*

Not a lie.

Granted, my parents or either one of my sisters will happily watch him, but that won't give me a chance to see Dorothy again before work on Friday.

Dorothy: *Sure! (beaming emoji with smiling eyes) What time? I get back from gleaning around eight. (high-five emoji)*

Me: *I have an appointment at seven. (thinking emoji)*

Dorothy: *Oh. Bummer. Sorry. (slightly frowning emoji)*

Me: *What do you have going on at seven?*

Dorothy: *Gleaning. (apple emoji, cookie emoji)*

Me: *Could you skip it one night?*

Dorothy: *Sure, I'll let the poor, homeless, hungry people know I can't help feed them because you need me. What is your appointment?*

Me: *Massage.*

Dorothy: *Oh! Yes, sounds super duper important.*

Me: *Calling you now. PICK UP YOUR PHONE!*

I call her and she answers on the first ring.

"What is your deal? Texting was invented so people wouldn't have to actually have verbal conversations."

"Hi, Dorothy. I've missed you too. Have you had a good week so far?"

"Sure, make me sound insensitive."

"What is your aversion to phone conversations?"

"Ugh! It's just a time thing. Small talk. Chitchat shit that drives me crazy."

"So talking to me drives you crazy?"

"No. Not yet, but if you refuse to text with me, it might get to that point. And emojis give context to words better than I can do with inflection. So when you take away my emojis, there's a good chance of you misinterpreting the true meaning behind my words."

"I'll do *anything* if you skip one night of gleaning to watch Roman for me."

That is code for I'd do *anything* to see her Thursday night.

"Um ... again, no emojis makes this hard for me, but your *anything* sounds sexual. Are you pimping yourself out for a babysitter for your son? Gosh, what kind of massage is this that you're getting?"

"Please."

"You sound desperate."

"Pretty please."

"Yeah, that's better. Not near as desperate. Eye roll emoji."

I laugh. "Did you just verbal emoji me on the phone?"

"Yes. High-five emoji."

"Enough emojis. The inflection of your voice is just fine for me. Just so you know, the please and pretty please is Roman. He's begging to spend time with you again."

"Wow, and I thought I sucked at lying. I know it's past his bedtime."

"He told me everything he wanted to say to you before he went to bed."

"Okay."

I choke on my next breath filled with more begging. Okay. She said okay. "Okay, yes you'll watch him?"

"Yes."

"He'll be so excited."

"Okay."

Yeah, a few emojis with that monotone *okay* wouldn't be the worst thing. I mentally insert my own smiley face and high-five emoji after her okay.

"Can you be here by six-thirty?"

"Okay."

"Great! Goodnight, Dorothy. You're the best."

"Okay …"

I wait for the line to disconnect.

"Goodnight, Eli."

Yes! High-five emoji.

✧ ✧ ✧

DOROTHY ARRIVES BY six and sits in her car until six-thirty. I let her because I think maybe she needs that thirty minutes alone in her car. It feels good to nudge her toward her limit without completely pushing her over the cliff. Great things happen when she allows herself to venture out of her daily norm—like doggy style sex and oral sex.

Yes, I'm *still* thinking about that. I'm certain I will think about that day every day for the rest of my life.

"Dorfee!" Roman tackle hugs her again, only she's ready for it this time and stays on her feet.

"Little Romeo! Are you excited to hang with me tonight?"

"Yes!" As quickly as his excitement starts, he runs off to play, much like a dog greeting someone then running off when they realize no one brought them treats.

"Hey." I take in her jeans, floral shirt, and green Nikes that match the stems on the shirt. It's my first time seeing her in jeans. They're not as inviting as her very accessible skirts, but she looks hot as hell just the same.

"Hey. So are you leaving his car seat ... for emergencies?"

"9-1-1 is the best choice for emergencies."

"Yes, but if you get in an accident or my mom or dad choke on something and die, I wouldn't want to wait until you got home. And 9-1-1 is not a taxi service." She shoves her hands into her front pockets, then her back pockets, then she folds them over her chest. Very odd for her.

"Yes. I'll put his car seat in your car right now. Just don't forget to have me get it out when I get back."

"Cool." She brushes past me and slips off her shoes.

Something feels a little off about Dorothy tonight,

but I can't quite figure it out. And I need to get to my appointment, so I switch the car seat and give her last minute instructions.

"There's a list of numbers on the counter. He's already had dinner, but there's also a list of snacks he can have, but don't give him anything later than seven-thirty. Bedtime is eight. There's a list of that routine as well. Going pee is at the top of the list. Make him go first thing and again one more time before you actually put him in bed.

"Eli, I can read. And this is not my first time babysitting. Go." She glances at her watch.

Again, I feel like something is not right with her. She gives off a nervous vibe that's different than her other vibes.

With Roman in the other room, I move in on her, hoping to erase the weird vibe with a kiss. She stiffens at first. Then she grabs my shirt and lets me kiss her, allowing her tongue to slide against mine.

Fuck the massage. I want to put Roman in his bed and get Dorothy naked in mine. When I release her mouth, my nose rubs against hers as I whisper. "Maybe when I get back you can kiss me ... lower."

She rubs her lips together and lifts her gaze to mine. A few seconds later, they widen a fraction as my intentions must make their connection in her brain.

"Oh ..." She shakes her head. "No. I'm good."

I chuckle, stepping back, feeling the burn of rejection. Maybe I should have texted that to her. Maybe she might have inserted a winking face emoji. Maybe the one with the tongue sticking out. Maybe an eggplant emoji.

Maybe … my blowjob days are over.

I sigh. "Well, thanks. See you in a while."

She glances at her watch again, chewing on her lower lip, and nods. "Okay."

"Bye, Roman. Keep an eye on Dorothy." I slip into the living room where he's surrounded by Duplo Legos and give him a kiss on the top of his head. When I get into my car, I whisper on a laugh, "Oh … No. I'm good." My ego-crushing laughter continues as I pull out of the driveway. "You've lost your game, man. It's just … gone."

✧ ✧ ✧

AFTER MY MASSAGE, I have a string of missed calls, messages, and texts on my phone from Julie.

> *Why does the hospital transporter have our child at the farmer's market?*
>
> *Where are you?*
>
> *Why aren't you answering your phone?*
>
> *Why didn't she know where you're at?*
>
> *Did she have a car seat for him?*
>
> *I'm taking him with me since he's on my watch again tomorrow anyway.*
>
> *Dammit, Eli! Why did MY child have a fit when I tried to take him with me? OMFG, I'm so embarrassed that he threw a tantrum because he wanted to stay with her. A police officer asked HER if everything was OK, like I was trying to abduct my own child!*

WHERE THE FUCK ARE YOU?

I call her on my way to my car.

"Jesus! Where are you, Elijah?"

I rub my forehead. "I had an appointment. Calm down. What's going on?"

"Are you fucking the transporter girl? Is that why she was at brunch on Sunday and at the farmer's market with Roman tonight?"

"If only that were your business. Do you have another question for me?"

"That's my son. You can't leave him with just anyone. She had no fucking clue where you were."

"She said that?"

"She said you had an appointment. I asked where, and after a few minutes of this deer in the headlight look, she shrugged. How is she supposed to get ahold of you in an emergency if she has no clue where you are? How would she get ahold of me or—"

"I got a massage. I tweaked my back on my hike the other day. And for the record, Dorothy has a full list of names and numbers, including yours, to call in the event of an emergency. Roman and I have been spending time with Dorothy for almost six weeks now. She's not a random stranger. She's a nursing student and an EMT. I'm completely confident in her ability to keep our son safe and act appropriately in an emergency."

"Are you dating her?"

"So we're done here. Good. Thanks for calling, Jules."

I back out of the parking spot and drive home, organizing my thoughts to tactfully find out why the hell Dorothy had Roman at the farmer's market. When I pull into the garage, the car seat is next to the back door.

I stop at the car seat, bending down to inspect it closer. The straps look dirty. And when I feel them, they're sticky with white smudges like adhesive.

"What the hell?" I mumble before going into the house.

Dorothy looks up from the sofa and holds a finger to her lips. "He's asleep," she whispers.

But he isn't asleep in his bed. And he isn't in his pajamas. He's asleep on the sofa with his head on her lap, food on his face, and a pile of books around him.

She smiles, stroking his hair.

I ease into the chair opposite the sofa and rest my arms on my legs, dropping my head for a few seconds to rake my fingers through my hair. "Dorothy ..." I whisper, shaking my head. "What were you thinking taking him to the farmer's market?"

When I glance up at her, I expect guilt and remorse. Nope. Instead, she twists her lips to the side and releases a slow breath as she eases Roman's head off her lap. Without looking at me, she shuffles her socked feet to the kitchen, so I follow her.

Dorothy turns toward me and leans against the counter. "You talked with Dr. Hathaway." She scrapes her teeth along her upper lip while nodding slowly, contemplatively. "Yeah, that was really awkward. She wanted to take him home with her. I figured that would be fine, I mean ... she's his mom. But he didn't want to go, and it just escalated. And I kinda felt bad that I couldn't remember where you said you were going. Sometimes I space off certain details. Anyway ... she just kept asking over and over. I'm not used to seeing her so on edge. Boss Bitch usually shows such authority and control. Like ... I felt really sorry for her." She shrugs. "What was I supposed to do?"

"Um ..." I cough sarcasm. "Maybe *not* take him to the farmer's market. Get him to bed on time in his pajamas and with his face washed. Basically follow the instructions I left for you to follow."

"I glean on Thursdays."

"I understand that. But I asked you to watch Roman instead tonight."

"You begged me to watch him. And so I did. You never told me I couldn't take him with me."

"You didn't ask."

"I didn't know I needed to ask."

"I don't buy it. That's why you wanted the car seat."

"I wanted the car seat for emergencies too. I wasn't lying about that."

"Just about going to the farmer's market."

She shakes her head. "I didn't lie."

"Have you ever heard that omission of the truth is the same as a lie?"

"Nope. Never heard that. And it makes no sense."

"Dorothy ..." Resting my hands on my hips, I drop my head and ease it side to side.

"I have photos of him in my little red wagon, riding with all the sacks of leftover food. Wanna see? He told everyone we passed that we were *cleaning*. Oh my god ... it was so cute." She pulls her phone out of her pocket.

"No. I don't want to see pictures of you doing something you weren't supposed to be doing with my son. *And* ... I don't want to think about you driving a vehicle with my son in it. You drive way too fast, run red lights, and completely get distracted when you're driving. I'm not just upset that you took him to the farmer's market. I'm upset that you took him anywhere. And I'm upset that you put me in a really uncomfortable position with Julie."

"Daddy?" Roman stumbles into the kitchen, rubbing his eyes. "I pee peed."

Sure enough, his pants are soaked, and I suspect my sofa cushions are too.

"I'll clean everything up." Dorothy pushes off the counter and heads toward Roman.

"Just go, please. I'll get him cleaned up. Thank you for ..." I shake my head again, feeling a headache coming on. "Watching him."

"I will. I ... I'll clean him up. Like uh ... like it didn't happen. I'll just clean it up." She takes Roman's hand.

"Dorothy, are you listening to me? Please just go home."

"I think you're mad. So I'll clean him up. Problem solved."

"Dorothy!"

She jumps. Wide eyes unblinking at me.

Roman's lower lip pushes out and tears fill his eyes. "Daddy ... why are you mad at Dorfee?"

Fuck ...

"Okay. S-so ..." Dorothy stutters and surveys the room like she's looking for something. "I'll just ... go. Bye, Romeo."

"Bye, Dorfee," he murmurs, blinking several times without releasing any actual tears yet.

As she passes me, I grab her hand to stop her and blow out a long breath. "I shouldn't have asked you to watch him tonight. You had plans, and I didn't respect that. So all of this is on me, not you."

She keeps her gaze at the door and says nothing, so I release her hand because I don't have time to deal with her *and* get Roman cleaned up and in bed.

No time for patience.

No time for reflection.

No time to plan how I will handle Julie in the morning.

So I act on impulse and do the things that need to be done first, starting with my soaked child.

The door clicks behind Dorothy.

"Let's get you cleaned up, buddy." I remove his clothes over the tile floor in the kitchen.

"Daddy, I rode in red wagon."

"Oh yeah?" I force a little daddy enthusiasm even though I feel none.

"I did. I did ... and Dorfee pull the wagon and I go wee! And ... and we gots food. Lots of food. We were cleaning!"

"That's great, Roman." I pick him up and carry him upstairs. "Are you going to shower with me?"

"And Dorfee and me gave *all* the lots of food to people, Daddy."

"Uh huh …" I set him down and turn on the shower to warm up while I undress. "Let's see if you have any more pee pee." I set him on the toilet, and sure enough, more pee.

He giggles. "It's lemon … ade. Me and Dorfee had lemon … ade. Purple lemon … ade."

"Lavender lemonade?"

"Yes. Labender lemon … ade. It was yummy."

I usher him into the walk-in shower.

As I shampoo his hair, he glances up at me. "Daddy, some … some people have no food."

I pause my motions for a few seconds before returning a slow nod and resuming the sudsing. "That's true."

"Is sad, Daddy. Dorfee say is sad. But me and Dorfee gave … gave people food. All the lots of food. Dat … dat make people happy."

I'm an asshole.

When you meet someone who is essentially a better human than ninety-nine percent of the population, it's hard to not occasionally show your asshole side. By default, their selflessness will be misread as selfishness. Tonight, I thought Dorothy was being selfish with her insistence on going to the farmer's market.

I was wrong.

She was being completely selfless in her actions. And at the same time, teaching my young child a very valuable lesson and me as well.

CHAPTER EIGHTEEN

She's Mine

Dorothy

"Good morning." Mom smiles, cinching the tie to her white bathrobe.

"Thanks for this," I mumble over a mouthful of leftover fried rice.

"You mean my lunch that you're eating for breakfast?"

"Oops." I grin.

"How was the market?"

"Good. I took Romeo with me. Put him in my little red wagon. Look." I pull up the pictures on my phone. "He's so stinkin' cute. He also kept eating the food we were gathering. The vendors went crazy over him. And I got us lavender lemonade, and he tried to eat the sprig of lavender, but spit it out onto the leg of a lady passing us. That was a little embarrassing."

She laughs. "I'm sure. Did Eli enjoy the market?"

"Oh." I shake my head, shoveling in more food. "He

didn't go. He had an appointment. I was babysitting Roman for him. I also ran into Dr. Hathaway. She seemed a little confused or worried about me being there alone with Roman. When she tried to get him to go home with her, he was all, 'No! I stay with Dorfee!' Oh my god, it was just ... crazy. I didn't know what to do."

"So did he finally go with her?"

"No. Because this police officer came over and basically asked me if 'my son and I' knew her. Like ... can you imagine how horrified she must have been? I felt really bad for her. But I didn't know what to do."

"What did Eli say when you told him?"

I cringe. "I don't think he was happy. He didn't *exactly* know I was taking Romeo to the market with me. He kinda freaked out when he got home."

"Dorothy Emmaline Mayhem, you took his child without asking?"

"No. I didn't *take* his child. He begged me to watch Roman. No big deal. Like, his son was fine. Yes, he wasn't in his jammies and his face was a little dirty, but he was safe and sleeping on the sofa. I mean ... isn't that what should be important to parents? That at the end of the day, their child is alive and safe at home? Like ... he sees this bad shit all day. He sees kids die and parents grieve. But he freaks out about a trip to the farmer's market that ended just fine. I didn't know what to say or do. This morning while I was showering, I thought thank god he didn't know about the car seat."

"You didn't use a car seat?"

"No. Of course I did." I rinse off the fork and put it

in the dishwasher. "I just couldn't figure out the stupid harness system. It's like it was too loose, and then I tried to tighten it and Romeo said it was too tight. And just when I thought I had shit figured out, I realized there was like ... a strap with a metal part at the end that needed to go somewhere, but hell if I knew where. So I tried again, and all metal parts were stuck in some sort of latch place which is good, right? But things were too loose, so I found some duct tape in Eli's garage, and I taped together the loose straps until I felt confident that everything was secure and tight."

"Oh my god ..." Mom covers her mouth. She laughs so hard she snorts. "Dorothy ... oh my god. You didn't. Please tell me you didn't duct tape that man's son to his seat."

"Not Roman. I taped the straps. And it was a bitch to get that tape off there when we arrived at the market."

She wipes tears from her eyes. "What about going back home? The tape couldn't have been as sticky."

I roll my eyes. "Duh, I took the whole roll with me." I glance at my watch. "I need to brush my teeth and go."

"I love you. I just really love you." She continues to laugh.

"Yeah, yeah. Love you too."

✧ ✧ ✧

Elijah

"WE NEED TO talk." Julie stands at the doorway to my office, dressed in a knee-length skirt, a white blouse revealing a bit of her new cleavage, black heels that make her legs look ten miles long, and a white lab coat. She's also wearing that same look she wore the day she asked for a divorce.

I close my laptop and lean back in my desk chair. "So talk."

She steps inside my office and shuts the door behind her before taking a seat on the other side of my desk. "I live with this guilt from leaving you. And when we got divorced, I swore to myself that I'd never be petty over little issues with Roman. So I don't want to come across like I'm trying to cause trouble. I'm not. I just had a bad feeling in my stomach yesterday when I saw your friend, Dorothy, with Roman at the market. I wasn't trying to be confrontational at all. I simply asked about your whereabouts. I honestly assumed you were there. It was just really disturbing that she seemed so ignorant on the subject. My mind went into this mama bear protective mode, and I could imagine her turning her back on him for two seconds and having no clue where he was either."

"Jules ..."

"Just ..." She holds up her hand. "Please hear me out." Taking a deep breath, she meets my scrutinizing gaze. "It could happen to you. It could happen to me. Responsible people have bad things happen to their children. But *we* navigate this world with a fierce, protective love for him. And I know your family and my family share that love too. You know I hate that you send him to daycare where the people taking care of him do so because they are getting paid, not because they love him with their whole being. But at least he's in one spot. And there are rules and security. But some girl that you've known for two seconds should not be allowed to gallivant around the city with our child. And I don't care if it makes me sound like a cold, untrusting bitch. What you think or anyone else thinks doesn't matter to me. Roman is my only concern here."

"Are you done?"

"No. I want a legal agreement that lists the people who are allowed to be unsupervised with Roman. And the list has to be mutually agreeable for every name on it."

I grunt a laugh. "And you don't want Dorothy on that list."

"Are you marrying her?"

"For god's sake, Jules. Marrying someone doesn't magically make them more trustworthy."

"Uh …" she laughs. "I disagree. I'd like to believe that neither one of us would marry someone unless we completely trusted them with Roman."

"Well, I completely trust Dorothy." I hate the lie. I mostly trust her. I feel pretty fucking guilty for not being able to completely trust her, but I sure as hell won't let Julie see an ounce of my doubt. It doesn't mean I'm planning on leaving Roman with Dorothy again anytime soon. But I want the decision to be mine, not something mutually agreed upon between Julie, me, and our lawyers.

"So you know everything about her? What's her favorite color? What hospital was she born in? What's her mother's maiden name? What school did she attend? Childhood pets? Does she have any cavities? What medications does she take?"

"Enough …" I rub my forehead. "If I hired a professional nanny, I wouldn't know or give a shit about her favorite color."

"True. But she'd come with references. And you could do a background check. Drug testing. All the things a responsible parent would do before hiring a nanny. So if you don't know her well enough to marry her, and you haven't conducted a thorough background check on her, then you better always be with her when she's with Roman."

"Julie—"

"This is nonnegotiable, Eli. I'll be the bitch if that's what it takes to keep my son as safe as possible. I'm a little disappointed that you're not showing the same level of responsibility. And if you can't do this on your own, I'll make sure a judge makes you do it."

My phone vibrates with a message from my nurse. I stand and slip on my lab coat. "I have to go. Have a fucking fabulous day, Jules. You sure have made mine."

"Why do you make me the bad guy?" She follows me out of my office.

"Because every day I can manage to find something seriously wrong with you is one less day that I have to wonder if something is seriously wrong with me." I keep walking toward the elevator without looking back.

After checking in on a patient who was readmitted earlier this morning, I make my way to the lab to check on Warren and review some test results.

"How's it going?" I ask, walking into the lab.

Warren pushes his chair away from the counter to let me look at the computer. "I think it's going really well."

It is. We're seeing massive destruction of cancer cells without major side effects. We still have a lot of testing to do. But small victories matter.

"Willow said she saw Dorothy Mayhem with your son at the farmer's market last night. Is she babysitting for you now too? Man, that girl can juggle a lot. Has she by any chance said anything about me? She's taking the whole hard-to-get game to a ridiculous level."

Great. There were witnesses. I hope that doesn't get around to Julie. I know she'll start pulling people into her office to interrogate them.

"I had an appointment. She watched him for me. It's not an actual job for her."

"Don't you have like a million family members always fighting over who gets to watch him?"

Yes. I do. But I didn't need a babysitter, I needed Dorothy naked in my bed. But that all went to shit. I question if I'll ever see her naked again.

"Mmm ..." is my only answer as I inspect a few slides.

He leans against the counter a few feet from me. "I wonder if she's a flowers kind of girl. I mean, at first I thought she might be a fun time, you know? But the more she dismisses me, the more I want her. And I think she's hell-bent on busting my balls until I treat her the way she thinks she deserves to be treated. Ya know?"

"Like an intelligent woman with morals and high standards?"

Warren laughs. "Sure. Something like that. So what do you think? Flowers? Chocolates? Cookie bouquet? Singing telegram?"

I tell myself there's no reason to not tell Warren the truth. But the *real* truth is that there's a million reasons to not tell Warren about me and Dorothy. I don't need rumors going around because rumors always escalate to the most ridiculous stuff. And the last thing I need is Julie catching wind of something that isn't true about Dorothy.

"Maybe she's legitimately not interested. I realize that's not what your ego wants to hear. But you can't be a god to every woman."

"If you're a Christian who believes in one god, then it's possible I *can* be a god—the god—to every woman."

"In that case, send her a cookie bouquet from Bloomin Bakery."

"Oh yeah. Those are the best."

"They really are."

"I wonder if it's too late to get one ordered for today? I'd love to get her thinking about me today. That leaves two more days to seal the deal."

"And by deal, you mean politely ask her out on a date, not make her an on-call room conquest, right?"

"Sure." He smirks.

I want to punch him. Why does my instinct to protect Dorothy make me rabidly violent?

✧ ✧ ✧

Around four o'clock Dorothy knocks on the door to the lab. Warren lets her in. A large cookie bouquet hides her face.

"I can't accept these. I mean, I ate one but only as payment for my time to deliver them to you."

He takes the bouquet from her. "Why not?"

She shoots me a nervous glance before tipping her chin up and addressing Warren again. "I *get* the sexual innuendo. These cookies in exchange for my cookie. Well, I don't want to share my cookie with you. So, nice try."

While they work out their cookie issues, I sneak one out of the cellophane wrapped bouquet and take a bite.

Mmm ...

They are my favorite cookies in Portland.

"Dammit ..." Warren looks at his phone. "I have to go. Those cookies have nothing to do with your cookie. In fact, they weren't even my idea. Dr. Hawkins made the suggestion when I said I wanted to send you something. So now do you think *he* wants your cookie?"

"Yes."

I choke on my cookie as she deadpans her answer.

A cackle makes its way out of Warren as he covers his mouth with his fist and shoots me a look accompanied by an eye roll. "Sure. Sure he does. I'll send you something less sexual tomorrow, Mayhem, like a rosary." Warren leaves the lab.

"Hey, 'Dr. Hawkins,' why would you tell Warren to send me a cookie bouquet?"

I pop the last bite of cookie into my mouth. "Why are

you air quoting my name?"

"Because you're weird with your name. Eli. Elijah. Dr. Hawkins. Just so many rules to figure out."

"At work, Dr. Hawkins is great. Without the air quotes. And I suggested Warren send you a cookie bouquet because I knew you wouldn't accept it, and I thought Bloomin Bouquet's cookies sounded really good today. I missed lunch with my mom. I'm kinda hungry."

"Why did you miss lunch with your mom?"

"Because I had sex with Dorothy Mayhem at my mom's house last weekend. And I knew that's *all* she'd want to talk about today."

"Maybe you needed to talk through your anger over me taking Roman to the farmer's market. Maybe she would have told you something really profound like 'Eli, you should be thankful your son is alive and free of cancer. I bet a lot of your patients' parents would love for their biggest problem to be that their child didn't put on pajamas before falling asleep, or that he wet his pants after too much lemonade because he was healthy enough to go to the market."

Red face.

Shaking balled-up hands.

Clenched jaw.

Dorothy Mayhem is seriously pissed off. Not something I've seen before. She doesn't stutter once. Every word feels planned and rehearsed. Did she recite this speech all night?

"I get what you're saying, but it's not that simple."

"It is that simple! He's alive. You have a living,

breathing child. Stop fucking away the minutes of your time with him by worrying about the stupid stuff."

I stand, moving closer so she'll lower her voice and so she can hear my words and feel their gravity.

"Maybe he's not dying today, but that doesn't mean I'm not in danger of losing him. Julie doesn't want you alone with him unsupervised."

"What?" Dorothy jerks her head back. "Does she know we had sex?"

"Serial killers, rapists, and child molesters have sex. It's not a ticket to sainthood."

I hate Julie for being right. Does that make her reasons for leaving me right too? Is she just always right? I hope not. But she is right about Roman and us protecting him needing to be our number one priority. There is no way I will tell her she's right. But … she's right. And nothing Dorothy can say will change that.

"You think I'm a serial killer, rapist, or child molester? Seriously?"

"No." I return a sad smile. "But if you were, I wouldn't know it. The truth is, there is so much I don't know about you. And I can't be guided by blind instinct, or insane moments of passion. I have to always keep a clear head when it comes to Roman. And I haven't done a good job with that."

"Because of me."

"No. Yes … I … I'm not saying any of this is your fault. I approached you. I invited you to do things with us. I asked you to watch him last night. It's me. I need to be more mature in my thinking. Not be so impulsive."

With slightly narrowed eyes, she observes me. Then she nods slowly. "Okay. Yeah, it was a mistake."

"Mistakes happen." I shrug, giving her my best understanding smile, hoping it beams like her favorite emoji so she'll know I'm not mad at her, and I don't blame her.

"So we act like it never happened?" she asks.

"Yeah. I think that's a good idea. I don't care to dwell on it."

Dorothy's gaze shifts past me. "Were the cookies really your idea?"

"Yes."

Her lips corkscrew. "Okay." She grabs the cookie bouquet and leaves.

I shake my head, with a grin affixed to my face. That could have gone badly. She came out fighting, but in the end, I feel we've reached a compromise. She took the cookies before I had a chance to snag one more, but I can't get greedy with my victories.

An hour later, Warren returns with a bounce in his step and humming a tune.

"Thank *you*, Dr. Hawkins."

I glance over at him with a lifted brow. "For what?"

"The cookie bouquet suggestion. Once *Ms. Mayhem* realized it wasn't my idea, but I made the effort to take your suggestion and get it for her, she gave me the thumbs-up."

Inching my chair to the side to face him straight on, I cock my head, eyes narrowed. "Thumbs-up for what exactly?"

"Tuesday night I'm taking her to dinner."

What ... the ... fuck?

"You're kidding."

"No. I wouldn't joke about this. That girl has been a brick wall for weeks. Then out of nowhere, cookie bouquet equals date for Dr. Warren. Booyah!"

I glance at my watch. "I'm going for coffee."

"I can get you one."

"No. I don't want you having anything to do with my coffee." I push through the door.

"Dude!" He laughs. "That's a bit harsh."

Harsh? Harsh will be when I beat the living shit out of him for not backing the fuck off Dorothy. Harsh will be losing my job for said beating. Harsh will be trying to keep custody of my son with an assault conviction on my record.

I message her.

Me: **Where are you?**

She doesn't answer in a timely manner. And by timely, I mean within seconds. So ... I call her.

No answer.

But my phone vibrates with a text.

Dorothy: **Working. Not allowed to take calls on the clock. Not really supposed to be texting either. (shrugging emoji)**

"Wilma, how would I find Dorothy Mayhem?"

She glances up from the desk outside my lab. "The transporter?"

"Yes."

"What do you need, Dr. Hawkins?"

"I need Dorothy Mayhem."

"I have a few minutes. I can help you."

"Great. Tell Dorothy Mayhem to come here."

Her eyebrows snake together. "Um …"

"Two words, Wilma. Dorothy. Mayhem. Can you do that for me?"

She nods slowly, pulling her phone from the pocket of her scrub top. "What do you want me to say to her?"

"I don't know. Request something."

"For who?"

I shrug, jaw clenched with irritation. "Doesn't matter."

"I think it does. You see, you order something like a scan, and she comes to transport the patient. Or equipment. Do you need an ultrasound or something?"

"Fine. A CAT scan."

"For who?"

I grumble. "It. Doesn't. Matter."

"But it does. I have to enter the order into the system under a patient's name."

"Jesus …" I run my hands through my hair. "No one is getting an actual scan."

"But you just said—"

"Never mind." I stomp off. "I'll find her myself." It's not easy tracking her down, but eventually I catch her returning a patient to their room on the second floor.

"What the—" She stumbles as I back her into the wall, hovering over her without actually touching her.

"I need a word with you."

"I'm working."

"I'm not asking. A word. Now. Or I make a scene. Do I need to make a scene?"

"I'd rather you not," she says, eyes shifting from side to side.

"Move." I nod toward the empty room several feet behind her.

Keeping her gaze on me, she backs into the room as I move toward her, a slow dance of distrust.

I shut the door and lock it behind us. She stares up at me with unblinking eyes.

"You have a *date* with Warren?"

She dips her brow in confusion and nods once.

"Why?" I partially yell because I don't appreciate being blindsided like this.

"Um ..." Her eyes shift side to side. "Because he asked me and bought me a cookie bouquet. And ... I thought he might be a good way for me to get over us."

"Over us? What does that mean?"

"Wow ..." She clears her throat and swallows hard. "When you said you didn't want to dwell, you really meant it. Well, you kinda ended whatever it was we had like..." she checks her watch "...an hour ago. So I figured I could spend weeks journaling and obsessing over what exactly went wrong, or I could move on quickly to distract my thoughts. So I chose to move on quickly."

"What are you talking about? I didn't end us."

"You did. You called us a bad decision. I said *mistake*. You said, 'Mistakes happen.' And you said you didn't want to dwell on it anymore."

"I was talking about last night!"

She jumps. I don't mean to scare her, but I hate feeling so out of control. I hate the idea of losing her. But she acts like everything is already lost.

This makes me so fucking angry with myself, with Warren, with Julie, with … the world. I'm pissed at the world for no other reason than it nearly brings me to my knees to think of Dorothy and Warren together.

People aren't property—things to possess. But at this exact moment, my mind says, "Fuck that." Dorothy Mayhem belongs to me. Period. I own her awkward moments, her goofy, loud laughs, her robotic seduction, and every single inch of her body, leading straight to her G-spot, which … Yes. That belongs to me as well.

"I was talking about last night," I say with a little less desperation and aggression. "It was *my* mistake. I didn't need a babysitter. I have a long list of eager family always ready and willing to watch Roman. I've never needed a babysitter. I just …" I scratch the back of my neck. "I just wanted to see you so badly. And I didn't know if you'd say yes to me, so I took the chance that you'd say yes to Roman."

Her eyes narrow. "You used Roman to get to me?"

"Uh … *yes*. I have no shame when it comes to you." I brush my lips against hers.

To my surprise, she doesn't stiffen and take time to decide if she wants to be kissed. Instead, she grabs my lab coat and pulls me to her, opening her mouth to me. I kiss every inch of that mouth like I own it too while Dorothy makes little humming noises.

"M-my phone?" She breaks the kiss and grabs her phone. "I have to go."

I nod, trying to suppress the inclination to tell her to ignore her phone, take off her clothes, and let me find *all* the spots that bring her pleasure. "Okay."

She nods, rubbing her lips that hide a tiny smile. "Okay."

"Tomorrow, pack an overnight bag, and come to my house after work."

Her gaze shoots up to mine. "Oh … um …"

I smirk. "For *Roman*. Please …" I wink.

"Are you using him to get me to come over?"

"One hundred percent. And with no regrets." I chuckle, ducking my head to kiss her neck, to smell the coconut along her skin while my hands palm her ass.

Her breath hitches. "Oh … uh … so you're inviting me for a sleepover?"

"Mmm hmm …" I torture myself by taking one last taste of her skin, one last squeeze of her curvy, firm ass.

"Okay."

"Yeeesss …" I slide my hands just past her ass to the back of her legs and lift her up, pressing her back to the door, positioning the head of my erection right between her spread legs.

"I have to go." She grabs my neck to steady herself as I maneuver her hips to … well, torture my dick some more. "If…" her voice takes on a needy, breathy intonation "…if you don't stop right now, I'll have to find a place to masturbate because I won't be able to stop thinking about the orgasm you *almost* gave me."

Yeah, neurotypical people don't say that. I sure as hell would never confess to a woman that her flirting and teasing will require me to go masturbate. God knows I did it after every fake playdate when I first met Dorothy. And after she leaves this room, I will grab that cup of coffee I said I was going to get, go back to my office, lock the door, shut the blinds, and rub one off. But *never* would I confess that to her or any other woman.

My forehead drops to her shoulder. "Killing me, Dorothy. You're killing me."

"I have to go. If we wait, someone will ask where I've been. And I won't be able to lie."

Thunk.

Thankfully, she lands on her feet when I let go of her like taking a pan from the oven without oven mitts. I don't need her telling people about me groping her in an empty room while inviting her to spend the night with me. And that's how she would phrase it, I have no doubt about that.

"Get to work. Go, go, go!" I unlock the door and give her a gentle nudge.

CHAPTER NINETEEN

Wonder Woman

Dorothy

INSTEAD OF DEALING with an onslaught of questions, I text my mom after I get to work.

Me: *I won't be home tonight. Been invited to have a sleepover with Roman. Love you.*

Come to find out, Eli isn't working today. Just as well. I have enough issues focusing on my work while my mind keeps wandering to the sleepover. Roman will freak when he sees my pajamas. I have drawers of clothes that I convinced myself I needed at one point and time, but they're far from practical. However, I keep them on the off chance that the right occasion will present itself, and I'll have the perfect outfit.

Presenting … a sleepover with Romeo.

Perfect!

After work, I swap clothes in my car. No one at the hospital needs to see my pajamas, although part of me wants to show them off. I'm a little surprised Eli is letting Roman have me over tonight since I get off work at eight, which means I don't arrive at his house until almost eight-thirty. But it's a Saturday night, so I assume Roman gets to stay up a little later.

So many assumptions. Being an Aspie isn't always hot chocolate and marshmallows with rainbow sprinkles. No. Oftentimes it's showing up to a Star Wars themed party dressed as Mr. Spock, greeting everyone with the Vulcan salute.

"Hey!" I grin proudly when Eli opens the front door. My smile vanishes. "Is that the best you've got?" My gaze makes a critical inspection of his faded jeans and plain white tee. Poor Romeo needs a fun adult in his life, one who knows sleepovers involve at least a onesie with critter feet.

"I … I'm …" Eli's eyes widen, jaw unhinging as I step inside and slide off my jacket. His gaze sweeps along my red, knee-high socks that look like boots, my tiny blue shorts with yellow stars, my fitted, red tank top with the Wonder Woman logo, and my fancy tiara.

"Bor … ing." I roll my eyes at his attire, brushing past him and dropping my bag by the credenza. "Where is he?" I make my way to the kitchen, where there are two glasses and a bottle of wine—an odd choice for a sleepover. Hopefully he has apple juice for Romeo. But Eli does score big when I notice the large pizza box from my favorite pizza place.

But pizza has to wait. I want to find Romeo.

"Where's my little Romeo?" I circle to the living

room.

No Roman.

"Wonder Woman is here." I sneak up the stairs to his room.

No Roman.

After staring at his perfectly made bed inside his dark room, I turn in the doorway. Eli stands at the top of the stairs, nose wrinkled and teeth wedged into his bottom lip.

"He's playing hide and seek, huh?" I whisper.

Eli eases his head side to side, his gaze making a hungry inspection of me.

My posture slumps. "Then where is he?"

"Um …" He clears his throat. "Julie has him this week."

"What? But you invited me here *tonight!* I have it on my calendar. I can show you."

"No … I …" He rubs his mouth, and I swear he does it to mask his grin.

That makes me livid.

"I asked you to stay the night with me."

"A *sleepover.*" I hold out my arms.

Hello!

Seriously, did he miss my pajamas? Pajamas equal sleepover.

"*You* called it that." He shakes his head.

"You said *for Roman!*"

"It was a joke. I had just told you how I'd shamelessly used him to spend time with you. And I smirked and winked when I said it because it was a joke. I thought you knew it was a joke and that Julie had him this week."

My mind explodes. I can't formulate a single coherent thought.

Anger.

Confusion.

Embarrassment.

Stupidity.

So many emotions. I don't know how to deal with them. What to say. Or what to do next.

"I ..." I shake my head, jaw slack. "I missed that joke then. I miss a lot of humor."

"I'm really sorry. Can we just let it go? I have pizza and wine. And *I* want you to stay tonight."

Oh god ... sex. He invited me over for sex!

Suddenly, his sexy jeans and crisp white tee make sense.

"I have to run home." I make a straight line to the stairs, but he blocks me from going down them.

"What? No. Why? Did you forget something? I have an extra toothbrush. Just stay."

I look up, giving him a huge duh look. Clearly, I'm the only one who can see the obvious. "This is not the outfit I would wear to spend the night with *you*. I have one that will work better. I'll drive home and get it. But right now, I am not dressed for sex and seduction."

"Oh, Dorothy ..." He chuckles, stepping toward me. "I believe you are."

I step back.

He steps forward with a look in his eyes. I've seen it before. And I'm *not* wearing the proper clothes for what that look means.

Our little dance ends in his bedroom with his bed hitting the back of my legs, preventing me from taking another step.

I gulp, like the big twenty-ounce gulp.

Run!

Yes, I want to run, fast like Wonder Woman or even leap out the window. But part of me wants to stay because Eli smells like those familiar herbs, one of the rare scents that I like. And he looks sexy, not like he can save the world or anything spectacular like that, but definitely like he can bring his A game in bed.

"I look … um …" My eyes close when he ghosts his lips along my cheek to my mouth.

"Fucking spectacular." He kisses my top lip before teasing his tongue along the seam of my mouth.

I have no bra on under my tank top. My nipples are usually well-behaved. Eli manages to bring out their wild side, and this is a little embarrassing to me. And I don't like the way my shirt rubs against them in their erect state. Too itchy.

Then there's the underwear situation. Yes, it's a *situation*. Wonder Woman underwear that looks like boys briefs, but they're not for boys. Really. I bought them online, and it specifically said *youth girls'*. (Petite peeps like me can wear some youth-sized clothing.)

If he sees them, he might be offended. Wondering if I'd planned on showing Romeo my undies.

I had no such plans. But it could look that way.

I only wore them because I have them. And for my

own personal feeling of awesomeness, I wanted to feel as much like Wonder Woman as I could.

Turning my head, I break the kiss. "This shirt is scratching my nipples."

He studies me for a few seconds and grins, grabbing the hem to my shirt.

"No." I hug myself to keep him from removing my top. "I need to change my underwear first."

His eyebrows shoot up his forehead. "Did you have an accident?"

"No." I jerk my head back.

"Well, no underwear is required for what I have planned."

I roll my eyes. "I just don't want you to see mine."

"Streaks?"

"What? No!"

"Holes?"

"Ugh ... no!"

"Now you *have* to show me." He slides his thumbs under the waistband of my shorts. I bat them away.

"Oh for fuck's sake, Eli! They're Wonder Woman briefs. I was *not* going to show them to Roman. I'm not a child molester. I wore them because I had them, and they go with the rest of my outfit."

Eli's smile swells to his ears. "Jesus ... I am one lucky guy tonight. We'll get to those special undies in a sec. I'm more concerned about your nipples." His hands return to the hem of my shirt.

I reach for my tiara.

"Is that itchy too?" He focuses on my head.

"No."

"Then leave it on." His mouth twists into a wicked grin as he slides my shirt up, easing it over my head without disturbing the tiara. "Sit."

I sit on the edge of the bed, feeling quite agreeable at this point because my nipples are so happy to be freed from the itchy cotton shirt. He palms one of my tiny (yes, tiny) breasts and strokes my nipple with the pad of his thumb as he kisses along my neck to my mouth.

Fact: If done properly, a woman can have an orgasm just from nipple stimulation. Our nipples are a minefield of nerves that send sensations to the same parts of our brains as the clitoris and uterus. Years ago, I read a study about it published in the Journal of Sexual Medicine. I immediately conducted my own experiment and confirmed the accuracy of the published results.

As Eli moves his mouth to my chest, giving Tiny Breasts some expert attention with his tongue, I feel confident that he, too, has read that same article because before long ... I have my first orgasm of the night, sitting on the edge of his bed.

He looks quite pleased with himself. I'm pleased with myself too, but not for the orgasm. I manage to not ruin the moment by informing him that I'm very responsive like that, which means it doesn't take much to pleasure me, and it also doesn't take much to over stimulate me to the point where I want to crawl out of my skin.

Let's hope that doesn't happen.

"Niiice ..." I say with a labored breath and heat trapped in my cheeks while we grin at each other.

"Enough with my nipples. Now move along to something else."

Eli chuckles while standing. He shrugs off his shirt and unfastens his jeans. That's when it hits me ... we are seconds and mere inches from his exposed cock hanging or probably bouncing at eye level (mouth level) with me. I jump to my feet which makes his eyes widen with surprise.

Is it hypocritical or maybe just really unfair of me to want him—ask him—to go down on me, when I have no desire or intention of ever reciprocating? Probably.

It's not that I haven't studied blowjobs. I have. And if I can turn off my brain, my taste buds, my sense of smell, and numb my gag reflex, I know I can give as good a blowjob as the next person. But that switch doesn't exist yet—maybe with future medical and pharmaceutical advancements. So Eli is stuck with the woman who has a hypersensitivity to everything. And while I have no actual data to back it up, I feel certain that a lot of Aspies probably get an F in oral sex.

Before Eli can question my quick move to my feet, I kiss him. That I can do. That I actually really like doing.

And to ease the sting of the blowjob ban, I slide my hand down the front of his briefs and wrap it around his cock. My hand can't smell it, taste it, or gag on it. So I know I can and will stroke it all night if that's what it takes to keep that thing out of my mouth.

"Goddamn ..." he seethes, breaking our kiss and resting his forehead on mine just below my tiara, watching me stroke him. I don't mind watching either. I'm pretty good at it.

Eli grabs the back of my head and smashes his mouth to mine, moaning into our kiss, rocking his pelvis into my hand. "Take off my pants," he mumbles against my lips.

Shit!

That's classic code for getting a woman to squat to pull said pants down, only to stab her in the throat with a cock.

I tear my mouth from his and remove my hand from his pants. He watches me with hooded eyes while wetting his lips. Eli looks drugged. And hot. He looks really hot. But not even the sun is hot enough for me to fall for the take-my-pants-off trap. And the tight-lipped smile I give him should clue him in about that. He has to know I'm on to him and his amateur tactics.

I kiss his chest and his arm, slowly moving to his back where I kiss between his shoulder blades while wrapping my arms around him, scraping my nubbins for nails along his chest. And then ... I squat into the safe zone. My hands curl round the waistband of his jeans and briefs, pulling both down in one moderately smooth motion. As I kiss the backside of his legs and over his firm ass, he steps out of his jeans and turns toward me.

A tiny smile pulls at his lips as he grabs my ass, jerking me closer to him. "Why the grin?"

I removed your pants without swallowing your dick! I'm pretty fucking proud of myself.

And that's exactly what will come out of my mouth if I'm forced to give an answer. So I raise onto my toes and kiss him instead. Hugging me tighter, he lifts me off the floor and lays me in the middle of his bed.

Kneeling between my spread knees, he peels off my socks and tosses them over his shoulder, wearing a cocky grin. "I fear I've wasted my whole life setting the bar too low for my fantasies because you're the ultimate wet dream right now." He kisses along my calf, making a slow ascent up my leg while sliding my shorts down a few inches, just enough to reveal my girl-boy briefs. "Perfect." He grins, completely removing my shorts and sending them to collect on the floor with the rest of my clothes.

"What?" I ask as he rakes his gaze over my body without moving another muscle.

"You're beautiful, Dorothy. And I just want to look at you. Just for a few seconds, I want to commit this to memory."

It sounds sweet. It really does. But I'm sprawled out on his bed wearing nothing more than Wonder Woman briefs and a tiara. Kinky? Fetish-like even? Maybe. But *beautiful* is hard to believe, probably because I see *parts* more than the whole of things. Beautiful what? Eyes? Skin? Hair?

"Are you a little kinky, Eli?"

His lips twitch, eyes filled with unspoken words. I need those words. Forcing me to guess shit usually ends in disaster.

"Define kinky." He leans forward and kisses my abs, teasing his tongue along the top of my Wonder Woman briefs.

I close my eyes as my fingers curl into his hair, urging him a bit lower. He runs his nose along the crotch of my briefs, driving me mad with the warmth of his breath.

"Eli ..." I lift my hips from the bed. Yes, I realize it's the equivalent of him stabbing at my mouth with his cock. I never claimed my reasoning was fair.

"Not yet ..." His mouth denies my request as it kisses its way up my body. "If I give you that now..." he brushes his lips over mine "...I'll have to wash my mouth out with soap and water, and brush and floss my teeth before I can kiss you. And right now ... I want to kiss you."

I grin. "Solid point."

Eli kisses me, it feels different than his other kisses—a weird clash of patience and desperation. Maybe it's his naked body hovering over mine. Maybe it's that we're on the verge of having sex totally naked in a bed that doesn't belong to his mom.

His hands explore my body. Mine rest on his arms. Eli lets things build slowly as if he wants to draw out the moment. The journey seems to matter to him. I, on the other hand, have laser focus on the destination.

I hate that I have two modes: Don't touch me. Or ... Give me an orgasm now.

Foreplay is simply an overabundance of touching.

"Put on a condom."

"I will." He takes his sweet time working his mouth back down my body.

I grimace, clenching my hands to prevent myself from reaching between my legs and getting myself off. Yes, something I would have done and often did do years earlier. The look of shock guys would get on their faces after I'd pleasure myself and hop out of bed before they wrapped it up and made an attempt to stick it inside of me was truly priceless.

But Eli is not just a random guy I plan on using for a quick orgasm. And I want him to think I'm good at sex—not just with myself, but with him too.

Again, he lets his mouth hover between my legs as he slides a finger under my briefs, teasing my clit. My hand covers his as I jerk my pelvis, guiding his finger inside of me.

Yes!

He's slow. My hips rock against his hand at a much faster pace. His thumb finds my clit as he kisses my inner thigh, teasing it with his tongue.

Are we done kissing? I feel like we are. If he can add his long middle finger and move his tongue up two inches, including it in the mix, I will see stars.

"Let me get the condom."

What?!

He sits on the edge of the bed, retrieves a condom from the drawer, and rolls it on.

I shimmy out of my superhero briefs. "Hurry up."

His body vibrates. "We have all night."

No. We most certainly *do not* have all night. There's pizza downstairs. I have my meds to take. Face to wash. Teeth to brush and floss. And *if* he can work on his efficiency, we might have it one more time, but there's no way we're dragging out this one time. All. Night. Long.

No fucking way.

So … I attack him. That's really the best description.

I push him back on the bed and kiss him hard while lining up his cock. Then I sink down as we seethe in unison.

"Find it, Eli." I grin, holding up my wrist and setting my sexual activity function on my watch.

He rolls his eyes. "It's not a race."

"I disagree." I start moving at a brisk pace.

He grabs my hips to slow me down, but I keep pace, chasing that orgasm, angling forward to keep my clit rubbing against his pelvis. And as I approach the coveted finish line, he lifts me from him, as if he knows.

"What are you doing?" I protest.

He flips me onto my back—pinning my arms to the bed beside my head—and settles his hips between my legs, sliding back inside of me. "I'm *finding it,* Mayhem. Better keep up." He smirks before kissing me and *seriously* pounding into me.

Game on!

Until … it's not.

Eli manages to find the perfect angle that denies me the friction I need, and he has my hands pinned to the bed so I can't help myself.

"You're terrible at sex." I scowl at him as sweat beads along his brow while moving above me, clearly burning more calories and approaching the damn finish line that I can no longer see.

"I'm really not." He grins, releasing my arms.

My hands fly straight to his hair. Balling them into fists, I jerk it as hard as possible. "Fucker …"

He cuts me off with his lips covering mine and his

tongue filling my mouth as he slides his hand between our pelvises and delivers a spectacular orgasm just seconds after he climaxes. Eli just *has* to win.

CHAPTER TWENTY

Dorothy Defined

Elijah

WELL, THAT WAS a first.

Even the times I had angry sex with Julie, it wasn't all that angry. More like make-up sex with a bit of attitude.

Dorothy Mayhem sex involves a playing field—maybe a battlefield—a time clock, and placement medals.

Before I can hook an arm around her and pull her next to me, she's out of bed and back into her superhero pajamas, minus the tiara that fell off while she rode me like a true immortal.

"Wow ..." She bends down and cocks her head to look at the stack of books on the side table by the chair in the corner of my bedroom. "You have a lot of books on autism. Do you think Roman is on the spectrum?"

I sit up and reach for a tissue, my briefs, and jeans. "No."

Dorothy eases into the chair and inspects the books

one at a time. "*Autism in Heels*. Sounds like something for a woman."

I wait on the edge of the bed, jeans pulled on, hands folded between my legs.

She glances over at me, eyebrows peaked in question. "Are you reading these because of me?"

I nod, wondering what's going through her mind. Do I need to apologize? Fish for some pathetic excuse?

Dorothy tosses them onto the ottoman and rubs her lips together. "What do you want to know? You don't need a book. All you have to do is ask me."

Dropping my head, I massage the back of my neck. "I wasn't looking for answers. I was looking for insight. I was looking *for* the questions I never would have thought to ask until after I screwed up. Until it was too late."

She nods slowly, forehead wrinkled. "I bet it was frustrating reading these. Because for every three things that you could relate directly to me, there had to be at least one … maybe two that don't quite fit. I know this because I've read all the books. I think even this one." She picks one of the books up and glances at the back of it.

I look up at her and whisper, "Yes."

"If I picked up a book about men, would all the stereotypes apply to you?"

I shake my head.

"If I figure you out, will that mean I know everything that makes Dr. Warren act the way he does?"

I shake my head.

"The spectrum is *human*. It's not autism. Doesn't matter what the so-called experts say. But I owned the label years ago anyway." She giggles. "Imagine being my parents ... sitting around a table with your ten-year-old kid (after years of being told girls don't get autism), and the doctor finally says, 'Yes. The diagnosis is Asperger's.' And your kid yells out, 'Oh great ... now I have ASS BURGERS.'"

I bite my lips together, until my face turns blue.

Dorothy smirks. "It's okay. You can laugh. It's pretty funny."

I fist my hand at my mouth and laugh until my stomach hurts, just like I did in the back of her Audi when she said "snacking on Dorothy." It's not me laughing at her in a mean way. It's her making me laugh in the most refreshing way. After Julie left, I wondered if I would ever laugh like this again.

Roman makes me laugh, and it's real. And it feels good. But it's bittersweet because every time he does something cute or funny, I want to call Julie's name and tell her to come watch him or listen to him repeat it. But Julie isn't here. We are no longer a family unit. And that always steals a tiny piece of joy from the moment.

"My parents tell that story all the time. It took me years to see the humor in it. But now it makes me laugh. Humor can be difficult for me. Laughing at myself never came naturally. I can do it now, but only because I learned to do it. Through many meltdowns and tears, I forced myself to laugh it off. And journal. I work things out that way. And sometimes I talk stuff through with my parents. They aren't board-certified talk doctors like your mom, but they suffice. They help me put things into perspective. Tell me when I've overreacted in a situation or underestimated the importance of doing or saying more."

I make my way to her, removing the books from the ottoman and sitting on it, resting my hands on her legs, hoping it's okay. She places her hands on top of mine. I need this. I need to know that I can touch her—at least sometimes—and that it's okay. Some things in these books worry me. They make me think she will never want to be touched. Never *truly* want to have sex.

"I don't read those books to figure you out. I read them to learn more about a part of the human spectrum."

She glances up at me and smiles.

"It never hurts to study different perspectives. Right?" I ask.

"Right."

"Think it's too late for pizza?"

Dorothy's jaw drops as she gasps. "It's *never* too late for pizza."

"Okay, Wonder Woman. Let's eat." I stand, taking her hand and leading her to the kitchen.

She piles half the pizza onto her plate.

I chuckle. "Worried I'm going to eat more than my share?"

"It happens a lot to me." She grabs her bag and fishes out a pill container.

"Cholesterol meds for all the cheese you eat?"

"Not yet." She smirks as I hand her a bottle of water.

"Anxiety pill. Sleeping pill. Multi-vitamin. Magnesium. Turmeric. What do you take?"

I grin, carrying our plates to the table. "I'm going to self-medicate with this bottle of pinot."

"Yuck. I hate wine." She dives into her pizza.

"Noted. In fact, I'd like to take more notes, if you don't mind."

Dorothy glances up at me with half a slice of pizza hanging from her mouth. "About what?" she mumbles.

For the next hour, I interview her, preparing to pass any and all Dorothy Mayhem tests should the occasion arise again.

Favorite color: Red

Place of birth: Portland, Oregon

Date of birth: May 6th, 1989

High school: Riverdale

Mother's Maiden Name: Crowley

Childhood pets: Two dogs, both Cavalier Spaniels—
   Jax and Bailey

Cavities: None

Medications: Protected by HIPAA

Favorite pastime: Tie between Xbox and bingeing on
   Netflix

Favorite Series: Game of Thrones

Favorite musical artist: Taylor Swift

And then there are so many things that she can't answer about herself. I'm okay with that because I want to discover her, not study her.

"Come to bed." I hold out my hand as she yawns just

before midnight.

We trudge our way up the stairs.

"Shower with me?"

"Sounds crowded and messy."

"You haven't seen my shower. It's large and clean. And if we find something that's dirty, I have lots of soap to use on it."

"Is this your way of suggesting sex again?"

At the top of the stairs, I pull her to me. "Would that be so bad?"

"No foreplay."

"Said no woman ever." I laugh.

"Welp, I'm a woman, and I'm saying it."

"I feel like you're just using me for quick orgasms."

She walks toward my bathroom, pulling me behind her by nothing more than her index finger clasped to mine. "Would that be so bad?" She shoots me a flirty grin over her shoulder.

Dorothy … Dorothy … Dorothy …

CHAPTER TWENTY-ONE

Missed Goodbyes

Dorothy

WORST NIGHT EVER.

Plot twist—great sex ends in restless sleep. At least for me.

The firm bed.

The itchy sheets.

The nightlight from the hallway.

The extra body heat.

It doesn't work for me.

By four in the morning, I give up. Why torture myself any longer?

"Eli?" I say.

No answer.

"Eli!"

"Jesus!" He jumps once from my slightly elevated volume and a second time when he opens his eyes and sees my face an inch from his face. "Whoa …" He jerks his head to the side and sits up in bed. "What's going on?

Why did you yell at me? What time is it?" He looks at his watch on its charger by the bed.

"I'm going to go exercise."

"What? It's 4:00 a.m. on a Sunday."

"Yes, but I have to work."

"Not until eight," he replies in a raspy voice as he rubs his eyes.

"I can't sleep. So I might as well go exercise."

"I'll go with you."

"No. I'm going to the gym. You're not a member at my gym, are you?"

"No …" he murmurs on a yawn.

"Okay. See ya."

He grabs my arm.

"We're not going to kiss."

"Morning breath?" He laughs.

"Yes." I wrinkle my nose.

"How about an awkward hug?"

"Why does it have to be awkward?"

"It doesn't. It's just a high probability." He pulls me into his body and hugs me. I try to mold my body to his without falling on top of him. But with him leaning against the headboard, I don't know where to put my arms. So I just stick my butt out and let him hug my torso while my cheek smashes uncomfortably into his shoulder.

He releases me.

"What do you mean?"

"Nothing." He grins. "Drive safely, okay?"

"Okay."

"Dorothy?"

I turn at the doorway. "Yeah?"

"I'm flying to San Francisco tomorrow morning for a two-day conference. I'll be back Wednesday."

"Okay. Um … should I tell Warren about us? Because right now he's expecting me to go to dinner with him Tuesday night."

"Probably not quite yet. I have to work with him, and he asked you out just days ago. I'm not sure how well he'll take the news. Maybe give it time."

"Act normal?"

Eli chuckles. "Sure."

"You're laughing because I'm not normal."

"Dorothy, I lost all sense of normalcy before you came along. No judgment here."

"Okay. Bye."

I stop by the gym and burn a quick six hundred calories. Eli will get the notification as soon as he checks his watch. This makes me very happy.

The happiness doesn't quite balance the disappointment that I feel over *hating* his bed. I know he will ask me to stay over again. And I also know I will say no. Unfortunately, I have bigger problems.

Warren.

"Good morning." He slithers up beside me as I pay for my coffee in the cafeteria.

"Dr. Warren." I smile. Okay, it's a grimace I try to sell as a smile.

Thankfully, Dr. Warren is so full of himself, he buys it. "I have reservations at a very popular restaurant. I think you're going to be quite pleased."

Act normal. Don't tell him.

Easier said than done.

"Only if you tell me the name of it."

"Nope. It's a surprise."

"I don't like surprises." I take quick strides toward the elevator.

He stays hot on my heels. "You're going to like this one."

Nope. I won't like it. I'll just make sure to eat dinner before going out.

"By the way ..." I turn after stepping into the elevator.

He follows me, bringing his overpowering scent with him. "Yes?" He flashes me his expensive smile.

"We won't be having sex on our date."

"No?" He cocks his head to the side. "You sure about that?"

I stare at the digital floor numbers as the elevator ascends. "Positive."

He takes a step back and slowly inspects me over the lid of his coffee cup. After a few seconds, his face morphs into something like recognition. "Oh ... I get it."

He does?

How can he so quickly tell that I had hot, pounding, multiple-orgasm sex with Dr. Hawkins? Am I glowing?

"I'll wait." He winks, stepping off the elevator a floor before mine. "Message me your address, Dorothy. See you Tuesday."

Elijah

MONDAY MORNING I fly to San Francisco for the two-day conference. When I messaged Dorothy Sunday night to tell her goodbye, she gave her usual "Okay, goodbye" reply. She needs her space. I respect that, but it doesn't make me crave time with her any less.

I tell myself I'll be cool and not text or call her while I'm traveling, but I can't lie ... I'm a little disappointed she makes no effort to communicate with me. Again, I have to remember Dorothy is not Julie or any other woman I have ever known. So while this is ninety percent a really great thing, I have to deal with the ten percent that sucks. And her lack of need for regular contact with me is that sucky ten percent. It makes me feel needy, and I'm really not a needy person.

"Welcome back. How was the conference?" Warren asks Wednesday morning before rounds as he sips his coffee in the lounge.

"Fine." I glance at my tablet. "Brandon's last day of chemo. God ... I need this to work."

"He breezes through everything. I see him getting back on the field next year." Warren stands and pulls on his lab coat.

"Mmm ..." I nod, opening a bottle of water. "I hope so."

"So ... any suggestions for a second date?"

"What are you talking about?" I ask without glancing up from my tablet.

"I took Dorothy to dinner last night. I'm thinking a play or something like that for our next date."

I lift my gaze slowly to meet his smirk. There is no way I heard him correctly.

"Say that again."

"Which part?"

"All of it."

"I took Dorothy to dinner last night—"

"Dorothy Mayhem?"

He laughs. "Uh … yeah. Dude, you were here last week when I sent her the cookie bouquet that *you* suggested. Remember?"

I nod slowly, clenching my tablet with an iron grip while gnashing my teeth.

"Where you going?" he asks as I pivot and exit the lounge.

Dorothy has school, but I *have* to text her even if she doesn't respond. It's either a text to her phone or a fist in Warren's face.

Me: *We need to talk about your date with Warren.*

It takes her an hour to respond. While in the middle of rounds, I glance at my phone screen.

Dorothy: *Ugh! He took me on a FONDUE DATE! (five vomit emojis)*

"Dr. Hawkins?"

I return my attention to the patient's mom. "Yes?"

Warren has the nerve to frown at me, the way I used

to frown at him before I banned him from being on his phone during rounds.

"School. Will she be able to stay in school while receiving radiation?"

I can't stop thinking about Warren and Dorothy. Even as I spew off my answer to the mom, a woman who deserves my full attention, I can't shake the anger.

✧ ✧ ✧

Dorothy

AFTER CLASS, I respond to Eli's last text which was:

> Dr. Hawkins: ***I'm either coming to your house or you're coming to mine, but we are talking tonight.***
>
> Me: ***I'm taking Gemma to car wash dog wash night. (water emoji, dog emoji, car emoji)***
>
> Dr. Hawkins: ***Gemma and your dirty car can wait. I can't.***
>
> Dorothy: ***The free dog wash is only on Wednesdays. (shrug emoji)***
>
> Me: ***I don't give a shit.***

Someone is in a bad mood. I'll pass on that. I shake my head.

> Me: ***Call me tomorrow after the market. See... I'm letting you call me. (smiley emoji, high-five emoji)***
>
> Dr. Hawkins: ***I'm going for a run. After I shower,***

I'm coming to your house. Deal with it.

He really needs to add some emojis. In my head I imagine angry emojis, but he has no reason to be angry ... at least, not with me. Maybe he has issues at work or with Dr. Hathaway and needs someone to talk to.

Me: *Okay. (smiley emoji, high-five emoji)*

After car wash and dog wash, I take my routine walk, eat dinner, shower, and play Xbox, waiting for Eli. At 10:20 p.m., my phone chimes. Stomach-flu Hailey from the ICU messages me—well, it's actually a group message. I *hate* group messages.

Hailey: *OMG – Dr. Hawkins is seriously injured!*

I stare at my screen, not fully believing what's popping up—the long string of responses from everyone else in the group text. I have nothing to say because my brain is stuck in denial.

WTF? What happened?
Is he going to live?
When? What happened?
OMFG are you serious?
Deets ... we need ALL the deets.
He fell off a ledge on a trail.
Had to be airlifted.
Took two hours to get him out.
Really fucking steep cliff.

They're taking him to surgery now at General.

I'm off in ten. I'm going straight there to find out more. I'll update soon.

After reading all the texts from the group, I run straight to my parents' bedroom and throw open the door.

They look up from their adjustable bed, illuminated by the TV screen. *Grey's Anatomy*. Always *Grey's Anatomy*.

"What's wrong?" Mom asks.

"Dr. Hawkins is going into surgery. He was jogging. Fell off the steep ledge of the trail. Hailey sent out a group text. He was supposed to come see me tonight. I've been waiting for him. I don't know what to do. Stay? Go? I'm not family. I know they won't tell me anything. Hailey will give better updates to the group text. But his parents will be there. Oh my god … poor Roman. He's with Julie, but still … she'll take him to the hospital, right? Or maybe not. I mean, if it's bad, it could scare him. He's three. Oh god …" I blink and feel a lot of tears fall down my face all at once. "What if he doesn't live?"

It's like they're in bed one minute, and in that single blink, they're hugging me.

"Go," my mom says. "You definitely should go. I'll drive you and stay with you until we know how he's doing."

I nod, batting away the tears. "Okay."

We drive to General, and we're met with an overcapacity waiting room of family, coworkers, and friends. I'm completely out of place—more so than usual. There's no place to sit, so Mom and I huddle in a corner next to a window.

"I can get us coffees?" she suggests.

"Okay."

After she leaves to grab us coffees, a tiny peephole forms in the throng of people, and on the other side of the room, I make what feels like accidental eye contact with Lori Hawkins. She looks oddly calm. No real decipherable expression on her face. Not that I'm an expert at that.

She slowly stands, releasing Kent's hand, and worms her way toward me. "Dorothy, dear ... come sit with us." Her arms embrace me. I stiffen. After a few seconds, I flatten my hands and give her a few comforting pats.

"They're trying to stop the internal bleeding. He was unresponsive when they arrived with him. God ... we're just so lucky someone happened to see him go over the edge, otherwise ..." Her voice cracks.

Otherwise, he would have died and it would have taken days if not longer to find his body. *Those* lines I can read between.

"Where's Roman?"

"He's at home with Julie's mom, Peggy. Come on." She takes my hand and pulls me to the other side of the waiting room.

Kent gives me a sad smile as Lori introduces me to Eli's sisters, Kendra and Molly, their husbands and children. Julie is on the other side of Kent with red eyes and a tissue wadded in her hand. I smile at her. She glances in the other direction and wipes her eyes. Kent rests his hand on her back and rubs circles on it while she leans into him.

"Sit, Dorothy. I've sat far too long. I think I need to take a walk. Kent, message me if you hear anything." Lori releases my hand and points to the seat on the other side of Kent.

"My mom's here. She drove me. She went to get coffee. I'm good. I don't need to sit right now."

Lori nods. "Okay. I'll be back in a little bit."

Here I stand ... in front of Eli's family and Dr. Hathaway, who is either really sad about the accident—too sad to even smile at me—or she's still upset about the farmer's market incident. I can't blame her either way.

"Hey, here you go." Mom hands me a cup of coffee. I turn toward her and take a few steps back to distance us from Eli's family.

"I guess you're not going to introduce me, huh?" Mom gives me a look. The you-have-poor-manners look.

"Lori took a walk. Dr. Hathaway is on his dad's right, crying. I know Kent's name, but I already forgot Eli's sisters' names and the names of their spouses and kids. I would epically fail the introduction."

"Fair enough." Mom nods.

"I should have just gone to the cafeteria with you. We're just going to wait here now for who knows how long, and eventually a doctor will come out and either say he's dead or alive. Either way, I won't be allowed to see him very soon, so ..." I shrug.

"He'll be fine. We have to believe that."

I nod.

During the three remaining hours of surgery, I take the opportunity to introduce my mom to his family. After Lori comes back, we grab an early morning breakfast sandwich and a Dr. Pepper, and take a long walk around the block. Then two doctors come out to let his family know that they stopped all the bleeding. He has two fractured ribs, a broken fibula, a multitude of cuts and puncture wounds, and cerebral edema.

It's a miracle he survived the fall. At least that's the chatter going around the waiting room. And as bad as the list of injuries sounds … in the larger scope of things, they are minor injuries. He doesn't need surgery for the fractures. And as long as the swelling in his brain goes down without any complications, he should make a full recovery.

The doctor said it will be another hour before family can see him, and even then, he probably won't be conscious.

"I'm going home. I have school. I'm here if you need me. Just let me know. I can help with Roman or … whatever." I nail my exit speech after practicing it during the last hour of surgery because I knew I wasn't staying. In fact, I'm dying to get out of this waiting room.

"You should come back with us." Lori gestures toward the ICU.

"I'm not family."

"Dorothy …"

"I'll check in tomorrow after school."

Lori frowns. "Okay. We'll make sure someone contacts you if anything changes."

"Great. Thanks."

I power walk straight out of the hospital.

"I noticed Dr. Hathaway was next to Eli's dad, getting ready to go back with them to see Eli. Is she really still family?" Mom asks.

"I don't know. I don't care. He probably won't wake up while they're there. No need to stand in the corner of the room, watching a machine help him breathe."

"Why was he planning on visiting you so late?" She follows me out the door.

"He wanted to talk. At first, he made it sound like he wanted to talk about my date with Dr. Warren. But I don't know why that would be. I think it must have been something else because his messages seemed urgent." I get in Mom's Ford Escape.

"Wait ... you went on a date with Dr. Warren?" She closes her door and starts the car.

"Yes." I lean my head against the head rest. "I was going to tell you about it, but you were asleep, and then I just forgot about it, more like blocked it from my memory. He took me for fondue. I just couldn't. It was so gross. I can't believe those restaurants are even legal. It's just a melting pot of nasty germs. A haven for chronic double-dippers. I'm not gonna lie, my stomach hasn't been right ever since. I think I caught something. Tomorrow I'm going to request blood and stool tests. Legit, I ate one bite, the first one, but you know they don't wash those pots between customers. They just pour in more milk and cheese, crank up the heat, and assume it will self-decontaminate from the heat. Wrong!"

"Wait … did you and Eli break up?"

Wow, she doesn't seem to care about my fondue distress at all.

"No. I mean … I don't know what we are or were. It's not like we talked about it. We have sex. Good sex. But I'm not sure mutually sharing autonomic nervous system responses necessarily makes us a couple."

"Autonomic what?"

"Orgasms. We have sex. I told you last Sunday that staying the night was a complete disaster. We're not spooning and whispering I love you's. It's like hooking up, but with food, and sometimes a playdate with Roman. And he didn't want me to tell Dr. Warren about us, and Warren had already asked me out and I'd accepted. So what choice did I have? I went on the awful fondue date, but I told him with plenty of notice that we would not have sex. I'm not interested in having sex with anyone but Eli right now."

"Yes, Dorothy." Mom laughs. "Sex with only one person. It's called monogamy. You're in a monogamous relationship with Eli. You're a couple. You're his girlfriend."

I wrinkle my nose, not really believing her reasoning, even if it does kind of make sense when I repeat it in my head.

"Whatever."

CHAPTER TWENTY-TWO

Could It Be Love?

Elijah

L IGHTS.
   Way too bright.

Beeping.

Way too loud.

Pain.

Way too excruciating.

Fuck …

Everything hurts. Even my eyelids protest, especially my left eye. It takes me a little bit to realize I can't open it.

My throat …

Something's in my throat.

The sounds. My eye. My throat … I'm in the hospital. What happened?

The echo of voices thwarts my attempts to think back … to remember what happened.

Jesus … am I even alive? My head …

Yeah, I'm alive. Dead people don't feel this kind of pain. Death doesn't exactly sound terrible at the moment.

"Eli?"

Fucking hell! Ya mind not shining that light in my eye?

"Eli?" Mom.

My mom is here.

I force my right eye open a little more. The room dims a bit like someone dimmed the lights or shut the shades. The tube down my throat prevents me from thanking whomever did that, but I'm nonetheless thankful.

Mom ... Her pensive face comes into focus.

"Eli. They're going to remove your breathing tube."

That's great. Except I know from my medical training that removing tubes is not exactly the best experience for the patient. I like being the doctor. The patient? Not so much.

I follow the instructions as if I don't know them plenty well.

Suction.

Deflate.

Remove.

I cough a few times before they put an oxygen mask over my mouth and nose.

Mom smiles as Dad comes into my line of sight. My one-eyed line of sight.

"Do you know what happened?" Mom asks as a medical team mills around my bed, checking vitals, monitors, reflexes.

My head eases side to side. It's stiff. But it moves, so

that's a really good sign.

"You fell while out on the trail. It was a long fall. You're going to be fine."

I don't remember that. Maybe that's for the best. I just remember Dorothy and Warren and their fondue date. Date ... how could she have sex with me and go out with him two nights later? Ha! I don't like that memory, but it sure as hell feels good to know I have memories. So my head injuries can't be that severe.

"How ... long?"

"Two days." Mom smiles again. Of course she smiles. I'm alive and only have been in a coma for two days. Good news indeed. It could have been two years. Two years for Roman to forget me. Two years for Julie to remarry. Two years of not saving young lives. Two years for Dorothy to fall in love with Dr. Warren.

"Kendra and Molly will be here soon. Julie was going to get Roman dinner and take him to Peggy's, but your dad just texted her, so she's on her way now with Roman. He hasn't been to the hospital since your accident. We didn't want him seeing you unconscious."

"Good," I say in a hoarse voice.

"Dorothy said she'd check in on you after the end of her shift. I messaged her and she sent a string of emojis. She seems pretty excited to know you're awake."

"Okay." I inwardly smile because it's hard to actually form one on my face. My lower lip hurts. It's probably cut or stitched or ripped off. I'm not sure.

While we wait for the rest of my family, they remove my oxygen mask and give me some ice chips. Mom continues to quiz me on my accident, but I can't remember it. I remember everything else she asks me, which seems to please her and the other doctors.

"Daddy!"

Julie keeps a firm hold of Roman's hand as he tries to sprint toward my bed. "Remember, Daddy is a little fragile right now. We have to be careful with him." She lifts him up and sets him on the side of my bed. She smiles at me. It's filled with a little sadness, but mostly relief. And for the first time in what feels like forever, I don't sense anything like resentment or guilt. It feels like the way my wife used to smile at me.

"Your eye. Daddy, look! Your eye is scary."

"Yeah, well, it will get better soon. I won't look scary forever."

Julie uses one arm to keep Roman from getting too rough around me while her other hand squeezes mine. Tears fill her eyes. "I was so scared, Eli."

I squeeze her hand back. "I'm sorry."

She quickly wipes the stray tear from her cheek and laughs. "Don't apologize. I'm just …" She swallows hard. "I'm just so relieved you're here. It could have …" Her words break as more tears fill her eyes.

"Hey." I squeeze her hand again. "It's fine. I'm fine."

My mom hands Julie a tissue while Roman tries to climb off the bed.

Later my sisters and their families arrive. Everyone seems relieved to see me awake. Lots of tears. It must have been bad. Again, I'm happy for the tiny bit of memory loss.

"Dorothy, no! Come back here," my mom calls, slipping out of the room. "Don't be scared off. It's just family. Come in, dear." She ushers Dorothy into the room.

Dorothy still has on her work scrubs, red with a royal blue undershirt and royal blue Nikes. Tucking her hair behind her ears, her gaze darts around the roomful of people. Her discomfort can't be as bad as mine, but I still feel a pang of unease on her behalf.

"Dorfee!" Roman runs to her and gives her a high five.

Julie's expression stays neutral, like she's trying to act unaffected, but even with only one working eye at the moment, I don't miss her tiny flinch.

"Little Romeo, I've missed you." Dorothy smiles at Roman before finally giving me her gaze.

I need those honest eyes on me. They tell me everything she's afraid to say.

"I fear we're going to get in trouble for having too many people in here. Why don't we grab dinner?" Mom suggests.

Everyone says goodnight to me while Dorothy backs into the corner of the room like she's trying to disappear.

"Come here." I hold out my hand after the door to the room closes and it's just us.

"Thanks for not dying." She laughs nervously while taking my hand.

"You're welcome." I ease my hand up so our palms are flat against each other.

She stares at our hands as I lace our fingers together.

"I love you."

Her gaze shoots to mine, eyes wide, lips parted.

"I do. And I tried to die without saying it. And that was just stupid on my part. So in case I throw a clot or take some unexpected turn, I just want you to know. I love you, Dorothy Mayhem."

It's not that I intend for my declaration to be a surprise, but clearly it's quite the shocker. I chuckle then grimace. My ribs aren't ready for laughter. "It's not a question. Okay? It requires no answer, no acknowledgment."

She nods slowly, returning her gaze to our interlaced fingers. I bring them to my face, gently brushing my lips (kinda swollen lips) over her fingers. Dorothy has a way of taking away my pain, and I feel certain she has no idea the effect she has on me.

"I fear I could fall behind with closing my rings for a while."

A smile forms along her perfect lips. "Ya think?"

"I'm glad you came over the other night. I might need those memories to make it through the healing process."

Her cheeks bloom red. "I was reading about orgasms."

Yeah, I love her. And I feel certain I will die a happy man if she starts every conversation with "I was reading about orgasms."

She continues, "You know the Lazarus reflex?"

"Yes."

"Well, did you know that if you were only being kept alive by machines, so basically dead, that as long as your sacral nerve is being oxygenated, you can be stimulated to have an orgasm? Like giving a dead person an orgasm. That'd be the way to go out, right?"

It all hurts so bad, but so very good at the same time. My grin pulls at my swollen lip, and my laughter pulls at my fractured ribs, but I welcome the pain because Dorothy Mayhem makes life pretty fucking amazing. "Do I want to know how this all came about?"

She shrugs. "Just something I thought about when they didn't know if you'd wake up."

"Were you going to suggest I get one last orgasm before they unplugged me? Please say yes. If you do, I think I'll make sure you're legally responsible for making all final decisions for me if I go under again."

Dorothy giggles. "I've seen ultrasounds of babies masturbating in the womb. It's only fitting to go out with the same simple-minded pleasure with which you came into this world."

The question begs to be asked ... why was Dorothy so thoroughly researching orgasms? But I don't ask the question because it's Dorothy Mayhem. I expect the unexpected from her. It's one of the things that made me fall so fast and so hard for her.

"You should sleep. And I haven't been home yet, so lots to do before work tomorrow."

"Like masturbate?"

"What? No!" She releases my hand and curls her hair behind her ears again.

"Rumor has it I could be in this joint for another week. Think you could smuggle in a pizza some night?"

There it is … that smile. God, it's oxygen. "Maybe."

"Drive safely, Dorothy."

She nods, lips twisted as her gaze makes a slow inspection from my toes to my head. Then she leans over and kisses my cheek. "Goodnight," she whispers.

I take a slow breath as she walks to the door and close my eye when she disappears around the corner.

"Eli?"

I open my eye again.

She peeks her head around the corner, teeth planted into her bottom lip.

"Yes?"

"I do too."

"You do too?" I ask.

"Love you. I think I love you too." She shrugs. "So now you know, just in case you don't wake up in the morning."

How incredibly morbid … and … *perfect.* Three words don't fit Dorothy. A simple "I love you" would not feel right coming out of her mouth in this moment. Nope. It has to be six. Six is infinitely better than three.

I think I love you too.

CHAPTER TWENTY-THREE

Homebound

Dorothy

I KEEP MY routine for the most part. I *need* routine, especially with Eli in the hospital and his family visiting at randomly different times. Several times I consider suggesting we make up a schedule so his room isn't stuffed to the limit with visitors. But they seem to enjoy the large gathering, and so does Eli. So I never get the nerve to say anything.

On his last night in the hospital, I stop by after my shift, assuming—hoping—the later hour will grant me some alone time with Eli.

No such luck.

Instead, his parents and Julie are here, discussing his home care. They smile when I slip into the room, even Julie's smile looks a little more genuine.

"Hi, sweetie." Lori smiles.

They continue discussing who will take care of Eli until he can get around on his own.

As I take a seat in the corner of the room, Eli winks at me before returning his attention to his mom.

"I'm taking off two days a week to be with you. Your dad will take a day off too. Molly is going to see about taking one morning, but she's not sure yet. I really think we should consider an in-home nurse just during the day. And I'll stay over during the nights." His mom brushes his bangs away from his face.

"I can do two days. And I'll do nights and weekends too," Julie announces.

"Jules …" Eli starts to speak.

"It's fine. I've already arranged for two of my colleagues to cover some days for me until you've recovered. Then my mom can have a break from watching Roman. She and my dad have been wanting to take a vacation anyway. And Roman can take a break from daycare." Julie rests her hand on Eli's arm.

As for me … I want to slink out of the room before anyone looks in my direction.

Too late.

Eli studies Julie with an unreadable expression before sliding his gaze in my direction. "Know any good in-home nurses?"

"Oh—" I do. I know several.

But Julie cuts me off. "Eli, don't be ridiculous. Why would you want that? I'm giving you more time with Roman. Quality time. It's the perfect solution, but you'd rather have some stranger help you to the bathroom? In and out of bed?"

Yes. I indeed need to get out of here. I like Boss

Bitch. I love world renowned Dr. Hathaway. But Julie, Eli's ex-wife, doesn't make my favorite people list with her offer to help him to the bathroom and in and out of bed.

His parents and Julie follow his gaze, which happens to be on me like I'm the one with a decision to make. I don't even want to be here, let alone weigh in on decisions.

"Thoughts, Dorothy?" Eli asks me.

Wow! No pressure.

"Roman would love spending more time with you." I make the mistake of giving Julie a quick glance. "*Both* of you." My grin feels extra toothy. Extra everything. Do they notice my level of get-me-the-fuck-out-of-here discomfort? "I bet he'll find it really fun. Lego time. Watching Kratt Brothers. And whatnot."

Okay! Is everyone happy? Great. Can I leave now?

I hate conflict, so much so I have a terrible track record of putting myself in really uncomfortable positions to avoid dealing with certain situations. My parents find this particular trait frustrating. They think I constantly give up my own happiness because I don't want to risk the chance of conflict. What they don't really understand is avoiding conflict makes me happy.

"Do you want to talk privately about this?" Eli asks me, therefore three sets of eyes are on me.

"Not particularly."

"Can you give us a minute?" he asks.

Lori and Kent don't blink, they just nod and make their way out of the room. Julie ... well, she shows a bit more reluctance to leave. Or maybe her hand is stuck to

Eli's arm.

"Jules, please."

Jules ... I kinda hate that he has a nickname for her. No nicknames for me. Nope. Just Dorothy. Some people try to call me Dot or Dottie. Those choices don't sound as smooth or as cool as Jules. And I just hate Dot and Dottie. So I have to stick with Dorothy.

Jules squeezes his arm and nods. "I'll be right outside."

"Thanks."

He watches her leave the room before giving me a solid grin. "Did you have a good day?"

"Did you clear the room just to ask me that?" I shuffle my sneakers toward him, sitting on the edge of his bed.

He rests his hand on my leg. "Sure. But for the record, I was planning on asking them to leave anyway, just to look at you without being interrupted."

"Your eye looks so much better."

"Better to see you with, my dear."

I giggle.

"I wouldn't be okay with your ex-husband staying with you if you were unable to take care of yourself."

"I don't have an ex-husband. Never been married."

His mouth quirks up a bit on one side. "What I'm saying is, it's okay for you to not want Julie to stay with me and take care of me. I'll hire an in-home nurse."

"You'll get to see Roman every day if she stays with you."

"True, but at what cost?"

I shrug. "Sounds like no cost. I don't think she's going to charge you."

"You know what I mean. What will be the cost to us?"

"My life won't change. I have school and work. And you'll get to see Roman *every day*. I'd think you were crazy for passing up this opportunity. I'm jealous you'll get to hang out with him every day. He's way cooler than my classmates or anyone at the hospital."

"You're sure … about Julie?"

I laugh. "She's my idol. I'd choose her to watch me if I were out of commission."

"Gee … thanks a lot."

"Anytime, Dr. Hawkins."

He rolls his eyes.

"You'll come over, right? Dinner? Movie nights? Pasta? Xbox?"

Just the four of us. Sounds super awesome. Super awkward. Super unlikely.

"Did you catch the part where I said I have school, work, a dog, two emus, and aging parents?"

"Did you catch the part where I love you? The part that craves time with you?"

I sigh. "I'll visit when I can." I mean it. I also have a busy schedule.

"It will be awesome having Roman around more again. God … I miss him so much when he's with Julie. I just…" a tiny frown steals his smile "…miss him."

CHAPTER TWENTY-FOUR

Remember When

Elijah

MY FAMILY HAS a coming home party for me the next day. Dorothy has to work. Roman goes crazy over the balloons and cake, and Julie wastes no time rearranging things around the house, including shit in my kitchen and bathroom.

"I'm so glad you're home … and alive. But you should rest now." Mom kisses my cheek as everyone funnels toward the door.

"Need help getting him upstairs?" Dad asks Julie.

"I think I've got it. But thank you."

Roman gives everyone goodbye hugs and kisses. A few minutes later, it's just the three of us. It immediately feels weird and familiar at the same time. It's not the house we lived in together, but most of the furniture is the same. Julie wanted a complete break from our life together which included a new home and all new furnishings. I wanted a better view, and an easy commute, but was fine with the old furniture. I knew Roman would work hard on destroying it anyway.

"I forgot how comfy this leather recliner is." Julie plops down in the brown recliner while I stay perched on the matching sofa with my casted leg on the coffee table.

"Well, you can't have it now" I grin.

She rolls her eyes. "I said it's comfy, not stylish."

"Suits Roman and me."

I wait for her comeback. It defines the previous year. Little jabs here and there, but rarely anything like a boxing match. We manage to always bring it back to Roman. We're in it for him. I often wonder, if we hadn't had Roman, would she have left Portland? Would I have ever seen her again?

There's something different about her right now. So much of her feels familiar, like the Julie I fell in love with twenty-two years ago. But on the outside, I don't recognize her—the red hair, the breasts, the clothes that hug her curves a little bit more than the comfortable, sensible outfits she wore when we were married.

"Mommy! I'm hungry." Roman zooms down the stairs and barrels toward her, jumping onto her lap.

"Oopf!" She hugs him, rocking him a bit as he hugs her back.

My world.

My life.

Right here, but not completely real anymore. For a moment, when Julie glances at me and smiles over Roman's shoulder, I feel like the previous year never happened, like maybe I didn't just wake up after an accident, maybe I woke up from the nightmare that my wife left me.

In the very next blink, I think of Dorothy.

"Hey, buddy. Can you bring me my phone? It's on the kitchen table."

"I get it!" Roman wiggles down from Julie's lap and runs into the kitchen.

"So … what sounds good for dinner?" She stands, sliding her hands into her back pockets which press her new chest out, showing off the goods.

"We can just order something to be delivered."

"No. I'm here. I fully intend to make meals. Clean house. Maybe knit something." She winks.

When she was pregnant with Roman, she took up knitting. That Christmas everyone got scarves and mittens.

"As I recall, the last time you took up knitting, the house never got cleaned and we always ordered delivery."

"True." An easy laugh bubbles from her chest. "I'll try to show a little more restraint this time."

"Here, Daddy." Roman brings me my phone.

"Thanks, buddy."

"You going to help me make dinner, mister?" Julie ruffles Roman's hair as they both head toward the kitchen.

Dorothy has three more hours of work, but I can't resist texting her on the off chance that she might break the rules and text me back.

Me: **What are you wearing?**

She doesn't respond right away. That's fine. I have nowhere to go and all the time in the world. Twenty minutes later, she texts me.

Dorothy: **Scrubs (shrug emoji)**

Me: **What's the color combination today?**

Dorothy: **I'm working**

Me: **Two words. I know you're wearing two colors. Be quick and sneaky. Type two words to me. (folded hands emoji)**

Dorothy: **Green white**

Me: **Grass green (grass emoji) or surgical green (stethoscope emoji)**

She doesn't answer. I frown. Kudos to Dorothy for taking her job seriously.

While Julie and Roman make dinner, I lean my head back and close my eyes. I dream of jogging along my favorite trail, the windy, narrow paths. Nothing but miles of trees, deep ravines, and the trickling of tiny waterfalls.

"Daddy!"

I jump, cringing as my wounds protest.

"Don't scare Daddy, silly. Remember we have to be really really nice to him." Julie hooks Roman around the waist with her arm and kisses him on the cheek as she scoops him up into her arms. "Let me get the wild man his food. Then I'll help you to the table. Unless you'd rather eat on the sofa."

"The table is fine. If I eat out here, Roman will want to eat out here too. And that will turn into an unbreakable habit."

Julie nuzzles Roman's ear as he giggles. "So very true. I'll be right back."

We eat tacos.

I think of Dorothy and her love of tacos ... and all food really.

After dinner, Roman sits between me and Julie on the sofa (my leg propped up on the coffee table), and we take turns reading him his favorite stories.

At eight o'clock, Julie takes him upstairs to tuck him in bed.

Dorothy: **Surgical green**

I smile as my phone chimes.

Me: **How was work today?**

Dorothy: **Same as every day. How are you feeling?**

Me: **Like I fell into a steep ravine.**

(Three rolling on the floor laughing emojis)

When can I see you?

Dorothy: **IDK**

Me: **Not an acceptable answer. (neutral face emoji)**

Dorothy: **Your house is only twenty minutes from my school. I have a 2.5 hr break between classes on Mondays. I could bring you lunch. And Roman. And Dr. Hathaway.**

I stare at the last line of her text. Julie is living with

me. Helping me. Allowing me more time with Roman. I'm grateful. Of that, there is no question. But it doesn't bode well for my time with Dorothy.

Me. My son. My girlfriend. And … my ex-wife.

But maybe that's it. I mean … I've seen it before. I've seen those rare instances where couples divorce. Share custody. And actually remain friends. Friends with each other. Friends with each other's new love interests. Maybe it doesn't have to be an awkward situation. Maybe it can be an opportunity.

After all, Julie left me. There should be no jealousy on her part. And Dorothy idolizes Julie, so they stand a good chance of becoming friends.

> Me: **That would be awesome. I'll pay you back.**
>
> Dorothy: **Not concerned about the money. I'll text you the menu so you guys can decide what you want. I can be there by 11:30. (high-five emoji)**
>
> Me: **Sounds perfect. Can't wait to see you! (high-five emoji, heart emoji)**

I start to type "I love you," but delete it. She knows. I told her with no uncertainty exactly how I feel. No need to suffocate her with the words. But damn! I sure do feel them.

> Dorothy: **Love you! Goodnight! (Face blowing a kiss emoji, sleeping emoji)**

"What's that grin all about?"

I glance up as Julie takes the last two steps. A curious

grin on her face.

Our newfound friendship doesn't seem ready for me to tell her I can't stop grinning because Dorothy Mayhem loves me. And she said it with emojis too. Yeah, I'm over the fucking moon, ready to bust out of my cast and do a happy dance.

Okay, maybe not quite yet. My body needs a little more time to catch up to my emotional enthusiasm.

"Just reading a message." I toss my phone on the sofa beside me.

"From your mom?" Julie sits at the opposite end of the sofa, hugging her knees to her chest.

It's hard to not stare at her. I'm still not used to her new look, and she's had it for months.

"No. It was Dorothy. Her shift just ended. She's stopping by tomorrow between classes, bringing all of us lunch."

Oh … and she loves me.

Julie rolls her lips together and nods. "That … sweet."

I ignore the way she makes it sound like Dorothy is a neighbor girl bringing by a May Day basket for Roman.

"As grateful as I am for what you're doing, I can't help but wonder if it won't put a kink in your personal life. I hope you know that my family can help. Definitely on the weekends. If you want to make plans or even stay at your place on the weekends, I'll be fine. You know my family would take care of me and Roman."

"Wow! I haven't been here a full day and you're dismissing me?" Julie's eyes widen.

"No." I chuckle. "I'm just thinking ahead is all. I feel like we all agreed to this arrangement without giving it thorough consideration."

"Well…" her lips twist as she averts her gaze to the coffee table "…my personal life isn't as exciting at the moment as what you probably imagine."

"I try not to imagine your personal life."

She ignores my jab.

"I was seeing someone. I didn't tell anyone. Never introduced Roman to him." She glances at me with a flat smile as if to make me feel guilty for Dorothy's and Roman's relationship.

Fuck you. Dorothy's amazing. It's your own fault you're not finding people who adore our son like Dorothy does.

"He went back to his family."

"Is that code for you had an affair with a married man?"

She jerks her head back and shoots me a scowl. "No!"

Really, how was I to know? In all fairness to me, Julie's favorite line is "You just don't know me anymore."

"They were divorced."

"And now they're back together?"

She nods, resting her chin on her knees. "And for the record … as I've said before, even if you didn't believe me … I never cheated on you. I didn't leave you because I was having an affair. There was no one else. I didn't leave you for another man, I left you for me."

I nod. "I forgive you."

"For leaving you?"

"No." I narrow my eyes. "I don't think leaving me

requires an apology. I mean ... we apologize for things we regret, right? I've never felt that you regret leaving me. But I have always felt your regret for hurting me. And for that, I forgive you."

As I shift my gaze to meet her teary eyes, she quickly wipes them. "You don't know how much I've needed to hear you say that."

"Well, I'm sorry I couldn't say it sooner."

She leans back and runs her hands through her hair. "I was struggling in ways you didn't know."

"What do you mean?"

She shakes her head. "Nothing. It's not the time to discuss it."

"Look at me. I'm a pretty captive audience at the moment, completely dependent on outside help to even make it to the toilet ... which by the way, I'll need to get to one soon."

"Oh!" She jumps up. "Sorry. Jeez, of course. You drank tons of water with dinner and your pills, of course your eyeballs have to be floating."

"It's fine. I think I'm good if you just hand me the crutches."

"You still need help because of your ribs."

I'm a mess and still really fucking weak, so I don't protest.

She walks right beside me as I hobble to the main floor bathroom.

"Do you need help getting your pants down?"

I give her a quick glance. Is she blushing?

"I'm starting to think I should have hired someone ...

a professional."

"I'm a doctor, in case you didn't get the memo. That makes me a professional. And I've seen it all."

"That's why you turned your back on me when I undressed to put on a gown after the coffee incident."

"You didn't need my help undressing, so it wasn't helping, which meant I just would have been watching you undress. *You* know the difference."

I have to pee. Badly …

"Just look away." I pull down the front of my sweatpants while she helps me balance, turning her head in the opposite direction.

I grab her shoulders, feeling a bit fatigued just from the trip to the bathroom. A slight bit of nausea sweeps over me too, from the pressure on my surgical wounds.

I pee for what feels like ten minutes. "I'm not doing so well."

"Oh!" She jerks my pants up.

Jesus … I didn't ask her to do that. What was the point of looking away?

"Let's get you back to the sofa. Can you make it? Do I need to help you ease to the floor?"

"Sofa. Go …" I tilt my chin up and focus on my breathing.

Julie grips my waist, and we let one crutch drop to the floor as she helps me hobble back to the sofa.

As soon as my butt connects with the cushion, I lean my head back, sweat beading along my brow.

"Good?"

I whisper a quick, "Yeah."

She returns from the kitchen a few minutes later with a cold washcloth for my forehead and an electrolyte drink.

"The more I drink, the more I'll have to pee." I take a sip.

"I'm going to grab a catheter kit tomorrow. I think that will be easier."

She's joking ... at least I think it's a joke.

"So ... I think you're sleeping downstairs tonight."

I grin on a tiny laugh. "Yeah, we're not tackling the stairs quite yet."

Julie sits on the opposite side of the sofa again. Our grins fade after a few seconds, leaving us with nothing to say in a silent room.

"I was scared, Eli."

My gaze finds her. But she stares at her hands in her lap.

"I let you go, yet I was so damn scared of losing you when they took you into surgery. All of my reasons for leaving you felt ridiculous and petty. This boulder of regret landed on me, and I could barely breathe. I thought ... this is it. This is God's way of testing me. You know? Like really testing me to see if I truly believed I could live without you. If I really *want* to live without you."

No. I can't let her think like this. Nope. It's too late to have these thoughts. So I smile on a sigh. "Well, good thing I'm okay. You worrying and overthinking things ... thinking God was speaking to you ... well, it wasn't that at all. Just good old fear. A very normal reaction to traumatic situations."

Julie glances up at me for a few seconds. I don't want her looking at me like she's still overthinking things.

"Can you get me my toothbrush and toothpaste? A bowl and some water? I think I'm done making trips to the bathroom until I absolutely have to pee."

She takes a few more seconds before nodding. "Yes. I'll get you fixed up."

CHAPTER TWENTY-FIVE

Firsts

Dorothy

Eli messages me their orders. I pick up sandwiches and cookies from my favorite cafe and drive to Eli's house.

"Dorfee! Roman hugs my legs as soon as Dr. Hathaway opens the door.

"Hey, little Romeo!"

"Careful, wild man. She has her hands full. Hi, Dorothy." Dr. Hathaway smiles. A real one, I feel pretty sure of it. I've seen her smile in professional situations, her confidence shines. That's the smile she gives me.

"Hi."

"It's very kind of you to bring all of us lunch. What do I owe you?"

I follow her inside, slipping off my tennis shoes. "Nothing. Really. It's fine. I can afford it."

She questions me with a look that I ignore as I set the sacks on the counter and slip off my jacket. "What can I get you to drink, Dorothy?"

"Water is great, thank you."

She pulls all of the food out of the sacks and sets each wrapped sandwich on a plate. "Yours must be the egg salad."

"Yes."

"If you want to set the plates on the table, I'll go help Eli get to his chair."

"Oh … yeah. Or I can help him. I'm a lot stronger than I look," I say.

"Just grab the plates."

Okay then …

I move the plates to the table, where she has a bowl of cut up vegetables and a bowl of grapes. I consider my feelings about eating food prepared by Boss Bitch. Since I'm on the fence, I decide to stick to my sandwich and cookie.

"Hey …"

I turn toward Eli's voice as Dr. Hathaway helps him to the kitchen table.

"Hey! How are you feeling?" I ask.

"Good."

"Weak," Dr. Hathaway corrects him with side-eye.

"Good and weak." He eases onto the chair, and she props up his cast on a stool.

"You don't have to eat at the table," I say, taking a seat next to him.

"I do. Otherwise, Roman would think all meals for eternity can be eaten in the living room. Julie sneaked me breakfast on the sofa before Roman woke up."

"Roman, come eat!" Dr. Hathaway calls.

He runs into the kitchen.

"Bib, wild man." Dr. Hathaway puts on his bib. "Where are you going?"

He runs to the other side of the kitchen and pulls out another bib. "Dorfee, here's your bib."

"Buddy, no …" Dr. Hathaway and Eli disapprove in unison.

"Fantastic. I was wondering where you put my bib." I take the bib and tie it around my neck.

Eli and Dr. Hathaway look at each other and then at me. I return a satisfied shrug and unwrap my sandwich.

"Mmm … this is a really good sandwich." Dr. Hathaway rolls her eyes like eating gives her an orgasm. "Reminds me of the sandwiches we had at the little hole-in-the-wall place just down from our hotel when we went to London right before I got pregnant. Remember?"

"Oh yeah." Eli nods. "Best sandwich ever. This comes close though. Good find, Dorothy." He winks at me.

"You ever been to London, Dorothy?" Dr. Hathaway asks.

"No. I'm pretty much a homebody."

"Oh, that's too bad. There's so much to see in the world." She wipes her mouth and takes a sip of water.

I finish chewing my food … thinking of an appropriate response.

"When I get better, we should go somewhere. What do you think?" Eli asks.

"Me too! I go somewhere wif Dorfee."

Dr. Hathaway clears her throat. "You'd stay with me,

wild man. We'll go someplace together. Maybe back to Disney World."

"If it's my week with him, he could come with us," Eli informs Dr. Hathaway.

"I suppose. But I don't want you taking him to London. I want to be with him the first time he sees London."

"Well, what if I want to be with him the first time he sees London?" Eli gives his rebuttal.

Me? Oh, I just keep eating. In fact, I can't eat fast enough.

"I don't think you honestly care. I just think you're acting like you do because you know how much it means to me." Dr. Hathaway wipes her mouth.

"Yes, you and your need to experience all of his 'firsts.' Did you ever think I wanted to be with him for his first visit to Texas? Doesn't seem fair given the fact that you made the decision to have him half the time. That means you should be fine with half, the way you make me have to be fine with half. And maybe his first time in London won't be part of your half."

"Eli—" Dr. Hathaway narrows her eyes.

"Maybe …" I interrupt before fully swallowing. "You could take him to London together."

I focus on the now. How to get out of an uncomfortable situation now. Not later when the three of them are on their way to London and I'm at home, being Dorothy homebody and feeling like I had a hand in putting their family back together.

Nope. I favor the now.

Just stop arguing in front of Roman now.

"Oh my gosh ... we should, Eli. We should take him together!" Dr. Hathaway beams.

Eli ... not so much. A piece of lettuce hangs out of his mouth, mid chew.

Someone should high-five emoji me. Problem solved.

Eli finishes chewing his bite and shifts his attention to me. "You think I should go with Roman and Julie to London? Just the three of us?"

"Sure." I move my gaze to the cookie on my plate. It's half gone already. "You both seem to like it. And I hear they have great sandwiches there." I glance up.

Seriously?!

No one laughs. I perfectly timed that joke. How could they miss it?

Eli grunts and returns to eating his sandwich.

"You really wouldn't mind?" Dr. Hathaway asks me, with big eyes and a tiny grin.

"Why would I mind?"

"No reason." She shakes her head.

Roman steals the conversation with why he wants to be a honey badger, and that gobbles up the rest of lunchtime.

"Why don't you take Roman outside to play for a bit?" Eli asks Dr. Hathaway.

She looks at Eli and then at me as she finishes wiping Roman's face and hands. "Yeah. Sure."

"I can take him out to play for a bit. I have about thirty minutes before I have to head back."

"No." Eli pushes his plate away from the edge of the

table. "Julie will do it." If his face were an emoji at the moment, it wouldn't be a favorite of mine. I prefer happier emojis.

Dr. Hathaway and Roman go outside while I sit at the kitchen table under Eli's bad emoji gaze.

"I don't want to go to London with Julie and Roman. I want to go with *you* and Roman."

"Okay. But I don't care as much about seeing London as what Julie—Dr. Hathaway—does. And she's Roman's mom, so it makes sense that she should see London with him instead of me."

"Maybe that's the problem. Maybe I want you to care. I want you to care enough to not go on dates with Dr. Warren. I want you to care that my ex-wife has moved in with me for the next couple of months. I want you to care that I'm officially dependent on her for my basic needs. I want you to care that she pulls down my pants to get my cock out so I can take a piss!"

I curl my hair behind my ears. "I didn't know she did that for you."

"Well…" he coughed a laugh "…now you do. So do you care?"

"Yes."

"Well you have a terrible way of showing it."

"Different," I whisper.

"What?" he asks in a clipped tone.

"Nothing," I murmur while looking at my watch. "I uh … should go."

"Five minutes ago you said you had thirty minutes, but now you need to go?"

"I don't know why you're so angry. I'm sorry. What did I do?"

"Tell me what you said."

"About what?"

"I said you have a terrible way of showing that you care. And you said something after that. What did you say?"

"I said different. I have a different way of showing that I care. Not a terrible way. Just because I don't act like you or every other neurotypical person out there, doesn't mean that my actions are wrong or terrible. It just means they are different. Can I go now?"

"Dorothy ... I need to know where your head is on this. Where your heart is on this. Because I get this feeling that Julie is having regrets about us. Regrets about leaving me. And while at first I thought it was just shock from the accident, I'm not so sure anymore."

"Regrets? As in she wishes she wouldn't have divorced you?"

Eli shrugs. A few seconds later he nods.

"Okay."

"Okay? Really, that's your response?"

"Eli ... I ..." I close my eyes, but it doesn't stop the pain in my head. "I'm going to play the Aspie card here. I didn't know what that meant five years ago, but I get it now. It's when I feel like everyone is waiting for me to *get* or see something that's so obvious, but I don't see it. And it's not because I'm not smart. I know I'm a smart person. I have the grades to prove it. It's that I've missed a cue or failed to make an important connection, and everything after that point is ... well, pointless. So if you're 'beating around the bush,' then you need to stop. You need to be very specific and very direct."

He studies me under his scrutinizing gaze for several seconds. "Fine. Literally until the moment I stepped onto that elevator with you, I've wanted my life back. I've wanted Julie to wake up and realize what a terrible mistake she made. And maybe that makes me pathetic, but I don't care. I don't regret loving someone so deeply. I don't regret having a child with her. And I don't regret thinking that fifteen years of marriage and a child is worth fighting for until you know without a doubt that there's absolutely no hope."

"More direct." I glance at my watch.

He sighs. "I love you."

"I know."

"And I choose you."

"Okay."

He grimaces. "But if six months from now, you don't feel like I'm the one for you anymore, I'm going to look back and wonder if I blew my last chance to have my family together again."

"Is there a question? If so, you should ask it now."

"Am I it for you? Could you see yourself with me twenty ... thirty years from now?"

I laugh, shaking my head. "We've known each other for less than two months, and you're asking me about twenty-thirty years from now? I've changed professions three times in eight years, but after six ... seven weeks of knowing you, I'm supposed to make a twenty ... thirty-year projection?"

"No," he whispers, staring blankly at the middle of the table.

"That's a relief. I'm going back to school. I have a test this afternoon. And now I have a headache, so I'm going to go take something for it so I can focus on my exam."

"I'm sorry." His gaze lifts to meet mine. "Your headache is my fault."

"Probably." I shrug. "It's fine. Nothing a couple of ibuprofen won't handle. Need help back to the sofa? Or do you want Dr. Hathaway to help you?"

"I just need you to come here." He holds out his hand.

I rest my hand in his.

"Come here." He tugs my hand.

I unfold from my chair and take the two steps to stand next to his chair.

He releases my hand, reaches up to fist the top of my shirt, and pulls me to his mouth. It's a slow kiss, but I tell myself I can spare an extra minute or two for a slow kiss.

"Uh-hem …"

I pull away and rub my lips together while embarrassment crawls up my neck.

Dr. Hathaway stands in the doorway, holding a plant in one hand while covering Roman's eyes with her other hand. "Delivery. From one of your patients."

"Mommy, move your hand!" Roman pushes her away.

"So …" I work my way toward the nearest exit. "I have to go. Bye."

"Bye, Dorfee!" Roman is the only one to tell me goodbye.

Eli and Dr. Hathaway are too busy having a stare-off.

CHAPTER TWENTY-SIX

It's Still You

Elijah

"ROMAN, NAP TIME," Julie says while glaring at me. "I don't want a nap!"

"Then go have some quiet time with your toys in your room, otherwise ... it's nap time."

"I go to my room." He pouts, dragging his feet up the stairs.

She knows he'll go to his room and play if nap is the alternative.

"Really, Elijah? In front of our son?"

I wet my lips, still tasting Dorothy on them. "I thought you were outside."

"Well, we weren't. And if you're not ready to explain to Roman why you're kissing Dorothy, then I suggest you not kiss her if there's even a remote chance he could catch you."

Julie definitely wouldn't want to know that I went down on Dorothy in her bedroom while Roman played

Xbox within hearing distance of Dorothy's moans—things that wouldn't get me nominated for Father of the Year.

"Understood. Maybe this weekend you can take Roman to your house Friday and Saturday night, and I'll get someone else to stay with me."

"And by someone else, you mean Dorothy?"

"I mean my mom and dad can come over during the day."

"And at night?"

I shrug.

"You'd rather make out with your new girlfriend than have your son here?"

"Oh, Jules ... you do not want to go there with me."

"Go where?"

She is here.

At my house.

Helping me do things like take a piss and brush my teeth.

I could slay her with a brutal dose of reality. But I don't. For once, possibly the first time since she left me, I take the high road.

"Could you please help me to the sofa? I'm a little exhausted from ... everything."

"Yeah," she says. Her expression falls into one of resignation.

After she helps me get situated on the sofa, she checks on Roman.

"He fell asleep on the floor." She grins, coming down the stairs. "Like literally in the middle of his Legos. So I covered him with a blanket. I knew if I tried to move him into bed, he'd wake up." Julie picks up the dishes from lunch and brings me my medications with a glass of water.

"She calls you Boss Bitch."

Julie pauses for a second. After a few blinks, she hands me my pills. "Who?"

"Dorothy. I'm pretty sure it's a good thing."

"Mmm …" She nods. "Usually."

"You're smirking. You know it's good. You know it's a compliment."

"It's … a nice compliment. Yeah."

"She knows your stats. Listened to you give talks. She pretty much idolizes you as a doctor. How does that feel?"

"How does it feel to know your girlfriend looks up to me—at least professionally?" She sits on the sofa, angling her body to face me. "It feels good. And a little weird."

"Does it make it harder for you to dislike her?"

"I don't dislike her."

"You dislike her with me."

Julie presses her lips together and flips her long, red hair over her shoulder. "I didn't say that."

"You didn't have to say it. I can see it. Why? Is it Dorothy in particular, or would it matter who kissed me?"

"I don't know," she whispers, averting her gaze. "I don't know about anything anymore."

"What do you mean?"

"The definition of Hell: Having everything you *should* ever want and still wanting more." She runs her fingers through her hair, drawing in a shaky breath then blowing it out slowly as emotion turns red in her eyes. "I wasn't happy and I didn't know why." She quickly wipes away a tear. "We had a baby. A *baby*, Eli. And it wasn't enough. Wh…" she clears thick anguish from her throat "…what kind of person throws away *everything* because it's not enough? I actually had tests done—hormone tests, brain scans—I honestly thought something was physically wrong with me to feel so incredibly dissatisfied. So … angry."

Still, after all the pain and anger, I still break inside watching Julie grasp for that invisible thing that tortures her.

"Everything irritated me. I constantly felt on the verge of either starting a fight or having a complete breakdown. And you were the recipient of *all* of it. Even when you didn't realize it. For two years before we separated, I resented the way you combed your hair, the way you laughed, the childish voice you used when talking to Roman, the scent of your cologne, the rhythm of your words, that stupid pause you take before answering a question, like your mind is always on a two-second delay, the way you slurp your smoothies and stir your coffee, just … every damn thing about you drove me to the verge of insanity. And without one single shred of reason."

I think regaining my memories from falling into the ravine would hurt less than her words. And yet, I know she isn't saying them to hurt me. Still … they rip open old wounds, ones that can't be repaired by the expert hands of surgeons. I hold onto my words and mask my reaction.

"I hated myself. I just ... hated myself for hating you. I hated myself for wanting out. I felt like the worst mother, the worst wife and daughter, the worst friend ... I felt like the worst h-human." Her words fall apart. "And I just needed out, but I didn't know how to tell you that. You were perfect. And I wanted nothing to do with you. What does that say about me? There were times I actually hoped you'd cheat on me so I could have an out. But not Elijah ... nope. You would never do that. And even *that* irritated me. Who thinks that? What sane human being hopes their spouse will cheat on them?"

I don't know. Maybe that means I'm sane. But I refuse to make that wager. After all ... I've done some mildly insane things with Dorothy in the past few weeks.

"So I pulled the plug on our marriage. And I changed everything I hated about myself on the outside, but it didn't change how I felt on the inside. I signed up for classes like pole fitness, and I tried speed dating. Then I went through three different psychiatrists, tried healing touch and meditation. When that didn't work, I downloaded an app for hooking up and I fucked ten strangers in less than two weeks."

I flinch. Even with the rumors, it still knocks the air from my lungs hearing her confess *everything* to me. I much prefer the I-was-a-butterfly-you-were-my-cocoon analogy.

"Still ..." Her blank, glassy-eyed gaze remains affixed to the window or maybe the wall. I can't tell. "I didn't feel better. I just simply felt alone. But alone felt numbing. And that lack of feeling was better than hating myself. And then one day, I met Nick at a yoga class. I didn't care for the class, but I liked his smile and the way he looked at me when he didn't know I was watching him."

Julie chuckles. "So we started dating. The good kind of dating where you leave all your baggage behind. We didn't ask each other about our jobs or siblings. I didn't tell him about Roman or my failed marriage. He didn't tell me about his three daughters and his ex-wife who was diagnosed with cancer two months after he asked her for a divorce. You see, we lived in the moment. Moments filled with questions like, 'What do you think of that waitress's purple eyeshadow or where should we go for ice cream? Should we get a tattoo? Do you think anyone could hear us if we fucked in that bathroom?'"

"Christ, Jules ..." I close my eyes.

"I never smoked a joint or shot up or even got a prescription for an antidepressant. Yet, I felt high all the time with Nick. He gave me what I needed before I even knew myself what that was. And I gave him a life without questions or guilt. We didn't have to fit because we weren't trying to be anything more than a moment."

When I open my eyes, Julie blinks and the tears break free. This time, she makes no effort to stop them or bat them away.

"Sometimes we would meet for coffee and just sit in the back corner of a cafe and drink in complete silence until one or the other stood from our chair and walked out. That's messed up, right? Meeting up with someone just so you don't have to sit alone and drink coffee. But it was perfect—a time and place to just *be* without feeling alone. Without feeling the need to pollute the air with words."

"What happened, Jules?"

She pulls the sleeve of her long-sleeved T-shirt over her hand and uses it to wipe her cheeks. "Three weeks ago, we were sitting in our usual cafe, in our usual spot, drinking our usual drinks. He got up to leave first. But instead of brushing his fingertips along my arm, his unspoken 'goodbye, see you tomorrow,' he instead stopped just inches behind me so our backs were to each other. And he told me." She wipes more tears.

"Told you what?"

"*My ex-wife's name is Jennifer. She has her first chemo treatment today. My girls are Elisha, Kylee, and Becca. It's time for me to go home. Thank you for this. I will never forget it.*" She sniffles, shaking her head, eyes rolling to the ceiling. "He went from a beautiful mystery to an ugly reality. But I need reality. For the first time in three years, I'm ready for reality. It finally *fits*. The switch flipped. And everything that tore me apart before Nick, feels like the only thing that can put me back together. Like the poison is the cure. Like it's time for me to go home too. Only … mine is no longer waiting for me."

We sit in silence for many minutes as her confessions hang in the air with nowhere to go.

"You're my reality, Eli. You're my home. You. Me. And Roman. And I don't deserve you. I don't deserve a second chance. But I want one. And I have to…" she pulls in a shaky breath to steady her words "…I have to believe that our love that has spanned more than two decades and the creating of another life is greater than my months with Nick and your weeks with Dorothy. I have to believe that these other people came into our lives to bring us perspective and bring us back together."

I'm tired. My pain medication has kicked in and done its job. The part of my brain that processes mind-blowing confessions is out of commission. So I lean my head back, close my eyes, and succumb to sleep.

CHAPTER TWENTY-SEVEN

I'm Here for You

JULIE AND I don't speak of our conversation for the following two weeks. We fall into a routine of meals, laughter with Roman, television, patient updates from the hospital, and visits from family. The silver lining is my dad's willingness to help me bathe. He pretty much treats me like a vehicle. I feel thoroughly bruised from the high pressure setting he chooses on the bath hose nozzle. But ... I don't have to deal with the awkwardness of my mom or Julie bathing me.

Dorothy? Well, she won't answer my calls, but she offers short one and two-word texts in response to my texts.

> Me: **How was your day?**
> Dorothy: **Fine.**
> Me: **Can I see you soon?**
> Dorothy: **Not sure.**
> Me: **Are you okay?**

Dorothy: **Yeah.**

She offers enough emotional reassurance to make any desperate man jump off the side of a tall building. But I'm not that lucky, because I can't move my fucking body far enough on my own to even get to a tall ledge.

I feel like she's running from me, and I can't chase her. My injuries prevent me from physically going to her. And I fucking hate it. She won't talk, won't come see me, won't offer any reassurance that we're okay.

How ignorant of me to think we're okay. We're not okay. I grilled her about a stupid imaginary London getaway, and then I pressured her to tell me her plans thirty years into the future. Of course she ran. Any person in their right mind would run and never look back.

"If you don't stop frowning, that line on your forehead will only get deeper." Mom winks, glancing up from her knitting. She's keeping an eye on me while Julie and my dad take Roman to the park.

"My fall didn't take my life, but it feels like it ruined it. I can't work. I can't navigate. I can't bathe on my own. I can't …" I shake my head. Depression works its way into the fourth week of my healing process.

"Yesterday, since you haven't been bringing me Friday lunch," she smirks, "I walked over to the hospital and left a message for Dorothy. She messaged me back and agreed to have a cup of coffee with me on her break."

I'm shocked. And a little pissed off that she waited a full day to tell me this. But mostly I'm painfully envious that she saw Dorothy.

"How is she?"

"Better than you." Mom chuckles. "She's Dorothy. Focused on school and work. I think that's a good focus for her right now. Those are things she can control."

"What is that supposed to mean? She could come see me. God knows I've been trying to get her to commit to even a quick phone conversation."

"Maybe now is not the best time to talk with her."

"Whose side are you on?" My insides tighten, pulling at healing wounds, making new emotional cuts in my heart. I'm ready to crawl out of my skin. I need out of this cast, out of the house … I need out of my mind.

"Yours, dear. Always yours. Whose side are you on is the only question that matters."

"Side? How do you figure that I have a side to choose?"

"Because Julie talked with me."

Silence steps into the room, surrendering only to the hum of the furnace kicking on. Julie told my mom. Why did she do that when I gave her absolutely no response to her confession? Not a single word.

"You've wanted this since the day she left you. You've wanted her back."

"Ye—ah … I sure have. Even when I've hated her, I've still loved her."

"That speaks volumes." She sets her knitting to the side.

I fiddle with the drawstrings to my gray hoodie. "It really does. It proves that I'm an expert doormat. A crippled, lovesick man who refused to accept reality and move on."

"Well, yes, those would be your sisters' words. They'd try to disown you if you took Julie back."

I nod.

"I've hated the pain you've held on to by trying to hold on to her, but it's one of the most incredible qualities about you. Your love is so unconditional. Your wedding vows meant something to you. And the way you fought for your family broke my heart, but it also gave me unfathomable pride. It's easy to love someone when they love you back, when they want you, when they need you. It's not near as easy to have that same deep love when they seem to despise you or when they kick you out of their life."

"Do you think it's Dorothy? Is this jealousy Julie's feeling?"

"I don't think so. I think this was going to happen with or without Dorothy. I'm sure seeing you with Dorothy makes Julie feel anxious, like she needs to do something quickly before she loses you for good."

I lean my head back, rubbing my hand down my face on a grumble. "Oh man ... fuck my life."

"What can I do? What do you need from me? Your *mom*."

"I need to get out of here."

"Where do you want to go?"

✧ ✧ ✧

"YOU'RE NERVOUS." MOM shuts off the car.

I stare at the front door to Dorothy's house. "No. Maybe. Well, it's because she lives with her parents. If they're here, they'll answer the door. Then I have to explain myself to them. That part makes me a little nervous."

"For what it's worth, I'm out of my comfort zone here as well since I'm the mother dropping off her injured thirty-eight-year-old son with an overnight bag. *Hi, could you look after my boy? He needs help getting around, going to the bathroom, and cooking food. Here's my number. Call me if he's a burden.*"

I laugh. "Yes. This is crazy. Hopefully my patient transporter, EMT, nursing student girlfriend will show up and demonstrate her caregiving skills."

"Maybe I should stick around."

"That would be safe. But I don't want to be safe. I don't want her to feel like she has an easy out."

"Eli, you need to let her go or seriously hold on to her, but don't string her along." She rests her hand on mine.

"I know."

She helps me out of the car as best that she can and situates my crutches under my arms. Yes, I'm stubbornly using both crutches even with my ribs protesting. Physical therapy has helped.

It takes us forever to get to the door, three knocks before Kellie answers the door, and one huge breath of courage to deliver my speech.

"Oh my gosh, Eli! W-what an unexpected surprise. Dorothy didn't say you were coming. She's not even home from work yet. Come in. Do you need some help? Hi, Lori. So nice to see you again."

"It's so nice to see you too. Sorry for the unexpected disruption."

"It's no problem. Have a seat wherever you'll be most comfortable. Actually the most comfortable chair is in Dorothy's game room, but there's only one."

"Perfect." I work my way to the game room and her expensive reclining chair with all the bells and whistles.

"Oh ... okay. Can I get either of you something to drink while you wait?"

"I'm not staying." Mom wrinkles her nose while depositing my overnight bag just inside the door to the game room as I ease into the soft fabric, letting my crutches drop to the floor on either side of the chair.

"Oh." Kellie narrows her eyes at my bag before shifting her attention to my mom and then to me.

"Dorothy hasn't been able to make time to come see me, so I thought I'd surprise her. But since it's late, and I can't drive, I brought a bag. I'll figure out how to get home tomorrow. Hope this is okay." I smile.

Kellie grins as if my intentions are quite clear. She most likely knows enough about the previous weeks to know that Dorothy simply isn't ready to see me. "Sounds like the best idea I've heard in a long time."

Yeah, she knows.

"Great." Mom clasps her hands next to her chest. "Looks like you're good, Eli. So ... I'll head home."

"He's in good hands." Kellie winks at my mom and walks her to the door.

They murmur a few more things to each other, but I can't make out the words. After the door shuts, Kellie brings me some water and a bag of microwave popcorn.

"Dorothy really misses Roman." She hands me the popcorn and stands next to the chair, tightening the sash on her robe.

"He adores her. She's his superhero. I'm sure he would love to show her his Flash costume that my mom and Julie bought him for Halloween. He's going to have it worn out before he gets a chance to go out trick or treating in it."

Kellie laughs. "Oh Dorothy would love to see it."

"Kellie, I'm ... I'm sorry. I feel like I'm failing Dorothy at the moment because I'm injured and dealing with my ex-wife living with me again and my family always around helping me. I just ..."

"Dorothy thinks you belong with Dr. Hathaway." She blurts the words out so quickly, it takes me a few seconds to process them. "I want to believe that she'll tell you that to your face, but it might come out as a different version. However, those were the words she said to me. And it's not because she doesn't like you. She does ... so much so. But ... you need to know where her head is right now, and I fear she won't be able to adequately articulate her thoughts. You see, her grandfather cheated on her grandmother many years ago. Not just cheated, he fell in love with another woman. My brother was three at the time—Roman's age. I hadn't even been conceived. My father left his new love to go back to his family. My mother took him back. Had she not taken him back, I wouldn't be here, therefore Dorothy wouldn't be here. She knows the story. It's been retold to her many times."

After careful thought, I return an easy nod and a tiny smile. What can I say? Maybe nothing. Maybe the right words don't exist. "Thank you for telling me that."

She smiles. "Thank you for loving my daughter."

Outwardly, I keep a soft smile. Inside? It feels like a jagged piece of metal being shoved into my heart.

"Yell if you need anything. I'll be going to bed soon, but I'm a light sleeper. And Dorothy should be home soon too."

"Thank you."

CHAPTER TWENTY-EIGHT

Fuck the Truth

Dorothy

Y^{*ES!*} Barbecue jackfruit sandwich *and* apple pie leftovers in the fridge. It's enough to keep me from taking a walk. With it getting darker earlier, I find it less appealing to take walks on the nights I get home close to nine from the hospital.

After throwing the leftovers on a plate, grabbing a fork, and a glass of water, I make my way to my game room.

"What the fuck?" I flip on the light to the room, seeing a figure in my chair.

"Hello to you too." Eli pushes the button on the side of the chair, bringing it to an upright position. Then he shuts off the TV before I can register what he's watching.

"What are you doing here?"

He grins. "I'm here to see you. Is that apple pie?"

I glance at my plate. "Yes."

"I love apple pie."

"So?"

Eli chuckles. "So get your ass over here and share some with me."

"It's only one piece."

"Hence the word share."

My nose wrinkles.

"I won't go down on you until after we share the pie." He winks.

I squeeze my legs together.

"I'm joking. Do I look sexually active yet?" He gestures to his cast.

"How's Romeo?" I sit on the arm of the chair, with my plate on my lap.

"You mean The Flash? Because that's who he is now that he has his Halloween costume early." Eli brings up a photo of Romeo Flash on his phone.

"Oh my god, he's so adorable." I tap the prongs of the fork against my lower lip while grinning at the picture.

Eli sets his phone down on the other arm of the chair and exhales an audible breath. "Julie wants me back."

Ugh. My appetite begins to wane. Not because I wasn't expecting the conversation, I just thought he'd wait until I ate my sandwich and made him beg for pie. "She's smart. Even if it took her unusually long to come up with the right answer." I shrug. "All that matters is that she did."

"The right answer?" he asks.

"Duh. You and Roman. Choosing your family. Of

course it's the right answer."

"For whom?" Eli's eyes narrow.

"For Roman. And maybe for you and maybe for her too, but definitely the right choice for Roman."

"And what about Dorothy Mayhem?"

"What about me?" I take a bite of my sandwich.

"You said you thought you loved me too."

"So?" I mumble over cold barbecue jackfruit.

"And Roman likes you. A lot."

I swallow and nod. "True. But I'm not his mom. Dr. Hathaway is his mom. And she should get to see him every day. So should you. And now that she's back in the game, it's kind of a no-brainer."

"What if I choose you?"

"Then you're an idiot."

"Why?"

I hate his line of questioning. It's stupid and completely pointless. "Because you have the chance to be with Roman every single day. Nights too. All the weekends and holidays."

"But I want you."

I stand and slide the plate onto my entertainment console, making a loud *clank*. "You are a stupid fucking idiot!" I grab the back of my neck with both hands, digging my fingers into the muscle along my neck to ease the tension. "If I could choose Roman over you, I would in a heartbeat. Does that make you feel better? Does that ease your decision? He's three, and smart, and funny, and he says all the cute things. And that smile …"

I wipe my cheeks, narrowing my eyes at my hands, a

little confused and surprised to see tears. The sting of my eyes and the trickle down my cheek went unnoticed amid my anger. "That smile is *life*." I wipe my hands on my pants. "So why in the hell would you choose to live half a life when you can have it all?"

Eli pinches the bridge of his nose. "Why are you doing this to me?"

"Doing what?"

"Making me feel like a terrible person." He rubs his eyes and looks at me. They're red.

"I'm not," I whisper.

"You are. Because you're using my son as leverage to take yourself out of the equation. But this isn't an equation or a poll where everyone gets a vote. This is my goddamn life!"

I jump, hugging my arms to my chest. I've seen Eli slightly upset before, like when I agreed to go on a date with Warren or when I suggested Eli and Dr. Hathaway take Romeo to London. But those were nothing compared to Eli's clenched jaw and tear-filled eyes taking me hostage in my own home. I can't move. Not a single muscle.

He swallows hard, keeping his jaw locked and managing to blink several times without shedding those tears. "You've made me feel like a truly awful father. And I know that's not what you meant to do, but you have. The guilt, Dorothy … you're fucking killing me with guilt. You've turned loving you into a fault. An epic error in judgment. A choice …" He shakes his head and sniffles. "You weren't supposed to be a choice. Not you. Not

Roman. But you've laid it all out there. If I *choose* you, that means I'd have Roman part-time. But that makes me a 'stupid fucking idiot' in your eyes. So what's the point?"

What did I do wrong? How do I excel at always messing things up? I spend so much time planning my moves and my words. I journal them and bounce them off my parents. How did a move that felt so selfless turn me into a monster? The judgmental enemy.

"Just ..." I ease my head side to side, grimacing from the pounding inside of it. "Just tell me what you want me to say ... what you want me to do."

He hangs his head, closing his eyes.

I glance back at the door. Eli brought a bag, but who brought Eli? I look at my watch. It's almost ten o'clock.

What would a neurotypical person do?

I'm not sure. This exact scenario hasn't played out in the movies or my novels quite this way. I mean ... given his complete demeanor, I assume he might want to storm out, get in his car, and squeal his tires.

But he can't storm anywhere. I'm not sure he can even stand on his own.

No car.

My drive is gravel so no pavement for squealing tires.

That leaves me in uncharted territory with only one question.

What should I do?

Pie.

You can't go wrong with pie, especially apple pie. I slide the plate from the console and kneel on the floor between Eli's legs, giving the table his casted leg is on a tiny nudge. He opens his eyes, sharing a lifeless expression.

I think I put that on his face. Another example of my plans not at all going how I imagined they would go. So I fork up a bite of pie and hold it up to his mouth. After a few slow blinks, he takes the bite.

That brings a tiny smile to my face, even if he isn't finding a single shred of happiness.

Because of me.

I take the next bite. The following bite includes the largest chunk of apple, the best bite of the whole slice. Slowly, I move it toward his mouth, hoping he pays attention to my offering, a peace offering of sorts.

He takes the bite, but his emotionless gaze remains affixed to me. Such a waste. I might as well have taken the bite for myself.

My bite.

His bite.

Mine.

His.

Yep, I take the last bite of crust, the one that's a little crunchy but sweet with a thin sticky layer of apple filling clinging to it. Something tells me Eli wouldn't appreciate it as much as I do.

With the pie gone, things get awkward again.

Nothing to say.

Nothing to do.

Yet a crippled man remains in my game room with his overnight bag by the door. And I need a shower. And my meds. And I had planned on working a few things out in my journals. But that's all gone to Hell with the addition of Eli to my Saturday night. He's about to quickly find out I have no fucking clue how to be a hostess. I don't study things I never plan on doing, and inviting people to stay at my house is pretty high on my Unnecessary Skills To Learn List.

"Eli—"

"Shh ..." He eases his head side to side. Taking the plate from me, he sets it on the arm of the chair and leans forward enough to slide his hand behind my head and pull me forward. We meet in the middle, a breath from our lips touching. "Just tell me you still think you love me too. Nothing else. Just that."

I know it's a mistake to fall in love with Dr. Hawkins. I know he's bad news. Bad for my heart. Bad for my schedule. Bad for my train of thought.

But I do it anyway.

"I think I love you too ... still."

A barely detectable grin breaks through his pain-etched face just before he kisses me.

Well fuck.

This isn't part of the plan. I'm supposed to step away. Yes, out of the equation. But he does this thing where he cradles my head in his large hands and kisses me with his demanding lips. For a final goodbye kiss, it feels highly inappropriate. Too much tongue for goodbye. And then I moan. Cries, maybe even whimpers, seem more appropriate for a final kiss.

Not moans.

But I do it anyway.

"You can't choose me," I say as soon as the kiss ends.

Eli rubs his lips together and nods slowly. "I won't. I'll wait for you to choose me."

"What?" I rear my head back. "I already made my choice. I chose Roman having his parents back together. I chose Roman's dad not kissing me like he'd rip off my clothes if he could."

He grins. And if I wasn't so relieved to see him not looking at me like I took an axe to his heart, I would be upset that he's not taking things seriously.

"It wouldn't be in record breaking time, but don't fool yourself, Mayhem. I could rip your clothes off and locate your G-spot even with only half of my body working. If a resuscitated corpse can have an orgasm, imagine what I could do with two fully functional hands, my mouth, and a headful of dirty thoughts."

Well ... gulp ... damn!

"Can you do me a favor?" he asks.

I shrug. Blind promises aren't my thing.

"Can you let me recover? Can you give me a few meals with you, maybe a couple cups of coffee, maybe a playdate or two with Roman before you make your decision?"

"I told you—"

He kisses me again.

If I didn't love his mouth on mine so much, I'd be offended that he keeps cutting me off.

"I won't change my mind," I say as I pull away.

He kisses my nose and then my forehead. "Then it won't hurt to wait until I'm recovered. Besides, you can't dump me right before the holidays. That's just cruel."

I roll my eyes.

"I'll take that as a yes." He smiles.

"Whatever. Clearly you don't know how my brain works. But ... you'll find out." I climb to my feet.

Eli grabs my hand and kisses the inside of my wrist. "Clearly you don't know how my love works. But ... you'll find out."

"Where did you plan on sleeping when you showed up uninvited and unannounced?"

"Your bed. I let you sleep in mine. You owe me."

"My bed is smaller."

"Then you'll have to let me hold you so neither one of us falls out."

"If we zip in, that won't be an issue, but you put off a lot of body heat, so zipping in could get too hot."

"Zip in? What are you talking about?"

"I'll just show you." I pick up his crutches. "You can lean on me too. I'm a lot stronger than I look."

✧ ✧ ✧

Elijah

DOROTHY HELPS ME to her bedroom via the bathroom for a quick piss and teeth brushing. I didn't get a chance to inspect her room as much during my previous time there.

"It's not a twin bed."

"No." She unzips her bed. Not a sleeping bag. Actual decorative sheets and bedspread, all-in-one thing that goes on like a fitted sheet, but it all zips up. "It's for people who don't like to make their beds or lose their covers off the side in the middle of the night," she explains while helping me into bed.

"I'm overdressed for bed."

Dorothy twists her lips. "Did you bring pajamas?"

"Yes, they're called underwear, and I already have them on. I just need to remove my shirt and sweatpants."

"You mean me. You need me to remove them for you."

"Yes."

She eases my shirt over my head. "Did Dr. Hathaway do this for you at your house? Undress you?"

"Yes."

"Humpf."

"Did you just humpf my answer?"

"No." She slides my sweatpants down my legs, over my cast, and then pulls off my socks.

"Jealous that someone else has been undressing me?"

"No." She folds my clothes and sets them on top of my bag. "Do you need extra pillows for your leg?"

"An extra one for my leg would be great."

She positions a pillow under my leg and zips my side of the bed. Let me repeat ... *zips* my side of the bed.

"I'm going to shower, brush and floss, and take my pills. You good?"

"I'm *zipped* up in Dorothy Mayhem's bed. The only way I could be better is if you tied me to it and had your way with me—gently and with utmost caution for my injuries, of course."

Dorothy returns a blank expression. I think she gets

my humor, minus actually finding anything humorous about it. "So you're good. Okay. I'm going to shower."

By the time she makes it through her nighttime routine, I start to drift off to sleep.

"I can unzip just the bottom if you need air on your feet."

I blink open my heavy eyelids, bringing wet-hair Dorothy Mayhem and her oversized Taylor Swift *Reputation* T-shirt into focus. "To keep my feet from getting claustrophobic in your zipper bed?"

"To allow cool air to your feet to help regulate your body temperature." She unzips the bottom of the bed. "I can leave it like this or actually let your feet out like this." Peeling back the bottom covers, she exposes my feet. My good one and the one with just my toes sticking out from a blue cast. So many options and unexpected surprises with the zipper bed. Same goes for Dorothy Mayhem.

"However you sleep in here will be just fine with me."

"Oh." She shakes her head. "I don't actually sleep inside it. I sleep on top of it so it's always made up. If I get chilly, I grab a blanket. I just hate dealing with making beds."

I never let on to her just how much emotion I feel right now. She'd interpret it as me getting emotional over a zipper bed. It's not that. Well, it is that. It's everything. The twenty-year-old version of me might have found zipper beds a hard limit. I might have run away from a zipper-bed girl without looking back. I mean, she has a zipper bed. Just imagine what other oddities rule her life.

Right now, it crushes me to imagine the day might

come where nothing fantastical like Instagram emus, chicken-less soup from a can, and zipper beds won't be part of my life—that *she* won't be part of my life.

Because ... She. Chose. My. Son.

Dorothy put Roman above everyone else. And in doing so, she made me love her in a way that rips the air from my lungs, shackles my heart, and claims my soul.

"So you don't care?"

Quelling my aching emotions, I grin. "Just get in bed."

"Okay." She shrugs, flips off the light, and slips onto the zipper bed next to me, pinning me in since she's on top of the bedding and I'm zipped inside of it.

I have her exactly where I want her, and I can't really touch her. So I close my eyes and just find comfort in her proximity.

"I love you," I say after several minutes of her fidgeting, hoping it distracts her from the discomfort of sharing her bed with me, maybe calm her nerves a bit.

"Okay ..." she replies in a breathy voice.

"*Are* you okay?" I try to pull down the covers, but I'm zipped in tightly and her weight beside me thwarts my attempts.

"Yes ..." She swallows so hard I can hear it. And I can hear her shallow breaths, slowly quickening.

I turn my head toward her, squinting to see her face in the darkness. Jutting my chin to get as close as I can. Her face comes into enough focus that I can see her eyes close, her bottom lip trapped beneath her top teeth.

You have got to be kidding me!

"Are you…" I squint a bit more, nudging her body with my elbow to get her attention "…getting yourself off?"

"Yeah …" *Pant. Pant. Pant.* "No …" *Pant. Pant. Pant.* "Maybe … oh god …"

"This is not happening," I mumble.

"Fu … fuck, Eli!" She grabs my thigh, holding it for dear life as her pelvis lifts from the bed.

I realize she doesn't want me to read books on autism and generalize her into the typical stereotypes. But the part about some Aspies struggling to exhibit appropriate behavior in certain situations seems to fit Dorothy to a T. And I think I realized it the day she casually got naked in the back of her car at the pizza place.

It feels like weird timing. *If* I were going to masturbate in bed without including my partner, I think I would wait until they're asleep.

After her hold on me relaxes, along with the rest of her body, she releases a contented sigh.

"Why? Just … why?" I whisper, staring at the dark ceiling, praying that it won't take all night for my erection to die down.

"It helps me relax so I can get to sleep easier. I usually journal before bed, but I didn't figure you'd want the light on."

"Well…" I adjust my uncomfortable erection "…you thought wrong."

"Okay. Sorry." She rolls to her side, planting her ass against my hip. "I'll journal next time."

CHAPTER TWENTY-NINE

My Baby Girl

Dorothy

"OH ... CRAP ..." The alarm on my phone chimes. "Shit ..." I cringe, peeling myself from Eli's torso. How did this happen? He had surgery less than a month ago. And I'm on top of him!

Before I can completely ease off his body, he blinks his eyes open.

"I'm so sorry. Did I hurt you? I don't remember crawling onto your chest. It's not like me. I just—"

"It happened early on."

"Oh jeez." I wrinkle my nose, leaning over to shut off my alarm. "So I woke you up?"

"Yes." He grins on a small yawn, covering it with his fist.

"Did I hurt you?"

"No." He chuckles. "You're a featherweight."

"Did you get back to sleep easily?"

"No."

"Eli … I'm so sorry. I'm not used to sharing space. I've never shared my bed with someone else."

He runs his fingers through his dirty blond bedhead, leaving his arm resting behind his head, flexing his muscles.

God … he's so hot.

"I struggled to stay awake."

I shake my head. "You mean, fall asleep."

"No. I could sleep forever with you on me like that, much like I can with Roman. But I didn't want to go back to sleep. I wanted to smell your hair. Absorb the warmth of your body. Feel your heart close to mine." He offers a sad smile. "I wanted to make a memory that time can't erase."

I let his words swirl around in my head, finding a way to make sense of them, finding a place to keep them. But they don't fit in my mind, so I tuck them away in my heart because that's where they landed when he said them. "For the record…" I grab workout clothes from my closet "…loving you has been unexpectedly good."

"Good?" He chuckles.

"Perfectly adequate."

"Doesn't get any better than that." He pushes to sitting.

"Let me help."

"I'm good. Well, if you could unzip the bed, I'd be good. I just need to make my way to the bathroom."

I unzip his side of the bed. "How are you getting home? Don't you have brunch today?"

"Mom is bringing brunch to my house. My sisters

and their families are coming over too. This is really the day for you to skip work to come to brunch."

I help him get up and situated with his crutches. "Sounds like the perfect family gathering. Roman should be pretty excited. And Dr. Hathaway, I assume, will be there. So that's good … oh … was she at your house last night? I mean … how did you coming over here go over with her?"

"I don't know." His words are a bit strained as he takes his first few steps toward the bathroom with the crutches. "I didn't tell her I was coming here. It was a spontaneous, last minute decision. They were at the park. But my mom went back there after she dropped me off here, so Julie found out eventually."

"I bet she was pissed off. I hope not at me. I didn't invite you over last night."

Eli glances back over his shoulder. "If you didn't look up to Julie, at least on a professional level, would you still think I should be with her?"

"If you could love each other, then yes. For Roman … absolutely."

"Jesus …" he mumbles, continuing toward the bathroom.

"What?" I follow him around the corner.

"If you're not going to let me be with you, then stop making it so easy to love you." He pushes the door shut behind him.

I leave. He seems a little upset. I thought we were okay, but maybe we're not. When I get to work, Mom messages me to let me know that his dad picked him up.

I really should not have fallen in love with Dr. Hawkins. What was I thinking?

✧ ✧ ✧

Elijah

I NEED A shower.

Instead, I receive the Sunday brunch welcome wagon as soon as my dad helps me inside my house. I feel like an errant child who just got dragged home from a friend's house after breaking curfew. Except my mom took me to Dorothy's house, so I have no reason to feel guilty.

"Hey." I give my family a tight-lipped smile as I enter the family room filled with my sisters, their families, Mom, Roman playing with his older cousins, and Julie.

Julie … she shifts her gaze to the floor as soon as I look at her. She makes me feel guilty, which is insane. Julie has no right to make me feel guilty for anything. But this voice in my head (Dorothy's voice) keeps scolding me for pining after another woman when I have the opportunity to put my family back together.

For Roman. Anything for him.

Mom and my sisters have smirks on their faces, like I got away with something, and they're dying to know the details. The details? Ha! That's easy.

I poured my heart out to Dorothy and she rejected me.

The apple pie was good.

And from the way it sounded, her orgasm was too.

That pretty much sums up the previous evening.

"I'm starving," I say, instead of explaining my absence.

"Yes! Let's eat." Mom herds the gang into the kitchen until I'm left alone in the living room with Julie.

"How was the park?" I ask.

"He had fun. Wet the bed, probably from too much water. I already have it cleaned up."

"Thanks."

She nods.

"Are you going to avoid looking at me all day?"

She lifts her gaze, wearing a forced smile, a mask that does little to hide her anger or disappointment. I can't tell which one. "Good morning, Elijah."

Hurt. She's hurt.

Julie has no right to be angry. I know this, and I can tell by the somber expression on her face that she knows it too. But heartache is immune to reason. That, I know all too well.

"Good morning."

She clears her throat. "How is Dorothy?"

An instant smile comes to my face, in spite of the immediate pain. "She's good."

Julie presses her lips together and nods. "That's good." Her words carry no bitterness.

The women in my life have a knack for being their most amazing selves when I really need them to show me their dark side. Their anger. Their jealousy and selfishness.

"She thinks I should try to put my family back together—for Roman."

Julie's gaze snaps up to meet mine as her lips part. "Wh ..." She shakes her head like she can't believe what I said. "Well, what do *you* think?"

I glance over Julie's shoulder to my family gathered around the kitchen island, filling their plates with food, filling the room with laughter, and filling my heart with memories and reminders of the life I've wanted for so long.

"I think life is pretty fucking complicated."

She blinks several times and slides her hands into the front pockets of her faded jeans before tipping her chin toward her chest. "It is," she murmurs.

"It's painful to have everything you ever thought you wanted, yet feel like it's not quite right. Like something's missing." I ease onto the sofa, leaning the crutches against the arm of it.

Julie grunts a laugh, keeping her gaze pointed at her feet.

"*Of course* you know exactly how I feel. Except you haven't experienced it from the other side of the equation—the lonely side."

She glances up, eyes wide. "The lonely side? Oh, Elijah, you are so very wrong. There is no feeling of loneliness that's greater than feeling like nobody understands you. The desolate hell of needing something that makes no sense to the rest of the world. Of realizing that, if you find the courage to choose yourself, you will be alone. Free ... but so very alone."

"Am I supposed to feel sorry for you? Because I—"

"No," she interrupts with complete conviction in her

voice. "I want *you*, Eli. Not your pity. Not your sympathy. I just don't want you to think that the confusion, the depression, the feeling like I wanted to crawl out of my skin ... out of my life ... was some fantastic walk in the park for me. And I'm not blaming anyone but myself, but it wasn't easy. Do you know how many times I contemplated taking my own life? Do you?"

I flinch, choking on the lump in my throat that grows a little more with every word of her revelation.

Julie blinks back her tears. "Be..." emotion trips up her words "...because I couldn't figure out what was wrong with me. Why was I so unhappy with my life? Why did this perfect life feel like a goddamn burden? I felt so inadequate as a mother, a doctor, a wife, a person ... Do you know what it feels like to feel like a failure as a human being?"

My jaw clenches as my eyes burn with unshed tears.

"It's so ... fucking ... lonely," she whispers before sucking in a shaky breath and looking at the ceiling like her tears can defy gravity if she just keeps looking upward.

"You two going to eat with us—" Mom stops as her gaze ping-pongs between me and Julie. "You know, your dad turned the porch heaters on. We're all going to sit out there and eat. You both take your time." She rests her hand on Julie's shoulder for a breath before disappearing into the kitchen.

"You should see someone," I say with resignation. "My mom. Julie, you could talk to my mom. If you're depressed—"

"Don't." She brushes off my efforts to show concern.

"I've already seen someone. I'm already taking medications—mood stabilizers, antidepressants. And I hate it. I hate them and what they mean. I hate that something is wrong with me. But I'm taking them for Roman because he deserves to have a mom who is present and reliable. And I've been going to therapy. Granted, it's only been a month, but I'm doing the work."

I rub my forehead. Bipolar. She's bipolar, and I didn't see it. How did that happen? How the hell did I miss that? "Why didn't you tell me before now?"

"I didn't want you to feel responsible. Until I realized I did in fact want *you*. But I don't want you to come back to me out of some feeling of responsibility. It's not your problem. Not your responsibility."

"Jules, asking me to come back into your life makes it my problem, which makes it my responsibility too."

"*If* you come back."

I nod slowly. "*If* …"

Julie studies me for a few seconds. "Do you love her?"

"Yes," I whisper, because I do … I unapologetically love Dorothy Mayhem.

I wait for Julie's next question, readying myself for what will be my difficult answer.

Julie will ask me if I still love her.

And I will say yes.

In spite of everything—the blindsided abandonment, losing my marriage, losing time with Roman, the jagged words—I love Julie Hathaway. For over twenty years, I honestly felt I was put on Earth to love her. It's just that simple.

Or so I thought …

But Julie says nothing. And that's fine.

I don't need her to know at this point that I love her. Just like I don't need her to know that I spent the year after our divorce hating her to the bone, but somehow still loving her right down to my soul.

It's complicated.

"Can I bring you a plate of food?" She smiles. Not a great smile, more like her dog died, but he'd had a good life so all will be fine eventually.

I know that smile too well. It's the one I wore on my face for months after she left me. "Thank you. That would be great."

CHAPTER THIRTY

Dorothy

"DID I DO something wrong?" Warren follows me to the elevator from the cafeteria after my break. He grins as if he can do *no* wrong.

It's been six weeks since the fondue date from Hell.

Six weeks since Eli's accident.

And three weeks since I've seen Eli. Not that he hasn't made ample attempts at calling and texting me. He has. I've just been busy.

Busy with school.

Busy with work.

Busy biding my time until he heals. Then I will, once again, tell him to go back to Dr. Hathaway, and that messy lust and love chapter (and by chapter, I mean a dozen or more journals) can be stamped complete.

The End.

"Um, yeah," I answer, staring at the elevator doors while rolling my lips between my teeth and drumming my fingers on my arms hugged to my chest.

Go away. Go away. Go away.

"Well, are you going to tell me exactly what I did that has earned me the cold shoulder?"

What I did sounds singular. I have an entire journal of all the things I find "wrong" with Warren. Where am I supposed to begin?

"You took me on a fondue date."

He steps close, hovering just behind me. It makes me itchy. I have to be allergic to him. A hookup in the on-call room could put me into anaphylactic shock.

"You didn't like the fondue? Or you had *other* things in mind that didn't include dinner?" He lowers his voice with everything that comes after the word *other*.

I push open the door to the stairs, unable to wait another second for the elevator. Warren follows me.

Idiot.

"Dorothy, come on. Just tell me."

I hold my coffee in one hand and ball my other hand into a fist as my feet stomp up the stairs. "A fondue date is equivalent to unprotected sex with a stranger on a first date. It's gross and just asking for trouble. Yet, that's where you took me. And I only went out with you because the person I was having sex with at the time didn't want me to tell you, so I kept our date to keep from having to explain why I couldn't go on a date with you. And I have more ... just so much more I could say about your deep character flaws and questionable taste in everything from cologne to your brand of shoes. But this year I vowed to be more reticent with my negative opinions."

"Christ, Mayhem, you are one hell of a ballbuster. And who are you fucking that knows me?"

"No one. I'm not sexually active at the moment." I glance at my watch as it pops up with an activity notification, asking me if I'm doing a stair climbing workout.

"But who *were* you with when we went on our date?"

"Not saying."

Please shut up before I blurt it out because I can't keep secrets!

I pull open the door to the fifth floor. Warren stays on my ass, and I know he doesn't need anything on the fifth floor.

"But clearly you're no longer together. Right?"

"Yes. No. Ugh … he was in an accident, so things are complicated."

"An accident?"

"Go away, Warren." I double my speed down the hallway, but his legs are so much longer, it's useless.

"The only person I know who has been in an accident is Dr. Hawkins. But that's ridiculous so—"

"Why would that be ridiculous?" I whip around, glaring up at Warren as he holds his coffee out to the side instead of ramming it into my chest.

The cocky grin falls right off his genetically gifted face as his eyes widen, jaw unhinged. "No way. There's no way you and Hawkins were …" He shakes his head.

"Well …" I clear my throat and take a step backward, diverting my gaze to the nurse passing us on my left. "I didn't say it was him. I just asked why it would be so ridiculous."

Warren cocks his head to the side. My skin turns red as he studies me. I refuse to look at him, but I know he's visually interrogating me.

"Holy ... shit ... it's true. You and Hawkins."

"Nope." I shake my head. "At least ... not anymore." And *that* is my biggest fault. I absolutely cannot lie to save my life, or Eli's life, or a small village of starving children halfway around the world. And while I hate lies because I can never see past them, I envy those who can do it so well.

I turn and keep walking. Warren doesn't follow me. I think he can't move his legs after my unintended confession leaves him paralyzed with disbelief. Knowing he knows will drive me insane, so I have to confess to Eli that I let it slip.

Me: ***Dr. Warren knows we had sex. I told him we are not having sex now. Hope you're not mad.***

It takes him less than ten seconds to respond, probably because he has nothing better to do than sit on his butt all day.

Dr. Hawkins: ***Hi. Do I know you? I feel like you're someone I used to know and call and TEXT a lot with no reply. Hmm ... let me think.***

I roll my eyes just as he sends a second text.

Dr. Hawkins: ***Actually, I'm livid that we're not having sex now. Why is that?***

Squinting my eyes, I dissect his response to sort fact from fiction. He's joking. Right?

Me: *You're in a cast. You had surgery for internal bleeding. You're back with Dr. Hathaway.*

Dr. Hawkins: *I fucking miss you so much I can't breathe.*

I frown.

Me: *Okay. I have to work. Take care.*

✧ ✧ ✧

Elijah

"Why the long face?" Julie asks, glancing up from her spot on the floor next to Roman.

They're putting an elephant puzzle together on the coffee table next to the sofa. It's been a lazy Sunday afternoon of books and puzzles with football, hot chocolate, and cookies. Julie looks comfortable and completely at home. Her easy smile gives me a glimpse of what our life might have been had we not divorced.

"Sorry." I recover with an easy smile that mirrors hers. "I didn't mean to have a long face. I'm just a little tired."

"Then take a nap."

I shake my head. "Tired of living on the sofa. It's not fun. I miss running and working. I miss driving and chasing Roman."

"I'm sure, babe. But tomorrow is your day."

Babe.

Yes. Tomorrow I get my cast off. No more crutches. And then what?

"Look, Daddy!" Roman jumps up and down after fitting the last piece into the puzzle.

"That's amazing, buddy. Good job."

He jumps up on the sofa. Julie no longer stops him. She knows I've healed enough to handle his full body excitement. As Julie climbs up next to us, I give Roman a big kiss.

"Mommy help too! Give Mommy a kiss too!"

My smile fades a bit, but Julie's expression beams with hope. Why? Where was this hope when I wanted it? When I felt like I needed it more than anything?

"Kiss Mommy!" Roman slaps my cheeks, pushing them into fish lips.

"How about I give Mommy a high five."

I hold up my hand.

Julie laughs.

"No. Kiss her!"

"Okay, buddy. One kiss." Julie pulls him away from me.

What? No. Fuck no. Not one kiss.

She leans, grinning. "For Roman," she whispers before pressing her mouth to mine.

I don't move, and she doesn't really move her mouth much either, but she also doesn't pull away. It's more than a peck. It's as if she's waiting to see if I take the bait.

My head jerks to the side as Roman claps. "Yay! Kisses for Mommy!" He jumps off the sofa.

Julie looks at me, keeping her face right next to mine.

"Eli …" she whispers.

"Put him down for a nap."

"Eli—"

"Jesus, Jules … Just do it."

She nods slowly, rejection ghosting across her face.

As soon as they reach the top of the stairs, I grab my crutches, tie my right shoe onto one of them, and make my way outside, ordering a cab to pick me up down the street. If it doesn't show up by the time Roman goes to sleep, I don't want Julie seeing me waiting in the driveway.

Forty minutes later, I'm dropped off at the hospital, my hospital.

"Dr. Hawkins! Good to see you!" one of the ER nurses greets me.

"Thanks," I mumble, making my way to the elevator. When the doors close, I message Dr. Andrews, the pediatric oncologist.

> Me: **You working?**
>
> Dr. Andrews: **Hey! Leaving soon. You coming back to work soon?**
>
> Me: **I'm on my way up. I need a favor.**

Dr. Andrews went to school with Dr. Warren. He's single and works a ton of hours. And he'll do what I tell him, so I don't have to deal with colleagues of equal rank refusing to do me this little favor.

"Dang … still in the cast, huh?" Dr. Andrews greets me at the elevator.

I work my crutches toward the nearest vacant room. "Yeah, but not for long. I'm scheduled to have it removed tomorrow."

"That's great. So what's the favor?"

I ease onto the table. "I want you to remove it now."

He laughs. "But you just said it's coming off tomorrow. I'm not your doctor, and what's one more day?"

"One more day is my sanity. So either you can remove it, or I will remove it, but it's coming off now."

With little resistance, he grabs his tools and removes my cast. "You might still need crutches." I untie my right shoe from the crutch, slip it on, and loosely tie it. "Yup. Thanks. Bye." I hobble toward the elevator and take it down to my office.

Me: **Come to my office.**

Dorothy responds quickly.

Can't. Busy.

Me: **It's not a request. It's an order.**

Dorothy: **You're not my boss.**

Me: **Actually, I do have authority over you. So get your ass to my office!**

She returns the middle finger emoji.
So ... I wait. And while I wait, Julie messages me.

Just tell me you're okay.

I feel bad. In spite of everything she did to me, I still feel bad. Julie is bipolar. She's trying to put her life back together. And the fact that she wants me in it ... well, the timing is just terrible.

Me: ***I'm okay.***

And that's it. That's all she says to me. Once again, she's making it hard to find myself in this life. She's making it hard to hate her and easy to come back to our life. I'm just not sure if that's still my life.

Knock. Knock.

"Come in."

Dorothy opens the door. Pink scrubs, gray undershirt, gray Nikes, her hair pulled into a ponytail, and a scowl on her face. "You need to promise me right now that I won't get fired for being in your office instead of where I'm supposed to be."

"I promise." Well, I'm ninety-nine percent sure she won't get fired. I've been here long enough to have some pull.

Dorothy closes the door behind her and takes a seat, looking out the only window in my office, the one that has a great view of downtown Portland.

I lift both of my legs onto the desk so she can see that my cast is off. She makes a quick glance in the direction of my legs, then her gaze meets mine.

"You're better. Good to know. I choose Roman. Go back to your wife. Are we good? Am I dismissed now?"

"No. We're not good."

She blows out a long breath. "If my grandfather would have chosen his mistress over my grandmother, my mother wouldn't have been conceived. I wouldn't exist. My father wouldn't have found the woman he loves so much. I'm not a believer in fate, but I believe some things just make sense. You and Dr. Hathaway make sense. Giving Roman a home with both of his parents makes sense. We don't make sense."

"First…" I ease out of my chair, limping a bit to make it around the desk so I'm leaning back against it while standing in front of her "…we make sense. It's nothing that can be put into words. I just know we make sense because I *feel* it. Second, you're not my mistress. Julie divorced me. And you never would have been my mistress. I'm not that man."

"But she wants you back."

"And for a year after the papers were signed, she could have had me back. But then you walked into my life and changed that."

"I didn't."

"Dammit, Dorothy!" I slam my hands beside me on the desk, and she startles. "You get to decide if you love me, if you want to be with me. But it's not okay for you to make decisions for me and my life. But…" I lean forward, resting my hands on the arms of her chair "…if you love me, then *be with me.*"

Her forehead wrinkles as she clenches her teeth, emotion filling her eyes with unshed tears. I don't want to hurt her. I want to love her. I can't find my breath when I imagine her with anyone but me. It has to be me. She has to let *me* love her.

Drawing in a shaky breath, she brushes away a tear

before it meets her cheek. "You're going to remember me as the person who gave you back your life. That's how I want you to remember me. Years from now you're going to have a perfect life. A wife. Roman. Maybe even a little brother or sister for him. A dog. Possibly an emu of your own. Or an alpaca. And you'll smile thinking about this moment when patient transporter, Dorothy Mayhem, insisted you not give up what is most likely your last chance at taking back your life … the perfect life. Can you do that? Can you remember me like that?"

"Don't give up on me. Please …" I rest my forehead against hers and close my eyes.

Dorothy rests her hands on my cheeks. "I'm not. I'm your greatest warrior. I'm your Wonder Woman. I'm fighting for you when you're too stupid and blind to see what's right in front of you."

"No." I roll my forehead against hers. "You don't get it. *You're* the one who is too stupid to see it. You're the one who will remember *us,* and you'll see how *you* made the choice. Not me." I grab her face the same way she's holding mine. "Look at me."

Dorothy forces her watery eyes to meet my gaze.

"This is *your* choice. It's always been your choice. Because I made my choice the second I got into the backseat of your car."

More tears roll down her face. "I choose Roman," she whispers.

I press my lips to hers, holding her firmly to me, committing this feeling to memory. "He's not yours to choose," I whisper, releasing her and tearing my face from her grip.

She chokes on a sob as I grab my crutches and leave my office.

CHAPTER THIRTY-ONE

Dorothy

"WOW! REALLY, DOROTHY? Where have you been? I know you're an adult, but we've been—" Mom's hand covers her face when I look up, letting her see my swollen eyes from crying.

All. The. Tears.

I left the hospital at eight. Worked out for two hours. Then sat in my car outside the gym crying for two more hours.

"Dorothy…" Mom scuffs her slippered feet across the floor and pulls me into her arms.

I don't even cry. Everything feels numb, like all my feelings resided in my tears, and I have no more tears left—and no more feelings.

Not joy.

Not love.

Not anger.

Nothing.

"What happened?"

"He hates me."

"Who?" She pulls back, holding me at arm's length.

"Eli."

"No." Mom shakes her head.

I nod slowly, still feeling no emotion. No tears. No smiles. Just nothing.

"Why do you think that?"

"I chose Roman instead of us. How is that wrong?" I manage to furrow my brow because I still don't get it. I'll never get it.

"It's not wrong, baby girl. It's brave. It's honest. It's kind beyond words. And Eli can't understand because he loves you. And speaking as someone who loves you very much, I know he's hurting because the idea of living without you is pretty unbearable."

I turn toward my bedroom. "Goodnight."

"Dorothy ..." She follows me to my room.

"He said it was my decision. And I chose Roman. Then he said Roman wasn't my choice to make. And he blames me. But it should have been his choice. Julie and Roman or me and part-time Roman. But he kept trying to make the wrong choice. And I can't live like that. That's too much pressure to not screw up and make him regret choosing me. Too much pressure to be something good enough that he doesn't miss Roman when he's not with him ... when he only has me. And what if he doesn't have me someday? I could die. Or move. Or be spectacularly me like I've been with all of my relationships ... all of my *failed* relationships. Then what? Dr. Hathaway is not going to wait for him forever."

Mom gets a clean nightshirt out of my drawer and one of my favorite pair of practical, boring white panties. "Go shower. Get some sleep. Clarity will come with time. Forgiveness will come with time. So don't watch the clock. Do your thing. Live your life. Then one day you'll realize that this was nothing more than an experience to help you deal with something else down the road. Eli is extremely lucky to have had you in his life, even if it was only temporary."

I nod. Taking the shirt and panties from her. "I hope so."

✧ ✧ ✧

Elijah

"HI." JULIE SITS up, rubbing the sleep from her eyes. The blanket falls from her body and off the sofa onto the floor. She checks her phone on the coffee table. "One a.m. Are you okay? Her gaze lands on my leg as I limp into the room without my crutches, slipping off my hoodie.

"No. I'm not okay." I ease into the chair across from the sofa.

She retrieves the blanket from the floor and wraps it around her again, nestling into the corner of the sofa, red hair messy from sleeping. "Want to talk about it?"

"No." I stare blankly at her.

"How did you get home?"

"Cab." I scratch my forehead, pinching my dry eyes shut for a few seconds.

"I guess you don't need to get your cast removed tomorrow."

I shake my head.

She blows out a slow breath. "Have I lost you, Eli?"

How do I answer that? The answer should be glaringly obvious. Right? I mean ... she divorced me. How can you say you've lost something you willingly, even eagerly, gave away—released, let go?

"You made me feel like nothing. Less than nothing." I grunt a laugh. "I mean ... is that even possible? I think so. It wasn't that you just didn't want me, it's that you despised me. And I get it." I finally glance up at her, meeting her anguished expression. "You had ... you *have* something going on that's out of your control. But I didn't know that. And neither did you. And that nothingness radiated to every cell in my body, taking over my existence. And for so long I felt like only you could bring me back to life. I felt like I would never be me again without you."

I shake my head slowly. "God ... I felt like you were this force by which I lived my life. And when you left, it felt like the sun stopped shining. Like I didn't know how to exist in a world that didn't revolve around you. I let you be my everything. So when you left, I had nothing. Except Roman. And for so long I clung to him for the wrong reasons. He was you. The only piece of you I still had. A tiny sliver of my existence that you didn't ... that you couldn't take away."

"Eli ... I'm sorry."

"Don't be sorry. God ... don't apologize for being bipolar. That's fucked-up. It would be like my patients apologizing for having cancer. Apologizing for suffering. Apologizing for dying."

"What happened tonight, Eli?" she whispers.

My gaze affixes to the coffee table. "I lost Dorothy." Pushing out of the chair, I hobble to the stairs and climb them, slowly and awkwardly, but I do it by myself. After a long shower, I floss and brush my teeth, crawling into bed around two a.m.

Just as I start to drift off to sleep, the other side of the bed dips. Julie slides in next to me, wrapping her arms around me, her front to my back. I close my eyes again and fall asleep.

The next morning, I wake up a little after six to an empty space next to me. It takes me a few seconds to get my balance when I stand, pulling on a white T-shirt. As I navigate the stairs, the aroma of coffee greets me.

"Morning." Julie's already showered and dressed for work in a navy pencil skirt and light gray button-down shirt. Her hair is neatly pulled back into a ponytail.

"Morning." I take a seat at the table.

"So ... we need to make some decisions."

Decisions. I kind of hate all decisions at the moment. I don't even want to make a decision on what I'm going to wear today, let alone make any sort of life-changing decision. "What decisions?" I murmur.

She hands me a cup of coffee, brushing her lips along my cheek for a soft kiss. I don't think I want her kissing me. But I did want it for so long, the foreign feeling of not wanting it is messing with my head.

"Your mom is coming over today. So even if you decide to come into work, she'll be here with Roman. But we need to set a schedule. My mom is used to watching Roman every other week, so I don't know how she'll feel about watching him full-time. She's been used to having lunch with friends on her weeks off, or taking short trips with Dad. But what I'm really thinking is we should consider scaling back our schedules like we discussed doing right after Roman was born. Well …" She sits across from me. "I adjusted my schedule and you just made sure you didn't work more than forty hours a week. But what if we tried to each work four days a week. I could take Thursdays off. You could take off Fridays. If your mom is willing to watch Roman on Mondays, then my mom could do Tuesdays and Wednesdays, and he wouldn't have to go to daycare. Also my mom will still have days off to do other things, including her getaways with my dad. What do you think?"

What do I think? I take a sip of my coffee. Well, I think I miss Dorothy.

"I can't do this now." I bow my head, scratching the back of it while closing my eyes.

"Oh … well. Okay. We can discuss this later when you're not so groggy. Do you want to ride into work with me?"

I used to … I used to want her next to me in bed. I used to want her good morning kisses. I used to love commuting to work together, especially on the days that we couldn't keep our hands off each other—during the early years, right after we both got our jobs at the children's hospital.

The reckless behavior.

I used to drive seventy-five ... eighty miles per hour with Julie's head in my lap, her mouth on me. Sometimes I had to pull over behind an old building or along an empty trailhead because we just couldn't wait ... because we *needed* each other in every way possible.

The feeling of needing Julie has consumed my entire adult life.

"I don't know how long I'll be there today, since they're not expecting me until Wednesday. So I'll drive." I try so hard to sound normal. To sound okay. But I'm not okay.

Dorothy ... everything with her is okay.

Beautiful. Exhilarating. Heart-stopping. Soul-reaching. *Okay.*

"Okay. I'll check in on you. Maybe we can grab lunch if my schedule allows."

No. Julie isn't allowed to say okay. It's not her word. It loses all meaning coming from her lips.

"Maybe." I force a smile before taking a sip of my coffee.

"Oh, your mom is here." She sets her coffee cup in the sink. "Since you're driving, I'm going to take off. Kiss Roman for me."

I nod.

How is this happening? How is she standing in my kitchen, acting like we're a family, giving me exactly what I've wanted forever? How is it possible to feel so suffocated by my dreams?

"Good morning, Lori! Have a great day," Julie's

cheery voice grates along my nerves.

"Someone's in a good mood." Mom lifts an eyebrow in surprise after Julie shuts the door.

We haven't seen this Julie in a long time. It's great, right? I mean it should be *everything*. But it's not.

"Yup." I take another sip of my coffee, resting my elbows on the table.

"Your cast is off, yet your appointment to get it off is today. Want to talk about it?" She takes a seat next to me, setting a glass bottle of green juice on the table and her purse on the floor.

"Nope." I move my attention from her to the window, not really focusing on anything in particular. That's the problem. Nothing in my life feels in focus.

She rests her hand on mine. "What do you want, Eli?"

I grunt. "The impossible."

She returns a half-hearted laugh. "Well, I taught you to reach for the stars. I guess I should feel some pride in your predicament. Can you define the impossible?"

I rub a hand down my face and blow out a long breath. "I want Roman every day. I don't want to miss out on a single thing. And I want Dorothy. And I don't want to hate Julie. And I don't want her to hate me. And if I'm making a wish list, might as well add curing cancer to it."

"What's your plan B?"

Allowing a tiny smirk to grace my face, I give her side-eye. "That's what I'm trying to figure out since Dorothy removed herself from the equation."

"I'm sorry, Eli."

"Yeah, me too."

"So where does that leave you and Julie? She seemed pretty happy a few minutes ago."

"Yes. She crawled into my bed last night and wrapped her arms around me, releasing this content sigh like all is right again in the world. This was after I told her Dorothy left me. I just lay there wondering how my life got so messed up. And I feel like something is wrong with Julie for wanting to be with me when she knows I'm in love with Dorothy. But then …"

I laugh a crazy man's laugh. "But then it hits me. *I've* been the one for the past year, silently begging her to come back to me, love me, need me, raise Roman with me, while knowing all along that she didn't want me."

"Yes. It's ironic. And painful. And I wish I had a brilliant answer for you, but I don't. However, if Dorothy is truly out of the picture, then you need to decide where to go from here. You need that plan B."

CHAPTER THIRTY-TWO

Goodbye

"WELCOME BACK." DR. Warren glances up from the computer in my lab, giving me a faint smile.

"Thanks." I planned on arriving a little earlier, but Roman woke up and I decided to have breakfast with him and my mom.

Warren's gaze lands on my leg and my slight limp. "Sure you're ready to be back?"

"More than you can imagine," I murmur, swiping through a few charts and lab results on my tablet.

"Must have been hell, you know ... being nursed back to health by Dr. Hathaway *and* sleeping with Dorothy Mayhem."

I blow a laugh out my nose while glancing up from my tablet. "Alright, I suppose this is as good of time as any. Yes, I was involved with Dorothy. But I'm not now. And I apologize if you truly had real feelings for her that went beyond getting her under you in the on-call room."

Warren crosses his arms over his chest and nods once.

"What happened?"

"An apology. That's the most I owe you. I'm not telling you what happened between me and Dorothy."

He shrugs. "She'll tell me. I'm not sure she can keep a secret."

"Leave her alone."

Warren holds up his hands. "Whoa ... I'm leaving her alone." He glances over my shoulder and nods. "Speak of the devil."

I turn toward the window. Dorothy's talking to Willa. She grins at something Willa says. It makes me smile. I love seeing Dorothy happy. But her smile falters as her attention gets pulled toward something past Willa. Julie passes them, giving Dorothy a wide grin and a nod before she makes a quick left, coming into my lab.

"Doctors." She hasn't lost a bit of her early morning cheeriness. "Keisha Eldridge's biopsy came back. It's malignant melanoma." She shows me the results.

After looking over them, I hand them to Dr. Warren.

Julie smiles and runs her fingertips along my ear, messing with my hair. "You could use a trim, Eli."

My eyes find Dorothy. She drops her gaze, tucking her hair behind her ears as she brushes past Willa like she can't get out of here fast enough.

"Let's take Roman shopping next weekend for a new Halloween costume. He's already worn out his superhero costume. I knew he would. We should get costumes too. Remember we always talked about doing that?"

Warren glances up from Keisha's chart, raising a single eyebrow as Julie messes with the collar of my shirt. I used to love her messing with my hair and my clothes—anything to feel her touch. Where did it go? Why does her touch feel so wrong?

Dorothy Mayhem ruined me. Just completely ruined me.

But her words hold me accountable, like I owe it to her to give Roman the life she thinks he deserves. And he does deserve that life.

"Yeah." I pin the best damn smile on my face that I can muster. "He would love that."

"Perfect!" Julie lifts onto her toes and kisses the corner of my mouth.

I stiffen, feeling the full weight of Warren's scrutinizing gaze.

"Bye, Dr. Warren." Julie tosses him a grin before sashaying out of the lab.

"Don't say it."

"She's the mother of your kid. A successful doctor. Incredibly beautiful. What could I possibly say? Other than … it's obvious why you're no longer with Dorothy."

I take three painful steps toward him, grab his lab coat, and shove him into the wall. His eyes bulge from his head.

"Dorothy Mayhem is the fucking universe. She's what every other human could only hope to be. She's better than me, better than you, and better than Dr. Hathaway—added all together and multiplied times infinity. And even then … we don't come close to Dorothy Mayhem. So if I ever hear you say her name again, it better be in complete respect and reverence. Do I make myself clear?"

Warren blinks slowly before nodding. I release him, go tell Keisha Eldridge's parents that their daughter has a deadly cancer that's very rare in children. Then I layout her treatment options and give them very promising survival statistics while praying with them to a god that may or may not exist.

Dorothy was right … my problems are small even if in my heart they feel incredibly large and unbearable.

✧ ✧ ✧

THE NEXT TWO weeks turn into a blur as I acclimate back into working full days. I still go to physical therapy. But I'm back to walking normally. Warren and I make silent amends, focusing more on work and less on personal life.

Julie and her things continue to infiltrate my house, like she's moving in without actually announcing it or renting a big van to do it all at once. And I'm letting it happen because I don't know how to stop it or if I should stop it.

I hope one day soon I'll just wake up and everything will click. Julie will be the love of my life again. Roman will frolic around in bliss because he's back in a full-time, stable home with two parents tucking him in every night. My sisters will stop scowling at me during Sunday brunch because they'll accept my reasons for allowing Julie back into my life … my home … my bed.

And Dorothy …

Well, I have to believe that one day I will thank her.

One day I will stop missing her. One day it won't hurt to pass her in the hallway at the hospital. But that day feels unreachable right now.

After lunch with my mom, I grab a coffee to cut through the chill in the fall air and wait for the elevator to take me up to my lab.

"Shit!"

I glance over my shoulder just as Dorothy rounds the corner, holding out her hot coffee that she's dribbled down the front of her shirt. Before I can say anything, she glances up. From the size of her eyes, it's obvious she wasn't expecting to see me when she turned the corner.

"Hi." My smile reaches a new high, one it hasn't seen in weeks.

It feels good and awful. Refreshing and heartbreaking.

"Gulp."

I chuckle. That feels pretty damn good too. It just happens. I'm not doing it to play the part. I'm not doing it for her. It's for me.

The smile.

The laugh.

The warm sensation of contentment.

It's for me.

And it's fucking incredible, even if this moment passes in a blink. For now, I'm just going to keep my eyes open.

"Did you actually just say gulp?"

"Well..." she wipes her hand down the front of her scrub top, making the dripped coffee spread into bigger spots "...I uh, thought it first. Then it just came out."

"You might need a new top."

Keeping her chin tipped toward her chest, she continues to mess with the spots. "I don't have a matching top. Not one that will work with my undershirt and shoes."

More laughter fills my chest as my grin threatens to crack my entire face. "Sometimes you have to make the alternative work, even if it feels all wrong."

"Easier said than done." She looks up.

My words that were spoken with no great meaning, take on a life of their own. Sucking all the oxygen from the space around us. Echoing a very grim reality. Erasing my smile and silencing my laughter.

The elevator doors open. I step aside and let her go first. She pushes the button to the fourth floor. The same floor as my lab.

The doors close.

I move behind her to hide everything that's etched into my face.

I miss you.

I love you.

I'm living with the alternative for Roman ... and for you.

"How are you?" I whisper.

She doesn't have to say it this time. I hear her gulp. "Fine," she squeaks like it barely makes it past her throat.

Fine.

I don't like *fine* Dorothy. *Fine* Dorothy breaks my heart because I know her "okay" is spectacular, but fine feels along the lines of barely breathing. Does she know how incredibly fucking fine I am right now too?

The doors open.

She bolts out.

And I would let her go. I really would, but she lifts her hand and wipes her face as her feet move as fast as they can away from me.

I take one more sip of my coffee, toss it in the trash, and follow Dorothy, doubling her pace to catch up to her.

"Don't! What are you doing?" She tries to move past me when I get ahead of her and turn to stop her. I want to grab her. Shake some sense ... shake some more emotion out of her. But I don't physically touch her.

"A word."

She shakes her head.

"I'm not asking."

She bites her upper lip, but it doesn't keep her bottom lip from quivering or prevent the redness building in her eyes. I jerk my head toward the on-call room, and she leads the way, again wiping her eyes with her back to me.

A groggy resident lifts his head when I open the door to the otherwise vacant room.

"Out," I snap, holding the door open.

"But I just—"

"Out!" I blow out an exasperated breath, not feeling patient enough to explain my demand with more than one word, and definitely not patient enough to listen to his reasons for not getting out right this minute.

Dorothy turns like she's decided to flee as the resident slips on his shoes and slides past us with a grumble. But I step in her way again, taking several steps to force her backward as I close and lock the door.

She opens her mouth to protest again, I grab her face, lowering mine to her eye level.

More tears fill her eyes.

"I *need* you to be okay. I need it like oxygen."

"Eli …" she whispers, making a solid effort to keep those tears from leaking down her face.

"Tell me you're okay, Dorothy. Tell me you're okay, and I'll let you walk out of here right now."

"I'm fine."

"Not the same." I grimace, feeling her pain as if it were my own … *because* it is my own.

"I'm fine." She blinks, losing the battle with her emotions.

"Yeah…" I whisper, resting my forehead on hers for a few seconds before ghosting my lips along her tearstained cheek "…I'm fine too."

My pulse pounds so hard it's deafening. When our mouths lock, reality ceases to exist. I'm just so tired of doing the right thing when it feels so wrong.

When she unties my scrub pants, I let go.

I let go of reason.

I let go of worry.

I let go of everything that's not in this room … in this moment.

We tear apart long enough to discard our tops. Then our mouths collide again while my hands work the hook to her bra. Dorothy doesn't even try to speak. This is how I know she's *fine.* Because "okay" Dorothy would have lots to say. She would invite her conscience to come between us. Okay Dorothy would warn me that she's not wearing the right bra or underwear to do this.

I miss *okay* Dorothy. But the part of my soul that's been starving without her feels some gratitude for her pain because she's giving me this. She's feeding my soul, bringing me back to life.

Her hands slide into my hair, deepening our kiss, moaning into my mouth, pushing me back toward a single bed. We kick off our shoes. My hands cup her breasts.

"Eli …" She tips her head back, eyes closed, as I add her bra to the pile of clothes at our feet.

I slide her scrub bottoms and panties off in one smooth motion as my mouth covers one of her breasts. I can't get enough of her. My hands and lips move along her skin, desperate to consume every inch of her.

We fall onto the bed, both of us working together to get my bottoms and briefs off. With them still clinging to my right ankle, I settle between her legs, guiding her left knee toward her chest, and push inside of her. Our mouths crash together again.

Hungry.

Desperate.

The perfect union of all that we've held back.

The legs of the old metal-frame bed scrape along the floor as the springs whine beneath the thin mattress. Dorothy's fingers curl into my backside while I drive into her. I don't want it to end, but the *need* spurs me on. *She* spurs me on with her tongue mimicking our rhythm and her back arching off the bed, letting me know she's close.

I need. I need. I need.

I love this woman. She makes me crazy. All of my senses culminate in her presence. I am the best version of myself with her. I just … love this woman.

"Jesus …" she pants, closing her eyes as her head eases to the side and one of her heels digs into the back of my leg.

I press her other leg an inch closer to her chest, like my entire being wants to crawl inside of her … possess her.

Keep her forever.

My neck stretches back, face twisting as I release.

My mind and my heart instantly prepare for her to push me away, pull on her clothes in under thirty seconds, and run out on a wave of regret because the only thing that comes close to the size of Dorothy's heart is her conscience.

But … she does what she's always done best. Shocks the hell out of me.

Her eyes flutter open, lips curl into a perfect smile, and she cups the back of my head like I've done to her so many times. Then she pulls me back down to her for a slow kiss.

Our kiss ends when something on the floor makes a vibrating sound. It's one of our phones.

"Eventually," she whispers, brushing the pad of her thumb along my eyebrow.

I squint.

Her lips form a faint smile. "Eventually I'll be *okay*. And so will you."

A goodbye.

This is goodbye. A redo because the one in my office was horrible. But nonetheless, it's goodbye. I don't know if saying goodbye to Dorothy Mayhem can ever be anything but horrible.

I nod because all words remain congested in my throat.

CHAPTER THIRTY-THREE

The Man in the Yellow Hat

SEX ISN'T CLOSURE. It's not a goodbye. And it doesn't satisfy the heart. It's a false moment of hope where the body gets its way while the mind turns a blind eye to reality.

My reality?

I have a family.

Tonight I'm dressed as The Man in the Yellow Hat. Julie is a banana, and Roman is Curious George. Roman wanted us to be superheroes, but Julie fell in love with the monkey theme. I really think she was just pissed off that Roman insisted we be superheroes "like Dorfee."

Julie gives Roman a real banana as a snack before we head out and fill his belly with candy. I snap a quick picture of our little monkey eating the banana and send it to Dorothy because I know she'll love it.

Me: ***Not a superhero, but still pretty dang cute!***

It's the first contact I've made with her since the on-call room weeks ago, other than the occasional quick passing glance at the hospital. I'm not even sure why it's such a knee-jerk reaction to take the photo and send it to her. But ... it is.

"Your family is on their way over here. Who are you sending that to?" Julie rolls her eyes, peeking around me to see my phone.

"Jesus, Elijah ..." she whispers before I can get out of my message screen that has Dorothy's name at the top.

I turn toward her, but she's already halfway up the stairs.

"Hello? Where's George?" Mom calls, opening the front door.

My parents and sisters make their way into the living room, snapping lots of their own pictures of Roman and then of me.

"These are the best costumes!" My mom beams. "Where's Julie?"

"Bedroom." I gesture toward the stairs. "I'll go see if she's ready."

I take slow steps down the hallway to my bedroom. Our bedroom? Fuck, I have no idea. I close the door and slither my guilty ass to the doorway of the bathroom.

Julie glances up in the mirror, eyes wet, lips trapped between her teeth.

"I'm sorry." How unoriginal. Even with sincerity in my voice, the words sound empty.

"What are we doing, Eli?" Our gazes meet in the mirror. "Because I'm here, going through the motions, trying to put our family back together. And I thought that's what you wanted too."

"It is." I drop my chin, feeling too much guilt to even look at her any longer.

"What did I misread? Misunderstand? Because I thought you and Dorothy were over? I've been making meals and doing the laundry. We sleep in the same bed, but you never touch me. And I thought it was because of your injuries and maybe Dorothy too … I thought maybe you just needed time to let go. But messaging her pictures of Roman is not letting go."

I force my gaze back to her. And she doesn't look mad, she looks hurt.

She stares at her feet. "I get it. I ruined us. I've never expected anything from you. I bore the burden. But you begged me to give us another try. So I thought this was what you wanted. And since I've been taking my meds and doing the counseling, I've realized it's what I want too. But I can't do this if you're not all in. If you need more time, I'll give it to you. Just ask me. If you don't want this anymore, then just tell me. But please, I beg you … don't hold me at arm's length, making me look like a fool because you can't decide what it is you want."

I take off my yellow hat and run my hand through my hair on a deep sigh.

What I want.

I want the impossible.

"Daddy! Let's go!" Roman tears through the bedroom, ramming into my leg, thankfully my good leg.

Julie turns her head and blots her face.

"Okay, George. Let's go." I step out of the doorway.

Roman takes my hand and tugs on it as I try to lead him out of the bedroom. "Come on, Mommy." He holds out his other hand to her, and she takes it.

As the three of us stand here holding hands, Julie and I look up at each other.

"I want this," I whisper to her.

She gives me a quivering smile and nods. "Me too."

✧ ✧ ✧

WE TAKE OUR little boy trick or treating. I watch him giggle, and it makes me smile.

A real smile.

Julie plays chase with him between houses, as if our little monkey is going to gobble her up, and it makes me smile.

A real smile.

When we arrive home, we give him a bath, and more smiles and giggles ensue. And I think ... maybe I can do this. Maybe I can find my way back to this life. Maybe Dorothy is right.

"He's asleep." Julie sighs with a fantastic smile on her face as she shuffles into the bedroom, tossing her banana costume on the floor, leaving her in a black tee and yellow leggings.

I rub a towel through my wet hair, freshly showered. Julie's gaze slides along my bare chest to my jogging shorts. I hate that there's a part of me that feels like she has no right to look at me this way.

In or out, Eli. Make a decision.

For Dorothy, the day in the on-call room might have felt like the true severing of ties. But for me, it's this moment. It's this decision to take back my life, to give my little boy everything.

Julie takes away the space between us one slow step at a time. I've waited for so long to see this look in her eyes again, to feel wanted, to feel the undeniable pull that brought us together twenty-two years ago.

But still … I think of Dorothy. Maybe I'll always think of Dorothy. She will just have to be a scar, a permanent mark on my heart because I let her inside of me. And letting her go has been brutal and not without damage.

Julie rests her hands on my bare chest and presses her lips to my sternum. I close my eyes and slide my hand into her long, red hair. It's not as soft as Dorothy's hair. But the shiver it elicits in Julie is familiar. So that's what I cling to—the familiar.

She feathers kisses up to my neck. My grip on her hair tightens like the suffocating pressure in my chest. Her lips pause at the angle of my jaw, and she waits for me to look at her.

I do.

But just as quickly, I close my eyes and kiss her so she doesn't see the pain and regret in my eyes. I have to believe someday it won't be there.

Someday I will be *okay*.

Julie doesn't smell like coconuts. But that's fine.

Fine …

She smells like roses. I used to love the smell of roses.

I drop the towel in my other hand and grip her hip, inching my hand up to her breast. It's not familiar. It's larger than it was when I last touched her like this. And much larger than Dorothy's breasts, which I miss.

Julie's fingers trace my erection along the outside of my shorts. I'm clearly turned on, and that's good for us. I just really don't know if it's Julie or memories of Dorothy.

It doesn't matter.

This is my life now. I will embrace it.

I will love it.

Blocking all other comparisons from ruining this moment, I walk us to the bed. We don't rush anything, like there's a need to get reacquainted, a need to let our bodies find their old rhythm. Our arms and legs tangle together on the bed as we continue this slow kiss. I remove her shirt and bra.

Julie sucks in a deep breath and holds it, eyes filled with apprehension and regret as I stare at her new body. She doesn't say it, but I know she's feeling a certain amount of shame for not loving herself the way I always loved her. For thinking something about her was less than perfect. But perfection changes and so does how we view ourselves. And that's ... *okay*.

Just as I get ready to say something comforting, we turn our heads toward the door and the sleepy-eyed boy with vomit down the front of his jammies.

"Oh, buddy!" I climb off the bed as Julie quickly covers her chest.

"My tummy ..."

"Yeah, let's get you cleaned up," I say.

He cries a little then heaves, but I don't get out of his way quick enough to keep the vomit from landing on me. Without giving a second thought to what was about to happen before Roman got sick, we clean up the mess and tuck him into bed between us with a big bowl for any more messes.

CHAPTER THIRTY-FOUR

Oops ...

Dorothy

"WHAT ARE YOU doing?"

"Jesus!" I jump at the sound of Dr. Warren's voice. "Don't scare me like that."

He tosses his lunch wrappers in the garbage. "I ate my lunch, watching you pace a six-foot strip for the past fifteen minutes. What's up?"

"Nothing is up." I force myself to stand still, shoving my hands into the pockets of my scrub top.

Fifteen minutes. Fuck ... my break is up.

No. This is a good thing. I need to work. Work is good. I should think about work.

"Haven't seen you lurking around the lab as much. Does this have anything to do with the reconciled Hawkins-Hathaway duo?" Warren tips his chin up, eyeing me with suspicion.

"Oh. So the rumors are true? They're back together?"

He lifts an eyebrow. "Yeah ..." he says slowly.

"Good. That's great. Just as it should be."

Then the breakup and subsequent thirty-two journals used to sort out my thoughts weren't all for nothing. It's a silver lining. Silver linings are good.

Roman has his parents back together. *That* is all that matters to me.

Sort of ...

"How many cups of coffee have you had today, Mayhem?"

"One. Why?" I stop myself from pacing again. When did I even start pacing again?

He chuckles, pressing the button to the elevator. "No reason."

"He's happy. Right?"

Dr. Warren pauses, holding open the elevator doors. "Sure. I mean. They've all had gastrointestinal issues or food poisoning, vomiting-diarrhea shit stuff going on over the past three weeks. But I think everyone has recovered."

"That's good. Just in time for the holidays!"

He laughs again before stepping onto the elevator. "Sure."

"Wait!"

The doors close before I can stop them. I need to get back to work. My shaky finger pushes the button.

"Hi."

I look over my shoulder. "Hi." I practically choke on that one word as Dr. Hathaway gives me a polite smile.

The elevator doors open again, and I rush onto it, which is stupid since she's getting on as well. It's not like I can really run from her.

She presses the button to the sixth floor. Fantastic. That's where I'm going as well.

"How have you been?" she asks, and it feels real and kind. Not like she found out I had sex with Eli in the on-call room five weeks ago.

Not that I'm counting.

"Fine. I heard you've all been sick. Sorry. Hope it's all good now."

"Yeah." She shakes her head with a bit of relief. "That wasn't a lot of fun."

"I'm sure not." I reach into my pocket as my phone vibrates. When I pull it out, the other things in my pocket come out as well, dropping to the floor. "Crap." I bend down at the same time Julie does.

My hand goes for the wad of tissue (because I don't want her to touch my dirty tissues). She grabs a folded up ten-dollar bill and the one thing I really should have snatched up before her—but I didn't.

We stand at the same time, both of our gazes affixed to the pregnancy test in her hand. *My* pregnancy test. The one I took in the cafeteria bathroom twenty-five minutes ago.

The doors open and she slips the test into the pocket of her lab coat. Like ... what the fuck? That's my test!

"A word, Dorothy." She steps off the elevator, shoulders back, chin up like the boss bitch she is, making a straight line to her office with *my* pregnancy test.

What is it with the Hawkins-Hathaway duo and their constant need to have *a word* with me?

I was never sent to the principal's office in school. So

this is new for me. And it sucks because I'm not prepared for this. If she can give me a day, I'll be ready. Something tells me she's not likely going to grant my request.

"Close the door please."

I close the door.

She stands behind her desk, as any authoritative boss bitch would do, and pulls the test out of the pocket of her lab coat. After wordlessly staring at it for an eternity, she lifts her gaze to mine. "Please tell me you have a boyfriend."

I shake my head.

Her brow wrinkles as she returns her attention to the pregnancy test.

"When is the last time you spoke with Elijah?"

"Um ... on Halloween he sent me a photo of Roman, but I didn't respond. But not because I didn't think it was a cute picture. Roman is the most adorable little boy I've ever seen."

Dr. Hathaway grunts a laugh and nods several times. "And when is the last time you had sex with Elijah?"

It's not her business. I mean ... I don't think it's her business. I honestly don't know whose business is whose right now.

"Five weeks ago," I say because I can't lie to her.

Her head resumes its slow nod. She would have been a good principal or maybe even a prosecutor.

"What are your plans?" She pins me with a neutral look that makes me squirm.

"I peed on that stick less than thirty minutes ago. I don't have a plan yet."

"Are you planning on keeping it? Are you planning on telling him?"

"I …" I shake my head. "Of course I'm keeping it."

She cringes. "I didn't mean to imply that you shouldn't. I simply respect a woman's right to choose."

If only she respected my right to *my* pregnancy test.

"I'm sorry."

"For what?" Her head cants to the side.

Damn she's good. Solid. Unyielding. Formidable in her own way.

"Did you rape Elijah?"

"What?" My head jerks backward. "No!"

"Then why would you apologize for having consensual sex with him?"

"Because I gave him back to you so Roman can have a home with two parents who get to see him every day because that's the dream. And Roman is too young to live anything short of a dream if it's even a remote possibility."

I sigh, hoping my heart will settle down, hoping she'll let me leave so I can deal with this in some way that doesn't involve her giving me the third degree, demanding I make life-changing decisions right this second.

"You're right. Roman does deserve that. And I love Eli. And there's nothing I want more than this second chance with him."

I work my teeth into my bottom lip so hard I can taste blood. "I'm not taking him away from you, but I have to tell him. You know this, right? And we'll figure something out. But I'm not ready to tell him yet. If you want me to let you know when I'm ready to tell him, I can do that."

She turns her back on me and drops her head, cupping a hand on the back of her neck. "You can go now."

I don't need to be told twice.

✧ ✧ ✧

Elijah

"I NEED TO go." I unfold from the chair as my mom stands and makes her usual Friday trip around her desk to give me a hug and kiss.

"Thanks for lunch. We'll pick Roman up around five. I'm proud of you for giving Julie another chance. You are a kind man and an incredible father. So just enjoy your weekend alone with Julie. You both need this, especially after a solid three weeks of someone being sick in your house. Everyone will be well-rested and in a good mood for Thanksgiving next week."

I nod. "Yeah. Okay, then I'll see you later."

I head back to work. If I didn't know better, I'd say the universe is conspiring to keep me from having sex with Julie. And while I *still* can't get Dorothy out of my mind, I need to make an effort to move forward and show Julie my intentions are real.

So now that everyone is finally well, I'm sending Roman to spend the weekend with my parents while I work on my relationship with Julie—while I reconnect with her.

God … I hope it falls into place. I hope all the old

feelings come rushing back because I can't live a life with her if every damn day my heart beats for another woman.

I get home a few minutes before five, a little surprised that my mom and dad aren't here yet. "Hey." I smile at Julie when I walk into the kitchen.

"Hey." She returns my smile, but it's not quite as big as mine.

"Rough day?" I ask, looking over my shoulder as I wash my hands.

She sips a glass of red wine and shrugs. "You could say that."

My gaze makes a quick sweep of her body covered by the same clothes she wore to work—fitted black pants and a soft pink blouse showing a bit of cleavage. Her hair is down. And her lips are covered in red.

"You look like a million bucks." I mean it, and I feel a sense of accomplishment for saying it without tripping over any guilt.

"Thank you." Julie stares at her wine glass, swirling it a bit while I pour myself a glass of it. "I love you, Elijah." She keeps her chin tipped to her chest.

"I know." I lean against the counter next to her, brushing a strand of hair away from her eye, coaxing her to look at me again. Over the past few weeks, while muddling through a mess of sickness, I felt every breath of her love. The way she cared for me and Roman when she wasn't feeling well herself. I witnessed the woman I fell in love with so many years ago.

A world of vulnerability resides in her eyes and the deep lines along her forehead as she forces a smile. "I'm in. Even if it's a long shot at best ... I'm in."

I brush my hand down her arm. "What do you mean?"

"I mean I want a life with you. The one I took away. I want it back. I *know* I don't deserve it, but I want it. You. Me. Roman. There's nothing I want more. So I'll fight for us until I get my family back. Or..." she blinks, averting her gaze to the side "...until you tell me the fight is over."

"Jules ..." I brush my knuckles along her cheek, and she leans into my touch. "The fight is over. We're fine."

Fine ...

I inwardly scold myself for saying it. Even if it means nothing to her, it still means something to me. It means we're not okay yet. But I want to get there. I do.

"It's not. It's only just begun." She takes a step back and holds out her other hand.

It's a pregnancy test.

And it's positive.

She's pregnant. And we both know it's not mine. So it's his ... the man who left her to go back to his family. A million thoughts race through my mind.

Does he know?

Will he come back to her?

But she still wants me. She still wants me and Roman.

Tears fill her eyes.

"Jules ... everything will be fine. We'll figure this out." I take her glass of wine. She shouldn't be drinking wine.

She wipes her eyes before the tears escape, shaking her head slowly. "You don't even sound surprised. You knew ... she told you."

I squint. "How could I have possibly known you're pregnant with another man's baby? And who is 'she?' What are you talking about?"

"Oh my god ..." Julie whispers, covering her mouth with her hand. The tears win over and break free in a blink. "You ... you thought I ..." She shakes her head. "I ... was pregnant with his baby ... and you ... you were just fine with it?" Julie laughs. The crazy kind. The painful kind. The kind of laugh that scares me.

I reach for her, my natural instinct to comfort her and protect her, but she takes another step away.

"Only you, Eli ... only you love like that."

"Like what?"

"So completely," she whispers on a sob, "so unconditionally. You always do the right thing, even if it kills you."

"Jules, there's no right or wrong here. I'm just saying I support you no matter what you decide. But I don't think you should decide this without him. If I were in his shoes, I wouldn't want that."

"Jesus Christ ..." She puts her hand on her head and fists her hair, continuing to shake it like this is a reality she's not ready to face. After a few seconds of her doing something between a sob and that crazy woman's laugh, she grabs my hand, places the pregnancy test in it, and closes my fingers around it. Her painful smile fades into an expressionless face, drenched in tears, makeup smeared around her eyes. "It's not my pregnancy test. I'm not the one who's pregnant." She lifts onto her toes and presses a kiss to my cheek before grabbing her purse, slipping her feet into her shoes, and walking out the front door.

I open my hand and stare at the positive test. What just happened? It feels like someone just rammed a truck into my brain. Her words are there, echoing over and over. I hear them.

Julie's not pregnant.

It's not her test.

Dorothy ... no. Julie wouldn't have her test. It makes no sense, yet it's the only explanation that makes any sense at this point.

"Dorothy's pregnant with my baby ..."

CHAPTER THIRTY-FIVE

Guacamole for the Win

Dorothy

"ORVILLE GOT STUCK in Gemma's dog door again," Dad says, rolling his eyes after the waitress takes our order.

I convinced them to meet me for late night Mexican. Guacamole and chips makes everything better, even positive pregnancy tests.

"So what's up? You have exciting news for us?" Mom takes a sip of her huge margarita. "Early job offer? New boyfriend? Promotion at work?"

"Nope." I take a sip of my water. "Just pregnant."

Mom chokes on her drink. Dad doesn't move. Not a single blink.

"It's okay. You don't have to say anything. There's not much to say."

Mom clears the rest of her drink from her throat. "Not much to say? Dorothy, you're … pregnant? Well … um … do you not get what that means?"

The waitress brings our guacamole and chips. I dig right in. "Yes, Mom. I'm well aware of how babies are made. The developmental process. And the eighteen-plus-year commitment. But I already took the test. I already had my initial meltdown, followed by Dr. Hathaway stealing my pregnancy test and nine hours of denial."

"Wait ... what?" Mom reaches across the table to grab my hand, stopping me from taking a bite of my chip.

So I retell the whole saga.

Then we eat in silence because I know they have no idea what to say or do at the moment. That makes three of us. But I have roughly thirty-five weeks to plan everything out. It's no secret that I had no intentions of ever having children. Adopting, maybe. But not this.

And yet ... here I am. Knocked up by Dr. Hawkins.

"Don't wait to tell him," Mom finally speaks as Dad pays the bill. "If Julie hasn't already told him."

"No. Trust me. She didn't tell him. I honestly think she's hoping I don't tell him. I mean ... she has him back. Now here I am threatening to disrupt all of that, but not really. He can be as involved as he wants to be or not at all. I don't need him financially. And I'll figure it out. Right?"

And by right, I one hundred percent mean, "You guys have my back, right?"

"Of course." Mom scoots out of the booth after Dad. "But tell him, Dorothy. And tell him soon."

"I will. I *just* found out today. I haven't even confirmed it with a doctor. And I could sneeze and miscarry. Disrupting everyone with a 9-1-1 pregnancy alert isn't called for at almost ten o'clock on a Friday. But …" My nose wrinkles. "I'm pregnant. I'm … pregnant."

My parents nod slowly, showing a bit of relief in the face of my flash of panic—my *real* acknowledgment.

"This kid will get my genes. It's doomed. Eli will realize this too. He's smart. He studies things, like terrible things we genetically pass along to the next generation. He's not going to want this. And that's fine, right? I've got this. I mean … *we've* got this. Right?"

"Yes. Of course, baby girl. We've got this." Mom hugs me right after we exit the restaurant. "But *soon*. You need tell him soon."

"Yes. Soon …" I sigh. Soon as in January if I can keep my mouth shut that long. Thanksgiving is this coming week. Christmas next month. I'm not disrupting families over the holidays. Besides, that gives this little fetus inside of me time to decide if he or she is going to stick.

I get stuck at all stoplights getting out of Portland, so my parents beat me home.

"Oh shit …" I whisper when I see a blue Tesla and the outline of a man—the man—sitting on the steps to the front porch. I gun it to get pulled into the garage before Mom and Dad drag their asses out of their car. "Go in the back door. Go now!" I demand before I even get my seatbelt unfastened.

"He knows …" Mom shakes her head.

"We don't know that, but I just … just go."

"We're going … we're going." Dad pulls Mom's arm toward the back door to the garage.

I walk out front and lower the garage door at the keypad. My lungs and heart refuse to cooperate. It's hard to breathe as I take slow steps to the porch.

There he is ... sitting on the top step, wearing jeans and a hoodie. His elbows rest on his knees, hands folded in front of him. He has a thicker layer of stubble along his face, approaching the perfect length for a neatly trimmed beard. He's ... hot.

Yup, even now, in the dark, when he belongs to another woman, he's still a sight to behold.

"You should have messaged me. I wasn't expecting you. We went for a late dinner, since I don't get off work until eight. Mexican ... chips and guacamole. It was really good."

Eli runs a hand through his hair, dipping his chin and scratching the back of his head. "I know what time you get off work. But I didn't want to discuss our baby via text."

Gulp ...

"She told you," I whisper.

"The question is, why didn't you?" He sounds a little hurt or angry. Or maybe just tired. I really can't tell because it's dark, and I'm cold, and my pounding pulse makes it hard to hear well.

"I literally took the test this morning." I start pacing again. "I stuck it in my pocket. Then it dropped out of my pocket when I went to grab my phone. She was there. She took it and made me follow her to her office to talk about it. I didn't dream she would tell you today. I thought she'd have the decency to give *me* at least twenty-four fucking hours to digest the fact that my life is going to change forever!"

Eli stands, taking the three steps to meet me. "Why are you yelling?" He grabs my shoulders to stop my pacing.

Wow … I thought … I really thought I had this. I thought I worked this out in my head, very factually, very analytically. Yet, here I am breaking down. Here come the tears like rain that wasn't in the forecast.

"Because I'm pregnant. And I really wanted to give you the life you wanted—the life you deserve. And I know it took two to make this baby, but I should have never let it happen. It's just that I really wanted to be with you one last time. And now everything is ruined, and I'm trying really hard to pretend that it's not. But if Dr. Hathaway leaves you again because of this, I'll feel bad for like … ever." I cover my face with my hands and hold in the sobs, but they shake my body anyway.

Eli wraps me in his arms. "Oh my god, Dorothy … you're not even close to hitting the truth about what this means." He presses his lips to the top of my head.

I wipe my face, sniffling as I look up at him. The moonlight illuminates his face, and right now I want to be selfish, but I can't. I won't. "You just got your family back. Don't let this ruin that. Promise me you won't do anything stupid."

He rubs my cheeks with his thumbs, drying my tears and pushing away the hairs stuck to my cheeks. "Define stupid." A grin pulls at his lips.

"Stupid is thinking that I can't do this by myself. I can. And my parents are here. This baby will be loved and well cared for. Stupid is thinking I need you more than they do."

"Dorothy Mayhem, stupid is thinking that *I* don't need *you*. Stupid is thinking this baby is anything short of the best damn miracle I've experienced since Julie told me she was pregnant with Roman. Stupid is thinking I'm letting you make any more decisions for me." Eli's grip on my face intensifies as he leans down to force me to look him in the eye.

"The only thing that's been ruined is me. You ruined me the day you walked into my life, wearing those outrageous red Nikes. You ruined me for Julie and all other women. I'm the expensive vase you broke while shopping. I'm no good for anybody. I'm yours. You are stuck with me. So pick up the fucking pieces and deal with it because I'm not going anywhere."

"But Roman—"

He releases me. "No! No! No! No!" Brushing past me he walks a good twenty feet down my driveway, pulling at his hair. "Roman is perfect!" he yells … as if he's trying to wake up everyone in a five-mile radius. "He's happy. He's loved. He's well-adjusted. AND HE ADORES DORFEE MAYHEM!" Eli cups his hands around his mouth and tips his head back like an animal howling at the moon. "EVERYBODY LOVES DORFEE MAYHEM BECAUSE SHE'S THE VERY BEST HUMAN THAT EVER EXISTED! AND SHE'S HAVING MY BABY! I. AM. THE. LUCKIEST. MAN. ALIVE!"

Dropping his hands from his face, he marches back toward me. I can't even begin to explain how completely embarrassed I am right now.

"I choose you, Dorothy. I chose you then, even when you didn't choose me. I choose you now. I'll choose you tomorrow. But for the love of god, woman ..." He drops to his knees at my feet, literally resting his forehead on her tennis shoes, hands gripping my calves. "Would you please choose me? Would you let your own happiness matter for once?"

"Sweetie?" Mom calls out the door behind me. She sounds a bit worried. I can't imagine why that would be. "Is everything good?"

Wiping the last few tears from my face, I curl my hair behind my ears and squat down, running my fingers though Eli's hair as he breathes heavily with his forehead still resting on my shoes. "Yeah, everything is ... okay."

Eli mumbles something, but I can't make it out. He lifts his head slowly. "Say it again."

I let my smile show, but just a little.

He sits back onto his butt, evidently not caring that he's sitting in a mix of dirt and grass, but mostly dirt. Then he grabs my waist and pulls me to him, so my legs straddle his legs, so my nose nearly touches his nose. "Say it again."

"Everything is okay." My smile crawls a bit farther up my face.

"Again ..." he grins.

I press my palms to his very stubbly face and brush my lips across his lips. "Okay ... everything is okay."

"Because you love me."

I kiss his top lip. "Because I love you."

"Because you choose me."

I kiss his bottom lip. "Because I choose you."

"And we're having a baby."

I nod, kissing his nose, his cheeks, his forehead. "And we're having a baby."

CHAPTER THIRTY-SIX

Elijah

"OH ... MY god!"

Grimacing, I crack open one eye. My back hurts. I'm on my stomach. Rarely do I sleep on my stomach. Must be why my back hurts. A pillow lands on my ass—my bare ass.

Kellie stares at me, wide-eyed, with her hand over her mouth. And she starts to mumble behind that hand. "I was going to do a load of laundry for Dorothy. And I thought I'd wash the blanket that was tossed onto her bed, but I had no idea you were under the blanket. Oh my god ... why would she completely cover up a naked, sleeping man and then just go to work without saying anything?"

"Um ..." I squint, opening my other eye and rolling onto my back, keeping the pillow over my midsection. "We're talking about Dorothy ... clearly your guess is as good as mine."

We were zipped into her bed. And then we started

doing certain *activities* that required more freedom to move about the bed ... and the floor. Yeah, I'm pretty sure we were on the floor at some point. My mind is a little fuzzy because I don't think I got more than two hours of sleep. I have no clue when Dorothy even got up or how she's functioning on so little sleep.

"Thank you for loving my baby girl." She hugs a wad of dirty clothes to her chest.

I rub my eyes before lacing my fingers behind my head, meeting Kellie's huge grin and bright eyes. Julie's mom never thanked me for loving her daughter.

I return the smile. "It's truly a pleasure. And I ..." I cringe, feeling eighteen instead of thirty-eight. Maybe my naked body only covered by a pillow is what has me feeling a bit insecure. "I apologize for not being more responsible with your daughter. But I love her. And I'm going to take care of her and raise this baby with her. I have only the best intentions where Dorothy is concerned."

"I appreciate that. So much." She sits on the side of the bed.

Okay ... we're going to chat now, with me naked in Dorothy's bed. Nope ... nothing awkward at all about this. I scoot over an inch or two, keeping a firm hold on the pillow.

"A few years back, before her uncle died and left her all his money..." Kellie lets out a slow breath, looking out the slats of the window blinds "...I went shopping with Dorothy right around the time school was getting ready to start. We each grabbed a cart. I went in one way. She went the other way. We met back up a few minutes later. I had like four things in my cart. Dorothy's cart was *full*. Now ... things you'll find out about Dorothy, if you haven't already: She has backups of everything—shampoo, deodorant, toothpaste ... you name it. And not just one extra. I'm talking three or four extra tubes of toothpaste. So before I actually focused on the contents of her cart, I assumed she simply was having a moment. A little anxiety that required the comfort of backups.

"Nope ... I was wrong. Here's the thing, we spend so much of our lives as parents trying to make sure our kids are good humans. Then one day, without you really noticing, it happens. Dorothy's cart was full, but the stuff was not for her. Upon explanation, she told me there was a donation box in front of a children's house she passed every day on her way to work. It had been over a week and no one had donated. She's done some summer workshops with these kids ... the abused and neglected kids. And she said they had *less than* nothing, and nobody was helping them, not at all. Then she said she knew what she was doing wouldn't really make a difference, but she at least wanted to try. One minute I was worried that she was having an off day, preparing to interrogate her about taking her medications faithfully. The next minute, I'm standing in a store with tears rolling down my face."

She shrugs. "I'm happy to say that I have raised a good human who's now adulting better than me."

Yeah, I need a lifetime with Dorothy Mayhem. And I can't believe how close I came to letting her slip away from me.

"Anyway, I just want you to know that some days will be sheer madness. I mean ... god knows I love that girl, but she is clumsy and loud. Talks through movies, constantly being told to shush. And she's a hypochondriac. Always dying of something. She won't eat the last slice of bread, the last bit of peanut butter in a jar, the last cookie in a box. Nope. She'll just get out a new one. And the birds ..." Kellie laughs. "I asked her once if she wanted to put some seed out for the momma bird who had babies in a nest. Dorothy didn't even think, she just said, 'No. I believe in Darwin.'"

I chuckle. Does Kellie know that all of Dorothy's quirks that may drive her parents crazy make me love her just that much more?

"But then ... she fills a box for kids who have less than nothing."

But then that ...

Dorothy ... Dorothy ... Dorothy ...

"You did a great job raising her. She's perfect." I grin.

Kellie stands, twisting her mouth to hide her pride. "She's ... adequate." She winks and slips out of the bedroom, shutting the door behind her.

✧ ✧ ✧

MY MOM MESSAGES me a picture of Roman eating pancakes with a "Hope you and Julie are enjoying your alone time."

This means Julie didn't get Roman last night. So I drive to her house. After ringing the doorbell twice, she answers the door in a robe. Puffy eyes and a forced smile.

I step inside. "Jules …" I hug her to me.

She grips my shirt and silently sobs for a few minutes. There's not much to say. She knows.

This hurts.

Everything we had has changed, and it just doesn't fit right anymore.

"I'm t-too late." She pulls back and wipes her face.

I nod slowly. Just once. "It's not because of the baby. I don't want you to ever think I'm choosing this child I'm having with Dorothy over our child."

Julie turns, her breath shaky on a slow inhale as she walks toward the front window to her spacious great room. "I know, Eli."

"I want us to be okay, Jules. Maybe not today. Maybe not for some time, but I want us to give Roman the best of us apart and together. I don't want him to ever see me do anything but love you. Because I do … I love you with a part of myself that will always belong only to you."

She turns, blinking more silent tears that she quickly wipes from her face as she shrugs. "So that's what we do … we give him everything. Me. You. Us. And the woman who idolizes me."

"Jesus, Jules …" I shake my head and allow myself to return the same tiny grin she has on her own face. "Are you going to lord this over me forever?"

She laughs. It's still partially a sob, but I can tell she's trying so hard to make this right. "Yes. You'll get her love, but I'll get her respect."

My eyebrows shoot up my forehead. "You think she

doesn't respect me?"

"Well ..." Julie straightens her robe like she would straighten her lab coat, shoulders back, chin up. "I'm sure there's some respect there, but I don't think she could ever think of you as a boss bitch."

I have a million comebacks, starting with the fact that I'm pretty sure men can't be boss bitches. But I don't give her anything more than my silence and an easy nod. She's hurting. I know this because I recognize the false confidence. I've lived it for the past year. Letting go of your first love is pretty fucking painful. And as much as people might think she let go of me last year, she didn't. Not really.

This. This is her truly letting go.

This is me ... letting go.

"Eli ..." As more tears fill her eyes, I fight my own emotions, and she sees it. This time she hugs me.

This time she comforts me.

We hold each other for so long, I'm not sure what time of day it is. It's a silent goodbye. It's painful. It's exactly what it should be because we've been each other's world—each other's everything—for so long. I spent a lifetime with this woman.

Now, I kiss her on the cheek one last time as I release her, turn, and walk out the door to spend a lifetime with Dorothy Mayhem.

EPILOGUE

New Neighbors

Seven (ish) months later ...

"I'M A WHALE. A whale in a gown. A whale with a hat. How do you like that?"

"Are you ghost writing for Dr. Seuss?" I ask Dorothy, the mother of my child—a girl we were told. My superhero. My exercise buddy. My almost everything ... except Roman. Oh ... and she's not my wife.

Nope.

No marriage for Dorothy Mayhem.

Just as well. It would be a crime to change that awesome name of hers.

I adjust her graduation cap before kissing her coconut-flavored lips while holding Violet Riley Mayhem Hawkins in my hands as she kicks inside her mom's belly.

Yes, I'm getting ready to live a life of Riley and mayhem.

"Does this gown make me look fat?" Dorothy continues, frowning.

"Nurse Mayhem, I've had about enough of you insulting the woman I love. Can you give it a break? Put a smile on your face. And go plant your sexy booty in that chair to get your diploma."

"Think you'll actually stick with this one?" Her dad smirks, referring to her many degrees.

Dorothy shrugs. "I don't know. I'm kind of getting sick of the hospital scene."

I laugh to lighten the mood. Her parents? They don't laugh because they know she's not joking. I know it too, but this woman has my baby inside of her. I don't give a shit whether or not she gets an actual job as a nurse.

My Dorothy wanders through life. And as long as she always makes it back to me, I don't care if she spends an eternity in college, getting twenty different degrees, or pushing patients around a hospital, or gleaning every night of the week.

"Dorothy ... I will clap for you." Roman hugs her legs, and she bends down to hug him back. My son loves her, maybe more than me. She's worthy of that kind of love. She's just ... fucking perfection.

"Thanks, Romeo."

"Kisses for Violet." He presses his hands to her belly and kisses his baby sister.

"I'm going to cry ..." Kellie wipes her eyes.

"Please don't, Mom. I'm puffy everywhere else. Can you not make me cry with your sappiness?"

"It's happiness, not sappiness." Kellie rolls her eyes at Dorothy. "We're going to take Roman to find seats. I love you." She hugs her daughter.

Dorothy makes her usual awkward attempt to hug her mom back, but Violet has complicated things. As if that's even possible with a Dorothy Mayhem hug.

"Come on, Dorothy," one of her classmates calls, passing Dorothy to get seated in the auditorium.

"You good?"

She grins at me. "I'm okay."

I glance at my watch. "I'm going to watch from here so I can close my standing ring before you."

"Jerk." She frowns, pivoting to head into the auditorium.

I grab her gown, giving it a tug to stop her. Then I wrap my arms around her, resting my chin on her shoulder, my hands over hers on her belly. "Dorothy Mayhem," I whisper, "I am so proud of you. You are the universe. Unequivocally the kindest human I have ever known. Thank you for choosing me. This lifetime ... with me. I love you."

Her head tips back against mine. "I think I love you too."

"Okay." I kiss her cheek one last time before letting her go.

✧ ✧ ✧

THREE DAYS LATER, I take my Dorothy to the hospital at three in the morning, when her contractions get too close for comfort.

Only ... we don't make it there.

"Now, Eli." She shoots me a wide-eyed glance, ten

minutes from the hospital. Her hand slides up her skirt. "Eliii!" She closes her eyes, holding her breath. "I feel the head. Eli!"

"Okay, babe. We've got this. No big deal." I pull over on the side of the road.

"It burns!" She grunts, scrunching her face. "It *is* a big deal!"

I call for an ambulance.

"I'm going to move you to the backseat." I hop out, run around the car, and lift her from the front seat to the backseat.

"Eli!" She tucks her chin and pushes. "Oh god! Call an ambulance before this baby falls out onto its head! Eli … she has my genes. We can't let her fall on her head too!"

"Dorothy Mayhem …" I grab her hand, interlacing our fingers and squeezing until she gives me her eyes. "I know I'm not your favorite doctor … but I'm nonetheless a doctor. I called the ambulance. They'll be here soon. In the meantime … we've got this. I've got you. I've got Violet."

I slide off her panties, prop up my phone with the light illuminating Violet's crowning head. "She has a head of dark hair."

"H-how can you be so fucking CAAALLLMMM?" Her face contorts with another contraction as she pushes.

I know she's in pain. But my Dorothy has never been so beautiful. "I'm calm because I'm getting ready to deliver our baby. And you are the strongest person I know. So let's do this. Let's meet Violet."

Dorothy opens her eyes, tears running down her cheeks as she nods. "Thank you," she whispers between contractions on a labored breath.

"For what?"

"For letting me be me. Letting me be enough."

My own emotions burn my eyes. "You're welcome."

"Ouch … it's coming … it hurts. ELI!"

"Push, Dorothy … you've got this."

She pushes once, twice … and on the third push Violet's head is out.

"Stop, baby. Take some short breaths. Try not to push. The cord is around her neck." I feel for the cord, it's tight but not too tight. "Okay. Give me another big push."

Dorothy yells and Violet slides out. I unwrap the cord from her neck, and just as the ambulance's lights illuminate behind us, Violet lets out her first cry. It's a bit weak with a gurgle, but it's her first breath, and nothing since Roman taking his first breath has ever sounded so beautiful.

"My baby …" Dorothy reaches for Violet as several people crowd around the vehicle.

I can't even speak, I'm so fucking over the moon as I hand Dorothy our daughter.

It's funny how a year can change your world. And it's amazing how a single breath can take a life, give a life, and sometimes … save a life.

She is my breath of life.

✦ ✦ ✦

Dorothy

Three weeks later …

WE BROUGHT VIOLET home from the hospital two days after Eli delivered her in the back of my Q5. I really should have gotten the Q7.

Home … well it's his house off Skyline Drive. And our weekend home is forty-five minutes away, with a huge yard, a trampoline, and two emus. Gemma travels back and forth with us. And my parents spend more time sitting together on the sofa with me not there as much.

I'm a homebody. A creature of habit. I like the familiar. And Eli respects that. He honors every little quirky thing about my personality. My need for space. My need for expressing my emotions in emojis and sorting them in piles and piles of brightly colored journals.

"Julie is coming over." Eli frowns as he comes down the stairs from putting Violet down for a nap. He sets the monitor on the coffee table.

"She's just dropping off Roman. What's the long face about?" I ask.

We have a great relationship with Dr. Hathaway. And all the guilt I thought I'd feel over Eli giving up having Roman full-time was for nothing. Roman is a thriving young boy because all of us have worked hard to make sure he feels an abundance of love and sense of family.

"She's moving." He shakes his head. "We agreed we wouldn't do this until Roman is older. It's not a written agreement, but we both voiced it. I heard she was offered a job in New York. *New York*, Dorothy. That's too far. That's too many trips. He's supposed to start preschool this fall. How can she do this? How can she uproot him like this? There's no way it's going to work with every other week. I ..." He runs his hands through his messy—and yes—sexy hair.

I feel his anxiety, even if I don't know what to say. Is he going to ask me to move to New York too, so we're close to Roman? The idea evokes a nauseating anxiety because I know I'll say yes. It will kill me to leave my parents, my emus, my comfort zone, but I'll do it. I'll do it for Roman. And Eli knows this ... he knows my love for Roman is as great as my love for Violet. I don't see Roman as anything less than my own child. My buddy ... my little superhero.

My Romeo.

"So we go." Yep. Here I go. Avoiding conflict at all cost. "We move to New York."

"My patients, babe. This isn't just about Julie, Roman, you, Violet ... our families. It's about my patients."

I nod, easing out of the recliner and standing in front of him. I just ... lean into him. It's my way of offering a hug. Eli wraps his arms around me.

"Of course ... of course you'd say this. I love you so fucking much, Dorothy Mayhem."

The doorbell rings, and before Eli can answer it, Roman opens the door and runs inside.

"Shh ..." Eli preemptively shushes him as he picks him up for a big hug. "Violet is sleeping. How are you, buddy?" He buries his face in Roman's neck and kisses him over and over.

"Daddy!" He giggles.

Dr. Hathaway—yeah, she'll always be Dr. Hathaway, Boss Bitch to me—walks in behind Roman and grins at the display of father-son affection.

"Go play quietly in your room while I talk to Mommy."

"No. Listen, Daddy! We have a surprise."

Eli holds his finger to his mouth to remind Roman to keep his voice down.

"We have a surprise," Roman repeats on a whisper, cupping his hands at his mouth.

God … I love this kid.

Dr. Hathaway chuckles.

Eli gives her a hesitant smile, clearly not in the mood for surprises. Especially the ones that involve moving to New York. And I already know he's pissed, that she's gotten Roman excited about it.

"Come here, Daddy. Come here now." Roman tugs on Eli's hand, pulling him toward the door.

I glance at Dr. Hathaway.

She winks. "You look great, Dorothy. How's that beautiful little girl of yours?"

I know we're not supposed to let her butter us up, but I can't help my motherly pride when she asks about Violet. My daughter is the most beautiful little girl ever. I realize every mom says it, but it's actually true in my case.

"She's perfect."

"Grab the monitor and come with us." Dr. Hathaway nods to the baby monitor.

I hesitate for a few seconds before grabbing my phone. Eli uses the monitor, but I have audio and video of the nursery on my phone.

I follow them outside just as Eli and Roman cross the street.

"Must have sold," I murmur, noticing the house across from ours no longer has a *For Sale* sign in the yard.

"Daddy! This is Mommy's new house! You like it?"

Eli just ... stops, even with Roman tugging on his arm. After a few seconds he turns toward Dr. Hathaway.

She shrugs with a big smile. "It will make it easier for both of us to tuck him in at night. And for him to spend time with his sister. And for me to discuss cutting-edge medical research with Dorothy, when she's not busy being a superhero."

Yeah, he's in shock. He hasn't even blinked yet.

Me? I'm trying to play it cool, when really I want to ask how often she wants to get together to discuss this cutting-edge medical research. But I don't take this from Eli. It's his moment.

It's his world coming full circle.

"Are you okay, Eli?" she asks on a slight chuckle.

Roman continues to pull on one of his hands while he nods slowly. Something along the lines of the happiest emoji ever takes over his expression as he reaches his other hand to take mine.

"Yeah." He exhales a long breath. "Everything is definitely *okay*."

The End

Acknowledgments

This story is a labor of love. Thank *you* for reading it. Out of everything I've written so far, this one feels the most personal to me.

I have to start by thanking Shauna and Marley for so many inspiring, true stories that helped bring Dorothy Mayhem to life.

Thank you to Asher, my own little version of Dorothy, for reminding me every single day that the spectrum is *human*. It's not autism. I will always be in awe of your imagination and kindness.

My editing team ... I cannot say enough about the special humans who rake through my words, sort out the shit, and polish the rough spots. Max, Monique, Leslie, Kambra, Sian, Bethany, Sherri, Jyl, and Allison ... thank you!

Jennifer Beach, thank you for keeping me from falling apart on a daily basis and working your ass off to make Jewel E Ann look social, or ridiculous, in the case of newsletter face swaps. But more than anything, thanks for sharing your activity rings with me, and for letting me "win" on certain days to boost my aging ego.

Thank you to every contestant who participated in

my cover design contest. There were so many good ones, but Sign.Yra nailed the essence of Dorothy Mayhem.

My wonderful Jonesies, you are my safe place. Thank you for your daily love and encouragement. More than anything, thank you for supporting my chaotic style of writing—the whiplash from dark suspense, to romantic comedy. Your willingness to "go there" with me has made me a very happy writer.

Thank you, Kate Stewart, for being a sounding board when I'm on the edge of a cliff. You always pull me back to reality and remind me how incredibly lucky *we* are to have this opportunity to tell stories.

Jenn, Sarah, and Brooke with Social Butterfly PR, thank you for giving my stories visibility, for getting my book out there for the world to see.

To all my author friends … Yes, I'm excited to announce that I officially have friends. Thank you for letting me into your lives, cheering me on, sharing my stories, and inspiring me with your talent. You are too great in number to list by name, but I just want all five of you to know how much you mean to me.

Paul with BB ebooks, as always, thank you for your formatting services.

Finally, to my family, thank you for loving me as Dorothy *and* as Julie. I am blessed beyond words.

Also by Jewel E. Ann

Jack & Jill Series
End of Day
Middle of Knight
Dawn of Forever

Holding You Series
Holding You
Releasing Me

Transcend Series
Transcend
Epoch

Standalone Novels
Idle Bloom
Only Trick
Undeniably You
One
Scarlet Stone
When Life Happened
Look the Part
A Place Without You

Naked Love
Jersey Six

jeweleann.com

Receive a FREE book and stay informed of new releases, sales, and exclusive stories:
Monthly Mailing List
jeweleann.com/free-booksubscribe

About the Author

Jewel is a free-spirited romance junkie with a quirky sense of humor.

With 10 years of flossing lectures under her belt, she took early retirement from her dental hygiene career to stay home with her three awesome boys and manage the family business.

After her best friend of nearly 30 years suggested a few books from the Contemporary Romance genre, Jewel was hooked. Devouring two and three books a week but still craving more, she decided to practice sustainable reading, AKA writing.

When she's not donning her cape and saving the planet one tree at a time, she enjoys yoga with friends, good food with family, rock climbing with her kids, watching How I Met Your Mother reruns, and of course…heart-wrenching, tear-jerking, panty-scorching novels.

CPSIA information can be obtained
at www.ICGtesting.com
Printed in the USA
LVHW081021020521
686254LV00013B/861